The Provocateur

The Provocateur

A Novel by RENÉ-VICTOR PILHES

Translated from the French by Denver and Helen Lindley

Harper & Row, Publishers

NEW YORK, HAGERSTOWN

SAN FRANCISCO

LONDON

This work was first published in French under the title *L'Imprécateur*.

THE PROVOCATEUR. English translation copyright © 1977 by Harper & Row, Publishers, Inc. All rights reserved. Printed in the United States of America. No part of this book may be used or reproduced in any manner whatsoever without written permission except in the case of brief quotations embodied in critical articles and reviews: For information address Harper & Row, Publishers, Inc., 10 East 53rd Street, New York, N.Y. 10022. Published simultaneously in Canada by Fitzhenry & Whiteside Limited, Toronto.

FIRST EDITION

Designed by Sidney Feinberg

Library of Congress Cataloging in Publication Data

Pilhes, René Victor, date
  The provocateur.
  Translation of L'imprécateur.
  1. Title
PZ4.P6374Pr [PQ2676.I4]   843'.9'14   76–5555
ISBN 0–06–013337–6

77 78 79 80 81 10 9 8 7 6 5 4 3 2 1

*I realized in that dreadful instant
that the lives of myriads of men
weighed no more than a feather.*

GUSTAV MEYRINK, *The Golem*

The Provocateur

1 I am going to tell the story of the collapse and ultimate ruin of the French affiliate of the multinational corporation
of Rosserys and Mitchell, whose steel-and-glass office building
once stood at the corner of the Avenue de la République and Rue
Oberkampf in Paris, close by Père Lachaise cemetery.

At the time of the terrifying tremor and mass hysteria, I was a
senior executive at the firm, with the title of associate director of
human relations. For two years my duties had kept me from taking
part in top-level financial, commercial and technical decisions, but
the importance of my job was finally about to be recognized. A few
days before the first signs of catastrophe, Saint-Ramé, managing
director of Rosserys and Mitchell–France, expressed the intention
of making me director in chief of human relations.

Saint-Ramé, born in Poligny in the Indre, had a glittering array
of qualifications for his position. He was a graduate of the School
of Public Works and the Institute of Political Studies in Paris,

Master of Science from the Massachusetts Institute of Technology, licentiate, top rank, of the Boll Foundation, graduate of the Harvard Business School, Chevalier of the National Order of Merit.

"You're in, my friend," he said to me. "Human relations are going to develop spectacularly. The great corporations are on the verge of a nervous breakdown."

That's exactly what I did see and it almost drove me mad. Today, in the peace and quiet of my little white room, pampered and cared for, I feel better, and I manage one way and another to get through my long sleep.

I shall tell the tale of the collapse and ruin for the following reasons. In the first place, I've concluded that the experts' version of the affair is false. It is of course true that there are numerous tunnels, bottomless pits and huge dark caverns beneath the Avenue de la République, and I know of one slippery passageway that leads from the cellars of the company to the vaults of the cemetery. But everyone was aware of all that. In any case, the American and French experts had carefully studied the subsoil before deciding to build. The hypothesis that the earth subsequently sank is hardly tenable. At the time thousands of buildings were erected in Paris and elsewhere, many of them on much riskier terrain than Rue Oberkampf. So how could one of the most powerful companies in the world—which had put up office buildings and factories in almost every country on the planet—have been misled in France, in Paris, at the corner of the Avenue de la République and Rue Oberkampf? No, the truth lies elsewhere. Minds were viciously attacked before the foundation was. And no one who, like me, occupied an important post at the heart of the firm can agree that the rise of hysteria and the collapse of the walls were unconnected. I know that the former led to the latter and that the whole thing was premeditated. It is my duty to write the history of those lost souls, those savagely punished men, in order to save millions of others from one day sinking into corruption and mediocrity.

But I also have a second reason for setting it all down. It is now time for litigation. American and French courts are preparing to judge cases, estimate damages, determine liabilities. The publication of my work will clarify matters in the judges' minds. Not that I was a witness to everything. I did not see all nor hear all. I had to reconstruct whole sections of the affair from innumerable bits and pieces. For example, no one really knows what became of the imprecator after the officers of his company forced him into the open and tried to involve him in their disclaimers. On the other hand, the existence of the imprecations and the identity of their author, his dramatic appearances, the villainous tricks and perversions that ripped the heart out of the corporation—all these are true. I was involved in those incredible events and my mind still boggles at them.

The huge multinational American firm of Rosserys and Mitchell at one time enjoyed a phenomenal notoriety and even aspired seriously to govern nations. But it has lost its place in men's memories, and left no furrow in history. It is not superfluous to describe it briefly today.

The firm manufactured, crated and sold machines designed to clear, plow, sow, reap, etc. Its principal headquarters were in Des Moines, Iowa, that great state of North America. At first the company sold its machines within the United States, then it exported them and finally it built factories abroad.

By the time of the events related here, Rosserys and Mitchell had built factories not only in countries rich enough to buy the machines manufactured and crated in their territory, but also in poor countries without resources, for the simple reason that the salaries paid to workers there were lower than elsewhere.

The people who at that time strove for the summit operated by such subtle cogitation, such extensive knowledge, such well-tested techniques that they could proceed with haughty assurance. Their philosophy developed along these lines:

a) Let's manufacture and crate our machines in our country and sell them there.

b) Now let's sell our machines to foreigners who have money to buy them.

c) Let's manufacture and crate on the spot, in countries that can afford our goods.

d) Why not manufacture and crate our machines in poor countries and so get them more cheaply?

e) On reflection, why not manufacture the screws for our machines where screws cost least, bolts where bolts cost least, assemble where assembly costs least, crate where crating costs least?

f) And finally, why confine ourselves to the manufacture of machines? With all the money we earn, why not buy everything that's for sale? Why not transform our industry into a gigantic conglomerate?

The dry logic of this procedure masked a remarkable altruism. The construction of factories and office buildings over the whole surface of the globe brought work and food to people who needed them, added to their progress and well-being. So it was that those manufacturers, craters and sellers, the engineers of mankind's happiness, came to ask themselves what useful purpose was served by political parties and governments. And these neo-patricians, who knew the secrets of the human soul, answered themselves: "We who create riches turn over a considerable part of them to political institutions, whether duly elected or not, which redistribute them. We don't want to redistribute these riches ourselves, for then we'd be our own regulators. And the world, after so many convulsions, so much millennial anguish, has finally found the right road: to manufacture, crate, sell and then redistribute the profits. In short, just as very long ago church and state were separated, today we should separate law and economics. On the one hand, there would be much 'social' gain; on the other, much monetary. In a sense, temporal power would belong to the companies and the banks, and nontemporal power to the governments. The temples, churches, synagogues would turn it over to the great ministries."

Let us manufacture and crate in peace, they cried, let us sell freely, and in return we shall have peace and liberty!

Such grandeur of soul did not leave peoples and nations unmoved. Among them all, the United States of America was clearly the chosen people. The world forgot Judea. Little by little Jerusalem was replaced by Washington. Politics adapted itself to the new religion and created its high priests. What good would a manager be who hadn't read the Tables of the New Law? Then there erupted into the board rooms men of a new type, capable of conducting a government as skillfully as an enterprise or a great company. The word *management* discarded its century-old fancy dress, threw off its carnival costume and appeared in a cape of gold before the astounded citizenry. Once, people had asked whether a man was Christian or heretic, rightist or leftist, communist or Anglican. At the time of which I am speaking, they asked, "Is that man a good manager or not?"

Rosserys and Mitchell was one of the gems of that civilization. Thanks to its machines, superhuman work had been accomplished throughout the entire world. Wheat waved where Moses' footsteps had raised only dust. Millions of students learned that if they worked hard in class, later they might be employed by a firm like Rosserys and Mitchell International. To the generations of the young, men said, "On the day when the world is a single immense corporation, no man will go hungry, no man will go thirsty, no one will be sick."

For that was the time when the wealthy nations, bulging with industries, stuffed with stores, discovered a new faith, an enterprise worthy of the efforts exerted by man over thousands of years: to make the world a single immense corporation.

2

Oh, how vexing it is to look back! A man afflicted by some misfortune and recalling the days and hours that preceded it always has the impression that the tragedy was forecast. A crow perched on the balcony at his window, an antique cup broke, a leaf blew off his calendar, a sentence was overheard, seeming trivial and harmless one day, but on the next full of woe. So on the morning of the first crack, even before the employees had entered the building, a rumor spread through the cafés in the Place Voltaire where the personnel generally ate breakfast. It came to my ears as I emerged from the Métro at the Filles du Calvaire station, my usual stop. Chavégnac, assistant head of the Spanish-American section, hailed me and said:

"Portal phoned me last night to say that Arangrude was killed on his way home, on the belt parkway. Did you know?"

"No," I replied. "How did Portal hear about it?"

"From Arangrude's wife. She called last night."

As we made our way toward the glass-and-steel building we were joined by cadres, employees and brokers, who, seeing us approach, cut short their breakfasts to come hear the news.

I noticed that in this group of Rosserys and Mitchell employees, hurrying to keep pace with us, I was the ranking cadre. The idea that since I was responsible for the firm's human relations I ought to say a few words about this death occurred to me just as we reached the main entrance. Turning, I silenced the crowd with a gesture and said:

"It's true, ladies and gentlemen; yesterday death paid a visit to our firm."

And I disappeared into the lobby. My words were solemnly received; the group actually let me take an elevator by myself, which, in a company of that sort, was indisputably a mark of respect. A few minutes later, by telephone, Henri Saint-Ramé confirmed the death of Roger Arangrude, thirty-four years old, assistant marketing director for Benelux; graduate of the School of Advanced Commercial Studies in Jouy-en-Josas; former brilliant head of production at the Korvex Company, second in Europe for cellophane-wrapped pork products; dead, thirty minutes after his departure from the office, on the northern belt parkway, his temple crushed in a collision with a truck manufactured by the Sotanel Company, fourth in France, operating for the firm of Amel Frères, second in France in long-distance hauling. Tiresome as that recital may sound, it is word for word what the always efficient and self-possessed Saint-Ramé unreeled over the telephone. The premature demise of Arangrude would not be without effect on the company's organizational chart. I even foresaw a savage struggle, not so much to fill the post he had occupied as to assume the office Saint-Ramé had had in mind for him in the near future: marketing director in chief for the whole French affiliate.

Toward the middle of the morning I was summoned to Saint-Ramé's office. There I found Roustev, assistant managing director, former production manager, who had once expected to become manager of the company. At the last moment, however, he had

7

seen himself swept aside by the wave of young managers who had charmed North America. Saint-Ramé asked me the question appropriate to my position.

"How should Arangrude be buried?"

"Well," I said, "it seems to me we ought to consult his wife."

"Should I go and see her myself?" the managing director asked.

"I think you should express the company's sympathy and be the first to pay your respects to the corpse, or at least to the casket. But I don't think there's any rush. The family's certainly upset and as managing director you shouldn't risk a rebuff, or an outburst of hysteria."

"That seems reasonable to me. What do you think, Monsieur Roustev?"

"Seems reasonable to me too."

"Did his wife love him?" Saint-Ramé asked.

"I don't know, monsieur."

"Find out. A company funeral's full of traps. For management. The employees come to the church and you never know what to say or do. Should I deliver a eulogy?"

"I'll see Madame Arangrude and clear up these questions, monsieur."

"But it's not her I'm worried about, it's the other cadres. Some of them—some of the best of them—may strengthen their allegiance to the firm if they see that in a case of sudden death I myself speak a final word of praise in the presence of the employees. Brignon, for example. I hear Grant and Michaelson are trying to hire him away from us. I'm sure he'd appreciate the notion that his own posthumous homage would come from me, Saint-Ramé."

"I hadn't looked at it that way, sir. But come to think of it, a panegyric would certainly impress the executives and junior executives. Would you like me to write one out just in case?"

"Oh, no. Just give me his file; I'll do the rest. But first of all, see how the family feels, and make sure that death notices are posted on all floors, signed by me. Send them to the principal newspapers."

"Will the factory at Méligny be represented?"

"Oh, yes, the factory! By all means! Pick the best men, Roustev. It won't hurt the workmen and technicians to hear from my own lips, beside a premature grave, just what an assistant marketing director does."

As I left Saint-Ramé's office, I was besieged by a crowd of cadres, executives of my own rank. They thought I'd know something about Arangrude's replacement. I told them that the associate director of human relations, burdened with the responsibility of arranging a high-ranking cadre's funeral, needed to concentrate. Did that flatter them? Did they understand that if one of them should die I would show an equal diligence? In any case, they stopped bothering me and dispersed in twos and threes, whispering through the corridors. Back in my office I put in a call to the deceased cadre's home. I was surprised to get Mme. Arangrude at once.

"Madame," I said in appropriate tones. "All of us here are crushed by this tragedy. How are you bearing up under this terrible ordeal?"

"Oh, badly, badly! In front of the children I have to, but I don't dare think of tomorrow. My God—"

"Madame, I've just left our managing director. . . ."

"Oh, Saint-Ramé. What does he say?"

"Well, he asked me to come and see you about the funeral. When would it be convenient for me to call on you?"

"My husband's lying in the chapel at the Hospital of Saint-Ouen. I spent the night there and a part of the morning. I'd like to rest a little. Can you come this afternoon?"

"Certainly, madame. Would four o'clock be convenient?"

"Yes, four o'clock. Thank you."

"Courage, madame. Till this afternoon."

I hung up, pleased enough. This cadre's widow, despite her sorrow, seemed to feel unmistakable respect for our company. Had she possessed less self-control, I'd have been afraid she might shout hatred for Rosserys and Mitchell, holding them responsible

9

for the accident. Hadn't Arangrude been killed after an exhausting day of work?

It was eleven-thirty. I was just getting ready to tackle the day's correspondence and saw on the top of my desk, among notes and letters laid out by my secretary, a scroll of cream-colored parchment tied with a green-and-black ribbon. I thought it was another of those innumerable advertising gimmicks and I casually untied the knot and unrolled the parchment. How could I have guessed that this document marked the beginning of our troubles? Although my investigation later established that there was no relationship between the death of Arangrude and the appearance of the scroll, I still wonder about the coincidence. I was, in fact, one of the few to be immediately concerned with the parchment, which had been distributed to all departments. Others were probably too preoccupied by the fatal accident to take note of it. And this is what I read, printed in medieval black letters, with the title in green capitals at the top:

WHAT DO THOSE WHO RUN
ROSSERYS AND MITCHELL
REALLY KNOW?

At Rosserys and Mitchell, management knows how the economy functions. And since we live in a world dominated by economics, they have a privileged view of the workings of that world. You have all read, haven't you, that governing today means controlling the economy? Imagine how miserable we'd be if through some cruel stroke of fate the heads of state who meet "at the summit" were ignorant of economics. Even more, suppose that by some unlucky accident corporation presidents were ignorant of economics. We'd see the end of prosperity; and the glowing happiness that the citizens of the West, male and female, now find in eating more than they want, wearing soft, fur-lined coats, enjoying a great variety of goods and satisfying all their appetites, large and small, would be menaced. So when someone speaks to Henri Saint-Ramé of goods and riches, he knows, unlike the ordinary citizen, how to distinguish among these goods and riches. Those who do not know believe that goods include simply material objects: food, bicycles, etc. But there they are gravely mistaken; included as well are the services citizens purchase when, for example, they have to travel from one place to another. In this case citizens take a train, and the trip is an asset. Who would doubt that the lesson a schoolmaster gives his pupils is an asset? He who has not learned that there are two categories of riches, material goods on the one hand and nonmaterial goods on the other, how could such a person assimilate the principles of the law of supply and demand? In the marketplace the money of those who demand is exchanged for the goods, material or nonmaterial, of those who can supply them. Saint-Ramé has completely mastered this strange and subtle law. He knows it inside out.

What else does he know that the average man does not? He knows that a company manufactures and packages its goods and then sells them. Men and women buy these goods, but they cannot do so unless they have money. And this money comes from the company! That shows what a tricky closed circuit it all is. If the goods cost too much, no one can buy them; and if they do not cost enough, the company will not make money or be able to survive and consequently will not be able to produce more goods. To establish a just price is therefore necessary, a price that results from a direct confrontation of what is supplied with what is demanded. When the price of goods is low, more people want to, and can, buy them. At the same time, manufacturers would rather sell expensive goods than cheap ones; that way they make more money. If prunes, crab apples or forget-me-not buds cost 2.50 francs per kilogram, those who produce them will sell 200 kilograms; if on the other hand these material goods cost .60 francs, the merchants will sell 2000 kilograms. Finally, 1000 kilograms of these products will be sold at a price of 1.20 francs per kilogram, the intermediate price and intermediate quantity resulting from this famous law of supply and demand. It is what is astutely called the balanced price. As can be seen, mastering this law is no trivial matter. Which is why we must rejoice that men like

11

Henri Saint-Ramé keep unremitting watch over the proper application of so subtle and delicate a law.

Saint-Ramé, however, knows even more: most people, those who have not studied modern economics, reason as though they were living in the age of barter. They overlook the fact that goods manufactured today are complex and that muscular strength and intellectual brilliance are not enough. Machines are needed, coal, electricity, steel, wool, railways. Without these, corporations could not manufacture clothing, household goods or anything else. And so they have to buy these machines, this steel, this cotton, which calls for a surplus of energy and knowledge on the part of the directors. In short, the head of a company must have his eye on two markets at the same time: the one in which he sells his products and the one in which he buys machines and raw materials. And here we touch upon one of the most formidable distinctions current in modern economic theory: frozen capital and liquid capital. When a tractor emerges from the factories of Rosserys and Mitchell, it is essential to distinguish between the metal and paint of which it is made and the machines that made it. Metal and paint that Saint-Ramé bought are definitely lost to the company. They have been transformed into a tractor and henceforth they belong to the owner of that tractor. On the other hand, the machines have remained in the factory, where they continue to produce more tractors. Consequently one can state that metal and paint are raw materials which circulate from their points of origin to the foundries of Rosserys and Mitchell and finally arrive at the home of a peasant in the Beauce. It is therefore natural to call these assets liquid assets. As for the machines that remain at Rosserys and Mitchell, well, they constitute frozen assets, those that do not circulate. For scoffers we emphasize that the tractor, although it circulates about the peasant's vast fields of grain, is nevertheless an asset not liquid, but invested and durable, an implement that allows him to produce perishable foodstuffs. See how pernicious the economy of our times can be! Saint-Ramé is one of those who know this. And you, did you know it? Did you think economics was an improvised science? If Saint-Ramé were incapable of distinguishing between frozen assets and liquid assets, would you so much as get your salaries?

But the directors know much more than this and they know about far more complex matters. Have you ever heard of infrastructure? If you have, do you really know what it is? Saint-Ramé is one of those who know most about it. What does he know about it? He has clearly understood that for a company to be productive, more is needed than the work of men and machines. How could one manufacture without roads, without telephones, without electricity, without hospitals to look after the cadres, employees, salesmen, technicians and workers when they are ill? And if the state takes an interest in these questions, it is clear that there exists a productive relationship between the company and the state. So it cannot be doubted that Saint-Ramé has to keep not just two markets under observation from the corner of his eye, but three: the consumer's market, the raw-materials market and the one dominated by the administration. This indicates the extent of the knowledge that those in control must have.

One day I shall show you what they know about finance, for what I have written on the subject of machines, raw materials, the law of supply and demand, is nothing compared to this phenomenon: the economic and financial role of capital. Meanwhile let us pray God that our company will win the economic war for the greatest happiness of all men, and let us beseech Him to preserve the health of the leaders who watch over our growth and expansion. By revealing a little of what they know, and of their burden, I shall have contributed to the respect due them.

This text was unsigned. After reading it, I rubbed my chin in perplexity and indecision. Perplexity, for I did not completely grasp its purpose; indecision, because in my position as associate director of human relations it would be my duty to interpret it and eventually to decide whether or not to take action. What importance should I attribute to this curious screed? What repercussions would it have within the company? And, first of all, who in addition to myself had received it? I realized that this was the decisive factor in a future decision. I rerolled the parchment, retied the green-and-black ribbon and called my secretary.

13

"Mademoiselle," I said casually, "what in the world is this scroll?"

"It's sure to be an ad of some kind, sir. Everyone seems to have got one."

"Ah," I said, a little disturbed. "Did you get one yourself?"

"Yes, it was on my desk this morning. I haven't even unrolled it. But why? Is it important?"

"No, no," I replied hastily, "it's just amusing; a practical joke, no doubt. Thank you, mademoiselle."

So the scroll had been on everyone's desk when the offices opened. My brief conversation with my secretary had pointed up one of the difficulties of the situation: making too much of a stir about this would probably give it unmerited importance. And I was led for the first time to consider the meaning of the text. What did it actually say? Not very much. Nevertheless, reading it had produced an inexplicable feeling. Like all great companies, we are used to seeing trade-union manifestoes, political pamphlets and even revolutionary tracts from time to time. But I for one had never seen this kind of text before. It was actually the absence of any clear purpose rather than anything it said that vaguely troubled me. After meditating for a few minutes, I decided to make a tour of the offices. As I was closing my door, I thought of the coincidence between the appearance of this bizarre text and Arangrude's death, considering it, almost despite myself, very strange.

The corridors of Rosserys and Mitchell were astir with excitement. I joined, one after the other, several groups of headquarters cadres and discovered that this effervescence reflected a struggle between Roustev's clique and that of Saint-Ramé for control of the post Arangrude had occupied. I visited an office of the accounting department and there learned that the employees were upset by the accident. They couldn't stop talking about the dangers of automobile travel. Everywhere I saw the scrolls, but I didn't see a single one that had been untied. Some had simply been tossed into wastepaper baskets. The personnel, always disinclined to examine advertising prospectuses, were probably even more uninterested on this day when the death of the assistant marketing director for Benelux was absorbing their attention. I concluded that the only attitude to adopt was, first of all, not to talk about the scroll. Nevertheless I owed a report to Saint-Ramé and I went back to my office to phone him. There I found my secretary and my assistant in a state of hilarity. This made me quite certain that in one sense or another, the text would not leave the personnel unmoved. Therefore, before calling Saint-Ramé, I decided to exercise my function by feeling out the situation.

"What's going on here?" I asked.

My two co-workers recovered themselves as best they could and Loval said, "Sir, it's this paper, this scroll we found on our desks this morning."

"What of it, Loval?" I said severely. "What's so extraordinary about this scroll?"

"I don't really know, sir—nothing, I suppose. It's nothing special, I admit, but when we read it, it made us laugh out loud."

I foresaw that by putting these two at their ease I might obtain valuable insights and so I exclaimed:

"I'm not criticizing either of you for a minute. We certainly have a right to laugh here at Rosserys and Mitchell. Of all the companies in our country, this is the one where you have the most fun! I admit that I found myself smiling too as I read the scroll. . . . What it says is so preposterous!"

Thus encouraged, Loval interrupted me. "You know, I didn't find it preposterous, but what amused me was thinking of Monsieur Saint-Ramé's face when he read it."

Damnation, I thought, this is getting serious. "Monsieur Saint-Ramé? What sort of face would you expect?"

"I don't know, sir, but you might say that whoever wrote this was making fun of him."

"But he does just the opposite," I said. "He writes that managing a corporation isn't easy these days, that it takes vast knowledge."

"Yes," murmured Loval, suddenly very serious. "That's true."

15

"Loval," I asked on a sudden hunch, "did you know the substance of what was written in that scroll before you read it?"

A minute or two passed before he blurted out his reply. "Sir, this seems silly, but it's as though I knew it without knowing it."

"Come, come, Loval. Certainly you knew the law of supply and demand at least."

"Yes, sir, yes," he answered quickly, as if fearing he had disappointed me by his ignorance. "I knew it without anyone's having properly explained it to me."

"And in this scroll, Loval, was it well explained?"

"Oh, yes, sir, very well. It's as though I understood it better, as though someone had taught it to me."

"But, Loval—and you, mademoiselle—why do you consider it funny?"

"Only because we know that Monsieur Saint-Ramé understands all this, and so it seems funny to congratulate him for knowing it."

"Thanks, Loval; thanks, mademoiselle. Get back to your work and let's not talk anymore about it; you can see it's hardly worth a thought."

They left. I was by no means convinced of the conclusion we had reached in our conversation. Loval and my secretary had given me a clue. From that instant on I was persuaded that the corporation of Rosserys and Mitchell–France was harboring a redoubtable adversary in its bosom. I telephoned Saint-Ramé and immediately obtained an emergency interview.

3

I confess that when I entered Saint-Ramé's office for the second time that day I was far from foreseeing the scroll's disastrous consequences. I explained to our managing director, however, the reasons for my concern.

Saint-Ramé remained silent for a moment. Then he said, "You've verified the fact that everyone got this?"

"Yes, sir."

"Do you think that it was someone in the company who wrote and distributed it?"

"I believe so."

"Why?"

"Because it names you specifically."

"Yes, but . . . after all, I'm fairly well known, the head of a corporation. Reporters quote me in articles about the consumer society, and even the trade unions pillory me."

"That's true, sir. We can't be sure that this is by one of our

17

personnel; only it's not so much an attack on you—that's the bizarre thing about it. It's almost a defense."

"Yes, I noticed that. Very odd."

"Remember, sir, we may know more when we've read the next installment."

Saint-Ramé gave a start. "The next installment, did you say?"

"Yes, it's practically announced in the text. He even tells us what the subject will be: 'The Economic and Financial Role of Capital.' "

Saint-Ramé removed his eyeglasses, something he seldom did and which always signified profound reflection. At the end of several minutes, he murmured, "You're right. This text is really very odd. What the devil can it mean?"

Suddenly I had an inspiration. I'd ask his secretary to read the text and give me her opinion of it. During this time, Saint-Ramé would be hidden behind the door listening. Obviously playing any sort of comedy was not at all characteristic of Henri Saint-Ramé, who was not noted for his sense of humor. Therefore I made my proposal cautiously. To my astonishment, he quickly cut me short and said rather brusquely, "Come on, let's not waste time. What do we do?"

"Well, sir, you hide behind the little door that opens on your secretary's office. I'll go in through the hall door and you'll listen. When you've learned enough, have me called."

I left his office and went into his secretary's.

Mme. Dormun was a cultivated young woman who spoke several languages and was married to a government employee in the Ministry of Finance who calculated the taxes on gasoline and fuel oil.

"Good morning, Madame Dormun. How are you?"

"Not bad; the boss is in a good mood today," and coming close to me and lowering her voice, "He's having lunch with Taboul, the undersecretary in the minister's cabinet." Then, in her usual tone, "Arangrude's death made him very sad. It's not going to be easy to find someone here for the marketing director's job. What do you think?"

"I agree with you, it won't be easy. . . . Look here!" I exclaimed innocently, pointing at the scroll on a corner of her desk. "Did you get one of those too?"

"What do you mean? Oh, that scroll! Don't even mention it. I'm swamped with ads. As if Monsieur Saint-Ramé had time to read all that junk!"

I picked up the scroll, unrolled it and pretended to read it.

"Why, this is odd," I said after a moment. "Hold on—read it yourself. This is different from the usual prospectus."

Mme. Dormun read the parchment through first rapidly, then more slowly. Finally she asked me, "What in the world is it?"

"Haven't the faintest idea. Fairly comical, don't you think?"

"Why, no. I don't see anything funny about it! The unions will be furious."

"The unions?"

"Yes! They're being told that our directors know everything and that the employees know nothing at all!"

"I hadn't thought of that," I said honestly. "Seemed to me the text was making fun of Monsieur Saint-Ramé by caricaturing his knowledge."

"I don't think so. It's true he knows all this."

"Yes, but it's a bit simplistic. He knows this and a lot of other things."

"That's exactly what this says, and it's only the beginning. In time we'll realize that you have to know much more complicated things all the time to run a corporation."

"But after all, Madame Dormun, the way these things are put is so elementary. . . ."

"Not at all! I'm sure our people are going to learn a lot they didn't know, or only thought they knew."

After that I was impatient to rejoin Saint-Ramé and I quickly brought the conversation to an end. I found the managing director annoyed that he'd lent himself to the experiment and disconcerted by the results.

"Well," he said, "your secretary laughed and mine takes it so seriously that she worried about a reaction from the unions. What do we make of that?"

"Well, sir, the whole thing is highly ambiguous."

"That's putting it mildly. You know, I have an idea. Let's drop it now; there'll always be time to talk it over. Whatever it is, we have no way of keeping the personnel from knowing about this . . . paper. When they've all read it, we'll see; meanwhile try to get an idea, discreetly, of who its author is. . . . Before you leave, tell me: Whom do you see here for marketing director?"

"Maybe Brignon, sir. He's head of the French marketing division."

"Brignon," muttered Saint-Ramé. "Why not? Good education, good experience, aggressive; still, he's a bit young, and he's only been in this job a short time. Anyway, we'll see. Have you given instructions for the death notices?"

"Yes; they'll be posted late this afternoon."

"Good. When do you see the widow?"

"At four o'clock."

"Excellent. You'll tell me all about it tomorrow morning."

I took my leave and just as I closed the door I thought I heard a loud burst of laughter. Amazed, I hurried back into Mme. Dormun's room.

"Was it you who laughed?"

The secretary stared at me in astonishment. "No, it was Monsieur Saint-Ramé. He has a right to, hasn't he? Besides, I thought you were with him."

"I was with him," I stammered. "Yes indeed. But I thought you laughed too—you know, about that text."

"Oh, that damned paper! I swear, it's going to keep you awake!"

I smiled foolishly and closed the door. On my way to my office, I was stopped by a man from the engineering department. "Sir,

they've been looking for you. You're wanted down in the basement. It seems there's a crack."

"A crack!"

"Yes, sir, a great crack in one of the walls of the east subcellar.
A weight-bearing wall."

"Thank you. I'll go at once."

Before going down to the basement, however, I felt a need to
be alone for a few minutes. I returned to my office, walked to the
window and contemplated the view. The glass-and-steel office
building of Rosserys and Mitchell–France dominated the Place de
la République, the Place de la Nation, the Place de la Bastille, the
Place Voltaire. How many prestigious names! I thought of the
poets buried at the foot of our fortress in the confines of Père
Lachaise cemetery, where the cadres of the firm of Rosserys and
Mitchell were accustomed to stroll on fine days, as if in a park.
How sinister all this suddenly seemed to me! But now it was my
duty to examine the crack. I closed the window and left my office.
In the elevator plunging toward the entrails of the building, I bore
with me the image of three or four large tombs. Arangrude's
death, the scroll and the crack constituted a series that was begin-
ning to make me ill at ease. Do I today exaggerate the uneasiness
I felt then? Truthfully I do not believe so.

4

Be that as it may, I proceeded to make a minute inspection of the complex of basements (I had never before explored them so thoroughly). The building took root on a spot where in earlier times a great many dead had been buried. During its construction an ancient cemetery had been brought to light, made up of numerous galleries and supplied with water from little subterranean lakes. The authorities of the City of Paris had demanded that the catacombs and ossuaries be respected on both sides of the ground acquired by the Americans, which had led the architects to wall off the entrance to the subterranean preserves. For this purpose special stone had been imported from Pennsylvania. Rosserys and Mitchell made use of these cellars to file its archives and to house the great computer, and they had built an immense library which served also for New Year's celebrations and the company's official ceremonies.

When I'd finished my inspection I directed the responsible

members of the maintenance department to inform the Paris master architect and to keep me posted about his diagnosis and intentions. Should I or should I not ask Saint-Ramé for another emergency appointment? It seemed to me that this was useless, and dangerous because of what he might think of me. Mightn't he get the idea that my nerves were shot and that the moment had come to replace me? I chased away these evil thoughts and at the same time revived my sense of humor by going to the washroom. If tomorrow I should read LONG LIVE THE ROLL! on its walls, would my duty be to report it to Saint-Ramé? Reinvigorated, I went out to lunch.

The memory of luncheon on the day of that first scroll is engraved on my mind.

They are all there, the people who worked then for Rosserys and Mitchell–France, content, joyous, hurried, fat, famished, each rushing for a place in the restaurant or bistro suitable to his salary and rank.

Here is the cadre Brignon, one of our country's brightest marketing hopes, chief of the French marketing section, now candidate for the post that Saint-Ramé had had in mind for poor Arangrude. But how young he is, really!

He comes up to me and greets me with a low bow.

"Good morning, sir."

It's not that he's in awe of me, or afraid of me, but he knows he's been drawn into an unforeseen struggle, and doesn't want to neglect the marginal support of an older man who meets with the managing director at least once a day. They used to say that Brignon was the only cadre in the company's European sales department known and admired by the engineers in the research center at Des Moines. This reputation rested on his feat as a young man, a feat that deserves to be commemorated. An engineer in Kansas had offered American headquarters the patent on a reaper-thresher with vertical intake. Research and Development was excited and urged its purchase. But then it met with opposition from the salesmen: they claimed no country in the world could use it. The new machine was unanimously declared *unsalable*. Brignon persuaded Saint-Ramé to take an interest in this machine on behalf of the French affiliate by showing him how it might be sold in the Vosges Mountains on the eastern slopes of the Central Massif. Des Moines authorized the experiment and it was successful. The future of the machine was assured: arguing from the French success, the heads of Rosserys and Mitchell offered the machine in all countries with terrain like the Vosges. Des Moines congratulated Saint-Ramé, and the American engineers asked the name of the young architect of this success. It was thus that Brignon saw a bright future opening before him.

"Hello, Brignon."

"What are you doing for lunch, sir?"

"As a matter of fact, I hadn't given it a thought."

"Portal, Chavégnac, Le Rantec and I are lunching together today. Would you care to join us?"

"Very much, Brignon, but I'll be a little late. I have an errand to do. Where are you going?"

"We're lunching Chez Baptiste."

"Ah, Chez Baptiste. Very good, Brignon. Thanks, I'll be there soon."

Before joining them I wanted to drift around the place, shake hands with some of my colleagues, feel the company's pulse, sniff out further effects of the business of the scroll. Chez Baptiste was one of those restaurants suddenly adopted by the journalists of the business world, and thus brought to the attention of senior executives and their bosses. Most cadres were avid readers of articles recommending its special goat cheese, black pudding, little wine, excellent chocolate, and even mustard. And they would say proudly to their guests, "Try some of this mustard. It's unusual. Made by hand in the mountains."

Actually the journalists repudiated in private the products they touted to the public. At Chez Baptiste the lunches were expensive, the seats uncomfortable, and the owner bullied you. But festoons of Lombardy sausages hung from the ceiling and dandelion salad was a specialty.

Memories, memories. There we are at the table, Chez Baptiste. Suddenly my juniors pepper me with questions about the paths to power within giant multinational corporations. I don't dare talk about the scroll. Either they haven't read it or they don't dare mention it either. I answer in language I know will please them.

"Well, the first way is to master some technique. Can a factory manager for Rosserys and Mitchell rise to the top? Yes, he can. The second way is through finances: can the financial director rise to the top? Yes, he can. The third way is through sales: can the director of sales and marketing rise to the top? Yes, he can. Finally," I said, preparing my grand point, "we come to a new concept, distinct from all the others, borrowing a little from each —that is, the concept of *administration.* An administrator is neither financier nor technician nor salesman, but I think he's a little of each. Moreover, schools in America teach administration and in our own country such schools are springing up, growing, and may in the end displace all other schools. The path of administration leads to what is called *management.* Management consists in stripping all emotional factors, as far as possible, from plans, figures, organization, transactions. In short, from all imaginable decisions. So for a great manager there's no difference between religions, political regimes, labor unions, etc. This is why all the managers in the world think alike: management demands the most absolute neutrality, radical noninvolvement. The problem is to find out whether an enterprise is profitable or not, whether it can pay for itself. What difference whether the directors later call themselves rightists or leftists? The result is a general leveling off of ideas. Political antagonisms give way to a peaceful circulation of capital and merchandise, which can lead only to global harmony and fraternity."

"Is Saint-Ramé a manager?" asked Portal, chief of Italian-Belgian-Low Countries exports.

I saw the trap and replied with a smile. "Oh, he's a manager, but a great manager."

On these ambitious faces I saw signs of real admiration. Had I not made a subtle reply? Without contradicting myself and without compromising myself? It was something they'd have to learn in order to attain the heights someday.

"When will they bury Arangrude?" asked Brignon.

"I don't know. Probably tomorrow morning."

"Should we go to the funeral?" Chavégnac asked.

"You'll be informed at the proper time."

"Just how did he die?" asked Portal.

"His right temple was crushed . . . in a collision with a Sotanel truck."

"Sotanel?" said Brignon. "A good outfit. I have a buddy there on my own level, six thousand francs a month. It's the fourth largest French manufacturer of heavy machinery."

"Branches in Benelux," Portal insisted.

"The truck belonged to Amel Frères."

"Amel? That's a good outfit too . . . the second long-haul carrier. Operates in Benelux too."

"Poor Arangrude," sighed Brignon.

"He had children?"

"Two."

"And his wife?"

"I'm going to see her this afternoon."

A cloud now passes before my eyes and I can no longer distinguish anything but their frozen silhouettes. After this luncheon, instead of returning at once to my office, I went for a walk in Père Lachaise. . . .

Without pausing to wonder whether executives would be forgiven for wandering through vast cemeteries during working hours.

5

The widow was tired. She was wearing a skirt with black and white stripes, a black blouse with a high black collar, white shoes, a black foulard wrapped around her hair. The Arangrudes occupied a five-room apartment in the Saint-Cloud hills. They had bought it on credit. I knew a lot about their situation. In my capacity as associate director of human relations, it had been my duty to supervise their dossier. The company had advanced them the money to make up what at the time was called the personal contribution. It was, in fact, entirely impossible for cadres, even home-office executives, to buy an apartment; they cost too much. So cadres went into debt and for twenty years made astronomical monthly payments in order to live in a fashionable neighborhood. This requirement made displays of independence difficult. And when a marketing director lost his job, he simultaneously lost his illusions about the role he had thought he was playing in contemporary society.

What was to become of the widow Arangrude and her children? They would have to sell their color television, their stereo system, their Scandinavian furniture and Norman glassware, their wooden forks hand-carved by Eskimos, their chandeliers designed by American prizewinners, the husband's big car, the wife's small car, the handbags and ties imported from Macao by a minister's wife who had a shop in Saint-Germain. They would have to recover— from agents and credit organizations—as much of the invested money as possible while hoping for a rapid resale of the apartment; then they would have to say goodbye to all the wives of the cadres they knew and their friends; cancel the lease on the summer villa; dismiss the maid and the part-time girl from the Alliance Française. And finally they would betake themselves to the provinces, where rents were cheaper, with a recommendation from Saint-Ramé for the widow's employment with a Marseilles subcontractor for Rosserys and Mitchell–France. The death of a cadre on the point of becoming a director. I was seated before her and she was speaking softly to me:

"My Roger is dead and I'm going to tell you who Madame Arangrude is. My father was an official of public works in the prefecture of Hérault. I took my bachelor's degree and my master's in Italian. I became a professor and taught in a college at Mulhouse. One Sunday I saw floats decorated with pork butts going by my window. On these floats men dressed up as sausages were seated in a circle on a cardboard imitation of a frying pan. It was such a funny sight that I burst out laughing. Suddenly the fattest pork butt raised an arm toward me and cried, 'Mademoiselle, come and eat me!' It was Roger. He'd organized this publicity stunt for the local company he worked for, which later became the Korvex Corporation. Later I went out to do some errands and I found the floats in the station plaza. Roger recognized me. We decided to meet that evening. That's how I became his wife. He was ambitious and intelligent; he worked sixteen hours a day. He boosted sales of pork products spectacularly in that area."

"Yes," I said gently. "He and Brignon were the only two headquarters executives who took a real part in mass commercial operations. Saint-Ramé knew about that exploitation of the pork products, and he often held your husband up as an example."

"The next year," the widow continued, "he was hired by Rosserys and Mitchell. I was happy to come up to Paris. We had our first child and our first salary of over five thousand francs a month. Despite his success, Roger always remained modest and a learner. He would study problems of machinery every night. Seeing him immersed in his sales curves and statistics, my admiration for him increased. That was also a period of monetary education for him. He didn't want to be outstripped by events, and so he read a great many articles about gold, the dollar, the franc, the mark—I don't know what all."

"The pound and the lira," I murmured.

"Ah, yes, the pound and the lira. He used to make fun of me sometimes because I would confuse them," she said, suddenly regaining a little of her gaiety at the evocation of these poignant memories. Then she went on. "He quickly learned what was meant by gross income, revenues, margins, profits, investment. You know, his ability to assimilate was prodigious. . . ."

Just then we heard a noise of cars stopping under the windows of the apartment with a great squealing of brakes. "Oh, my God," she whispered, "they're here. Forgive me for not telling you, but you understand, I was suddenly alone and so confused it never occurred to me to warn you. . . ."

"What's going on?" I asked, getting up from the pouf I'd been sitting on.

She burst into sobs and said, "They're bringing home his body."

"Ah," I said, touched and disconcerted. "They're bringing home his body."

This was something I really hadn't foreseen. I put my hand on her arm and, patting it mechanically, strove for the proper attitude. Certainly if I had been forewarned I would not have arrived at this painful moment. We had an appointment for four o'clock, and Mme. Arangrude had never mentioned her intention of having the body brought home. I was all the more surprised since this funeral custom seemed to me to have fallen into desuetude, at least in the city. As though she read my thoughts, the widow said to me, "I didn't know what to do. I was exhausted. I'd spent the night in the hospital. Toward noon they asked me if I wanted the body to be brought to the house. I said yes, without thinking."

Suddenly a disturbing possibility crossed my mind, adding substantially to my fears. I asked, "But are they bringing just your husband's body or the body in a coffin?"

"As a matter of fact," she said, "I don't know."

"You don't know?" I repeated, nonplused.

"No. I simply said yes. I told you I was lost, I don't know the customs. I beg you," she added, afraid to see me wriggling out of this intimate situation, "I beseech you, stay here with me. My parents are coming this evening or tomorrow morning. But I'm all alone. Don't leave me now."

"Don't worry, I'll stay, but I'll have to leave by six at the latest."

There was a knock at the door. I hurried to open it and found myself facing three men, two in white jackets, one in a black overcoat.

"Is this Madame Arangrude's?"

"Yes, she's here," I said.

"Where shall we put the body?"

"Is he in his coffin?" I asked.

"No; we had no instructions about that."

"Wait a minute."

I returned to the widow and explained to her in a low voice, "The body is not in a coffin. Where should they put it?"

Mme. Arangrude buried her face in her hands and whispered, "In his room, here on the left."

"Come on now, be brave," I said, a little unnerved by this incident. "Where are your children?"

"With friends."

"Good. Come and show these gentlemen the way."

With the help of the ambulance driver, the men carried the

30

corpse upstairs on a stretcher, covered with a white cloth. They set it on a bed. Then they announced they'd come back the next day to put it in a coffin.

And so we found ourselves, the widow and I, at the foot of Arangrude's bed, where he lay stark and rigid, an immaculate gauze bandage around his head. We sat in silence. It had been a long time since I'd had any contact with death. My last loss had been a cousin of my own age who'd drowned off Majorca during a fishing expedition organized by manufacturers of camping equipment. We meditated silently for a good quarter of an hour; it was the widow who broke the silence.

"Do forgive me, but I assure you it isn't easy for a woman to find herself rudely thrust into this kind of misery. The authorities, the hospitals, are no help; they ask you a mass of mechanical questions, act accordingly, and don't bother to explain anything. They said to me, 'Is the body to be taken to your house?' I said yes."

"Actually," I remarked, "it's not a bad custom. As a child I went to the wake for my grandparents and for a neighbor. I wasn't left with awful memories. Perhaps, since the body is here, his closest colleagues should come to the wake. Would you like me to speak to Monsieur Saint-Ramé about it?"

"Oh, I don't want to bother anyone."

"I think many of them would like to pay their last respects."

"Do what you think best, monsieur. I'd like you to take care of it, if that's not an imposition."

"Oh, no! After all, am I not associate director of human relations? That's why I made the appointment with you. I wanted to raise the question of the funeral service. Where are you going to have your dear departed buried?"

"In the Saint-Cloud cemetery. Later his father may want to take him home, but just now we have no family vault there."

"And do you want the ceremonies to be private or could his colleagues, friends and associates be present?"

"I see no objection to that."

"Monsieur Saint-Ramé admired Roger Arangrude tremen-

31

dously. As you know, he intended to make him marketing director for the whole company, which is a very important position. Don't forget, Rosserys and Mitchell is the largest multinational corporation in the world."

"I know," said the widow, with a strange glance at the dead man.

"Monsieur Saint-Ramé would be pleased to deliver an oration at the tomb of this peerless colleague. What do you think?"

"I think Roger would have been happy to know that."

Silence returned. This was the second time that some strange power had tried to lull me into a sort of torpor, a detachment from the rational, mechanized world in which until now I'd earned my living so successfully. Earlier, at the window of my office, I'd felt the same impulse tugging at my spirit. And now at the bedside of this dead cadre I had trouble bearing up under the cumulative weight of these events. Was it written somewhere that this day should be fateful for me too? Could I have suspected for an instant when I got up that morning that I'd be confronted by a series of problems so strange and disagreeable as the death of a ranking colleague, a scroll containing a text halfway between a practical joke and a disguised warning, a crack in the foundation, and above all this incredible misunderstanding that had transformed me into an undertaker, with the result that I sat here side by side with Mme. Arangrude, silent and uneasy, my eye immobilized by that horrible gauze bandage around the dead man's forehead?

Considerations of a more practical kind blended with this confused but real foreboding of a future full of snares and pitfalls. For example, how was I to proceed in informing Saint-Ramé and the chief cadres of the possibility of a wake? No one expected that, and I had practically guaranteed it. Was it actually obligatory to inform the managing director? After all, the cadres, colleagues and co-workers of the dead man had a right to keep Roger Arangrude company. I broke the silence by taking up the conversation interrupted by the body's arrival.

"What were we talking about just now?"

"I don't even remember. I was talking about him, us, about his beginnings, I think. But I don't want to bore you with all that."

"But it doesn't bore me at all. I think you were talking about gross income, margins, profits and your husband's ability to assimilate, how fast he learned things. . . ."

"Ah, yes. I was pregnant and we'd moved in a hurry and rented a small apartment in the Rue de Rennes. Roger promised me that soon I'd have a much handsomer and bigger apartment, that he'd waste no time in becoming a success at Rosserys and Mitchell. What's more, he kept his promise, as you know. . . . When I saw him there stretched out, rigid and stark white, with that gauze bandage around his head, I couldn't believe it. I had the feeling he'd get up and start talking to me about inflation, about the rise in prices. . . ."

"Oh," I said, "he talked to you about that too. . . ."

"Yes . . . and in these last days he was uneasy. Monsieur Saint-Ramé had designated him for promotion and he was afraid that the price of machines manufactured in France would rise so high they wouldn't be able to sell them abroad, and in Des Moines they'd decide to convert the factories into body works."

"He was a pessimist," I observed, "because he was aware of his responsibilities."

"You may well say so. He expected a great deal from Europe. . . . He used to say that if the United States, Europe and Japan could reach an agreement it would be possible to sell a great many more machines to the other countries in the world; he wanted to go into China, for as he often said, the Chinese are greatly in need of machines. You understand? He didn't agree with Chinese ideas but nevertheless he wanted to sell them machines. He was kind. . . . Perhaps one day he would have gone into politics."

"I'm sure the day will come," I said gravely, "when we'll sell many machines to the Chinese. . . . Now I must go if I am to get to Rue Oberkampf in time to alert my colleagues. . . . It bothers me, to leave you alone, but I'll come back tonight. . . . I'm deeply impressed by your courage, Madame Arangrude. Au revoir." She accompanied me to the door. In the street I hailed a taxi and gave the address of Rosserys and Mitchell.

When I got to my office I was surprised to find a dinner invitation from Saint-Ramé for that same evening. I asked my secretary how the managing director had sent his message.

"Madame Dormun telephoned," she replied.

At once I called Saint-Ramé's secretary, who confirmed the invitation, telling me I should go directly to the boss's home, since he was away from the office and had made no mention of returning before the eight-thirty dinner hour.

So I had been invited by Saint-Ramé to his own home for the third time since my arrival in the firm. The first occasion had been a large collective buffet dinner to celebrate the Order of Merit bestowed on him; the second, a more intimate dinner at which two of our departmental directors and their wives had been present. That affair was in honor of Bernie Ronson, an American celebrated for his theory of internal communications within giant multinational corporations. This time was I to be the only guest?

35

I regretted not having put the question to Mme. Dormun.

At the moment of writing these lines I remember clearly my morale in the late afternoon of that day: in a word, it was high again. True, I had no idea at the time not only that I'd be proved right but also that I'd survive to enlighten the new courts of law which would, long after, adjudicate the consequences of the failure of nerves and of walls. But the feeling of not being morally subject to grave reproach greatly sustained me and made me almost merry in the execution of the task I had to perform. It must have been six-thirty. The personnel were preparing to leave. I asked my secretary to do one more chore: call together the principal cadres of the company to hear an urgent communication. It was the sort of order of the day that the cadres loved. Of course, when the summons came from Saint-Ramé the excitement was intense. Nevertheless they must have become more or less aware that the associate director of human relations had been unusually agitated and, more important still, that he had been twice in conference with Saint-Ramé, a fact that heightened interest in my meeting.

They were, in fact, not slow to turn up, and a quarter of an hour later they were gathered in my office: Brignon, Portal, Terrène, Fournier, Sélis, Samueru, Vasson, Abéraud, Yritieri, Chavégnac, Le Rantec. I looked them over with undeniable satisfaction. You must understand what I mean: a director of human relations derives his influence from the connections he maintains or fails to maintain with the top executives, and not from the luster and nobility of his title. For the most part my activities had little effect on the cadres bent on improving their jobs. At best they showed me a courteous condescension, or again, as in the case of Brignon, they humored me just to be on the safe side.

But here I was, suddenly summoning all of them and ready with a surprise. I would inform them that over on the hills of Saint-Cloud, stretched out rigid and white, with a gauze bandage around his head, was their admired colleague. I was going to propose a wake. How could I fail to feel smug?

I began on a light note. "Good evening, gentlemen. Thank you for assembling so quickly and in such good number for this meeting—and I apologize to you for its impromptu character. But as you will see, we are ruled by events. You all know, I'm sure, that Roger Arangrude was killed last night on the northern belt parkway; his car collided with a Sotanel truck leased by Amel Frères, a firm well known to you all, second in France in long-haul trucking. His right temple was crushed, which resulted in instantaneous death. This allows us to believe that our dear colleague did not suffer, at which fact we may rejoice. Monsieur Saint-Ramé has charged me with the funeral arrangements, and in his name I went to the home of the deceased this afternoon to meet the widow and decide what part our firm should play in the ceremonies. Our general manager will probably deliver an oration at the tomb. However, final instructions will be given tomorrow morning, for they have not yet been decided. Monsieur Saint-Ramé has invited me to dinner at his house to do this.

"So the purpose of this meeting is not to supply you with directions, since they have not yet been officially issued. Meanwhile a sad and noble task awaits us all. Madame Arangrude wished the body of her husband taken back to their home, to their apartment, to their bed, rather than abandoned in the hospital's freezer. And so you will not be surprised to hear that at the precise instant I am addressing you, your dear colleague Roger Arangrude lies on his own bed, stark and majestic. I add that a gauze bandage is bound around his head, which accentuates the majesty of his death mask. Perhaps some of you will secretly be a little surprised to hear your associate director of human relations express himself in this way. No doubt my language is unusual; some will judge it pompous. But it's not my habit to speak so. It is events rather than my words that are unusual. Is it not strange that his wife, reviving a tender and poetic tradition, should decide to bring her husband home and keep him company for the last time? Is it not strange to lose so cruelly and so meaninglessly the man in whom our general manager saw the future head of marketing for our firm? Finally, is it not extremely strange that the deceased should be crowned with an immaculate gauze bandage?

"I myself would not have spoken in these terms had I not seen him, but I *have* seen him, gentlemen, and I am greatly moved. In the name of the company, I assured Madame Arangrude of our active support. I warmly expressed your condolences and your sadness. I promised her that tonight those on whom the growth and expansion of the corporation depend would visit her and stand in meditation at the bedside of him who was one of our best. That is why, gentlemen, I invite you to participate in this wake at a convenient hour. I ask only that you not all appear at the beginning of the evening; the night will be long and you'll have to come in relays. Don't bring flowers; they'd crowd the apartment. After dinner I myself will go to Saint-Cloud, where I'm sure to see most of you. That's all, gentlemen. If any of you wish further explanations, I am at your disposal."

I was not a little proud of this speech. The ranking executives of Rosserys and Mitchell were all at sea. I had left them uncertain about one important aspect of this operation: would Saint-Ramé participate in the wake or not? I knew my colleagues well and I was sure that more than the death of Arangrude or the gauze bandage, this was what upset them. Moreover, the casual announcement of my dinner at Saint-Ramé's forced them to reflect seriously about how they should behave. What was the associate director of human relations trying to tell them? Was this wake optional or obligatory? Was Saint-Ramé saying through my lips that the home-office executives should appear at Saint-Cloud and stay there the whole night? It was difficult for them to state the problem directly because of its manifest impropriety: If Saint-Ramé goes, I will go.

Vasson, head of exports to the Orient, spoke up. "What is the proper time to appear, sir, in order not to disturb Madame Arangrude too much?"

"In my opinion," I replied, enjoying a guilty satisfaction, "between midnight and four in the morning."

There was a silence. Vasson went on: "Is it permissible to bring one's wife?"

To tell the truth, I hadn't thought about that. Many of these gentlemen would have trouble convincing their wives that they weren't having a night on the town. Imagine explaining to your wife that you had to go to an all-night wake for a colleague in Saint-Cloud! On the other hand, I wanted to avoid a crowd. Unquestionably at the peak of my intellectual form, I announced:

"Those of your wives who have had occasion to lunch or dine at least once with the Arangrudes or *a fortiori* to spend the weekend with them may accompany you. The others, if they think necessary, can ask me to intercede with their wives to release them for the night."

It was then that the first skirmish of the day took place, on the subject of the scrolls, which everyone seemed to have forgotten. Le Rantec started it.

"Sir, if no one has any further questions about the wake, I should like to take advantage of this meeting to ask about a scroll I received this morning and read this afternoon and which I've discovered was received by all members of the company. I am well aware that my question may seem inappropriate at a meeting on so grave a subject as the death of our colleague, but I confess that this scroll troubled me and I am sure, moreover, that my thoughts are representative of the majority of those here, and even of the co-workers who are under our orders. May we talk about this?"

Le Rantec occupied an odd post, which was all the rage at the time in the majority of the important companies—that of secretary general. The opinions of the cadres on this subject were divided. Some thought that the position constituted a stepping stone toward control of those firms called holding companies. To be secretary general of a holding company apparently meant to be able to stick one's nose into everything and, by no means a negligible asset, to be present at board meetings (although as a subordinate) and so to gain the attention of presidents and administrators. The other cadres maintained that secretary general was a blind alley, a pompous title signifying nothing, a job as lackey to company presidents.

Le Rantec's question spoiled my good mood. I was uncertain how to handle it. It would have been easier for me to postpone a discussion of the scroll until later, citing the time, my dinner engagement and the solemnity of this meeting. But it was clear to me that Arangrude's death interested them less than the parchment. I was actually witnessing the first reaction of the principal cadres to the appearance of the scroll. What Saint-Ramé and I had been looking for with our secretaries I saw before me here: henceforth it was an established fact that the cadres of the general staff of Rosserys and Mitchell–France were concerned about that parchment. I decided to report this to the managing director. Then I made a show of consulting my watch and, citing my schedule, agreed to listen to a little more of this affair, but not too much. I said in a firm voice:

"Gentlemen, like you, I have seen this scroll. I should not have thought it worth discussion, in any case not this evening. Nevertheless it's possible that certain implications of the text have escaped me; I admit that I haven't spent hours interpreting it. I have approximately fifteen minutes left; after that, you understand, I must leave you. Are there any further questions about the wake? If not, I'm willing to have this incident discussed."

They were silent, which meant that the scroll was absorbing their attention. Arangrude was already dead and buried. I was seized once more by somber premonitions.

"Gentlemen," I began, "we have a quarter of an hour to exchange impressions of this tract, as you might call it. I take the liberty of reminding you that until now this scroll has not been discussed by any part of general management, and moreover, if this evening we only have fifteen minutes, that is due to the tragic circumstances of Arangrude's death and not to a deliberate attitude on the part of management, which, as you well know, is ready at any instant to discuss any subject. Monsieur Le Rantec, you raised the subject. I give you the floor."

40

Those who may be enraged to note so many lies on my part in so short a time must be indulgent; there were extenuating circumstances. In particular the tone, which I am striving to reproduce faithfully, was altogether normal at that time within company counsels. It fooled no one. The cadres assembled in my office did not believe a single word of what I told them on the subject of the scroll. The very fashion in which I had introduced the discussion, the circumlocutions I had used to assure them that the scroll had not caught the attention of general management, proved exactly the opposite. Obviously the reference to a policy of free speech within the company represented a discursive procedure, a verbal game, rather than a reality. It would not have occurred to any executive, even the most naïve, to take the words of the directors at face value. That is why the language I used at that meeting was not false; no one put any faith in it. On the contrary, each one was grateful to me for making such adroit use of the rules of communication in force at the time. Le Rantec began his speech:

"I believe that this text threatens to unnerve the company because it doesn't resemble any other known text. It's not a trade union tract, it's not a piece of political propaganda; it's a simplistic text without motivation. It's not signed, and nevertheless it's been distributed to everyone. Therefore I think: (a) that we ought to discover the purpose, if there is one, of this text; (b) that we ought to investigate how a tract or document of any sort can be distributed in such large numbers without the knowledge of the management. That's all I have to say," Le Rantec concluded, throwing back his shoulders in self-satisfaction.

"As to the intended purpose," I replied, "management will concern itself with that. But you yourself have pointed out how inconsequential the text is. So management will certainly need you all to determine why anyone should be interested in explaining to the personnel the mechanism of the law of supply and demand. As far as the inquiry goes, I'm altogether in agreement with you: it will be diligently pursued beginning tomorrow, without waiting for Arangrude's funeral."

Brignon came back to the content of the text. "You asked how it can provoke the interest of the personnel. Like you, I don't know. But I have an idea. This text is not solely a commentary on the law of supply and demand; in a number of places it cites Monsieur Saint-Ramé and it continually praises him. I noticed a striking contrast between the extreme simplicity, the exaggeratedly elementary character of the explanation of supply and demand and the excessive praises heaped on Monsieur Saint-Ramé for knowing it. Isn't this a way of mocking him, of caricaturing his knowledge? After all, admiring someone because he knows that a surplus causes a drop in price is astonishing. I'd be curious to know the opinion of my colleagues on that point."

This was the signal for one of the liveliest discussions among executives that I have been privileged to attend in the course of my varied and eventful career.

Sélis, assistant director of imports, thought he was being spoofed, for he was one of those with the greatest influence in the area of prices.

He shouted, "Come on, Brignon, you don't claim the law of supply and demand is adequately explained in that leaflet!"

"By no means," Brignon retorted in a sharp tone. "But let's say it's incomplete rather than false."

"You sound as if you think it's pretty good," said Sélis in vexation.

"Hold on, Sélis! I'm simply a believer, in this case as in others, in coldly analyzing a fact whether it's agreeable or not. I am not an eminent specialist like you on the mechanics of pricing. But it seems to me that what's explained in the text is correct."

"What's correct?" asked Sélis, really irritated now.

"It's correct to write that prices fall when supply increases and rise when there's a shortage."

"Exactly!" cried Sélis. "That's what everybody thinks! Even," he added morosely, "in big corporations like ours. You're stating a commonly held belief about pricing mechanisms that dates back to nineteenth-century liberals! In our day that law's become more complex."

"Interesting as this discussion is," I broke in, seeing that it was getting nowhere, "I remind you that we haven't met here to analyze the law of supply and demand. . . . Who wants the floor?"

"I do," said Fournier, head of the Department of New Machines. "I was happy to see the difference between material and immaterial goods in the text; you may not think so, but a lot of people don't know about that. I'm almost persuaded that our advanced-training service should emphasize it."

"I can't get excited about this," interposed Terrène, head of the French market and celebrated for his drawling voice as well as for his common sense. "I don't see how stating that a lesson in literature is an immaterial good and a sewing machine is a material good can advance our thinking and that of the personnel. Sir, I really think this text is a practical joke and that its author, unless he's just malicious, simply wants to make fun of us."

"Bravo, Terrène!" Sélis exclaimed. "That's my opinion."

"Gentlemen," I said, "I propose we postpone the rest of this meeting; I must now break off the discussion. No doubt I'll see you again tonight at Madame Arangrude's in Saint-Cloud; those who would like to accompany me may telephone me at my home up to eight o'clock. Good night, gentlemen."

They left. I heard their babble diminish.

I remember staying in my office for long minutes of meditation before going home to change for dinner. I was thinking about those young men who did not like one another. Their dislike was not founded on the usual causes—differences of origin, politics, race or clandestine domestic entanglements. Not at all. To the best of my knowledge no such conflict existed at the time. Their fundamental enmity stemmed from the fact that they were all headquarters executives—staff cadres, to use the term adopted by theoreticians; they were all alike, unaware or aware of just about the same things, dedicated to the same kind of success, subject to the same risks, quickly bound by the same limitations.

Hardly had one of them been recruited by the firm when, depending on his salary and position, he instantly became a colleague and an enemy. They all behaved like mastiffs guarding a small territory around their kennels. With men in this state of mind, the true purpose of a discussion became secondary, so it was possible to call a meeting with any agenda at all. The cadres' reaction to the scroll amply proved this. Ignoring the mysterious distribution of over a thousand copies during the night, they plunged ardently into the joys and subtleties of the law of supply and demand. Only too aware of these aberrations, I nevertheless felt uneasy and confused. If this incident was repeated, if a second scroll appeared, would intrigues and feuds tear the firm apart? I decided to talk to the managing director about it. Before leaving, I opened the window wide and contemplated Paris. People were going home from work. Streams of cars crowded the squares and choked the boulevards. Below me to my right, floodlights bathed the slabs and tombs in a delusive radiance.

I was shaving when the phone rang. It was Roustev, the assistant managing director. He was angry; he had not been told about the meeting I had just held.

"It seems to me," he growled, "that I'm at least as concerned as you in Arangrude's death. To begin with, give me some explanation of this masquerade."

"What masquerade?"

"You called a meeting of the senior executives to invite them to a wake, didn't you?"

"Yes, sir."

"Does Saint-Ramé know?"

"No, sir; I haven't had time to tell him. The body was brought back, and I happened to be there."

"Brought back where?"

"To his home."

"I don't understand a word of this. I'm going to telephone Saint-Ramé, and I hope he'll make more sense. Good night."

Roustev occupied a quite special position at the heart of Rosserys and Mitchell–France. Once there was a French entrepreneur who manufactured machines for public works. His name was Gabriel Antémès. Thanks to government sales earmarked for him, and to his lack of principles, he made a fortune. But he was not very intelligent. A good technician and shrewd, he owned two factories and had a weakness for the young and ambitious manager of one of them, who was named Roustev. One day he gave him his daughter, fat and badly brought up, in marriage. Among directors at that time Roustev was looked upon as the new star and future boss of the Antémès enterprises. But in this business, in order to survive, as people said in those days, one had to expand steadily. The government, to which Antémès owed his fortune, put pressure on him and, at the direction of the Minister of Finance, that grand falconer of banks, proposed a merger of Rosserys and Mitchell with Antémès. A year later, the latter fell under the control of the former. Roustev was supplanted by the modernist technocrat Saint-Ramé.

When the crack in the foundation appeared and the first scroll turned up, our company was still dominated by the nasty continuing battle between these two men. As I dressed, suiting my costume to both a dinner with our general manager and a wake, I mentally prepared the plan that I would propose to Saint-Ramé. . . .

It annoyed me that Roustev had been the first to talk to the boss about the wake. But knowing Saint-Ramé's contempt for Antémès' son-in-law, I dismissed that concern from my mind. The telephone rang again. It was Rumin, the company's uncontested labor leader.

"Sir," he said, "you've held a meeting on a subject of general interest. Why weren't the unions informed?"

This time I had to be heartier; it was part of my duties not to offend so important and touchy a personage. Saint-Ramé would never have forgiven me. So I explained at length how the idea of a wake had come up.

"I think it's a fine idea," Rumin declared, "and even if Arangrude was a class enemy he's dead now, and I think a wake'll take us back to wholesome popular traditions and introduce a little human warmth into an ordinarily glacial company. But what about the personnel? You don't think they're good enough to come to an executive's wake?"

"Oh, come on, Rumin, you see traps and insults everywhere," I cried, upset at the proportions my proposal was assuming. "I told you I didn't think it out beforehand. What would you have done, Rumin, if you'd been paying a condolence call on the husband of a junior-level secretary, fourth pay grade, and you'd suddenly seen the woman's dead body appear? And if on top of that you learned that the corpse's homecoming wasn't because the husband wanted it, but because he was half out of his mind at the hospital? Would you have left him alone? Wouldn't you have asked the dead woman's friends and colleagues to keep him company during the night? And do you think I would have telephoned you to complain that the Department of Human Relations hadn't been informed?"

"Right—you wouldn't have telephoned because you're going out to dinner! But let me tell you, the workers have a perfect right to mourn a fellow worker even if he happens to be a senior executive."

"Listen, Rumin," I replied impatiently, "do whatever you like! Show up if you think it's proper. Just let me remind you that in this matter Madame Arangrude's in charge, and not the company. Good night, Rumin!"

I banged down the receiver and took a deep breath. Things were turning out badly. The executives entangled in the business of the scroll, a union boss furious about the wake, an assistant managing director sweating with indignation. Rumin plagued me. He owed his rise to the top of the union hierarchy to an uncommon audacity and a consummate knack for the spectacular. He could smell out "profitable" conflicts, which made the directors look bad in public. He manipulated reporters as well as Saint-Ramé did. He was constantly fighting avant-garde battles—about the psychological effects of work, the organization of leisure time, etc. Many saw in him one of labor's future generals. If he detected a conflict of this kind in a petty incident like the wake, he was quite capable of parading his shock troops under the dead man's windows at midnight. Worried, I decided to ask my managing director's full support and to tell him point by point everything that had either intrigued or perturbed me in the course of that day. With a heavier heart than I'd expected, I put in my appearance at 12 Avenue Georges-Mandel.

That dinner and that wake are engraved in my memory. At Saint-Ramé's I had the excitement of meeting two extremely illustrious guests, whom I should never have dreamed of seeing that evening. Any headquarters executive would have rejoiced at this invitation to join the seraglio. But I was filled with sinister forebodings. Oh, my chieftains! Where are you now? Do you slumber in peace, or do you still wander blaspheming through the labyrinths?

7

Henri Saint-Ramé had invited Adams J. Musterffies, international vice-president in charge of European finances (who I knew was on a tour of inspection to London and Amsterdam), Bernie Ronson, Des Moines' representative in France, Mme. Musterffies and myself. Mme. Saint-Ramé and her daughter joined in the feast. I had never before been in such choice, intimate professional company. That damned scroll, I realized, had induced Saint-Ramé to consult Musterffies and to violate company protocol by inviting me to his house. I had, indeed, been summoned rather than invited. These gentlemen led me into the living room and anticipated my wishes by asking me to describe the events of the day. This method pleased me, for it allowed me to go into detail —that is, to justify myself completely. They listened without interrupting. To my relief, I felt that they held no grievance against me, but on the contrary were concentrating on the facts and trying to interpret them. The atmosphere was serious, at times tense, and

48

this filled me with pleasure. My function would emerge from this ordeal reinforced and enhanced. These men, preoccupied until then by the price of day labor in southern Mexico, were devoting their precious time to an associate director of human relations describing a crack in the basement wall and the cranium of a dead executive. Moreover, I spoke a remarkable American English, a fact that did not go unappreciated.

At the end of my account, a servant broke the silence. "Madame is served." We went in to the table. Avocado à la vinaigrette was served. Having talked a great deal, I fell silent, expecting to be questioned later. I made use of the moment to complete my psychological analysis of the situation. Saint-Ramé had reawakened my admiration. At the end of the morning I had had the impression that he underestimated that accursed text, and his quasi indifference had disappointed me. But his detachment had been a pretense to avoid upsetting his colleagues. Then, alone in his vast office, facing up to his responsibilities, he had decided to employ drastic measures. He had inconvenienced Musterffies, insisted that he hurry over from London. What a leader we had! Perspicacious and serene. Yes, an incomparable man.

After the avocado vinaigrette a leg of lamb was served, then string beans. My prestigious fellow diners delayed voicing an opinion. Suddenly Musterffies questioned me.

"Do you think that this text was composed and distributed by one of your fellow workers?"

"Honestly, sir, I could not assert that," I replied promptly.

I had had to make a delicate decision in a matter of seconds. On the one hand, not having relished at all the phrase "fellow workers," I was able to observe that this referred to Saint-Ramé's employees, and his alone, certainly not to mine. Was that a provocation? Was he trying to make me responsible for the troubles? Was his intention to dissociate Saint-Ramé, head of the firm, from the associate director of human relations, responsible within the company for events involving the personnel? And in that case was that the real explanation for my presence at this dinner? Not sure of

49

these hypotheses, I had decided nevertheless not to discuss the wording of the question just then, inasmuch as I would seriously risk offending its author. On the other hand, I knew that a quick reply, pronounced in a strong voice and neutral tone, pleased these transatlantic magnates, for it implied in their minds clear thought and a profound knowledge of the issue under discussion.

Ronson changed the subject and brought up the problem of French universities. "The only cadres correctly trained in this country have all studied in the United States. You, my dear Henri, are the most brilliant example I know."

"One might almost say"—Musterffies went him one better—"that once they learn our rules, they apply them better than we do."

"Like the Japanese," hazarded Mme. Saint-Ramé.

"Oh, yes, we have some excellent cadres over there," Musterffies agreed. "In my early days with the company I made a long stay in Japan, and I predicted in a report that they'd supplant us in trade. What can you expect? They don't have to pay the exorbitant salaries we do."

"And you're studying in the United States, Betty?" Ronson asked Mlle. Saint-Ramé.

"Yes, and when I come back to France and stroll through the Latin Quarter, it's as if I was back in the Middle Ages."

They laughed. And they went on with their conversation, paying no attention to me. For dessert we were served ice cream.

"So?" Musterffies growled suddenly. "You can't answer my question?"

Well, that was clear enough. How naïve I'd been! I'd thought that the highest officers of the company, worried by an unaccountable event, had come to an expert in human relations for clarification. But no, nothing of the sort. Surely they had conferred privately and decided to pump me. After all, wasn't I the man who'd sounded the alarm? The American's discourteous tone led me to a grotesque supposition. Did they by any chance suspect me of being the author of the text? Instead of distressing me, this idea made me bristle.

"Sir," I said very curtly. "I can't answer your question because nobody can answer it. Still, you insist on an opinion, willy-nilly, so here's what I really think. Either this is a practical joke, in which case I believe it originates outside the company, the work of a group of extreme left-wing students, for example; or we're dealing with a new kind of subversion aimed at the intellectual proletariat of the great corporations—that is, the majority of the executives, and more particularly those who package and sell—in which case I believe that the author is one of our employees. In this latter case, it is my opinion that if the culprit is not discovered this affair may assume major proportions. Finally, sir, I can assure you that I am not the author of this text."

They stared at me in stupefaction, then exclaimed admiringly. Mme. Saint-Ramé discreetly offered me a liqueur. Adams J. Musterffies chewed on his cigar and said to me, "I like the way you've reacted; if you're with us this evening, it's because we're disturbed. On the other hand, we know very well that we have one of the best directors of human relations here in Paris; the only one unquestionably better than you is in San Francisco—Frisco, as we call it—and what's more, he's better only because of his greater experience. Soon you'll be as good as he is. That's right, isn't it, Bernie?"

He winked at Ronson, who nodded. By a gesture to me, Saint-Ramé conveyed agreement and support. Now we were back to the situation as I had seen it at the beginning of the evening: I was an astute executive, recognized as such, and the company counted on me to elucidate the mystery. Nevertheless I remained on my guard. They had forced me to go too far for me to pour out my thanks.

"How do you think we ought to carry out the investigation?" Saint-Ramé asked.

"To begin with, the company ought to pursue the inquiry by its own means, especially since everything indicates that a second text is on the way."

"A second scroll!" cried Musterffies.

"It's quite possible," explained Saint-Ramé. "The author's said as much."

"I have my own idea about this text," Musterffies declared peremptorily. "It's a practical joke."

Then there occurred an unhappy interlude. Betty Saint-Ramé, whose pallor I'd noticed increasing for some minutes, was taken ill. She began to tremble all over, dropped her glass and slid to the floor. There she started to roll and writhe. A light foam appeared at the corners of her lips. She emitted horrifying groans. We grew fearful. Mme. Saint-Ramé telephoned for a doctor. The condition of the girl worsened with incredible speed. She fell into delirium. I heard incoherent fragments of speech: "Forgive . . . Dante . . . paradise . . . the demon . . . forty-five dollars and ten cents . . . Hooray for Los Angeles . . . zero."

The doctor arrived promptly. He refused to have her carried to her room and examined her in our presence. When he was through he said, "This isn't good. She'll have to be taken to the hospital." Then he spoke to Saint-Ramé. "I have something serious to tell you. Do you want me to do it here or in private?"

With a sudden access of pride, Saint-Ramé assured him, "I have nothing to hide from these people."

"Well, sir, your daughter's been taking drugs. Did you know that?"

"No," murmured the managing director. "Are you sure, doctor?"

"Yes, sir. Not only am I sure, but I know she's in a serious condition. . . . How old is she?"

"Seventeen."

"What do you do for a living, sir?"

"I run a corporation. Rosserys and Mitchell–France."

"Congratulations. But then it's not the first time I've run across a case like this. Last week it was the young son of the director of the Regional European Bank. I shall end by believing, gentlemen," he concluded sententiously, "that you manage your businesses better than you do your children."

A society doctor would never have permitted himself such liberty of language. But Mme. Saint-Ramé had hurriedly called the first doctor available; I learned later that this one had his practice in a working-class neighborhood.

Saint-Ramé, ordinarily so quick to react, was silent. The Americans had witnessed this scene without understanding anything, for their internationalism did not extend to learning the language of the countries where they earned their salaries. Elementary courtesy demanded that the essentials be translated for them. I was distressed to be picked by Saint-Ramé for that task.

"Shall I translate everything, sir?"

"Yes, everything." He excused himself and accompanied the doctor from the room.

Betty had calmed down a little. She was still stretched out on the carpet; her mother, Mme. Musterffies, a man-servant and a chambermaid were hovering over her.

"Is it serious?" Ronson asked me.

"Yes," I said. "It's drugs."

"Drugs?" Musterffies exclaimed in astonishment. "And what did the doctor say?"

"He said, 'You manage your business better than your children.'"

"Oh," murmured the two Americans in chorus. Later, two ambulance attendants took the girl away. The guests awkwardly said goodbye, and we found ourselves once more in the Avenue Georges-Mandel.

"This trouble's really upset me," said Musterffies. "I don't want to go to sleep. Besides, we haven't exhausted our subject. I have other questions to put to you. Do you want to continue this conversation at the hotel bar, or are you tired?"

"I'm more upset than tired, and I'd be happy to join you at your hotel. Where are you staying?"

53

"At the George V. Have you a car?"

"Yes. I'll follow you."

Musterffies signaled to his chauffeur. He and his wife and Ronson were swallowed up in the immense vehicle and waited until I was behind them. We then left for the Hotel George V.

8

The people who seek traces of what I was, and what I have lived through, visited me this morning. They are all kind attention. Nevertheless my writings leave them skeptical. From the beginning they made no bones about it. My story gave them lively pleasure and kept its audience gasping, but to take it seriously was risky. They ask me how far along I am, promise to return soon and to let me know the moment they learn anything new. Then they embrace me and give way to the doctor. Just as friendly, just as attentive, he examines me at length. Afterward he shakes his head. Nobody ever contradicts me. I have been told once and for all that my adventures are notable for their romantic quality but have no relation to known facts. I'm alive, I eat, I drink, but people and places I've named since my return to consciousness mean nothing at all. In the face of my insistence on naming precise locations, they sometimes feel doubtful themselves. On the other hand, apparent inaccuracies strengthen their incredulity. Thus I constantly allude to lawsuits, but no suit of this kind is being tried, nor is any in prospect.

I'm sure that they and I are equally confused and troubled. They cannot identify me or explain my presence. And I don't even know where I am. I've accustomed myself to this climate of uncertainty, and am determined to write. I hope to have the strength to push my work through to the end. What comforts me is that the extreme technical accuracy to which I adhere does not appear in any way to detract from the importance of creating a book. Either these people are lying to me and misleading me, or my writing seems to delight them. Why do they attribute such importance to so profitless and lonely an activity? Perhaps I shall learn this before death finally seizes me at the last line, at the culmination of my ultimate effort to intone the peroration.

On the night I was taken to the bar by the boss of the multinational corporation, I remember Mme. Musterffies left us about one in the morning and went upstairs to bed. We'd been drinking whiskey, and as if to celebrate the departure of his wife, the vice-president ordered champagne. The truth is that between our departure from Saint-Ramé's home and one o'clock in the morning, relations between the American couple had deteriorated. It seems that Betty Saint-Ramé's attack had stirred unhappy memories in the Musterffies ménage. Madame had been drinking steadily and so had her husband. They began to comment bitterly on the dinner under the impassive gaze of their sober compatriot, Bernie Ronson, the eye of Des Moines. I hardly understood their fragmentary, slangy conversation. Musterffies criticized his wife for their children's education and, slightly drunk, maintained it must have been the same in the Saint-Ramé household. Henri, a hard worker, a man irreproachable in every respect, had trusted his wife to raise their daughter, as was only natural—and look what had happened!

I was embarrassed by this thundering tirade, which attracted the attention of several rich night owls, fascinated by an American industrialist who was half drunk and perhaps on the point of divulging secrets. It was then that Mme. Musterffies angrily abandoned us. We three stayed on and champagne was served.

"You see, my boy," said Musterffies, patting me on the shoulder, "someday the Russians are going to demand more pigs and cattle from their government; and when their stores are full their economic system will collapse under the pressure of Ukrainian and Georgian housewives. The President of the United States himself told me that—right, Ronson?"

"Absolutely correct," the latter replied, still impassive.

I was intrigued by Ronson's personality. His official title was Representative of Des Moines in France. Each country outside North America did in fact have to maintain one American representative on its headquarters staff. Mostly they were the image of Ronson: cold, courteous, discreet. A few could speak the language of the countries to which they were sent, an exceptional ability for Americans at that time. What did Ronson do? It was said that twice a year he sent secret reports to Des Moines on Saint-Ramé and Roustev, on the political and especially the economic situation in France, on our competitors' activities, and on state projects. Actually Ronson kept up a close relationship with members in three or four ministries (Economics and Finance, Foreign Affairs, Information), sometimes with ministers or ranking officials. His relations with the American ambassador to France and with most of the ambassadors of the Western powers were close and well known.

We had barely emptied the bottle of champagne when Musterffies was shaken by an attack of hilarity, which increased my embarrassment. My head fuddled by excessive drink, I had trouble keeping my ideas straight. I shuddered, speculating on the fate important personages decreed for subalterns who had witnessed their high jinks or misdemeanors. Those in politics were often found in ditches or lying mutilated on deserted beaches.

"By God"—Musterffies hiccuped—"you French never change a bit! A roll of paper, a crack—all this in our Paris office, at Rosserys and Mitchell! And what do I do? I jump into a plane in London just to listen to this tripe! In another way, it's sensational! It's never happened before, to us or our competitors! A crack! Well, maybe that'll bring the whole thing down. Luckily we have our factories! With all our companies around the world, I'm sure we can put down the revolt. Everybody needs steel, castings, paint, gasoline. We have the best tractors on the planet. So the crack isn't going to keep us awake. And then there's this dead man. He's what's got you upset, I guess—who is he anyway? They told me about a dead man at Rosserys and Mitchell; you too—right, Ronson?"

"Yes, a dead executive—Arangrude. He was about to be made marketing director. He was killed last night in a car accident."

"And what was it Saint-Ramé said? Where is he now, this dead executive?"

"At his home, sir."

"Now I've got it. The cadres are holding a wake for their dead colleague. We've got to show up, by God! I'm passing through Paris, and I am sure if I go it will make an excellent impression on his co-workers! You understand what I mean, Ronson? Adams J. Musterffies in person at the bedside of the dead marketing director! Do you think the vice-president of Romney and Proudy would go out of his way to attend the wake of his French company's marketing director? After all, Ronson, what's a marketing director? You and I were that when we were young—when marketing hadn't even been invented! But we know what it is, all right, don't we, Ronson? You remember those times?"

Musterffies must have been recalling prodigiously comic memories, for his hilarity became contagious; the hint of a large grin appeared on Ronson's face. I myself, imagining the confusion that Musterffies would provoke if he arrived at the poor widow's house in this state, was, let us say, sobered. I sought Ronson's eye desperately, since he was in a position to exercise some influence on the vice-president and restrain him from this mad expedition. But Ronson appeared unmoved. If Musterffies, now more than half-seas over, persisted, my situation at the heart of the company would be seriously compromised. What a scandal! Suddenly my mind cleared and I saw the scenario of my dismissal unfolding.

Having taken the initiative alone in organizing the wake at the home of the deceased cadre Arangrude, I had escorted the international vice-president of our company to it, first carefully seeing that he imbibed copiously by dragging him through "gay Paree" after dinner at our managing director's home. By doing so I had betrayed everyone's confidence.

The vice-president urged us to hurry on so as not to be too late in arriving at the Arangrudes'. Then I made two attempts to save myself.

"If you will allow me, sir, it's my turn to offer a bottle."

"No, no, my boy. I'm the one who pays here!" he cried. "Come on, let's get a move on. I'd forgotten the dead man, one of our best cadres! If we wait much longer we'll be rude!" At these words he got to his feet, staggering slightly.

"It's just that I can't remember the address," I babbled.

"Never mind. We'll go to your office first and find it!"

"All right," I said in a dejected voice.

We departed, Musterffies unsteady on his feet, Ronson imperturbable, and I in anguish. The vice-president hailed a taxi and I called out the address: "Corner of Rue Oberkampf and Avenue de la République, near Père Lachaise cemetery."

The taxi let us out beside the cemetery. During the ride, the American chief had not ceased chattering about the entrance he proposed to stage at Mme. Arangrude's home. Ronson had emerged from his reserve enough to try to dissuade him from lining up the cadres on either side of the stairway. I myself repressed violent objections with great difficulty. I had delayed this imprudent expedition on the pretext of not remembering the dead cadre's address. And I was racking my brain for tactics to make use of this delay and lead Musterffies back to his hotel. At Rue Oberkampf I had a ray of hope when the vice-president expressed the desire to visit the cemetery; I calculated immediately that he would be there for the night and would end up sleeping on a grave. So we marched toward the main entrance, which was locked. I knew of another, however, also locked but

59

easy to open. Under my guidance we turned west. While we were following the wall I heard a sound from inside an imposing tomb some ten meters away. "Stop," I whispered, and we listened. The noise was repeated farther off, but more clearly. It did not escape Ronson, who at that instant raised his finger. Musterffies asked permission to urinate, which was granted. Did Ronson understand my maneuver? Had he realized that by choosing to walk in the fresh air at night I counted on awakening Musterffies' common sense and diverting him from his project? I couldn't make him out. Certainly he did nothing to hinder my efforts or compromise my chance of success. We started on, and just as we were passing the vault that noise reached my ears again. Musterffies heard it. He muttered, "There's someone inside there." The fact that he muttered instead of shouting reassured me a bit. A drunken man always talks too loud. One kilometer more, I thought, and he'll be sober.

"It must be a cat," I said.

"A cat in a tomb?"

"No, outside; it must have knocked over a flowerpot. Père Lachaise is famous for the number of cats that wander around it at night."

"Why, I didn't know that," muttered Musterffies.

This brief exchange encouraged me, and I quickened the pace. A quarter of an hour later Musterffies stopped abruptly and said:

"Okay, now I've walked enough. I feel much better; thanks for the exercise. Now let's go back to Rue Oberkampf and get the dead cadre's address. The night's getting on; if we delay much longer we'll arrive when they're putting him in his coffin."

Dazed, I stood silent for several moments. So he had not been deceived. Had his comments been kindly or menacing to me? We retraced our steps. I felt physically and nervously exhausted. I recapitulated my day and the events became confused. I too had been drinking, moderately but more than was my wont. I had assumed responsibility for almost all the day's decisions. A terrible desire to sleep overcame me and now it was I who lagged behind.

An exclamation from Musterffies made me jump. "We're there!"

We were on the Avenue de la République. Far off, I could distinguish the imposing, scintillating mass of glass and steel that was our office building. Musterffies had regained his energy and clarity. I followed him painfully. Absurd ideas crashed against my brain from time to time, like waves against a reef. Was it because he could stand late nights and drinking better than I could that Adams J. Musterffies was in control in Des Moines? Was Ronson a secret agent of the CIA? Had Betty Saint-Ramé died? Should the cadres line up on the stairway or in front of the elevator door?

"Well, now, associate director of human relations, you're asleep on your feet, darn it. Are you all right? We're nearly there and I just asked you a question."

"Excuse me. A moment of fatigue."

"Well, then, what do you think? Should the cadres be lined up on the staircase or in front of the elevator door?"

"I beg your pardon. You asked me that question?"

"You'd better wake up, my friend. As a matter of fact, I asked you twice."

"Aha," I said with a nervous start. "Do you really think they should line up?"

"Not to present arms, of course, but so that they at least know me by sight. I don't know them at all. Where would you make the introductions? In the dead cadre's apartment? That wouldn't be very proper. What's on your mind, anyway?"

"Nothing at all, sir. It's simply that I hadn't thought about it."

"Well, how the devil do you get into this dump?" Musterffies inquired, hammering both fists on the shatterproof glass set in the steel door. "There's a watchman here, I suppose."

"Yes," I said. "Several, as a matter of fact."

I pushed the doorbell.

"Open up!" I shouted. "Don't you recognize me? And the gentleman here is vice-president of the company!"

"Ah, you too? You've come for the wake?" one of the watchmen inquired as he unbolted the door.

"What wake?"

"You know, the wake."

"Yes, but how do you know about that?" I demanded, suddenly alert.

"Because they've been here at least two hours already."

"Who is here?"

"Well, now, the employees . . . The catafalque has been set up in the Great Hall."

"What's he saying?" Musterffies inquired. I translated the unlikely report.

"Let's go in," said Ronson softly. "We'll soon see."

We mounted the monumental marble staircase and emerged into the Great Hall. The spectacle before our eyes seemed to me unreal. In the center of that huge space rose a catafalque, encircled by imposing candelabra. Around it, silent, immobile, I recognized Brignon, Portal, Chavégnac, Fournier, Sélis, Le Rantec and their wives; then Samueru, Yritieri, Abéraud, Terrène and Vasson; then Roustev and his wife, Rosine Antémès. And massed in the background, Rumin and some fifty activists. Alone at the foot of the catafalque: Mme. Arangrude. They were all seated in red plush armchairs. Struck dumb, I contemplated this strange cathedral. The picture of death bivouacking at midnight in the headquarters of the French affiliate of Rosserys and Mitchell International danced before my astounded, melancholy eyes. I blinked and lost consciousness.

9

When I came to, I was in my office. Musterffies, Ronson, Roustev, Rumin and one of the watchmen were gathered around me.

"What happened?" I asked in a feeble voice.

Ronson answered. "You collapsed at the top of the stairway, probably from fatigue and excitement. You're hurt in the temple."

"The temple?" I repeated, recovering my wits bit by bit. Raising my hand to my head, I felt a bandage.

"It isn't serious," said Musterffies, "but you got yourself a nasty crack on the right temple. Thanks to this gentleman," he added, pointing to Rumin, "we managed to find the company clinic and tie a bandage around your head. Come on now, drink this; it'll wake you up."

He handed me a glass of whiskey and forced me to swallow it. My head was heavy but I felt no pain. The bandage reminded me of Arangrude. So now I looked like him. I found this thought disagreeable.

"How long was I unconscious?"

"About twenty minutes," said Rumin.

"Why and how did you happen to come here?" I asked.

"It was Saint-Ramé who had the idea," Roustev explained. "He sent for the funeral directors at company expense and they've handled everything."

"Who announced it to the personnel?"

"Saint-Ramé did that too," said Rumin, "and he was right."

"I didn't mean that I was against it," I sighed.

"Do you feel well enough now to join in the meeting?" Musterffies asked.

"What meeting?"

"Saint-Ramé, Ronson, Roustev, this gentleman Rumin and myself are going to meet to study the facts. Saint-Ramé has been at the hospital, but he'll be here shortly."

"I feel all right," I said. "In a quarter of an hour I'll be in perfect shape."

"Rest awhile. We'll go down to the hall to keep vigil at the catafalque, as long as it's there. . . ." And Musterffies made a fatalistic gesture.

"As soon as Saint-Ramé comes, we'll drop by for you. Would you like me to put out the light?"

I said hurriedly, "No, leave it on."

They left. I got up, opened the door of my office, walked to the washroom and looked at myself in the mirror. They had fitted me out with an enormous cloth bandage tied on any which way. Except for the extreme pallor of my face and this curious turban, I looked normal.

I dashed cold water on my face and returned to my office. Had Saint-Ramé really given these instructions? It seemed highly improbable to me. But he'd explain. What annoyed me was Rumin's presence at this meeting. If the meeting itself proceeded normally, that wouldn't be serious. But if on the contrary we were forced to conclude that for thirty-six hours the company had been the theater of bizarre and inexplicable events, Rumin wouldn't hesitate to demand a company commission of inquiry, legally constituted—that is to say, with him on it. In such a case I couldn't foresee the consequences. I was at this point in my cogitations when the door opened. Ronson announced that the meeting was commencing in Saint-Ramé's office. I had regained my sang-froid and my equilibrium. I consulted my watch: four-thirty. Soon eleven hundred people would be invading the building. Our meeting would absolutely have to result in an intelligent decision. Failing that, hysteria would overwhelm Rosserys and Mitchell International.

From the beginning the meeting took on a style and air that worried me and made me doubtful of its effectiveness. I was well aware that the presence of an officer of the union prevented the intimacy—that is, freedom of speech—that frequently obtained in the high-level councils of management. I am talking about the true councils and not management's pseudo meetings of senior executives and directors. I understood that Saint-Ramé was irritated at having to acknowledge the proliferation of events, in themselves minor, and to recognize as well that through Rumin's meddling the personnel had also become closely involved. For this reason, to deny reality, to behave as though one were getting ready to discuss increases in salaries, seemed to me a step that it would be unwise to take. The managing director's demeanor was quite formal; he opened the meeting with these words:

"Mr. President, I suggest we postpone the investigation this matter obviously needs, and concentrate for now on Arangrude's funeral. At present his colleagues, a delegation of the employees, his widow and his body are downstairs in the hall—in addition to the funerary paraphernalia. When I arrived I was able to speak briefly with Madame Arangrude. Her family and that of the deceased will be in Paris this morning. The obsequies are planned for tomorrow morning in the Church of Saint-Cloud. I've decided that our firm will bear the expense and I'm sure you won't object to that decision. On the other hand, we can't leave the catafalque in the Great Hall all day. I've made the necessary arrangements for the funeral directors to come this morning at six-thirty and take the coffin, the catafalque, the candelabra and the chairs and install them all in one of their chapels. The firm will pay for that too. These decisions will be communicated to those downstairs as soon as our meeting is over. And I propose to see you again at four o'clock this afternoon to examine various recent developments in our corporate life."

This monologue requires two comments from me. First of all, no one should be surprised at the personalized character, a trifle dictatorial, of the speech, even though it was delivered in the presence of Adams J. Musterffies, higher up in the hierarchy than Saint-Ramé. The managing director knew his American superior for what he was, and what he feared most was involving a member of the Des Moines staff in this somber affair. By expressing himself in this way, he confined Musterffies to the remote role of super-overseer, so Rumin couldn't take advantage of his august presence to fabricate an international scandal and so that in Des Moines they'd clearly understand that Musterffies, on his way to Paris, had barely been touched by this ridiculous affair.

My second comment has to do with the tactic adopted by the managing director. His choice was this: either to arrive in haste, unshaven, overcome by private and professional concerns, absorbed in the imbroglio and saying, "Gentlemen, this is no ordinary crisis I am facing, and we are all in the same boat. I should be grateful to you for an explanation of your presence here and that of this catafalque. I warn you, however, that whatever the reason, we must take rapid measures before the opening of the offices." Or on the other hand, he could take the classic approach of confronting a quite different situation. This he did. That night, Saint-Ramé lacked neither courage nor character, but he presided over the meeting as though he had been awakened by the an-

66

nouncement that the workers had taken over the company offices. Today I know why—but it is too late. What had to happen happened.

Rumin, dumfounded, said, "I agree with you completely, sir, about restoring the Great Hall to its proper use, but I have the impression that something's escaped me, that you're hiding the truth from me. What did you mean by 'various recent developments in our corporate life'?"

"My good friend Rumin, it's the wrong time of day for such discussions. I promise to give the whole afternoon to them."

"I have no intention of discussing the matter now, sir, but how can I take part in a debate that I'm not prepared for when you've had plenty of time to think about it? . . . What's the matter with everybody?" he added angrily. "This is all very strange. I don't mean to imply bad faith. Monsieur Arangrude died, and I asked for and obtained permission for the personnel to be represented at the wake; that's open to discussion, but the wake's open to discussion too! If relations were better between the unions and management, I wouldn't be so suspicious. But I'm obliged to be vigilant. Have you ever seen cadres holding a wake for a dead colleague in Paris? No! So it was disturbing. It would have been normal to invite me. Moreover, you yourself informed me of the change in orders, explaining that since there was to be a wake it had better be held in the company building since Madame Arangrude's apartment was too small. All this is very odd, but not tragic. The only two things that are really tragic," Rumin concluded, "are, first, that Monsieur Arangrude is dead—he was a senior executive, but that doesn't mean it isn't sad—and then, the company's constant distrust of the personnel I represent."

Saint-Ramé must have understood then that he had made a tactical error. On his face I read the fatigue and despondency he'd been trying to hide. He gazed steadily at Rumin and said, in a heavy silence, "Rumin, I didn't call you!"

"What do you mean!" The union leader sprang up, outraged. "I answered the telephone myself!"

"I'm sure you did, Rumin, but it wasn't me. . . . Someone must have been imitating my voice."

"Aha," said Roustev, insensitive to the general consternation. "That's where we have to start. If I have this straight, we've been acting out a masquerade; because you ordered me to come here too."

Saint-Ramé spread his hands, then joined them in a gesture of helplessness. As if remembering an anomaly, he turned to me.

"But you and Messieurs Musterffies and Ronson—someone telephoned you too?"

"No," I replied, "no. It was by accident. . . . I was trying to avoid . . . that is, we were ready to go to Saint-Cloud but I'd forgotten the address. Then Monsieur Musterffies suggested we come to my office to find it."

Saint-Ramé seemed quite intrigued. That was the least anyone could expect, so I wasn't offended to hear the same question put to Musterffies. The latter confirmed my version and took the opportunity to have the essence of Rumin's speech translated. He nodded his head for a time and became absorbed in meditation. Perhaps he was searching his rich past for some similar event. But this time he didn't call out to Bernie. On the contrary, he began to examine each person present with interest. Ronson bent toward Saint-Ramé's ear and the latter at once announced: "Gentlemen, till this afternoon."

We broke up. Rumin and I took the same elevator down without exchanging a word. I informed the cadres, and he the personnel, of the decision that had just been made. The union leader held out his hand and looked me straight in the eye.

"See you soon," he said. "I hope you'll be able to go to the meeting without your bandage."

I'd forgotten the bandage. I understood now why Mme. Arangrude had stared at me a few minutes earlier with such a frightened look.

The men from the funeral home did their work with dispatch. At six-thirty the hall was cleared. Standing alone where the catafalque had been, I wondered how to pass the time until nine o'clock. Sleep? By the time I got home it would be seven. I'd have to be up an hour and a half later. Nevertheless I was very tired. A voice behind a pillar made me jump. It was Saint-Ramé. He approached and said in a kindly tone, "Go on home, get some rest; sleep till noon. We won't need you before then. And change your bandage."

Not to be outdone, I asked, "How's your daughter?"

"Much better, thanks." Then he added in a slightly unsteady voice, "Much better than we are, at all events."

"What do you mean by that, sir?"

"You know perfectly well. Wait. Before you go tell me: do you know anyone in our company who can imitate my voice?"

I looked doubtful.

"In any case," he went on, "there's something to make our investigation harder: the man who wrote that imprecation spends enough time around me to imitate me perfectly."

"Imprecation?" I asked in astonishment.

"Yes, that text is a true imprecation, despite appearances; it's loaded with death. The worst of it is that we deserve it to some extent. Believe me, I've thought about it. We have an imprecator in our midst."

He waved to me and disappeared, hunched over, toward the end of the hall. I asked the chief watchman to call me a taxi. Day was breaking when, having removed the cloth bandage, I slipped under the blankets. And suddenly I had an impulse to consult the dictionary. Exactly what was an imprecator?

I leaped out of bed and ran to my bookshelves. This is what I read: *Imprecation: malediction. Rhetorical technique which consists in wishing misfortune to those about whom or to whom one is speaking. Imprecator: one who calls down imprecations.*

"Malediction," I muttered as I fell asleep.

10

That day I reached my office about two forty-five. At three o'clock I went up to Saint-Ramé's office. Ronson, Rumin and Roustev were already there. Saint-Ramé smiled at me and invited me to sit down at his left. This place was so unusual for me that the two old company hands, Rumin and Roustev, frowned. The managing director opened the meeting.

"Gentlemen, Adams J. Musterffies will join us in an hour. This time at my request his presence will be official. I believe our company has recently been the object of trickery and jokes intended to distract the employees from their work. Last night, for example, we were made fun of in circumstances that should have called for solemnity and reverence. I'm happy to see the workers joining with management on this occasion and I salute Monsieur Rumin. The associate director of human relations will explain to you in detail what's happened in the corporation since yesterday morning."

I then gave an excellent summary. During this, Rumin constantly took notes. Roustev himself wrote down several lines. Saint-Ramé spoke again:

"I thank the associate director of human relations for the conciseness and also for the warmth of his exposition. Two possibilities are now open to us. Either Messieurs Roustev and Rumin will complete the narrative by telling us how they were called to company headquarters in the middle of the night, or there may be someone among you who wishes to put questions at once. Which do you prefer?"

Roustev announced that the procedure was a matter of indifference to him, and that he would indeed have a number of questions to ask. Rumin fidgeted on his chair, a sign that he was deeply interested, which worried me.

"I should like," he said in an assured voice, "to have certain points cleared up. In any case, what I can do to complete the story we've just heard amounts to very little. Monsieur Saint-Ramé, or as I now understand it, someone who imitated his voice, telephoned me to announce that the wake would take place in the company hall and that it would begin at eleven o'clock. I had a tough time getting back to the members I'd called in the afternoon and told to assemble at Saint-Cloud. I had to post a man at the door of Madame Arangrude's apartment building. That's all I have to add, and I hope," he added in a tone rich with innuendo, "that the company directors will be able to tell us more, otherwise the personnel will end up with no notion at all of what's going on.

"Now, here are the points on which I should like clarification. If I followed you properly," he said, addressing himself to me, "you saw Monsieur Saint-Ramé twice yesterday—once about Arangrude's death and the second time about the scroll. So I'd like to know if you connect these two matters and if you consider that the distribution of this scroll is more important than the death of the cadre. A second obscure point, though you've explained it, is your arrival in Rue Oberkampf. It is incredible that the accident of looking up an address should have brought you straight to where

71

we were gathered around the dead man. Finally, I consider it indispensable that Madame Arangrude, despite the trials she has undergone, should come here herself to testify as to what happened, since she is at the center of these incidents."

Rumin, much pleased with himself, crossed his legs and lit a cigarette. At this moment the door opened and Musterffies appeared. Those present rose and paid their respects to the vice-president. With a paternal gesture the latter quieted the confusion raised by his appearance and the meeting resumed. Saint-Ramé gave a résumé of what had been said. The American thanked him with a noncommittal smile. Then abruptly he indicated that he was going to speak. He held a long conversation in English with Saint-Ramé on the subject of Rumin, which the managing director summarized thus to the union leader: "Monsieur Rumin, I've summed up your questions to Monsieur Musterffies. The president thinks you were perfectly right to raise them and congratulates you on them. He agrees that it is indispensable to send for Madame Arangrude immediately." Whereupon Saint-Ramé summoned his secretary and directed her to send his chauffeur to Saint-Cloud. After which, the managing director addressed the meeting again in French.

"While we're waiting, I can at least reply, Monsieur Rumin, to most of the points you've touched upon. This is the way I spent my time last night. At dinner I entertained Monsieur Musterffies and his wife, Monsieur Ronson and our director here present. We discussed arrangements for the dead cadre's funeral and then the possible origin of the scroll. Toward midnight my guests said goodbye and I went to bed. I was awakened later on by Monsieur Roustev, who was surprised not to see me at the wake in the Great Hall. I was truly stunned. I dressed hastily and betook myself to Rue Oberkampf. Now, is there a relationship between the curious events that surround the death of Arangrude and the existence of these scrolls? This is what I do not know, Monsieur Rumin, and I count on you in particular to enlighten us in the days to come."

"What do you mean by that?" asked Rumin, on his guard.

"Simply that your position allows you to gather information more easily than we can."

"But I'm not a spy, monsieur!"

"Don't lose your temper, Rumin. It's not a question of spying but of coordinating the efforts of personnel and management in these troubled circumstances. That's in everybody's interest. We shouldn't attribute more importance to these scrolls than they deserve, but we'd be irresponsible to treat this problem lightly."

"May I speak now?" Roustev asked bitterly.

"Why certainly, André," said Saint-Ramé.

"Here is my opinion," declared the assistant managing director sententiously. "There are a lot of funny things going on around here and not just today. There's plenty I could say about mistakes made over the last two years, but I shall confine myself to present events. Someone in this company is making fun of us all; he writes a stupid text, has it printed, finds a way—a remarkable fact, when you come to think of it—to distribute it at night to every desk, more than a thousand copies, and under the noses of the watchmen! What do these watchmen do? Do they sleep? We ought to stop dealing with this security company immediately and demand damages. Then this individual thinks up a macabre scenario, profits by the coincidence of his own troublemaking project with our cadre's death; learns that a ridiculous wake has been organized on the spur of the moment at the widow's home, imitates our managing director's voice and perpetrates these tricks: (*a*) in the name of Rosserys and Mitchell, he orders the funeral directors to install a catafalque, candelabra and easy chairs in the Great Hall, and to transport the body there; (*b*) he informs Madame Arangrude of an alleged decision by the company to hold the wake in Rue Oberkampf for the purpose of rendering official and spectacular homage to the deceased; (*c*) the unions, the cadres, I myself, are informed in the same fashion.

"What I've just said has been verified by me. You understand, I've made my own inquiry, and the widow will bear me out. So you can see a clear connection between these scrolls and that Grand

Guignol wake. This connection is the impostor, the troublemaker. It must be someone who knows our company from top to bottom and its chief officers as well. At odd moments I even have the feeling that he knows the directors' plans. We must unmask this individual by calling in a reliable private detective agency. This is a small part of what I have to say. Someday, I hope, a detailed analysis will be made of the carelessness which has created such conditions that suddenly the most powerful corporation the world has ever seen becomes a theater of collective mindlessness and a stage for a morbid and decadent drama."

When he was through speaking, Roustev threw a self-satisfied glance at the two Americans, and at his hated rival, Henri Saint-Ramé. I don't mind telling you that I was far from imagining the astounding and inexorable drama being played out before my very eyes on that deceptive afternoon. The sequel will provide extenuating circumstances for me. No mind, however alert, would have perceived anything nonhuman or supernatural. It would simply have noted, as I did, a surprising anomaly: André Roustev, the notorious anti-union man and extreme conservative, had not succeeded in keeping his grievances silent in the presence of Rumin. Ordinarily Roustev was able to conceal his grudges and hatreds; his patience and obstinacy, his taste for contriving machinations, his persistence, had given him a reputation among certain people. Less subtle than Saint-Ramé, probably an inferior manager, he was considered in Des Moines a more ruthless director, hypocritical and wily. This is why he was always kept in reserve, and not, as many cadres believed, simply on account of the family connection. Roustev abhorred conversations with the unions and, as far as he was able, torpedoed every move toward understanding and détente. Dominated by what bizarre force, by virtue of what sordid calculation, had the assistant managing director of Rosserys and Mitchell–France given way to his resentment? It seemed to me that his outburst surprised Saint-Ramé, Rumin and the Americans as much as it did me. Saint-Ramé must have had trouble maintaining his legendary self-possession, and

Rumin certainly helped him out by speaking first.

"I thank Monsieur Roustev for having been so frank and clear. A union leader's duty is to stay as far away as possible from personal conflicts and to concern himself solely with the interests of his constituents and the company. What matter from whose mouth truth emerges? Whatever the profound differences that divide the personnel from the assistant managing director, I find myself in agreement with what he said. In particular, I too think an inquiry ought to be opened immediately; but I'm for forming a balanced commission. A private detective agency should do its work under that commission's orders. Finally, I observe that another of yesterday's events has been passed over in silence: a crack appeared in the wall of the subbasement on the cemetery side. I learned of it by accident this morning and I regret to say that the information did not come to me from management."

"Monsieur Rumin," I said, "if you don't mind, we can't keep track of every little thing that happens in the daily life of a huge corporation like ours."

"You call it a little thing?" Rumin protested. "A crack one point six meters long and six millimeters wide?"

"Where did you get those figures?" I asked, somewhat taken aback.

"I got them from the engineering department, and what's more, I went down and verified them myself."

"Yesterday," I said, "the width of the crack was no more than three millimeters. I ordered the architect called in."

"He came late in the afternoon," Rumin agreed, decidedly very much up-to-date. "I checked that out too; but meanwhile the crack had grown larger and the man I talked to on the telephone was obviously worried."

"What's going on here?" the taciturn Ronson suddenly inquired.

I translated. At that the American's face became animated. He exchanged a few words with Musterffies, who then spoke to Saint-Ramé in bossy tones. That too was something new.

"What's all this about a crack? Have you been kept up to date?"

"No," replied Saint-Ramé.

I was grateful to him for not taking the attitude adopted by almost all bosses when lectured by their own superiors—that is, to turn sorrowfully toward their subordinates and heap the responsibility on them.

On the contrary, Saint-Ramé faced up to it.

"My associate director of human relations has gone through a trying day and night; this series of events involved no technical, financial or commercial aspects and so they were all in his province. He had to deal with all the problems at once; as far as the crack is concerned, he took appropriate action, and cannot be faulted for not telling me about it."

"Just so," said Ronson imperturbably, "but the fact is that this crack has grown larger. What do you make of that, Monsieur Roustev?"

This invitation posed a serious problem for anyone capable of deciphering what the corporate language of the time concealed by way of calculation and ulterior motives. Meaning all of us in that office, old wheel horses of intrigue. The son-in-law of Gabriel Antémès, that boor, regained an importance of which perhaps he had despaired. He did not exploit the situation but under cover of modesty gave the question a highly damaging answer.

"Well, this is a very serious problem," he growled. "And of course I wasn't told about it. To reply, I'd have to study the question closely, measure this crack without any preconceptions, confer on the spot with the experts. I won't conceal from you," he concluded, "that this event is more important in my eyes than the distribution of these devilish scrolls and the grotesque funeral arrangements made for the unfortunate Arangrude. And believe me, I regret that as much as you do, if not more."

This was shrewd. Roustev had interpreted Ronson's verbal warning with the speed of lightning. He had understood that the Americans were commencing to be irritated by the commotion over the cadre's death and the appearance of the scrolls. And he anticipated their secret worry by declaring that the announcement about a crack was more alarming than what ought to be dismissed as witch stories.

Musterffies was grateful to Roustev for his attitude. He announced dryly, "I agree with you, André. I think you and Henri should divide the task between you. You take the matter of the crack in hand and Henri will supervise the question of the scrolls and the funeral arrangements."

This division of jobs seemed wrong to Roustev, who now cynically pressed his advantage by proposing, "I question whether Henri alone will have time to deal with the scrolls; it seems to me that he and I should handle that together, while each works alone, he on the dead cadre's funeral and I on the reduction of the crack."

"That's the thing! Reduce the crack!" Musterffies exclaimed with satisfaction. "That's exactly what's needed. What do you think, Henri?"

Rumin, Saint-Ramé and I had been silent but attentive witnesses of this triple exchange. A kind of coalition had formed, embracing the Americans and Roustev. By a sort of natural reaction, another had sprung up to oppose it—Rumin, Saint-Ramé and myself. This is doubtless the moment to emphasize how strange the managing director's attitude appeared to those of us who saw him every day. His hands playing negligently with a pair of ivory dice, his eyes almost dreamy, he seemed serene rather than stolid. And replying to Musterffies, he pronounced this sentence, which was unexpected, to say the least:

"That's it; Roustev is right. *Reduction* is the proper word: isn't a corporation comparable to a human being in all respects? We have to reduce this crack as we reduce a fracture, and I don't doubt that André will prove himself an excellent doctor."

Personally, this response enchanted me. Need I say that the way he'd protected me by emphasizing my difficulties had filled me with gratitude and even admiration. He enchanted me also by the caustic use of the verb *prove*. It would indeed be Roustev's first successful operation, if he succeeded in reducing the crack. Finally, this way of replying indirectly to the question about the reassignment of responsibilities made it possible to say a "yes" full of humor and reservations. It was truly a masterpiece by a leader of the times. Obviously this achievement did not go unobserved by those present, who had confirmation right there, if they needed it, of our managing director's class. Rumin stared quizzically at Saint-Ramé. No one knew how to resume a conversation so brilliantly interrupted. Then Saint-Ramé's secretary entered silently and whispered a few words in his ear.

"Show her in," said Saint-Ramé in a loud voice.

And Mme. Arangrude appeared. She was invited by Musterffies to sit down. Then Saint-Ramé, after apologizing for disturbing her, said:

"Madame, can you shed light on the circumstances in which the body of our lamented Roger was transported from your apartment to the Great Hall of the company?"

"Oh, Monsieur Saint-Ramé, I can never thank you enough," replied the widow, who seemed somewhat recuperated from her weariness. "My poor Roger often said to me, 'Monsieur Saint-Ramé is truly one of the men the future of this country depends on, and he'll rise to the top, because he has heart.' If you only knew how much pleasure you gave me when I heard about your decision last night; how pleased Roger would have been! You know, I even think that you ought to tell all those people who believe big corporations aren't human; if you like, I'll authorize you to publish the photos."

"What photos?" asked Saint-Ramé.

"The photos that were taken just before you arrived; I was sorry you weren't beside me at the foot of the catafalque."

"Ah, yes, of course," said Saint-Ramé. "I'd forgotten they were going to take photographs."

"A half hour after your telephone call," she went on, "the undertaker's people were there. I didn't have to do a thing; in fact, I was relieved. I'd been worried about the arrival of my husband's friends in my apartment, a little small for that. I said to myself, 'Just imagine, they thought about that too.' If Roger hadn't been dead, I could almost have jumped for joy. I telephoned his family in the Ardennes to announce the news. 'Roger's going to receive his last respects in the Great Hall of Rosserys and Mitchell–France.' They could hardly believe it. I should like you, Monsieur Saint-Ramé," she said, "to thank all the personnel in my name and in the name of the family. Roger will be buried tomorrow at ten o'clock at Saint-Cloud. I know you're going to make a speech; the whole family will be there. True, this won't bring my husband back, but I want to show myself worthy of him; he wouldn't have wanted me to cry. It was doubtless to arrange the funeral that you sent me your car, Monsieur Saint-Ramé."

"Yes, it was for that; we'll all be in front of the church at Saint-Cloud at nine forty-five. I thank you for having come, Madame Arangrude, in the midst of all your exhausting duties. I'll have you driven back."

Saint-Ramé arose, as did the others. The dead executive's widow said goodbye and left. Our managing director returned in a couple of minutes, took his seat and gave a résumé in English. This allowed the enigmatic Ronson a chance to assert himself again.

"Who took those photographs?"

"As a matter of fact," said Roustev, "I remember several flashes from behind the big pillars."

"That's right," Rumin confirmed.

"But who took the photos?" Ronson insisted.

"I don't know," said Roustev. "It's always done; I thought it was part of the service supplied by the funeral home. It's customary at all ceremonies."

"We've got to question everyone who was in the Great Hall that night," Musterffies declared.

After consultation with the Americans, Saint-Ramé declared the meeting at an end.

"It's because I have to attend another meeting, with the cadres this time," he said by way of apology.

"Are you going to question them about the identity of this photographer?" Musterffies demanded.

"Yes, only first I'm going to telephone the funeral home about that."

Visibly in a bad humor, the Americans left the room without saying goodbye to anyone. I heard Musterffies growl, "Hell, where are we?"

11

From then on Rosserys and Mitchell–France was to become more and more entangled in a dense web of suspicion. It seemed clear that the company harbored a provocateur, and there were certain indications that he must occupy an important post. The first cadre I met upon leaving Saint-Ramé's office was Le Rantec, attached to general management. He was, as a matter of fact, the man I most wanted to suspect. Who was this Le Rantec? A man of medium height, swarthy, with very dark eyes, wearing dark striped suits. He prided himself on his economic know-how and in this respect he was a typical representative of a growing number of men between thirty and forty, all similar and all living by the same illusion: they professed to understand how to manage and how to produce profits. Did they really understand? They attributed whatever they liked to the men they claimed as their own: McLuhan, Marcuse, Galbraith, Bloch-Lainé, ephemeral idols of these ignorant admirers who had neither studied nor read them. Le Rantec had circumvented Saint-Ramé and the Americans. Within the firm he enjoyed a reputation for competence and intelligence. Anyone who examined his career closely would have discovered that the cadre Le Rantec had never done any managing or organizing, but he arranged numerous meetings for the benefit of the other cadres, meetings in which the words *cash flow, staff and line, international management capital, balance sheet, taxes, treasury, stocks, holding companies, Europe, America, Japan, Eastern bloc, China, export, import, optimization,* etc., poured forth glittering. And no one raised a hand to say: "Last weekend I read a work by Marshall McLuhan entitled *The Gutenberg Galaxy*"—or one by John K. Galbraith called *The New Industrial State,* or the one by Monsieur Bloch-Lainé on profit-sharing —"and it seems to me, after reading it, that their author maintained the opposite of what you say." Anyone who made such an objection would have been scorned by the audience, so completely was it assumed that the act of repeating *certain words* in front of a microphone was a sign of power and that doing so communicated knowledge.

Le Rantec, when I met him upon emerging from Saint-Ramé's office, was showing signs of agitation. For a moment I was afraid that the company, improperly and prematurely informed of the troubles into which it had been plunged, was already falling apart. But no. Le Rantec was whisking through the corridors muttering to himself about soybeans, beef prices, international economic relations. He truly knew very little, but only a keen observer would realize that.

"Have you seen this?" he said to me. "The import tax on beef has been imposed again. The price of cocoa and copper is going up. Soon our raw materials will be beyond our reach! I plan to set up a meeting with Abéraud and Sélis, and maybe even ask the boss."

There it was. This man, incapable of running a department or organizing a workshop, who had never received any serious economic education, who had learned by reading reviews how the national budget is worked out, this man proposed to call his colleagues together to consider the consequences of an increase in the price of raw materials.

"Soybeans! Beef! Ah, yes!" I replied to this factitious and untried apostle of the Harvard Business School. "You're certainly right. Raw materials are rising."

Probably he felt something like indifference in my reply, for he announced sententiously:

"I see you take this lightly; and yet economic policy is basic. How do you hope to play any role if your mind never goes beyond the limits of the company? I don't deny that pregnant secretaries and executive psychology are important problems, but in the final analysis it seems to me that we at Rosserys and Mitchell are directly concerned in present global negotiations."

"You're right," I said. "Too many cadres—and I admit I'm one of them—are ignorant about these difficult questions. Why, just to know," I added, "whether it's a good thing or not to revalue the franc! It's impossible to form an opinion without a solid economic education."

Le Rantec peered at me delightedly. He became amiable and even forthcoming. Taking me by the arm, he condescended to show an interest in me. "My dear colleague," he whispered, "you look worried. What's wrong? Trouble with the boss? I can take care of that if you like."

That's how alliances were formed in the companies of that time. I admitted my economic inferiority to the other cadres. In exchange they proclaimed me the best director of human relations.

Was Le Rantec the imprecator? I decided to take a chance.

"Listen," I said, "have you read the text of those scrolls that were distributed the night before last?"

"Yes; as a matter of duty. It's a ridiculous broadside, a student's practical joke."

"Could you have written it?"

"Certainly I could have written it!" he replied, bridling. "It's the ABC's of the economy, a description of a modern corporate environment, and the natural constraints on it. The consumers' market, the basic distinction between kinds of assets, the circulation of merchandise, the law of supply and demand. It's all a little oversimplified, but it's true. I can't wait for the next one; it's bound to be more subtle. When you come to financial and administrative institutions, things get complicated."

"You can't wait for the next one?"

"But of course. The author all but announced it. You've read this one, haven't you?"

"I've read it, but I'm not as comfortable with it as you."

"What's bothering you? I tell you, it's a student's practical joke."

"In that case," I replied, a little irritated, "go and tell the boss so."

I knew that would hit him. Le Rantec raised his eyebrows and asked, "Is the boss upset about it? He's talked to you?"

"I won't say he's upset, but he's officially instructed me to find out where that damned thing came from. Well, now, could you be the author?"

"What do you mean?"

"Just what I said."

"I could have written it, yes, certainly; but I don't like to think you suspect me of writing it, or even instigating it."

"I shall answer you like a police inspector," I said, adopting a light tone to keep him from spreading gossip. "I suspect everyone and no one."

Le Rantec gave me a bittersweet glance, then brusquely took his leave. The afternoon was well advanced. I was alone in the small, severe but cushioned executive lounge. My job promised to be difficult. Innumerable dormant quarrels would come to life, stretch and forthwith go to work: the struggle that pitted Roustev against Saint-Ramé, the latter against Musterffies and especially against Ronson, not to mention the rivalries between cadres, and between the bosses and the unions. But it seemed to me incredible, in fact revolutionary, that these battles should be waged over a crack in the subbasement, an executive's funeral or a practical

84

joke by some students. Would Saint-Ramé trust me with the key to his actions? And that crack? I hadn't examined it since yesterday. If I didn't go down there at least twice a day I'd be accused of negligence. That made me decide to inspect the foundations before returning to my office.

I met no one. The basements were plunged in darkness, which surprised me. I made my way toward the switchboard and using my cigarette lighter I found a cardboard notice: OUT OF ORDER. This was strange, and it reinforced my desire to examine the crack. Fortunately I knew the subterranean labyrinth of Rosserys and Mitchell's cellars as well as I knew my own pocket, and I succeeded in orienting myself by the illumination of my lighter alone. After walking four or five minutes, I perceived a wavering glow at the end of a corridor. "Damnation," I said to myself. "If I'm not mistaken, that's where the crack is." I proceeded slowly and—I don't know why—with a pounding heart in the direction of the glow. When I was a few yards away I put out my lighter and what I saw made me numb with astonishment.

The beginnings of a scaffolding surrounded the crack, showing that work had begun. But the planks were lighted by a dozen candles, which gave these beginnings a singular aspect, almost unreal, phantasmagoric. Had the workmen, surprised by a power failure, placed and lighted the candles? But where had they gone? I tried to think of rational hypotheses to explain this strange scene. Didn't I have a tendency to interpret too many things in a supernatural fashion? Who but the workmen would have been able to light candles here? I felt, absurdly, a connection between this crack, lighted as it was, and Arangrude's catafalque surrounded by giant candelabra. Suddenly I was frightened and rushed toward the recreation hall. The elevator from the basement had stopped at the door. The moment I got there the lights suddenly went on. Then, reassured and a little ashamed of my fright, I retraced my steps. The crack was there before my eyes, the planks as well. But the candles had disappeared.

12

Much later an official version of these facts was circulated and was accepted by the investigators who requested my testimony. The workers, surprised by a power failure, had used candles to mark the position of their scaffolding, and had knocked off until the lights went on again. My interpretation of the various incidents that marked the life of the company at that time was generally regarded as alarmist. Be that as it may, I'd seen the crack and realized that Rumin was right: the lengthening and widening were quite noticeable. I went back up to my office, and my secretary told me that a meeting of the divisional executives and heads of departments was to be held at four o'clock in conference room 4, in the basement—not far, in fact, from that crack.

Saint-Ramé presided over this meeting, with Roustev on his right and me on his left.

Oh, how I would have liked to speak to them! "Ladies and gentlemen, now that the tocsin has sounded, mobilizing our energies against this monstrous fissure, let him who wrote and distributed the text raise his hand! Let him who rolled the parchment and tied the green-and-black ribbon rise and denounce himself! He will be forgiven. Better still, his definite pedagogic talent will be acknowledged, and his evident desire to teach and popularize the difficult economics of our times. He will be thanked for having calmed our company's nerves. He will even be invited to continue this experiment in good humor, to write the sequel, and if he wishes, the French management and the home office in Des Moines will authorize him to distribute these talented scrolls at night. The use of the green-and-black ribbon will be continued. Every month his fellow workers, from the most humble to the most aristocratic, from the most stupid to the most intelligent, from the richest to the poorest, will receive, democratically, their scroll on economic science and management.

"He who has accomplished this, let him raise his hand! He will even have a bonus, because he has made an innovation. He will have invented a system of communication, internal and revolutionary. He will have discovered the solution to the problem inherited by our Western civilization, otherwise so enterprising— that of communication between men wherever they are, and particularly within giant American multinational corporations.

"I myself, associate director of human relations in a firm of this kind, am jealous of him. Ah, how I'd have loved to compose that text. How happy I'd have been that night in my little room in Rue Burnouf to write such a text, print it clandestinely and distribute it under cover of darkness, adroitly outwitting the vigilance of the watchmen. Where is he who wrote this, who rolled and tied it? Let him show himself so that he may be congratulated, so that he may be felicitated, so that his salary may be raised, so that he may be promoted and sent to complete his education in Massachusetts and return even more knowledgeable, even better informed on amortization and the movement of capital, on profit accounting, on reserves, on self-financing, credit, capital assets, margins, taxes, prices, taxes imposed on companies, joint-stock companies, obligatory loans! Let him who wrote it, rolled it, tied it, distributed it, rise, and let him be praised by all!

"And now, now that he has risen, let all rise too and observe a minute of silence in honor and in the memory of our dear Roger Arangrude, a man who, still young, made an immense forward stride in the marketing of cellophane-wrapped pork products. Once more and most sincerely I congratulate the man who has just stood up, the man who wrote, rolled, tied and distributed the scrolls, for he was not content with this achievement but went even further. What did he do? I will tell you: he conceived the idea of rendering a final homage to our dear Arangrude! He took the initiative with the funeral parlor and ordered a wake in our great marble hall! Just think of that! We had decided to hold a wake in Saint-Cloud at the home of the valiant Madame Arangrude, and he realized that the merits of this dead cadre justified rendering him homage here with us! And he executed his maneuver with an audacity, a precision that aroused the admiration of our leaders! It was thus that last night a catafalque was erected—I humbly admit without our knowledge but to our delight—within this building, giant candelabra were arranged, magnificent red armchairs installed. There the personnel, worthily represented by Monsieur Rumin and by a delegation of executives, offered their profound and discreet affection to the widow and the directors, whom President Musterffies willingly agreed to join. (Emotion ran so high that your poor associate director of human relations lost consciousness for a brief instant.) Tomorrow we will bury our friend with no superfluous frills but with strict formality.

"Moreover, to show that the homage rendered by us that night to the dead cadre was your homage too, we took the liberty, with Madame Arangrude's authorization, of ordering photographs. The man who just stood up is also the man whom we chose to photograph the catafalque. We shall display these photographs in days to come on bulletin boards reserved for that purpose in this building.

"Finally, ladies, gentlemen, dear colleagues, dear fellow workers, you will notice on your way out of this hall, at the far end of the corridor on your right, boards affixed to the wall. Do not be astonished, do not be dismayed; it is simply on account of the crack, which we are actively repairing under the distinguished direction of our Monsieur Roustev, who knows better than anyone else the problems of structural strength and of subcellars because of the education he earlier received from his honorable father-in-law, Gabriel Antémès, the celebrated entrepreneur. This, ladies, gentlemen, is what I have to say to you; and although it is not yet closing time, the company grants you permission to leave at once, which may perhaps spare you traffic problems."

Those are the words I should have dearly loved to speak at this meeting held to dispense information. I'm sure they would have disrupted the Machiavellian projects of the imprecator. Would he have stood up? One could dispute this point interminably. What I am certain of, alas, is that today it is vain to ask. I am convinced that if the American directors had had any idea of what was being planned, they would have agreed to talk in some such fashion in exchange for the preservation of the building and a stop to the aggression.

But there it is. The history of nations and of corporations shows that it is impossible to gain a hearing for premonitory warnings. Later on, as a result of the sad sequels, it is admitted that they were brilliant. Saint-Ramé, by far the most subtle of the directors and of those present, if he had not acquiesced in a strange destiny, would probably have arrived at a solution of this sort, with the complete elimination of the bloodsuckers of the general staff, the modern and dynamic pseudo cadres, the pseudo economists, the false experts. This usurpation by mediocrity, the danger it implies to the survival of the Western democracies' economic system—constantly threatened by revolt, stupidly obliged to shoot down young people or forbid access to public parks—is something capitalist leaders never understood until too late. They were doubtless deficient in intelligence and soul. To finagle a profitable stock transfer or destroy Salvador Allende in Chile was obviously easier than to formulate and apply a system of controls—so prickly in an affluent society—and save the free world by agreeing to sacrifice rugged individualism and put a stop to profiteering. Is a Swiss millionaire's freedom to horde the masterpieces of world painting deep in his steel-shuttered cellars in New York anything more than the freedom to amass personal wealth? Wouldn't he accept any dictatorship sooner than give up his fortune? Running a peacetime army is a delicate job, and unless it's done without demagoguery, it runs the risk of destroying a country from within as certainly as a barbarian invasion. The same thing holds for corporations. In serried ranks they rush toward bankruptcy, at a time, moreover, when their treasuries have never been so full.

The managing director began to speak and gave a full report to his audience. Yes, a crack had appeared. Yes, this scroll, no doubt about it, was odd. Yes, tomorrow Arangrude would be solemnly interred. Yes, there had been a funeral wake in the great marble hall. Ardently and thoughtfully I listened to these words. At bottom, Henri Saint-Ramé felt the same way I did. The difference between the speech I had imagined and his was small. This proved that we had arrived at the same diagnosis of the company situation, the remedies to be applied, the facts to be revealed and those it was best to disguise. What did that difference consist of? In a word, what Saint-Ramé could not and did not wish to utter that evening was the crucial statement that the man who had written, rolled, tied, distributed, ordered, lit the candles, should stand up, that he should stand up and be rewarded! Yet if he had risen, I believed that would have settled many things. Today, knowing what I do, I am convinced that it would hardly have been possible. The imprecator had already decided that he would nevermore stand up. The die had been cast: the giant corporation, American and multinational, would drink its cup to the lees.

13 At the end of this day, the second after the appearance of the initial scroll, I had a talk with the night watchmen of
our glass-and-steel office building and asked the man in charge of
the cleaning women to join us. I requested additional vigilance
and told of the two steps taken by the company—the employment
of six additional watchmen and the promise of a sizable bonus to
each of them if they surprised a man or a woman or a group
distributing tracts or prospectuses throughout the building during
the night. But I announced these measures without conviction. I
was sure that our adversary employed means unknown to us or
that in any case he possessed some enormous advantage over us,
the nature of which I could not guess. In a manner of speaking, I
was under a spell.

A telephone conversation with the director of our security firm
had informed me that the night watchmen working for Rosserys
and Mitchell had been with his company for a long time and that

they were bonded, so that it seemed unreasonable to suspect anyone of them. On the night of the distribution, they had seen nothing, heard nothing. To the question "Early in the morning didn't you notice rolls tied with black-and-green ribbon lying on the desks?" they replied, "No." Among so many papers of all kinds and sizes littering the desks, one more might not have attracted attention. I accepted this explanation the more readily since our fellow workers themselves, believing they were looking at a prospectus of some sort, had not been interested. Most of them did not become aware of the scrolls until midday. I was absolutely sure another would soon appear. I simply hoped that this time, with the watchmen forewarned and stimulated by the promise of a reward, the job of the imprecator would be made more complicated.

Nevertheless, fascinated by the course of events, I no longer doubted their almost supernatural character, which no longer would impress just myself but everyone else if a second operation was successful. I dared not face that possibility. It implied a stirring up of minds, perhaps a panic, the consequences of which could prove disastrous for the corporation. What if, for example, the rumor spread that the company had the evil eye? We'd suffer a drain of workers, a mass of resignations, we'd have trouble finding replacements; or alternatively we'd be obliged to offer salaries two or three times as high as the current ones, which would ruin the firm. It was at the end of that day that I became convinced of the economic gravity of the affair. If a second scroll appeared, the future of the French firm would be compromised. And who knew, since one thing led to another, and rumors flew beyond national frontiers, whether the multinational company itself might not be shaken?

It must have been after eight o'clock when, tired out by lucubration, I decided it was proper for me to leave my office. I put on my overcoat and left. It was the time when congestion eased in Rue Oberkampf, and that was not the least of the reasons that prompted executives to stay late at the office. Thus they killed two birds with one stone: they projected images of themselves as prodigious workers, still at their desks after the departure of the little people, and they avoided the nuisance of the traffic jams.

I walked at a swift pace toward Rue des Cendriers, where we senior executives parked our cars. We did not have parking privileges in the basement garage. Rue des Cendriers afforded the advantage of escaping the close attention of the police, for reasons unknown. It was a cadre who had been the first to discover this; the subordinate employees respected this usage and never parked their vehicles there.

I got into my car and was about to move off when in my rearview mirror I caught sight of silhouettes not unknown to me. I immediately switched off my lights and observed them. A group of men was advancing in my direction. I slid down in my seat and they walked by without seeing me. Cautiously I raised my head and identified Roustev, Brignon, Samueru, Vasson, Yritieri, Terrène, Fournier, Portal and Chavégnac. They went on up Rue des Cendriers, then turned to the right into Rue des Amandiers. What the devil did this expedition signify? Always inclined to dramatize, I did not for an instant think that they might have met simply to dine together. Whatever their project, I was certain that the recent events were the pretext for this unusual gathering. Something told me that my day was not yet over; the duty of an associate director of human relations was to get out of his car, overtake the group and follow it. I put on an old black waterproof cap which I always kept at the bottom of my glove compartment for bad weather in the country and turned up my coat collar. Thus accoutered, I sped in pursuit of my colleagues the senior executives and our assistant general manager.

In Rue des Amandiers I found no one. Bemused and vexed, I prepared to retrace my steps when I thought I recognized Sélis disappearing into a small adjacent street. I remembered that he had not been one of the original Roustev group and this gave me renewed hope. Perhaps he had an appointment with them. As I hurried toward the spot where he had disappeared, I heard a door bang and carefully noted the location of the sound. From the entrance of the Impasse Ronce, I approached it, hugging the wall of the building from which the sound had come. It was a four-story structure, square and massive. What were they looking for in that building? The impasse was deserted and I was assailed by uncomfortable feelings. Now that I knew where these gentlemen had betaken themselves, I was entitled to leave and to demand an explanation from them next day. This plan seemed wise and I withdrew.

I had walked hardly fifty meters when I heard a door open. I hid behind a car and saw Sélis emerge and examine the other buildings as though he was lost. After a few moments' reflection, he made his way deeper into the impasse. Just then a man emerged from a tiny tavern I hadn't noticed before and made off in the direction of Rue des Amandiers. That fellow, I said to myself, is Abéraud, our assistant director of forecasts, but he's going away. What's going on tonight in this Impasse Ronce, where the ranking executives of our corporation are creeping around like thieves? I thrust my cap into my pocket, turned down the collar of my overcoat and marched back to my car. Arriving home, I telephoned Saint-Ramé and told him in detail of the comings and goings of Sélis and Abéraud, and of the disappearance of the Roustev group.

"You're really sure of this?" the managing director asked.

"Sir," I replied indignantly, "I haven't lost my mind yet, although recent events have been enough to upset anyone."

"Don't be angry, my friend," Saint-Ramé said gently. "I don't think for a second that you're crazier than the others, but you may have been mistaken. That impasse—you yourself said—was dark."

"I couldn't have been mistaken about Roustev and his bunch; they went right past me on Rue des Cendriers."

"Yes, but you didn't see them again; maybe they were on their way to have dinner. The only ones you were able to make out in the Impasse Ronce were Sélis and Abéraud, and you might have been mistaken."

"It's a possibility, I admit. Nevertheless . . ."

94

"Listen," Saint-Ramé interrupted me, "you did well to phone me. I want you to know that this incident interests me. So don't feel apologetic at having disturbed me. But the simplest thing is to verify it tomorrow. I don't see what secret mission Roustev could have been given without my knowledge. Do what I plan to do: rest tonight. Till tomorrow."

I slammed down the telephone. Decidedly Saint-Ramé himself understood nothing. I was so furious that I almost hoped the imprecator would succeed in his designs—which I no longer doubted would be catastrophic.

Next day things worked to my confusion. Roustev had invited the principal cadres to dinner to sum up the situation. Which was, strictly speaking, his right. Apparent, too, was his determination to exploit the crisis in order to secure top place. The invitations had been issued late, which explained why four among us did not receive it: we had been unreachable. Sélis, Abéraud, Le Rantec and I myself were, it appeared, not to be found at eight o'clock. I had been in my office. Had they missed me by one minute? Sélis and Abéraud, adroitly questioned by Saint-Ramé, declared that they had spent the evening at home. Perhaps I'd been mistaken about the Roustev group. It's true that I'd lost Roustev on Rue des Amandiers when he turned right. Had they gone into the Impasse Ronce? I would not know until much later.

An immense crowd filled the square in front of the church of Saint-Cloud, overflowing into the neighboring avenues as they awaited the arrival of the hearse. Musterffies growled, "Who the devil are they burying?" There was good reason to ask. In whose honor had all these citizens come out of their way? Would the cadre Arangrude have imagined that on the day of his burial people would have put themselves to this inconvenience, would have crowded together and practically bowed down at the passing of his deluxe coffin, ordered and paid for by his powerful corporation?

There were not enough employees at Rosserys and Mitchell–

France to form this multitude, in which so many faces were unknown to me. With laudable consideration, Saint-Ramé had ordered death notices posted all over the building, inviting everyone to attend. In addition, Rumin, having smelled obscure maneuvers on the part of management, had sent his membership, which meant that two thirds of all the employees had come to the square. The principal newspapers carried an obituary notice: *Adams J. Musterffies, vice-president of Rosserys and Mitchell International in charge of European finances, the general management of Rosserys and Mitchell–France, the unions and employees of the company, announce with sorrow the accidental death of Roger Arangrude, director of marketing for Benelux, graduate of the School of Advanced Commercial Studies, killed on the belt parkway north of Paris about 10 P.M.* Under our notice was that of the family. And under that a third notice was worded thus: *The Korvex Company, second largest in Europe in cellophane-wrapped pork products and first in Africa, has learned with profound regret and great sorrow of the sudden death of Roger Arangrude, former brilliant production chief of this company (Korvébon Hams).*

Headquarters executives from all corners of Paris were there. I saw them from inside my car, identical, sharing the same feelings, deeply moved, some of them even wiping tears from behind the thick lenses of their eyeglasses at the passing of the hearse. Arangrude was taking on the aspect of a symbol: he was the first cadre without wealth to receive the funeral rites habitually reserved for the chieftains of the system. However, these unhappy executives had been duped. They had lost their imagination. They no longer saw the world save in the rear-view mirror of their cars.

At the cemetery Henri Saint-Ramé delivered a surprising speech, to which I paid insufficient attention. I now bitterly regret this, but I was truly disturbed that day by the arrogance and cupidity of the financial empires of the time, whose aberrations, whose mad pride, were leading to the destruction of the free societies from which they had emerged and which they pretended to defend and even to incarnate, from which they had filched their extravagant power. Millions of young people in the industrialized countries, disgusted by the assassinations perpetrated by these powerful international financiers and by their political insolence, disheartened at having to pay so dearly for the liberty to consume, innocently turned their hopes toward burlesque socialisms and ruthless dictatorships. At this time the democracies seemed to be exhausted. Thus a South American country called Chile was one day stabbed in the back by the financiers of Wall Street and their accomplices in the wealthy quarters of Santiago. The statesmen of the West, not knowing, because of their lack of imagination and of character, how to extricate themselves within their own countries from the menace of communism or revolution, trembled at the idea of risking an apology to the Chilean popular front by condemning the assassination. And so they chose cowardice. These considerations explain why I did not at the time pay attention to the ambiguous discourse pronounced by one of the most stereotypical leaders of the period at the open grave of his coworker and in the midst of a crowd of employees and cadres who had gathered in the cemetery of Saint-Cloud. Here in rough paraphrase is his panegyric:

The cadre who lies in this grave is not an ordinary cadre; first of all— and I pray Heaven not to think this arrogant—Roger Arangrude was a cadre of Rosserys and Mitchell. Brilliantly, for two years, he assumed responsibility for marketing our machines to our Belgian, Dutch and Luxembourg friends. He accomplished this mission with so much success that we were on the point of entrusting him with the crushing burden of marketing for our entire firm. Then one evening he was summoned by God on the northern belt parkway. One does not doubt for a moment that despite the magnificent future that was opening before him in his earthly life, God was planning a greatly superior one in His realm. This is the meaning that faith imposes, when one possesses it. And although it is not a part of my role, I take the liberty of reading you this comforting extract from a holy and beautiful epistle in which it is written that those who believe need never despair: "Behold, I show you a mystery: We shall not all sleep, but we shall all be changed, in a moment, in the twinkling of an eye, at the last trump: for the trumpet shall sound, and the dead shall be raised incorruptible, and we shall be changed. For this corruptible must put on incorruption, and this mortal must put on immortality . . . then shall be brought to pass the saying that is written . . . O grave, where is thy victory?"

Thus Roger Arangrude lives for those who have faith, but he is alive as well for those, many in number, who loved him and appreciated him. For his obsequies this crowd has gathered and it is here to listen and to meditate. Why? I am absolutely convinced that Roger Arangrude would have attained the heights of his profession. Cut down in full strength, he was still only at the threshold of celebrity in the business world. Then why has this sorrowing crowd gone out of its way to be here? I will tell you: it is quite simply because this morning we are burying an exemplary representative of our free industrialized civilization. I have had a long conversation with brave Madame Arangrude and what I learned decided me to speak to you in this tone, which you have noticed and which probably the majority of you consider unusual and informal. It is because, as I told you at the beginning, the cadre we are burying is not an ordinary cadre. However great his assiduity, his ardor for work, they never led him to sacrifice the things for which a man should live—that is, culture, meditation, love.

Roger Arangrude spent long evenings in the company of his wife while they read, turn and turn about, the classic poems of humanity. There were even certain evenings on which the couple tested their sensibility and intelligence on the texts of young unknown poets, into whose universe they endeavored to penetrate. Where are the cadres of our day who read poems? Roger Arangrude did not return home simply to dine in silence, kiss his children and quickly pick up a few commonplace political ideas from the newspapers; he did not spend every spare moment watching television with empty or gloating eye. Each year he read a dozen modern novels, three or four works on politics or economics, which he conscientiously annotated; during vacations he reread at least one great classical novel, and for all that, did he not work sixteen hours a day! The last book he reread was *War and Peace.* Where are the cadres who have read, not to mention *reread,* this extremely thick book? What does it matter to them how Tolstoy viewed Napoleon's invasion of his country?

Why did Arangrude reread Tolstoy? And by doing so could he contribute to an increased sale of machines? And then Roger Arangrude visited museums, attended expositions. It was a pleasure to his superiors to know when they listened to his luminous exposés on tomato paste that beneath his cranium that unceasing mechanism of commercial calculation was oiled by the sighs of Anna Karenina or the murmurs of Boris and Natasha. I for my part derived unforgettable comfort from this.

Finally, Roger Arangrude loved his neighbor. His wife was his principal confidante, his children his principal associates, his friends his principal partners. He never broached either at home or in the houses of others questions concerning our company. The highest salary in the world would not have made him renounce culture, meditation, love—in a word, his own personality. And so it is because a man so profoundly engaged in the customs of his century, so much a master of himself in his professional activities, situated at the heart of the most powerful multinational corporation of all time, nevertheless was able to remain himself in this bewildering epoch that I am justified in taking liberties with the usual rules for this kind of discourse. It is in this spirit that I bow before the grave of this man today, and that I say to him: Farewell.

As people left the cemetery after the oration were their comments spontaneous and favorable? Not at all. Most of the great crowd had been too far away from the grave to hear anything at all. As for those who had absorbed or rather followed this discourse word by word, they left in silence, heads bowed and hands clasped behind their backs. Only the Americans, incapable of understanding more than ten or fifteen words of French, seemed relieved to know that Arangrude was beneath the flagstones, well cushioned, safely screwed down inside his coffin. They were not jovial for all that, and an informed colleague could easily guess that now the serious business would begin. Des Moines had, without any doubt, been informed in detail about the agitation in the French firm and unless Saint-Ramé succeeded quickly in reestablishing calm, he would have to defend himself.

My certainty that a plan and not an accident had disturbed the company had increased during the last three days, but on the other hand, my ideas had grown confused. One point tormented me: had Arangrude really been the man Saint-Ramé so enthusiastically described? The widow had not talked to me about Tolstoy. If the principal cadres in the firm had left the cemetery in silence, probably they were asking themselves the same question. Whether the reply was affirmative or not, it would raise new and very considerable problems. Thus, if Saint-Ramé had received from Madame Arangrude details of her husband's private life, it was hardly characteristic of our general manager to take them at face value and draw a romantic picture from them. Why had Saint-Ramé suddenly testified to such a devotion to culture, meditation and love? Why, indeed, should he sketch a false portrait of the deceased?

So the silence of the cadres proved their incapacity to judge whether or not it was proper to manifest enthusiasm over this discourse. No one wanted to run the risk of expressing an opinion. The case was most unusual. Brignon and I got into Le Rantec's car and during the trip I verified the embarrassment which the oration had caused us. Although it preoccupied our minds, we did not speak of it at once.

When we arrived at Rue Oberkampf I saw the Americans' limousine pulling up (it had not escaped the traffic jams). Disinclined to mingle with my chiefs, I disappeared into the building. A quarter of an hour later I was summoned by Adams J. Musterffies to the small reception room. "Our troubles are really beginning," I said to myself, and went off to obey the summons.

14

The American was not alone. A monstrous individual lay sprawled on a sofa. He gave me a familiar wave of the hand as though we had been buddies in the army and said, "Hello." I returned his salutation. Then Musterffies asked me to sit down and said:

"I want you to meet Harold King Vosterbill—we call him King Voster back home. He's been our official private detective back in Iowa for almost ten years. Our dear Henri has secured the services of a French detective, who'll be officially in charge of the investigation. We Americans have great confidence in French private detectives. King's presence shouldn't be interpreted as any weakening of that confidence, but it seemed to us matters were so shadowy that it wouldn't be a bad idea to combine our forces and our information. Besides, King has to earn his salary!" This pleasantry released an uproarious outburst of laughter. "In this affair," Musterffies went on, "I've designated you as the pivotal person for three reasons: first, because of the position you occupy; the associate director of human relations is highly concerned in the case of a provocation that must spring from an unbalanced mind. Besides, you speak our language very well, which is indispensable inasmuch as it was decided last night in Des Moines that we Americans would supervise the investigation, to facilitate the work of our French friends Roustev and Saint-Ramé. Finally, I've been pleased with you at each of our meetings. You seem discreet, modest, but at the same time enterprising and courageous. Need I add that I'm sure of your innocence; perhaps in the last analysis you are the only one here free of all suspicion. As a matter of fact, we spent the crucial night together—at the hotel, taking our walk and at the wake. I was with you from eight-thirty, when we met for dinner at Saint-Ramé's. Now, on that very night a man, according to the evidence, made insane fun of us; by imitating our dear Henri's voice he sent Arangrude's body to the funeral directors, your fellow cadres and the union members to the Great Hall, having earlier distributed those diabolical scrolls.

"Yes, you alone, Saint-Ramé and Roustev—for my part I would add Rumin, contrary to Ronson's opinion—escape suspicion. You see, Rumin is a member of the French Communist Party, and that stupid distribution of texts doesn't resemble their methods. Aside from them, we're forced to suspect everyone. Saint-Ramé is in agreement with us on this subject. Where our opinions differ is in tactics. Back home in the States we are accustomed to drive straight ahead to our goal, not making a mountain out of 'what people will say.' A problem arises, it exists, it has to be resolved, and this alone is of importance.

"Here in France you are more prudent, more anxious to hush things up, to minimize an incident. If this were only up to us, we would announce to the workers straight out that an investigation was about to take place for the purpose of unmasking the person who is keeping us from working, from producing, from selling, from profiting and, thanks to all this, from paying our fellow workers, from giving them handsome bonuses in the summer and at the year's end. Henri prefers not to noise the matter about but to proceed more surreptitiously. His detective will supposedly be representing a Belgian firm that wishes to associate its fortunes with ours. This will give him every opportunity to enter our building, to wander about wherever he likes, to visit all the departments.

"King will be considered one of my assistants from Des Moines. Henri and I have agreed on a maximum of one week. If at the end of this time we have not unmasked the provocateur, then we will employ my methods. I asked you here to introduce King Voster to you and to let you in on our plans. Besides Ronson, Saint-Ramé and myself, you are the only company executive to be so informed. What do you think of all this?"

What judicious reply could I make to the vice-president? There was certainly no lack of ideas in my mind. My head was crowded with them, but they were tangled, a bit confused, contradictory. In my eyes the principal point of that long disquisition had been this: the Americans had definitely taken over. The emphatic allusions to agreement with Henri Saint-Ramé on this procedure demonstrated the point clearly. Musterffies and Ronson had communicated with Des Moines, probably before the preceding night, otherwise King Voster would not have been here so soon. From the beginning I had detected a conflict between the French managing director and his American superiors. And so the latter had in fact come to deprive him of his prerogatives, a fact that confirmed the seriousness with which the home office in Des Moines took the confusion that reigned in France.

I couldn't rule out the possibility that they possessed information unknown to me and of a kind that made them decide very suddenly to take charge. What possible grievances could they entertain against Henri Saint-Ramé to mortify him so openly? Could it be that on this occasion sordid accounts beyond the reach of an ordinary senior executive were being settled between these gentlemen?

At all events, the place was ill suited for reflections of this sort and I replied:

"Sir, I think the essential thing is to keep the provoker or provokers from doing more harm, and consequently, whatever the method chosen, I shall be at my post to carry it out. Just the same, I'd like to ask one question: Shall I myself participate in the investigation? For example, may I interrogate the personnel on the events that have taken place?"

"You're right to ask that question," said Musterffies. "I don't know what King thinks, but my personal opinion is that you ought to be empowered to interrogate your co-workers the senior executives under the seal of absolute secrecy. That way you may obtain valuable information without alarming the personnel."

The detective seconded his boss.

"When I talk to the executives, may I quote the directors and you in particular?"

"Absolutely," said Musterffies, "absolutely. You'll be my spokesman."

At this moment the door to the little reception room opened and Ronson appeared, his face gray and tense. He was surprised to see me there, and to my amazement shook my hand. Then he announced the news:

"Saint-Ramé's daughter has just died in the hospital."

I was frightened. There was something unnatural about this. For the first time, it occurred to me that before long all of us would die. As though in confirmation, Harold King Vosterbill's coarse voice rang through the room.

"Now let's hope we won't find her coffin tonight in the Great Hall."

I took my leave, sad and discouraged. A quarter of an hour later I was recalled to the little reception room. This time six people stared at me in silence. I remained standing, not knowing what to do. I thought it proper to offer my sympathy to Henri Saint-Ramé.

104

The latter, guessing my intention, gestured gently and said to me, "No, thank Heaven, my daughter isn't dead. She's been out in the country since yesterday."

I sat down on an ottoman. Ronson briefly informed me in rumbling tones, "Only about thirty minutes ago Henri's voice announced to me over the telephone that he was canceling a meeting so he could go to the hospital; his daughter had died. This was not true. That is why you have been called back. Have you told anyone?"

"My secretary," I murmured, suddenly terrified.

"Ah . . . what can you do?" asked Musterffies.

"I'll go at once and correct it."

As I was getting up, Ronson motioned me to stay. "Telephone her from here; it will save time."

I rushed to the telephone near the window and called my secretary.

"Mademoiselle? It's me. . . . Yes. Listen, I misunderstood something I heard. Mademoiselle Saint-Ramé is alive and well. . . . Yes. Have you told anyone? . . . Ah, good. So much the better. It was my fault, and I hope you'll excuse me. . . . See you soon."

I hung up. I was both uneasy and furious. After all, I had not made any mistake. It was a matter of course that I'd notify my secretary of Betty Saint-Ramé's death; it was even my duty. Musterffies gestured reassuringly in my direction as though he understood. I felt he was sympathetic. Ronson said to me, "Forgive us. You're not involved in this at all, but it was important to kill this false rumor at once."

"It was partly the result of our conversation," Musterffies added, in an almost friendly tone. "Someone here, as I've told you, is making fun of us. This time the provocateur acted audaciously: he telephoned on the inside line and not to just anyone, but to Bernie Ronson! In the end he'll betray himself. Who in this company is capable of imitating your voice like that, Henri?"

"Anybody who works with me or around me."

A man I had never seen before, catching my eye, smiled at me

105

and said, "We haven't been introduced. My name is Redan, private investigator."

"Delighted," I said, and introduced myself in turn.

"By the way, have you tried imitating our managing director's voice?" the French detective asked me, laughing, and seeing that I frowned, he explained, "You know, we won't get anywhere unless we relax and put ourselves in the place of the impostor."

So I imitated Henri Saint-Ramé's voice.

"Bravo!" cried the detective. "Bravo! Now do it again."

I obeyed. This time even the Americans congratulated me.

I left the room amid the plaudits of the detectives and the general staff.

Le Rantec was my first victim. I summoned him immediately and in so peremptory a tone that he appeared in my office a few moments later more flustered than indignant.

"Ah," I said, "my dear Le Rantec, I've got to go at this seriously now. No help for it. Forgive me for hurrying you, but time presses. And so, dear Le Rantec, imitate the voice of our managing director; imitate, don't protest. Bow to collective discipline, which alone will bail these floods of filthy water out of the hold of our flagship—bail, my boy, bail, as we're urged to do in a famous song; and afterward we'll have a drink! No, I beg of you, don't rebel, don't think I'm mad; on the contrary, I've been instructed to talk to you this way by our beloved bosses. Imitate Henri Saint-Ramé's voice. I'll give you two tries—how about it? . . . What business is it of mine? Don't be insulting, my boy. Am I not associate director in charge of human relations?"

"I'm going straight to Saint-Ramé and complain," Le Rantec said, beside himself with rage, and he left, slamming the door.

But he was quickly back again, escorted by the Americans, Saint-Ramé and Roustev, who clearly indicated by their attitude that the time for jokes had passed.

"Come, Mister Le Rountec," Musterffies insisted, "don't get on your high horse. Perhaps our friend in human relations didn't approach you politely, but he was right. He's in charge; he must

106

carry on the investigation and unmask the impostor. I myself have done the imitation and I'm going to repeat it now to put you at your ease and free you from any embarrassment. Now just listen: 'Allo, Mr. Le Rountec? Saint-Ramé here, your managing director. . . .' You see? I can do it; it's not bad. I might be the guilty man, Le Rountec! If Adams J. Musterffies were the guilty man, that would be colossal! Come, lend yourself to this experiment with good grace. And remember we can tell immediately if someone's purposely trying to do a poor imitation. That right, Bernie?"

"Sure," Ronson growled.

At this moment King Voster made his entrance. Le Rantec, choking with rage at the tone and language that we had been using, Musterffies and I, in the last five minutes, looked as if he was going to pass out at the appearance of the American detective. No doubt less at home than I among the company's jangled nerves, he thought he was going to be tortured in my office to compel him to confess. God knows, the simple evocation of Kentucky—the detective's home state—during the introductions was quite enough to make Le Rantec break down, groaning ecstatically: "Kentucky . . . the United States . . . those campuses across the sea. Next year I'll send my son. . . ."

This piety was of no help to him when he heard himself ordered by Musterffies to perform under the eye of King Voster.

"Come, come, Le Rountec, a surprise! What the devil, don't be scared of this man. He's one of my old colleagues, Harold King Vosterbill, in charge of digesting statistics for me, born in the same town as Ronson—isn't that true, Bernie?"

"Yep," growled Ronson.

Le Rantec obeyed and with a frightened air imitated the voice of Saint-Ramé.

"Ah, not bad, my boy, not bad. Once more now!"

The second attempt was adjudged excellent.

"It's not as good as our associate director of human relations, but it's not bad at all," Musterffies declared. It was then that Le Rantec understood that I had been subjected to the test before him.

107

"What! You did an imitation before me?" he whispered.

"Yes indeed," I replied. "You can see for yourself it's not I who am mad, any more than these gentlemen. By the way, our ranking executives are going to have to submit. You understand the imprecator is imitating the voice of our managing director in order to perpetrate his crimes."

"The imprecator?"

"Yes. The man threatening our enterprise, underhandedly organizing wakes, spreading false news, conceiving, composing, printing and distributing these accursed scrolls, is an imprecator."

And suddenly I was seized by the desire to turn the situation to my own advantage, to highlight my attachment to the company, my fidelity to the system, my devotion to our civilization. Never before had a representative of human relations had an opportunity to shine. And so I added, ostensibly for Le Rantec but actually for the benefit of the general staff, all present in my office:

"You understand, Le Rantec, that we executives are considered by our superiors as the indispensable pivots of the firm and they place absolute confidence in us. That's why we must overcome these trials together and accept the ordeal of an imitation. I don't suspect you. President Musterffies, Messieurs Ronson, Saint-Ramé and Roustev don't suspect you either. But our duty is to begin our investigation with ourselves. This is where our corporation needs not only skillful salesmen and astute technicians, but men of character and imagination. A mortal danger menaces our firm, or perhaps it's only an exaggerated practical joke, a crackbrained exploit; but as long as we haven't identified the crime or the jest, we'll have no right to weep or to laugh. The time has come when we must close ranks and support our directors.

"And let me tell you very simply: I see a kind of tribute paid to the powerful and benevolent firm of Rosserys and Mitchell in that this new evil has first manifested itself against it. Honor where honor is due. Adams J. Musterffies is here in person, among us, a vigorous potentate who has left his office in Des Moines to throw

108

himself into the heart of the melee and to guide us in this combat. Henri Saint-Ramé is his young and enterprising vassal. And we, Le Rantec, are among their chevaliers. Let us don our coats of mail, lower our visors, buckle on our cuirasses and charge straight at the monstrous beast that is attempting to pierce the very entrails of our goddess, swelling with abundance and generosity—Rosserys and Mitchell, the greatest manufacturer and distributor of machines of all time. Le Rantec, let's mobilize our companions. There are only ten of them. With us, that makes twelve, twelve headquarters cadres who by this evening will have done imitations. During this time our superiors will have taken their own measures to approach the personnel by a different method; the personnel are fickle and may fling themselves into anyone's arms, even the demon's.

"Just imagine, Le Rantec, that demon's chosen to make his home with us under the subbasements! Imagine, Le Rantec, that Satan's plotted against us, irritated to see that thanks to our machines, this Earth is being cleared of its brambles, of its jungles, to make place for soybeans and mustard! Here you have the vengeance of Satan, Le Rantec, who realizes that man has paid his debt and after having sweated, bled, atoned, has finally become happy. And so Satan emerges from his fiery lair and attacks those on whom depend the prosperity and happiness of the world. And among them whom does he see, Le Rantec, whom does he see? Somewhere in France he sees a glass-and-steel building at the corner of the Avenue de la République and Rue Oberkampf, not far from Père Lachaise cemetery. In flaming letters visible throughout Paris he reads: ROSSERYS AND MITCHELL. Ruthless and hypocritical, he tunnels beneath the earth, guided by all the damned souls in the cemetery, and God knows, Le Rantec, there are plenty. He penetrates the subbasements. Some night, I tell you, we'll see the tip of his purulent green tail disappearing behind a pillar of the great marble hall. There you have it, Le Rantec. Certainly I haven't talked to you as befits a cadre who insists on brevity and an increased profit margin, but I *have* spoken to you in the only way that seems to me worthy of the associate director of human relations!"

That is how I came to be appointed director. Obviously I had expressed myself in American. The firm's ups and downs had addled minds to the point where my discourse, which in normal times would have earned me a stay in the infirmary, not only flattered the chiefs but galvanized them. I noticed that the American detective no longer looked at me as he had before, and I regretted the absence of the French detective. Adams J. Musterffies rose and said, "Magnificent! I've discovered you today! I am now persuaded that you are just as good as the director of human relations in San Francisco. Henri, Bernie, André, let's promote him director! What does this word *associate* mean after all? Promote him, promote him!" he cried, a prey to ever-mounting excitement.

"Yes, promote him!" the others approved in chorus.

After the customary congratulations, they left the room highly pleased. Le Rantec did not move from his chair. Pale, not yet recovered from this stirring episode, he seemed to be asking himself whether what he had just experienced was real. Finally he rose, wiped his face with his handkerchief and extended his hand to me.

"I congratulate you too," he said in a faint voice. "I need to think things over. I'm going home."

And he left. I in my turn wiped my brow and opened the window. The fresh air caressed my face. Beyond the tall buildings, far off, I saw children playing in a schoolyard. I lit a cigarette. A strange silence enveloped our building, ordinarily so noisy. Below in the street, traffic seemed to me abnormally slow. Fatigue took possession of me. I suddenly became aware that an event of considerable importance had taken place. I was not thinking about my unexpected promotion, but about the language used for almost an hour. How strange that was! People as little given to fantasy as the Americans, Saint-Ramé, Roustev, had raised their voices, almost in

110

song: "Promote him, let's promote him!" They stopped just short of gamboling and pirouetting.

I leaned on the window sill. To my right lay Père Lachaise. Was a serpent with a long greenish tail hiding down there? Was an evil genius rejoicing at that very moment in the darkness of our building's subbasements because language itself had become infected? In a week's time, I asked myself in anguish, would my co-workers at Rosserys and Mitchell be expressing themselves in song? Who was staging this demoniacal opera? Where had the person hidden himself who had loosed these terrible disturbances?

Tonight as I write these lines, though I am very tired from my literary efforts, I have no desire to fall asleep. My memory of those moments is too vivid, the visions that accompany it are too terrifying. Tonight my sleep will be a nightmare. And I shall certainly be startled into wakefulness by the lively bubbling of dark whirlpools, frozen by the growling of cataracts that announce the onset of hysteria.

Now, this was the time when the rich countries, bristling with industries, stuffed with stores, had finally discovered a new law, a project worthy of the rude labors imposed on man, with man's consent for millennia: to make the world a single and unique corporation.

15 On the following morning eleven hundred persons employed at the headquarters of Rosserys and Mitchell–France received, at their homes, a scroll tied with a green-and-black ribbon. It was the second imprecation. In layout and typography it was similar in every respect to the first.

WHAT DO THOSE WHO RUN
ROSSERYS AND MITCHELL
REALLY KNOW?

Those who direct Rosserys and Mitchell know more than people think. And if certain co-workers underestimate their superiors' knowledge, this is due to the latter's exceptional modesty. As a matter of fact, those who today survey the vast horizons of the world and plan cosmic

112

projects, those who, thanks to their education, knowledge and audacity, no longer fear the mysteries of the universe, those in whose eyes Pluto is a storehouse of energy and no longer a magic point in the sky —these men, contrary to what one might expect, are modest and live frugal lives. Their knowledge goes unobserved. And so it can happen that the men and women who meet them on the street or in the corridors of the company no longer recognize them, or on the other hand, deceived by their amiability, their simplicity, their naturalness, the modesty of their dress, are misled and say to themselves: "After all, what do these men, our bosses, know that we don't know?" Well, among the words, the concepts, the formulas that brighten their daily lives and end up as second nature to them, there are some that conceal a complexity of which the common man has no proper idea. So it is, for example, with the following words: *capital, investment, amortization, concentration, revenues, funds, budgetary bloc.*

We have seen that capital can circulate, depending on whether it is liquid or not. But most of those who take orders stop short at this notion, whereas their chiefs press boldly on. How is capital acquired? How is one to deal with its depletion and renewal? Here are questions to which it is obviously especially hard to find answers. Those who direct us have found them. Let's take steel. It is a raw material that circulates, since if an entrepreneur buys steel to manufacture an automobile, the steel contained in the vehicle emerges from the factory and proceeds to circulate along the picturesque roads of our country. But to buy this steel the entrepreneur has to expend money. Now, this money that he has to have in order to acquire this capital in raw materials is called monetary capital. Well and good. But who is going to give the company this monetary capital? Why, it is our fellow citizens. For they are not going to spend all the money they receive in exchange for their work. They are going to save some. A part of this saving will be deposited in the banks and various financial institutions, another part will be devoted to buying stocks and bonds.

Ah, those stocks and bonds! The masses, unaware and unappreciative of the science of finance, have never grasped the basic difference between a stock and a bond. They are not aware that he who owns a stock is a stockholder in the company, whereas he who owns a bond is a bondholder. The stockholder is an associate, he is invited to act—his ownership is, after all, considered an action—and in this respect nothing distinguishes him from those who own or direct the company. To own a stock is to become an actor in the company with which one is associated. Consequently it is natural that the stockholders should share in the good and bad times. And in fact, stocks rise or fall as the case may be.

The bond, on the other hand, is more cross-grained, more cynical, than the share. A man lends his money to a company, which is then obligated to pay him interest each year, whatever its temporary condition. After that, at the expiration of the appointed period, it will return the money to the lender. Those who preside over the destinies of Rosserys and Mitchell are not content with assimilating these notions—they go into details and, by means of mathematics, they transform at will the impersonal power of money. It may happen that a company issues bonds at a price, E, below the price of repayment, R. Would you have suspected that? And do you know what the difference between R and E is called? It is called the repayment premium. Consequently if X is the number of bonds issued, the premium for the whole amount borrowed comes to $X(R-E)$. And have you any idea what an annuity is? Well, it is a sum paid annually. To pay in ten annuities therefore means that each year for ten years a sum is paid. Let us enter boldly into the complications that are the lot of those who direct the economy and learn in our turn that annuities can be either fixed or variable. Finally, let us humble ourselves by respectfully contemplating the formulas that make it possible to establish with precision the amount of a fixed annuity:

$$a = \frac{Ar(1+r)n}{(1+r)n-1}$$

where A represents the capital to be repaid, r the unit of one franc during the period specified, and n the number of periods. Now let us

114

return to the surface and pause over this notion of investment, the keystone in the arch of our prosperity. An enterprise having secured its capital, being obligated thenceforth to pay interest on its bonds and happy to have emerged from its solitude, marching forward under the protection of its squadrons of stockholders—what is it going to undertake? Well, then, it is going to invest.

Those who direct Rosserys and Mitchell excel in investing for our greatest good. They enlarge their facilities, modernize them, build new factories, increase their supplies. Here the vital thing is to have foresight. In the same way it is indispensable to foresee the wear and tear on machines and buildings. And so it is necessary to build reserves to renew the fixed capital. Where to find these reserves? Those who direct us have studied the question and they have solved it. They will include in the sales price of the product an amount that will represent the depreciation of the machinery. Just see how sometimes the most difficult problems yield the simplest solutions. Thus, for example, they figure that a machine will produce 200,000 units, after which it will be worn out or obsolete. If this machine costs 400,000 francs, you divide 400,000 by 200,000, which gives 2 francs. And the price of each unit will then include these 2 francs. This ingenious operation is called amortization. Investment and amortization constitute the two columns on which those who provide us with our livelihood rely. This is why they attach special attention to them. Each year our dear Henri Saint-Ramé, in the peace of his office, takes up his pen and calculates. He deducts the sum total of the amortizations from the sum total of the investments. He thus obtains, would you believe it, the net investment, an infallible barometer of the health and dynamism of a company.

This summary and intentionally eclectic survey of the mechanism of acquisition and employment of capital, this abrupt plunge into the profound depths of speculative and financial calculation, suffers, obviously, from all that has not been included, which is immense. Here we have dealt merely with a minuscule view of the phenomena that govern our world and the oppressive preoccupations they entail for our leaders, the impressive intellectual faculties they manifest. May my modest contribution to the explanation of their heavy labor be understood in this sense. I hope that without displaying misplaced admiration, our fellow workers of both sexes, now a little more aware of the virtues and crushing responsibilities of those who direct them, will naturally come to thank them by a discreet smile, by an affectionate wink, by some sign or other expressing their devotion and gratitude when by chance they meet them in the street or in the corridors. Shortly your admiration for them will exceed all limits when I briefly explain the generous, warm-hearted company table of organization planned by our good masters: staff and line, and objective management. Beyond question, emotion will then choke our fellow citizens and who knows but what they will privately wipe away a round and salty tear or two.

Meanwhile let us pray God that our company will win the economic war for the greatest happiness of all men and let us beseech Him to preserve the health of the leaders who watch over our growth and expansion. By revealing a little of what they know, and of their burden, I shall have contributed to the respect due them.

That morning at the hour when offices open, the residents of the Bastille, Nation, République and Père Lachaise quarters were fascinated to see crowds of people pressing against the doors of Rosserys and Mitchell–France, all holding rolls of paper tied with green-and-black ribbon. Although I had expected sooner or later to receive a second accursed parchment, my heart beat hard when I recognized it among the letters and pamphlets that filled my mailbox. Despite the fact that I was slightly late, I could not resist the desire to read it, and unrolled the scroll. The text taught me nothing. It continued to be simplistic, naïve and, according to me, ironic. I thrust it into my pocket and got onto a bus. During the trip I was secretly tempted to read it again, but I did not dare exhibit it in public.

As I got off my bus, I was once more calculating the pernicious effects of this clandestine action. A crowd of questions was swirling in my head and I had barely turned down Rue de la Folie-Méricourt when the answer to one of them came to me with no effort on my part: hundreds of employees of our company were streaming toward Rue Oberkampf, brandishing scrolls in the air. This showed that like me they had found them in their morning mail. Not wishing to be conspicuous, I quickly drew mine from my pocket. Unlike the bus, Rue Oberkampf and its environs constituted a territory within which it would be bad form to appear exempt from this prank.

As I was walking along I examined the scroll closely and discovered that it bore no postmark. The imprecator and his accomplices had distributed them by hand at various homes. Unless they had made use of a number of teams of distributors, this was almost miraculous. The employees of Rosserys and Mitchell live in almost every section of Paris, some scattered in the remote suburbs. It would be my duty, beginning this morning, to ascertain whether all the eleven hundred persons who worked in the office building had received their scrolls. Here was something that would delay the interrogation of the principal cadres. But after all, I thought, this change of method restored the author's human character and face. We were no longer confronting supernatural powers. Demon or phantom would have outwitted our night guardianship. The genius of the imprecator, checked by the teams of flesh-and-blood watchmen, was brought back to rational proportions. But to counterbalance these positive and reassuring reflections, there was the corporation itself: a company at the boiling point, to judge by the crowding and confusion that reigned at the doors of the Great Hall. What the devil, I said to myself, you might think they were having a holiday. They were exchanging opinions, exulting, palavering, asking each other questions, talking all at once.

"Tell me, Irene, did you see that bit about annuities?"

And they burst into guffaws.

"What do you think—is that formula right?"

"Tell me, did you see that twaddle about amortization?"

"Well, what about it? It's so. It's true that you have to amortize."

I made my way into the Great Hall. Rumin, Saint-Ramé, Roustev and most of the principal cadres were there. I had the disagreeable impression that the employees were taking liberties with the elementary marks of respect. I, who ordinarily attach small importance to such formalities, was shocked by their disappearance. The atmosphere was jovial. To Saint-Ramé I whispered:

"Sir, what should be done?"

"I think I ought to talk to them. What do you think, Rumin?"

"Sir," Rumin said, "it's not my job to make the personnel come in, for the good reason that I didn't order them out. I keep wondering what's going on here. I've been in touch with my central committee and they're not amused by this kind of folklore. People may very well say that we're behind this agitation. The unions don't put on side shows like this when they have something to demand. You ought to talk to them; I'll keep still but stand beside you."

"Where shall I speak to them from?"

"Maybe from my office, sir," I said. "The window is well placed at an ideal height, neither too low nor too high."

"Mine is as well placed as yours," Brignon objected, having overheard the conversation.

I threw him a look of contempt. At a time when the company was confronted with a difficult situation he could think only of increasing his own prestige. I promised myself to make him imitate Saint-Ramé's voice more than three times.

"Do you think they'll be able to hear me?" the managing director asked uneasily.

"I can lend you my bullhorn," Rumin proposed, "if it won't embarrass you. Ordinarily it's used to issue orders."

"Could anyone recognize it at a distance as being yours?" inquired Roustev.

"No; it's like every other bullhorn," Rumin assured him.

"By speaking from the window and using Rumin's bullhorn, won't I exaggerate this incident's importance?" asked Saint-Ramé.

"It seems to me," I said, "that it's been pretty well exaggerated already."

Roustev and Rumin agreed. Then Saint-Ramé led us to the elevator and we entered my office. Rumin rejoined us with his bull-horn.

"How does this thing work?" Saint-Ramé asked.

Rumin explained it to him. The managing director advanced toward the window, with Roustev on his right and Rumin on his left. I stood just behind the union chief. As soon as Saint-Ramé appeared, a clamor arose, which no one of us could interpret. Rumin frowned; Roustev sat there rubbing his chin.

"Ladies and gentlemen—fellow workers!" said Saint-Ramé. "This morning you found a scroll tied with a green-and-black ribbon in your letter boxes. Now I'm going to tell you something. I too received that scroll!" A thunder of applause greeted these words. "What's more," the general manager went on, "I have it here with me, in my pocket. . . . Here it is!" There was delirium. Fascinated, I put my head between Saint-Ramé and Rumin and what I saw left me dumfounded. A thousand arms were brandishing a thousand scrolls, saluting the general manager, who was holding up his own scroll for the crowd to see. Then I witnessed a sad spectacle: embarrassed and caught flatfooted, Rumin and Roustev slowly drew their scrolls out of their pockets and, refraining from lifting their arms, held them at the level of the railing. Once more risking a look, I thought I could distinguish Le Rantec in a frenzy a little apart from the mass, waving his scroll and slashing the air with it. Was it possible that the séance of the night before had somewhat unsettled his brain?

"Ladies and gentlemen," Saint-Ramé went on, "I will say no more to you! Whoever the author of this scroll may be, I congratulate him on his humor, his entertainment value and his flair for distribution! And now I ask you to go back to work, await the next scroll calmly and serve our firm as you have in the past. Raise it always higher so that more and more of our machines will be sold throughout the world, so that we can increase our investments steadily—the investments which are, as the author of this scroll properly emphasized, along with amortization the two pillars on

119

which the firm rests. And I am now going back to my office, where arduous tasks await me, among which the first priority is to make you happy!"

At these words the crowd gave the managing director an ovation and without further incident dispersed in orderly fashion into the building.

16

That morning for the first time the cadres and personnel of the company could note the war cabinet of Rosserys and Mitchell–France. It came into being as a result of that jovial and unforeseen manifestation under the window of my office. Saint-Ramé, Roustev, Rumin and I myself appeared before our co-workers, and they, prompt to seize on the slightest covert change that might mean an alteration in the hierarchy, did not fail to detect this one. That the union boss and the director of human relations had been so obviously invited to share the managing director's responsibilities testified to both the growing strangeness of the situation and the resultant scrambling of priorities. As a matter of fact, what use would the sharpest salesman, the ablest engineer, the shrewdest manager be in the discovery and capture of the imprecator? And weren't these operations urgent priorities? On their rapid success depended the continued growth and expansion of our firm and therefore the enlargement of its cash flow. For it

121

was this that the directors feared most: distracted from their jobs by the antics of the imprecator, the workers, losing sight of their essential interests—that is, the interests of their company—would work less well, package carelessly, sell half-heartedly, unintentionally lowering Rosserys and Mitchell's famous stock rating, and thus weakening the enterprise by striking at its heart: its cash flow.

I shall not here expand on the mystique of the cash flow, as someone else will soon do that in my place on the occasion of a stately and romantic imprecation. By way of compensation, I wish to linger over the prodigious embarrassment in which poor Rumin seemed to be floundering because he was shifting insensibly from union chief to director. He admitted to me that day that he no longer knew in which role to take his stand. His pathological distrust of our employers made him constantly suspect maneuvers on their part and he believed for a long time that the imprecations came from an autonomous, fascistic, secret union. I tried, not without some success, to show him how elusive were the problems we had to resolve and how in this respect directors and union men were in the same fix. Finally he accepted almost completely the arguments I presented to him and from that moment we collaborated effectively.

Saint-Ramé called us into his office about ten minutes after he had delivered his speech. Around the managing director I found Roustev, the Americans, the two detectives and the local commissioner of police, who had come to make inquiries.

"I have my orders," he said. "In case of a disturbance, an arrangement has been approved by the Minister of the Interior designed to guarantee the safety of the banks and great companies such as yours, should crowds attempt to destroy them."

Saint-Ramé thanked the representative of law and order and offered apologies in the name of the company for the traffic jams resulting from his employees' excitement. He gave assurances that this would not happen again but said that this morning cadres, employees, salesmen and directors were in a festive mood. The incident was closed for the commissioner of police. It was not for us, as is hardly necessary to say.

A long meeting began, more tense, more ambiguous, than all the preceding ones. Adams J. Musterffies, nervous and choleric, himself dictated the order of the day and directed the discussion. He interrupted the French directors brutally and frequently and he forbade me to talk during the first two thirds of the discussion. On the other hand, he lent an attentive ear to Rumin's opinions, which I was called upon to translate from the beginning of the meeting. One mystery was quickly cleared up—that of the distribution of the scrolls—but this only intensified another: that of the imitator of Saint-Ramé. About ten o'clock a man named Rabeau, in charge of promotional operations, asked urgently to see the company's officers. He had, so he informed Mme. Dormun, an important piece of information to communicate immediately regarding the distribution of the scrolls. Musterffies ordered him shown in.

Rabeau explained to us that Saint-Ramé had directed him to give an order to a company specializing in the distribution of promotional material, and he produced the memo about the operation. It was true, he admitted in reply to a number of questions, that it was unusual for the managing director to act in person, and to his knowledge this had been the first time; but Saint-Ramé had explained why on the telephone. He then showed the bewildered audience a sheet of paper on which he had written the notes taken by him in the course of that telephone communication. He deciphered them thus: "Get in touch with the Distribex promotion company and tell them to be ready for an important nighttime distribution. The material and the pickup point will be indicated later." The date specified coincided with that of the distribution of the scrolls, and this was why he, Rabeau, considering it an unorthodox charge on his department's budget, wished to be covered before paying.

"You were right, Rabeau," Saint-Ramé said calmly. "I did in fact give these instructions, but not about the scrolls; someone must have changed my order for his own purposes. Don't concern yourself further with this affair, and pay the Distribex bill."

Rabeau left and Saint-Ramé had a call put through to Distribex. This is what he learned:

"We mobilized sixty-four teams," the Distribex manager alleged, believing that Saint-Ramé wanted to haggle about price. "The operation was difficult, not because of the amount of material, which was rather small, but because of the widely scattered addresses."

"Where did you take delivery of the material?" Saint-Ramé asked.

"In your storehouse in the Impasse Ronce."

Saint-Ramé hung up thoughtfully, then explained: "We do indeed have an old storehouse in the Impasse Ronce; it hasn't been used for two years. We keep lumber there, and I've been trying to get rid of it for the price of the land; I haven't found a buyer yet. So that man imitated my voice again and used the Impasse Ronce with complete confidence, once he saw that security had been reinforced inside the building."

Then Rumin raised an incredulous voice: "What the hell is going on?"

We had forgotten that the unionist was not in our confidence. For several minutes uncertainty prevailed, the members of the general staff not feeling eager to reply. Ronson emerged from his silence to declare: "Well, since Monsieur Rumin is with us, and considering his rank in the union and his position in the company, I think it's advisable to tell him what we know. What do you think, Adams?"

Musterffies agreed and asked Saint-Ramé to do so. As the managing director talked, Rumin's face underwent one change after another. Finally, stunned and scandalized, heedless of his hearers' exalted rank, he barked, "Well, if I've got this straight, you're up shit creek!"

I stared at the tips of my shoes. The Americans, sensing that the brief phrase was full of meaning, demanded a translation. Roustev undertook this. Musterffies, suddenly relaxing, turned toward Rumin and said, "Absolutely. We are up shit creek and we count on you to get us out. You've expressed not only the fact but what we think, Ronson and I. We've never seen anything like this, and I can tell you now, my dear Roumine, since the start of this maddening affair I've kept in communication with my friends in Des Moines, who are making fun of me. Before this meeting I telephoned to the States. I explained what had happened and the president of our firm burst into laughter and asked me to be careful about my consumption of champagne! What do you think of that, Monsieur Roumine? Have I got where I am just to hear myself given advice of that sort, in my position and at my age? The thing is that over there they're reacting just as I reacted at the start: they are roaring with laughter! Now go tell them that the French firm is in the process of losing its grip!

"Do you know that at this very moment I have a report to study on the price of metals and the monetary variations linked to them? In 1939 aluminum in the United States was 70 percent more expensive than copper; in 1969, thirty years later, my dear Roumine, copper is selling in dollars for two and a half times as much as aluminum. And since the retail price index back home on the other side of the Atlantic stands at 300 percent, the present dollar is worth one third of the 1939 dollar! Isn't that right, Bernie? Applied to the current price of nickel in America, this calculation shows an increase of 45 percent! And this year I have those accursed miners from South America, Africa and Australia on my back. I made contracts with them in dollars, and now that we've devalued, they're furious. They say we're stealing their iron and manganese! Can you see me, my dear Roumine, stealing iron and manganese? What can I do if our dollar has bled itself white defending liberty throughout the world? Oh, I have my troubles, don't I, Bernie? And now all of a sudden someone imitates Henri's voice, installs a catafalque in the middle of our Great Hall, spreads false rumors, orders the distribution of satanic scrolls! And then one morning our employees demonstrate on our doorstep! Oh, over in Des Moines they think I'm amusing myself for sure; but if this continues I'll send for them. Let them sleep right here; they'll see! Keep this terrible news to yourself, my dear Roumine—you won't regret it."

After this declaration the vice-president crossed his legs energetically and threw a self-satisfied glance around the group. Saint-Ramé asked me to translate.

"The vice-president," I told Rumin, "agrees with your truculent but accurate diagnosis of the situation. He thinks that this has gone on long enough and he's irritated to be buried in chitchat when a difficult report on monetary fluctuations and the price of metals needs his attention. He thanks you for being willing to collaborate with management on this grotesque occasion, and in particular for keeping quiet about Arangrude's funeral and the presence of an impressionist in the company doing our managing director's voice."

Rumin listened, astounded but attentive. Then he made a gesture impossible to interpret precisely but which may have meant: "If we've come this far, let's push on courageously." That we did by analyzing the second imprecation. All the participants agreed that it was distinguished from the first by the tone of its conclusion. Manifestly, this time the author was mocking "those who know." An expression like "a round and salty tear" left no doubt whatever. Nevertheless the employees had not been taken in, and their respect for Saint-Ramé seemed intact. "Moreover," the managing director explained, "that was what dictated my conduct. As soon as I saw the crowd waving the scrolls, I chose the path of humor. What other attitude could have ended the general jubilation so quickly? As a matter of fact, at the end of my speech the employees went back to their offices with a light heart, visibly delighted at this unforeseen interlude."

Several times I was tempted to speak, but I was restrained by Musterffies, who urged me, with a gesture, to arm myself with patience. He did me a service, for I kept to myself the essence of

126

the reflections which these new events had inspired in me and their connection with earlier events that had rather intrigued me. For example, that storehouse in the Impasse Ronce, abandoned by the company because it was too small but which, it was hoped, could be sold to a real estate agent for the price of the building site. I had a clear memory of the evening when Roustev, accompanied by certain of his cadres, had gone off in that direction. At the time I hadn't thought of the disused storehouse. I was not very well up on the real estate holdings of the company and I only knew that here and there it owned storehouses and sheds no longer of use to it, which it was trying to sell at an advantageous price. If on that evening I had remembered the storehouse in the Impasse Ronce, I would have made a connection between it and the comings and goings of Roustev, Abéraud and Sélis. I was astonished that this connection had escaped Saint-Ramé, to whom I had reported by telephone. Did certain cadres of the company know more than I did? Or did the managing director have reason to claim that I'd been deceived both by the darkness and by my imagination? In any case, it was a strange coincidence.

The detectives presented us with a complete report of their activities since the previous day. One or the other had slept in the building and visited the cellars, and this led us to a discussion of the crack. Its repair, Roustev asserted gravely, was well under way. At the end of the week the crack would no longer be visible. When I finally had a chance to speak up, this is what I said:

"The company's interest and that alone must dictate all opinions, all attitudes, all decisions; therefore it becomes obligatory to communicate one's ideas truly, even if they are in apparent contradiction with those of others! That's what prompts me to suggest that the secrecy about the presence, and vile actions, of an imitator of our managing director's voice should be lifted. Otherwise we're exposing ourselves to mishaps indeed. If the personnel aren't alerted to the danger, the impostor will calmly pursue his sinister work."

My intervention was received in the most profound silence. I understood very well the objections to my proposal. No one who has ever directed an organized group of any sort would adopt a medicine possibly more harmful than the illness.

Ronson's eyes gleamed as if he were repressing a notion that the shock value of my proposal might break the offensive of those evil forces that were assaulting our company. And then Musterffies spoke:

"It's tempting. I'll go further: it's probably what we should do. But what would we be unleashing? We'd end up the butt of a hundred jokes." And it was then, in a low voice, that he gave us a piece of information of capital importance: "I must tell you the position taken by the multinational general staff in Des Moines. It is this: The events disturbing the French firm belong to the world of comedy; it would be indecent if these phenomena were not promptly put down. For the first time in their history our German factories are on general strike, which is damaging to us in ways you can easily imagine. How can you dream of squandering our time and distracting the French employees by joining this stupid game that's already lasted too long? The German problems, the monetary problems, the bad mood of our suppliers in South America and the Orient, and preparations for the presidential election in America, are enough worries to keep us plenty busy and to let us avoid concentrating our efforts in Paris at the corner of the Avenue de la République and Rue Oberkampf, not far from Père Lachaise cemetery. . . . Correct?" Musterffies concluded, addressing himself to me.

"Correct," I said, surprised at this flash of humor.

The matter was settled. The employees would not have access to the truth. Aside from the Americans, the general management and the two detectives, only Rumin and I would be kept informed. In some uncertainty, I asked for precise instructions about the ten cadres I'd have to ask to imitate Saint-Ramé's voice.

"If they question me about the reasons for this investigation, what shall I say?"

"Tell them," Saint-Ramé proposed, "that aside from the imprecations, the provocateur has made use of my voice to circulate false rumors—the death of my daughter, for example. That explanation should suffice."

The Americans and Roustev agreed, and the meeting came to an end. Just as I was closing my office door, Saint-Ramé took me by the arm and, making sure that we weren't overheard, whispered in my ear this inconceivable sentence, so uncharacteristic of the image his collaborators and I had formed of him: "Monsieur Director of Human Relations," he murmured, emphasizing my title, "Rumin is right: we're up to our necks in shit creek."

Having barely recovered from this vulgarity of speech on the part of my managing director, I was preparing to take care of various current problems littering my desk when my secretary told me that Brignon wanted to see me as soon as possible.

"He doesn't seem to be in a good mood," she said, raising her eyebrows.

"That's fine. I had to talk to him anyway. Have him come in and I don't want to be disturbed by anyone. I'm in only to the general staff."

Ten minutes later Brignon entered, limply shook hands and seated himself.

"My dear Brignon, I was just getting ready—"

"Yes, I know," he cut me short. "You were going to call me in to have me imitate Saint-Ramé's voice; that's why I wanted to see you. I have a mission to fulfill for my colleagues, who are also yours, if I may still take that liberty. If I've understood right, you and Rumin have been running the company since this morning."

I did not allow myself to be upset by this aggressiveness. I'd expected that the cadres in management and marketing would resist my suddenly being coopted by the managing director. On the other hand, experience had taught me that to retreat, excuse oneself, recant, brought nothing but trouble and and an immediate weakening of a captured position, whereas staunch resistance and if necessary a certain amount of self-assertion were admired by the cadres. Nevertheless Brignon was appreciably lucky: in my

129

own heart I disapproved of these forced imitations of Saint-Ramé's voice. I thought that this grotesque procedure, instead of clarifying the situation, would only aggravate and complicate it. And so, somewhat mollified by this consideration, I replied:

"Brignon, you must make an effort—I know you're capable of it—to enter a new world, the world of company psychology. Of course, if you go about announcing to all and sundry, 'At Rosserys and Mitchell they've gone crazy; just imagine, they're making us imitate our managing director's voice,' you'd be heard and we'd be packed off to the asylum! But I beg you to consider the context. In the first place, someone here is making trouble and in the long run can impose severe losses on the company by circulating false rumors; it's vital for us to unmask the impostor at once."

"Do you mean to say," Brignon interrupted, "that the senior executives are suspect?"

"Just let me get to the end of my explanation; I never said that —in any case not that way. Every employee is open to suspicion; that's the way a police investigation is ordinarily handled. The general management is making discreet but thorough inquiries among the employees, a delicate task involving real political risks. That's why Rumin was included in the operation, not without difficulty. And the senior executives are so far above the usual suspicions that in simple propriety and elementary fairness, Musterffies and Saint-Ramé decided that a colleague, the director of human relations, would serve better than a police officer. Can you see yourself, my dear Brignon, interrogated by a policeman, you who are certainly going to replace Arangrude?"

"Saint-Ramé told you that?" Brignon asked avidly.

"He didn't say it in so many words; but I don't see anyone else who could assume such a heavy responsibility at a moment's notice."

Brignon modestly lowered his eyes. I felt the moment was propitious to find out what he knew. "It's your turn, my dear Brignon; tell me what you all did."

"Le Rantec told us about his interview with you. We were incredulous and indignant. I don't think too much of Le Rantec, but as he talked we got the feeling we were all being attacked. We didn't attend schools, take courses in management, economics and organization, visit the United States and, some of us, study at Harvard or M.I.T. just to imitate our managing director's voice in your office at thirty or thirty-five years of age. So then we decided unanimously to refuse the experiment. And I was assigned to tell you so."

This was a revolt of the senior executives. They refused to imitate. I was relieved. I rejoiced to discover that our French executives knew when it was necessary to raise their voices, to preserve the dignity of man. The attitude of Brignon and his companions testified to a desire to live as dignified professionals and not to pay any price for promotion or simply to keep their high salaries. This being so, I too had a mission to fulfill and I had to accomplish it well. Brignon's anger had not wiped out either his memory or his hopes. Arangrude was dead and it was necessary to prepare the position he was going to occupy.

"Put yourself in my place," I said. "What would you have done? You have to make your colleagues carry out what is after all a formality: how would you have gone about it?"

Brignon hesitated, then he said, "First of all, tell me frankly what the situation is! I don't feel comfortable these days; what's really going on in our company? People talk behind their hands and a little too much for my taste about that crack, about intrigues, about plots involving the death of Arangrude. After all, since you're the director of human relations you ought to be informed, and I'm sure if you joined us by explaining the facts and your hypotheses objectively and in detail, we'd willingly lend ourselves to what's only a humiliating vaudeville act at the moment."

This proposal seemed to me sensible and judicious. But how was I to reply to it properly, especially if I was to keep secret what had to be kept secret? I took a deep breath and sent the ball back—

oh, how cleverly—into my colleague's court.

"Brignon," I replied, "how do you see the future of the consumer society?"

"What's that?" said the other in surprise. "How does your question answer mine?"

"Oh, my dear Brignon," I murmured, "alas! it does answer yours. I have the conviction that a subversive commando has chosen Rosserys and Mitchell to sharpen its teeth, that its objective is to sow trouble within our company, inject suspicion into the depths of our best minds, and that this aggression aims in the long run at the corruption of the wealthy and industrialized Western societies. Have you forgotten the imprecations? Did you notice the agitation that overcame the employees? Did you, as I did, observe the bizarre gaiety, the shocking humor that suddenly invaded the company? The truth is, Brignon, that the treatment inflicted on the Indians by American arms salesmen is being imposed on us: they make us drunk, they drug us, they place us in an untenable position, for it requires reflexes which we do not have or which we have lost. Yes, Brignon, believe me, in joining with your companions you weren't rebelling against an abuse of power—for you're accustomed to such abuses—but against hysterical behavior by the general staff. That's what you're afraid of: that madness will overcome the company that pays you your high salaries.

"Very well; let me tell you, Brignon, you are right: that is what you ought to be afraid of. Madness is stalking our company. It's not just at the door now, it's inside, it's uncoiling, it's insinuating itself, probably someplace under the subbasement, and *that's* what must explain the devilish crack! Oh, Brignon, have I answered you? And will you answer me in turn about the future you foresee for consumer society? Where, Brignon, shall we find material to feed our blast furnaces and the engines of our vehicles if, carried away by the madness of growth for growth's sake, we condemn ourselves to produce for production's sake? Where will we get the energy? And since to the masses those who govern and control manufacture seem to lack any alarm system, isn't madness the only brake left to us? If we go mad before the great political crises awaiting us, perhaps we'll succeed in avoiding them. What do you think, Brignon? Now do you agree to imitate the voice of our admirable senior Henri Saint-Ramé, born in Poligny in the Indre, graduate of Harvard, master of the ship after God and the Americans, who seems to me the only one of all the directors to foresee the nature of the evil that assails us and that will very soon devour us?"

Brignon had listened to my declaration with evident interest, somewhat tempered by his surprise at my theory, and now he stroked his chin in perplexity and concentration.

"Well, Brignon," I insisted, harshly this time, exploiting my advantage, "where would you go if you resigned? Would you explain to some other Saint-Ramé that people have gone mad at Rosserys and Mitchell and that the madness forced you out? Only to read in a trade journal that Portal has replaced you and Samueru holds the post destined for Arangrude? And this just when your salary is to be raised soon and almost dizzily. Why not answer my question about the consumer society?"

Brignon believed he saw a contradiction and immediately leaped upon it. "You talk to me constantly about the consumer society, but you're one of its main beneficiaries. So what do you have against it?"

"Nothing, my dear Brignon, nothing, but a fundamental difference separates us. At this moment I am charged with protecting that society by having you imitate our managing director's voice; now, if we've got to this point, we must have—you, I, the others and those in all the industrialized countries—committed a good many errors. We're dedicated in fact to manufacturing any product whatever, provided it's new, failing which our system is so constructed that it will fall apart from the slightest deficiency, the smallest mistake. The industrialist who doesn't find a new product and a new market for next year is condemned. Do you find that normal—ceaseless invention not to satisfy needs but to nourish the economic machine? Do you find it normal that our managers or

133

our comptrollers talk constantly of signals and instrument panels? Is our economic society to be considered a kind of Boeing 727? Should we forget that if an airplane flies, it's to transport passengers from one point to another and that alone justifies its manufacture? And if it's proper to watch the instrument panel and the signals, that's simply to make sure that it doesn't crash—that's in the nature of the operation but doesn't constitute a goal. To fly is not the goal of an airplane; that's simply its function.

"We're the victims of the combined pride and lack of imagination of the economists of the last twenty years—that's what I wanted to make you say, Brignon. The nerves of our society are strained, and it will not require much more for populations grown sleepy and compliant, like guests after a hearty meal, to surrender themselves helplessly to dictatorships. The imprecator is mad, that's true; but, Brignon, are you and your companions protected from this brand of madness? I'm not a specialist, either in economics or in politics; I've just told you my thoughts as a citizen. Perhaps they're yours as well? And in that case you and I would make excellent imprecators."

Brignon raised a transformed face. I had demobilized him. Then I remembered that he had been charged with a mission by his colleagues, and they'd be waiting impatiently for him to emerge from my office. Wishing to spare him an understandable embarrassment, I proposed that he dispense with imitating Saint-Ramé's voice and come back later after thinking it over.

"I don't want a pale imitation," I said jokingly. "What I need is a real Brignon, strong enough to stand an accusation."

He smiled. Then to my stupefaction, he said calmly, "No; I'm going to imitate Saint-Ramé's voice and I'll explain why to the others."

He did his imitation. His voice rose clear, almost childlike, and it delighted my ear. He imitated five times with taste and discernment. Bravo, Brignon! May your soul repose in peace. Your director of human relations has not forgotten you. He will never forget you. He will remember that in difficult and even dangerous circumstances you did not hesitate to sacrifice yourself to the successful progress of our company, Rosserys and Mitchell–France, affiliate of the giant American and multinational company whose Paris office building of glass and steel then stood at the corner of the Avenue de la République and Rue Oberkampf, not far from Père Lachaise cemetery.

17

Those who surround and look after me declare themselves resolutely optimistic about my condition. They even appear relieved, as though I had just rounded a difficult point in the progress of my illness. According to them, it won't be long before I leave, breathe the open air and resume my activities. But they always refuse to enlighten me about the sickness that struck me down, about the conditions of my recovery, about the true reasons for my hospitalization.

What delights me most is that the periods when I have the strength to talk are perceptibly lengthening. To be sure, I relapse very soon again into prostration, but I am no longer tormented at the prospect of submitting to those interminable periods of sleep. Formerly they tired me, now they refresh me. Moreover, it seems to me that I write better and better. The fantastic and cruel episodes no longer alarm me, they sow less disorder in my brain. What's more, by degrees the hysterical masses and the rotund directors who people my memory are becoming sympathetic. When I confided this to the chief doctor, he explained that a complete reconciliation between the world and me was in prospect. Thus as the book advances, we make our way hand in hand, it toward its conclusion, I toward recovery.

Well, then, I see myself once more stationed at the entrace to the Impasse Ronce, fascinated by a major piece of evidence: to wit, the strategic position of the Père Lachaise cemetery in the life of Rosserys and Mitchell–France and the role it played in recent events. In the first place, was it sensible to build the offices of a multinational company so close to such a vast cemetery? Wasn't it dangerous for the principal cadres and a good number of the employees to go walking there so often? Was frequenting such a place compatible with the toughness, the commercial aggressiveness required of responsible cadres? How could one wander past tombs and mausoleums and at the same time properly construct a promotional plan for our tomato-pickers or the conquest of the Bulgarian market by our presses and tractors? I had not waited for the troubles to put these questions to myself. Well before the crack, the death of Arangrude and the first imprecation, I'd toyed with the notion of prohibiting our fellow workers in the company, whatever their rank, from strolling in Père Lachaise.

Nevertheless I hadn't dared propose a prohibition, convinced that it would be rejected and that a good many people would accuse me of abuse of power or even of maniacal delirium. I don't wish any director of human relations to have to exercise his functions in proximity to a cemetery. However, as I was becoming aware of the importance of this proximity, a flood of details came crowding into my memory, intensifying my attention to this necropolis. The night when the Americans and I had walked along the wall, noises attributed to an animal had reached us. The disused storeroom almost touched the hermetically sealed black marble chapel of Alfred Chauchard, founder of the great storerooms of the Louvre. But was this a sufficient reason to forbid access to the cemetery? Once more I was in collision with the

137

incapacity of our directors to understand that only an uncommon line of thought, following irrational paths, would make it possible to get to the bottom of this kind of subversion.

Who today would reproach me for not having addressed a circumstantial report to Musterffies, including an ardent plea in which I would have adjured him to be on his guard against a cemetery? It was better to employ two incapable detectives and, for good reason, to establish a relationship between the growth and expansion of a multinational company and the shady movements of a phantom executive, of a fleeting assistant managing director, of a quasi-translucent imprecator, of a mysterious managing director, of a director of human relations on the verge of bewitchment. And here essentially was the key to this affair: its solution was unthinkable. *Unthinkable!* Therefore anyone who wanted to persist in his search for the truth would have to avoid all logic and accustom himself to envisaging the unthinkable, the inconceivable, the non-natural; in short, he would have to imagine. And everyone knows that imagination is the treasure least widely spread through the world, the rarest and also the most dangerous, and therefore the most hunted, the most spied upon, the most wrapped in mystery. Thus it was more through lack of imagination than through excess of cupidity that the magnates were losing the battle.

No, I thought sadly as I returned to my office, whatever the value of my intuition, I fear that it would only be mocked by these gentlemen. And so it is alone that I shall scale the wall of that cemetery this evening to follow through on my idea. God preserve us from being governed once more by those who possess the ingots and means of payment: they're the ones who no longer fear anything. But the demons are becoming restive; they're emerging from their dens and coming to sniff at the magnates' padded doors. In short, the demons too are growing bold.

Abéraud, a progressivist cadre from the Central Massif, was, as I have said, assistant director of forecasts. At the time of the imprecations and the crack, this graduate of the School of Mines, who had been attracted to the vast realms of commerce by high pay, enjoyed a strange reputation. Everyone knew that he would never rise any higher, a victim of the formidable self-defense of executives of that period, who used to ask sneeringly: "Does mathematics necessarily make good salesmen?" And more generally, this reasoning was applied to every individual who disembarked in the company carrying with him conventional university degrees. The commercial cadres would then suppress their mutual resentments, joining ranks which had been widely separated by harsh jealousies and vulgar backbiting. They would proclaim in the corridors:

"Well, now, everyone's raving about the new man; it seems he has a degree in law, a master's in physics, a doctorate in philosophy! That's all very well, but how do their science and culture help them increase sales? What's needed in our company today is simple people not given to hair-splitting! People think salesmanship's easy! Well, our new man will find out! Just let him tour the villages and suburbs, let him visit the millions of basic consumers, and maybe perhaps he'll understand that you can't sell if you fly too high! Fortunately our firms are not in the hands of intellectuals. What would happen to our consumer society then? There's nothing as valuable as a simple solid cadre who isn't perplexed by an eclipse of the sun or thrown into a reverie by a flight of butterflies, who instead of taking long views, sees at his own doorstep, at his very feet, men and women in cars headed toward our stores with loosened waistbands, farting from the pressure of heavy bellies."

And so Abéraud had been neutralized, and the company was pleased to have the honor of his presence at the meetings of Saint-Ramé's general staff. The latter never missed a chance to boast in public of his eclecticism and the boldness of his policy in hiring, citing the case of this mining engineer. At once Abéraud ceased to be feared by any of his colleagues, who thenceforth saw no objection to giving him precedence on the intellectual level: We have a fellow with us; devilish intelligent; too bad for him he

139

came here. It was, in short, an honorable sentence of death passed on the man now sitting in front of me, his eye singularly piercing and attentive. Was he a progressivist? So it was said here and there, and he himself had never denied it. In our epoch any judgment about an executive's political involvement was chancy. There existed, to be sure, parties of the left that demanded a more or less radical change in society, but it was becoming difficult to distinguish their adherents from other company personnel. Abéraud and Le Rantec strangely resembled one another and also all the others. Somehow long views aroused commiseration; calculating the rate of exchange of the lira or the crown evoked admiration and conferred a leader's distinction on the audacious anticipator.

And so without too much concern, people revealed political commitments as fluctuating as the currency of the Occident. Numerous senior executives made a show of it, boastful and impertinent, and playing on an easy paradox, whispered in the ears of their delighted chiefs that they were inclined toward the left. The chiefs, at the close of dinner parties in town, would whisper to enchanted fellow diners:

"You see that young man down there? He's my general secretary and I predict a splendid future for him. His salary is amazingly high for a boy of his age. Well, my friends, he's a member of the Revolutionary Socialist Party!" And pleased with the effect, the magnate would add: "Today there is nothing more to fear from the left; we've fashioned beds to measure for the Russians and the Americans, with fine linen and perfumed quilts; the only real threats are the niggers and the gooks. But," the marshal would continue, sweeping the table with his arm, "we'll send them a few tons of margarine each year and then, if we have to . . . well, you know what I mean!"

He would burst into laughter and imperiously demand the attention of the general secretary. The young man would then reveal his beautiful white teeth and laugh even louder than Voroshilov or Kaganovich in the presence of Stalin.

140

Had Abéraud acquiesced in this situation or was he planning revenge? Did he hope that Roustev would supplant Saint-Ramé? Having seen little of him, I knew no more than what I have set down.

"Don't take the trouble," Abéraud said to me, "to explain why you want to see me. I'm all up to date. I admire, let it be said in passing, your strength of conviction: Brignon went to see you furious and came back convinced and excited. So we agreed that for the imitations everybody was free to submit or not. On the other hand, we've decided to proceed immediately with our own investigations. . . . We don't despair, despite your recent promotion, of having you with us."

Abéraud settled himself in his easy chair and lit a small cigar. Thus he invited me to join their group. This proposal opened perspectives for me, but it required careful play on my part, delicate maneuvering between my colleagues and the firm's general staff, which had coopted me. How was I to extricate myself? Abéraud guessed my thought.

"I realize that it won't be easy for you to maneuver and join us; you may be too close to the general management. But aside from Le Rantec's resentment, no one among us doubts your capacities and good will. That much understood, we have a single and unique goal: to cut short the nonsense and jokes, which, if continued, will cease to amuse anyone."

"You're right," I said gently, "but let me reflect on the special aspect of our conversation. *A priori,* I don't see why a collaboration with Saint-Ramé and Roustev should exclude my participation in your investigation."

"Ah," said Abéraud, "would you like us to discuss it?"

"I would," I replied dryly, irritated at my colleague's assurance and his touch of arrogance. "As I understand it, you are entering into open revolt against the general management."

"It's something like that, except that our revolt isn't open. Our action, our annoyance, spring in the first instance from an understandable feeling: to contribute as quickly as possible to the struggle against our company's enemy. Also our decisions are not public; we have no intention of distributing a report rolled up and tied with a green-and-black ribbon, rest assured of that. In these circumstances one cannot talk about an open revolt; but we've been excluded from current operations and we don't understand why. Since things have not settled down, to put it mildly, we're beginning to ask questions. Moreover, we've thought about these scrolls and their distribution and certain points really appear very strange. Thus we have come to the conclusion that only a person or persons having access to the company's card catalogue and files could enjoy the liberty of movement indispensable to this sort of activity."

"Let me tell you," I replied, "that you're not the first to examine such a hypothesis, and it's precisely for that reason we're obliged to suspect everyone, beginning with ourselves. If you push this line of reasoning to the end, you'll all agree, with good grace, to do the imitations just as I have."

"What you're saying rather confirms me in my belief that you and the general management have lost your heads. These imitations are ridiculous and totally useless. It seems someone's imitating Saint-Ramé's voice, and you hope to discover him by forcing the cadres to lend themselves to a masquerade! It's not being suspect that annoys us, but the impression that the company's losing its marbles. We're not frightened by suspicions. But if you have them, take real measures, search our houses, see how we use our time, question our assistants, our families, our friends, but for pity's sake don't waste any more time and energy on these grotesque entertainments!"

Abéraud was right. While I listened to him, I got the full measure of the image, folkloristic at best, that management had projected since the beginning of these events. Caught up in the whirlpool of my daily tasks, placed despite myself at the heart of the melee, I had so far barely been touched by this feeling. Now I became acutely aware of it. The Americans' attitudes, particularly

142

Musterffies'; Saint-Ramé's speeches to the employees; the requirement that executives imitate their managing director's voice, appeared to me like worrisome symptoms of slovenliness. Confronted by Abéraud and his penetrating gaze, I felt ashamed to have accepted such a mission from the vice-president; but what cadre is there in these times who would have stoutly refused?

Abéraud broke the silence. "My personal point of view is that we have been deliberately excluded from current operations. I repeat, this is my personal point of view; you're the only person aside from my wife to whom I've communicated that profound conviction."

"And why this honor?" I demanded distrustfully.

"That's simple, my dear Director of Human Relations," Abéraud replied, smiling. "Only you can really help me. I'm certain you've been an involuntary witness to events, attitudes, speeches which will be valuable for me to interpret now; and I assure you, everything will be cleared up. You yourself haven't done it because your job's kept you in the heart of the affair. To solve a difficult problem you have to gain altitude and then speed, and finally swoop down on it like a falcon. . . . Now," he added, almost to himself, "perhaps the firm's interest, and therefore ours, is not to clear matters up but on the contrary, in the spot we're in, to thicken the darkness."

"But what do you want from me, anyway?"

Abéraud hesitated a second, then rose and went to the window, opened it and leaned out. "What were you doing the other evening in the Impasse Ronce?" he asked, turning abruptly.

I jumped. Had the man been manipulating me at will from the beginning of our conversation? I reacted harshly.

"And you?" I retorted. "I saw you coming out of the tavern!"

"Don't fly off the handle. I was indeed in that tavern, where I am accustomed to go every evening for a glass of wine when I leave the office. But have you and Sélis by chance discovered another tavern in that spot?"

"I beg you," I cut in. "This isn't the time for jokes. Who knows but what the fate of Rosserys and Mitchell–France is at stake at this very moment. . . ."

"As you say, my dear fellow, it's at stake, but only slightly; you won't persuade me that the real game isn't being played somewhere else."

"Where?"

"Ah! That's what we have to not only find out but prove," said Abéraud. "But with a minimum of reflection and intuition, we shouldn't need witchcraft to discover where. To prove it is an altogether different matter."

Suddenly impatient, I decided to be brusque with the fellow, to administer one of those homilies which I have a talent for. They have been successful in raising me to my important position, and had thoroughly traumatized Le Rantec and Brignon. This is what I said:

"Why all this peevishness and pride? You try to get around me and push me into your revolt. And why? Because I'm an embarrassment to you. You're eleven, you'd like to be twelve; and it infuriates you that I'm not in your power. You're the leader of the revolting cadres and you plan to avenge yourself for your disappointments and for your eviction from the path that leads to power. What were you looking for when you came to us? Would you know how to sell so much as a necktie? Where are your forecasts? What do you foresee? What have you ever foreseen? I'm going to tell you. You foresee that by exploiting these troubles you'll make up for lost time. Besides, you may be the imprecator! Your logic, your fussiness, your rancor, would be stimulus enough to make you find some diabolical way to inject a poison, an unknown virus, into the entrails of our company. You have a knowing air, Abéraud, and you deal in implications! Do you preach the false in order to learn the true, or rather, are you the man we're looking for?

"I recognize in you a sad specimen of the bored senior executive second class, ready always to betray and destroy without running much risk, but also to profit and to enjoy the abuse of the liberties the industrial democracies lavish on us. Now I see the light, an explanation of the agitation rising among us: you are provoking it. Your objective is to disorganize the company in order afterward to reorganize it for your exclusive profit. You hate Henri Saint-Ramé, you manipulate Roustev and your colleagues. Moreover, I am now entrusted with a new power and charged with a mission I shall accomplish at any cost: to make our headquarters executives imitate our managing director's voice. So I don't need any lessons or advice from you, and I ask, yes or no, are you willing to do the imitation?

"Shame on you, Abéraud, who vomit on our liberties, our growth, our expansion, our cash flow, our staff and line, our law of supply and demand, our prosperity, our surfeit and that of our people! Are you thin or fat, Abéraud? You're fat. Do you eat the choice cuts of beef, Abéraud, or tough utility cuts? You eat the choice cuts, Abéraud! And your salary, Abéraud—is it abnormally low, sadly average, or wickedly high? It's wickedly high. And you, Abéraud, you dream of the annihilation of our world, the firing of our oil wells, the poisoning of our animals, the withering of our green vegetables, the pulverization of our dried vegetables, the rotting of our fruit, the souring of our industrialized mayonnaise, the flattening of our many sparkling drinks, the drying up of our rivers. That, Abéraud, is what you dream of. And now, my dear Assistant Director of Forecasts, by virtue of the powers conferred upon me by our beloved leaders, in the superior interest of our firm, and also your own, I demand that you imitate the voice of Henri Saint-Ramé, managing director of Rosserys and Mitchell–France! How do you answer?"

"I answer," Abéraud said very calmly, "that my speech apparently had no effect and that you're going crazy. I've just verified our colleague Le Rantec's fears; we unjustly doubted his assertions, attributing them to a momentary explosion of anger. Now I discover that he was not mistaken and that his report was accurate. He swore to us that you had used a tone and language that ordinarily can be heard only on the stage or in a madhouse. According to him you made use of astonishing expressions, your eyes flashed suddenly with disquieting flames, you waved your arms wildly and you kept looking toward the window as if the idea of throwing yourself out of it, or throwing him out, had come into your sick mind from time to time. Brignon compared his interview with you to a torture session. He himself really believed that you were on the point of losing your mind and you frightened him so that he did an imitation several times! And now I too have heard extraordinary things.

"Let's pass over the substance—it's useless to discuss it here and with you. But the form demands attention and it's enough to astound any cadre in the world, whatever his function, salary or nationality. Something is unquestionably going wrong in this company; and if one takes your three hilarious and disjointed declarations, together with Henri Saint-Ramé's recent discourses, a certain alarm is justified. Le Rantec's brought us the formal proof that our general staff has not only accustomed itself to this bizarre language, but admires it and takes pleasure in it! You were even, it would seem, promoted under Le Rantec's eyes as a result of a flight of this sort in which you compared us to the knights of the Middle Ages! Are you aware of your present state of mind? Come on, react; don't sit there like an invalid after an attack! I don't take your opinions seriously. They're fantastic, incoherent, and not at all like you. I've always considered you a worthy man, though our respective functions haven't often brought us into contact. And you can become a great director of human relations if you demand a little more independence from your chiefs and if you make your colleagues more aware of questions they have a tendency to underestimate—beginning with me.

"What's really happening? What scares you and what worries the directors so much? Tell me the truth about that wake. Help us help this company and its employees; don't go on playing the game of this demon who, according to you, is my master and my best friend. We have better things to do, we executives, than to

146

putter about in the labyrinths of witchcraft. Join our group; you won't have to disassociate yourself from Saint-Ramé and Musterffies. In their interest, to serve them effectively, you ought to cooperate with us. What do you think? Have I shocked you? Have I been discourteous? What proof can I give you of my good will and the sincerity of my efforts to regroup our colleagues, to raise their morale—which I assure you is at its lowest point—to put an end to the panic and the disorder that are beginning to threaten our company seriously?"

His words touched me. The more so since I was ill prepared to reply, for I shared his views. On the evening of my promotion hadn't I been struck by the strangeness of the managing director's behavior and my own? But should I tell him about it? Wouldn't he think that my own awareness of my verbal anomalies proved that they were only another trick? And Saint-Ramé and Musterffies crying as they leaped to their feet under the fascinated gaze of Le Rantec: "Let's promote him, let's promote him!" Had they been scheming? And scheming what? I felt ill at ease.

"Would you like me to open the window?" Abéraud asked. "It's hot in this office; you'll breathe easier."

"Yes, that's just what I was about to do."

I got up and walked heavily toward the window. Abéraud followed me. I opened it. And we two put our elbows on the sill and contemplated Rue Oberkampf, and over to the right, the tombs and mausoleums of Père Lachaise.

"Have you noticed how close the Impasse Ronce is to the cemetery?" said Abéraud. "It's right beside it."

I gave a start. This man was diabolical. But this time I did not hedge.

"Yes, I noticed it just today, between noon and two o'clock, and I'm sure the clue to the enigma lies in that cemetery."

"Aha," Abéraud approved. "I agree completely. All the same, confess that you're a strange person. You move without transition from an inexplicable feverishness to a very impressive judgmental and deductive talent."

147

"I must be ill," I said coolly, in full command of myself.

Abéraud fell silent. After a few minutes he left the window, planted himself in the middle of my office and asked with disarming calm: "Well, then, do you agree to join our group—in your capacity as senior executive, of course, and not in your role as director of human relations?"

"And you," I replied, without too much reflection, "do you agree to imitate our managing director's voice, which is why I wanted to see you today?"

"Oh, if that's all it is," he replied in a light tone, "I've even had a lot of practice. Last night I amused myself by telephoning my colleagues in a disguised voice; they all fell for it. I'll show you. What do you want me to say?"

"Good Lord, I really don't know," I said, confused.

"All right. Listen." And imitating the voice of Henri Saint-Ramé, he said, "Monsieur Director of Human Relations, I'm happy that despite the delicate position you're in you've agreed to collaborate with us. Henceforth the company's twelve department heads will unite their intelligence and their energy, which are great, and there can be no doubt that they will secure rapid and spectacular results. To begin with, I inform you that our next meeting will take place this evening at nine o'clock in the back room of the Goulim Tavern, in the Impasse Ronce, not far from Père Lachaise cemetery. In the course of this meeting we will freely exchange views and information about the present state of the company. Those who wish to may dine after the meeting. Each cadre will pay his own check.

"I, Henri Saint-Ramé, rejoice to learn that my company's division heads have rallied to protect it from the pernicious machinations of villains hoping to release the morbid forces that every man harbors in the depths of his soul. We were good, and they would render us wicked. We were inflexible, and they would render us flabby. If I were the imprecator I'd panic to hear that Rosserys and Mitchell's twelve great lynxes are on the trail, ready to prowl the corridors and tunnels by night, the catacombs and basements; that their nostrils will quiver and flare at the scent of my silvery skin; that their ivory and iron fangs will gleam from their slavering muzzles at the sight of me; and that they will pursue me with unsheathed claws and arched backs even unto the kingdom of the dead, and there dismember me! How's that?"

"Fine," I gulped, overcome. And the assistant director of forecasts left, softly closing the door. That imitation already dripped blood.

Shame be upon us!

18

At nine o'clock precisely I knocked on the door of the Goulim Tavern in the Impasse Ronce. A face surmounted by a bushy mane appeared in the peephole and an oily voice inquired:

"Who sent you here?"

"I was invited by Monsieur Abéraud."

"What's your number?"

"What number?"

"Are you or are you not one of the twelve manitous of Rosserys and Mitchell–France?"

"I don't know what you mean by manitou," I said impatiently, "but I do in fact work for that company."

"Then you ought to have a number."

"No one has talked to me about a number. I was simply invited to a meeting by Abéraud. Has he arrived?"

"Yes, the manitou Abéraud is here."

150

"To hell with your manitous!" I shouted. "If Abéraud is here, go find him and tell him that the director of human relations is waiting for him!"

"All right, I'll go," growled the centaur, "but it's strange that you don't have a number."

Five minutes later he returned with Abéraud. The judas slid open with a dry click and the eyeglasses of the assistant director of forecasts glittered in the penumbra.

"Yes, it's him; you may let him in," I heard him say.

The heavy door turned silently on its hinges, then closed behind me. As soon as my eyes had adjusted to the semidarkness of the entrance, I barely repressed a start of surprise at Abéraud's costume. He was dressed in an ample dark cape that fell to his knees. In place of a tie, he wore a sort of neckcloth, bouffant and of green silk, such as I had occasionally seen around the throats of certain dandies but which I would never have imagined beneath the chin of a cadre of the general staff. Finally I noticed, pinned to the left side of his cape, a green plastic badge bearing the number 5 imprinted in black. Abéraud guided me along a corridor that zigzagged and seemed to descend steadily, and until we came out in an immense hall of irregular shape, he said not a word. Perhaps he did not wish to supply explanations in the presence of the servitor, who had been following us. Abéraud seized me by the arm and pulled me toward a red velvet banquette. There, making sure that no one could overhear him, he addressed me in a low voice.

"I'm sorry about your number. I was sure you'd come to our meeting, but I couldn't be totally certain; not being sure, I couldn't reveal our code. It's very simple. Henceforth we won't communicate within the company except by using numbers. This holds good, of course, only for subjects of our investigation. As for you, you have the number 7. Each one has the number corresponding to his seniority at Rosserys and Mitchell. The others are waiting for us in the rear hall, which I've reserved for our meeting. Since they weren't sure of you, they'll be happy that you've come."

151

"I have one question," I said. "What's all this about manitous?"

"Ah!" Abéraud exclaimed. "That's the taverner's idea. An honest fellow and a bit of an original; sometimes he calls his clients manitous, not as a tribute to their importance but to make them feel like sorcerers—you know that's the precise meaning of the word."

We walked across the room. Men and women were seated at the tables, veiled in smoke; I couldn't make out their faces. I was struck, nevertheless, by the large number of men with long wispy mustaches, unusual in those days, and women in long dresses with lace ruffles. I attempted a joke.

"Tell me, is this tavern a mustachio club?"

"Quiet," murmured Abéraud. "Don't laugh at these things."

Surprised, I fell silent, following my guide. Abéraud pushed gently against a tiny round door and I had the impression then that we were descending lower and lower. We proceeded, it seemed to me, for almost a quarter of an hour through a badly lit corridor. I no longer had any desire to talk, and I'd have been seriously alarmed by this place if Abéraud's presence hadn't constantly reminded me that the leading cadres of Rosserys and Mitchell–France held their meetings here. Suddenly my guide stopped and said to me in a low voice:

"Here's the cloakroom. You will change into your cape and put on your neckcloth and badge."

I made no protest. How could I, having come this far? My mission was to insinuate myself into this group of colleagues in revolt, and on that account I had to accept their rules and adopt their manners. No doubt they had excellent reasons for meeting at the Goulim and putting on distinctive uniforms and badges. I hadn't taken part in their deliberations, but I found it hard to believe that cadres like Brignon, Sélis or Le Rantec would have happily accepted a role in this farce without imperative, secret motives. Abéraud examined me from head to foot, adjusted my neckcloth and expressed his satisfaction.

"Of all of us, our costume is most becoming to you; you'll make them jealous. Follow me."

We made our way toward a massive square door, which Abéraud opened by leaning against it with his whole weight. There I found them. They were seated around a rectangular table in armchairs with very high backs. My appearance caused no comment, no movement, no astonishment. They've learned quickly to control themselves, I thought. Abéraud has more influence over them than I would have believed possible; a devil of a fellow. Abéraud waved me to the seat reserved for me between Chavégnac, Number 6, and Brignon, Number 8. Then he installed himself in a chair at the end of the table, facing Le Rantec, who, by his position, vied with him for the presidency. Abéraud spoke first.

"My dear colleagues, allow me to rejoice that we are twelve in number, for this confers a new and very particular cachet on our association. Indeed, twelve is by no means an insignificant number. Nor will it be for the adversary whom we pursue and who draws the essence of his strength and success from mystery. Since we have decided to meet him on his own ground, with his own weapons, it is not unimportant that he'll have to deal with twelve resolute executives who've adopted a ritual, an organization and a uniform and will soon have a plan of action. I rejoice too that the man whose collaboration has brought our number to twelve is none other than our eminent director of human relations."

At these words the cadres finally gave some sign of life by nodding.

"I don't think," continued Abéraud, "that it would be a waste of time to explain to our colleague what led us to adopt certain rules calculated, I feel sure, to astonish a cadre who was not prepared for them. This holds true for our choice of a place for our meetings, the wearing of our numbers and these characteristic garments. My dear Director of Human Relations," he continued in an almost suave voice. "I'm grateful to you for showing only brief signs of impatience from the moment you entered the Goulim until now, when you're a full-fledged member of our group. If you had protested we'd have understood, this atmosphere being planned to amaze honest citizens. You must understand, my friend, that while our directors and their detectives are awkwardly trying to elucidate our company's obscure and painful situation, we are embarked on the right course. That is not, however, an ordinary course. It takes tortuous twists and turns, it requires an effort of the imagination, it leads us by indirect but sure paths to the adversary's doorstep.

"If today the investigation has made no progress, this is due to two equally formidable facts: *(a)* the man who is attacking our company is almost certain to divert ordinary suspicions, and *(b)* the reasons for his aggression are exceptionally anomalous; it would be an error to look for them in some ordinary disappointment or simple rage. A co-worker dismissed, an embittered cadre, a small subversive group would be a shabby means of conveying that cold and demoniac hatred directed at our company. These considerations convinced us of the directors' inability to overcome this kind of evil. It's as though the adversary, before beginning his exactions, had injected into the souls and minds of our leaders a microbe or some annihilating drug. This means that an effective counterattack must be wily, insidious, quasi-magical. Furthermore, we consider it established that the subbasements of our firm and the underground passages of the cemetery hide enigmas that have to be resolved if we hope truly to protect our company. And so, my dear Director of Human Relations, we've made our home here at the Goulim, which by deep and winding passageways is connected to other passages, which we will explore together. Moreover, we have to discipline ourselves. We're so little used to reasoning beyond the limits of the imaginable that in the absence of a ritual we'd have been stopped short. We have to forge the soul of a commando. Respectable executives, well trained, in business suits, wouldn't have amounted to much in this adventure. That's why you find us so changed tonight. And you're right. We're no longer the same men. We've crossed a boundary, disdaining ridi-

154

cule. We wear capes, neckcloths and badges. In the army, in the church and at official ceremonies, what good are the uniforms and parade costumes if not to impress the priests, the generals, the statesmen, the faithful, the soldiers, the people with the grandeur of those tasks which it is the mission of a country, an army, a church to accomplish? Have you noticed our colors, green and black? They are those of the ribbon tied around the scrolls. We don't fear the man who has undertaken to make a martyr of our firm—his colors are ours. His punishment will be inflicted by us and not by a law that would not know what jurisprudence to invoke.

"And now our colleague Le Rantec is going to sum up what we think about the affair, after which we'll discuss what measures to take. Have you anything to say, my dear Director of Human Relations?"

This preamble had impressed me, because it had developed ideas familiar to me, which I'd been turning over for days but had never dared make public. I was sure that the company was struggling against strange enemies, and how often had I deplored the lack of audacity on the part of the directors, the small attention they paid to those forces concealed by man but not mastered by him, which are capable of breaking loose and casting him into madness. Even before the first symptoms of madness appeared I was a believer in the motto: *For abnormal situations, abnormal remedies.* The grinding sounds then rising to our officers' ears were not produced by the mechanisms of growth, of expansion, of profits, nor in truth by the employees' discontent or hatred, but from elsewhere. But where?

The home office in Des Moines, officially aware of the French firm's problem after the press got hold of it, also remained unresponsive to this maddening plaint, this wail rising from the mind of the ill and delirious company, indifferent to the maleficent waves undermining its foundations. So it was that, disregarding the tableau my colleagues had conceived, which couldn't be taken seriously, I listened to their words, and these appealed to my

155

intelligence. They themselves were not more sympathetic to me than before, but what they explained through Abéraud's mouth seemed to me very sensible and of an evident subtlety. They might indeed be right to try autosuggestion, to discard the outer aspects of executives—and to clothe themselves in garments that permitted them more easily to slip into their new skins as devil-hunters. For now no one, including myself, doubted that the adversary to be tracked down had borrowed his tricks from Satan. I admired Abéraud for having thought to explore this arduous path, and having rallied his colleagues. It was no small achievement, and from that evening on I would no longer withhold my admiration from the almost prodigious intellectual agility of our assistant director of forecasts. My hatred was born later on, but it came from a change in my opinions and my feelings, unforeseeable at that time, and due to the stupefying evolution of the affair. That's a different story. To Abéraud's concluding question I replied simply:

"Having listened to you, I can only offer a simple approval, supported by my personal analysis of the facts, which is very similar to yours. Now I understand better your concern over the smallest details and your dressing yourselves in this manner. I understand too why you've been at pains to take certain precautions in regard to me. I'm not angry on that account, and since in principle my collaboration with the directors must continue, I may be of great value through the information I'll have access to."

"In the name of our colleagues, I thank you," said Abéraud. "We shall make use of the various advantages that your present position offers. I give the floor to Number 9; we must get used to our numbers."

Le Rantec, Number 9, declared, twisting about: "Pursuant to the decisions made in the course of our last meeting, I got hold of a plan of the subsoil of our office building, thanks to one of my friends, a former pupil in the National School of Administration, who works side by side with the prefect. Before unrolling it and commenting on it, I think it would be well if Number 10 made a brief report on questions of stewardship. I propose this since, following our meeting, which will keep us late, we will have dinner, and I feel that then his statement may fall on deaf ears. What do you think, Number 5?"

Number 5 (Abéraud) agreed. And the floor was given to Sélis, Number 10.

"I call the attention of Number 7 [that was me], who is participating in our deliberations for the first time, and Numbers 2, 3 and 12 that at the close of the meeting they must give me their dues, the latter three because they've forgotten, the other because he didn't know. The sum has been fixed at 1500 francs. We have already incurred considerable expenses: twelve capes tailored by Zart and Lamer, Avenue Montaigne, of authentic draper's cloth from the village of Madre de Dios, cost 1100 francs apiece; plus twelve neckcloths of green English silk, cost 250 francs apiece; plus twelve engraved badges, cost 7 francs apiece. This makes a total of 16,284 francs. There remains, moreover, the sum of 1704 francs, which we shall owe for reserving the hall and cloakroom, and the bill for dinner. And so by tomorrow very little money will remain. Nevertheless, the haberdasher's charges having been paid once for all, I believe that from now on our finances will be in healthy shape, provided we stretch things a bit. Each of us might contribute a supplementary 500 francs tomorrow, which would permit us to operate until the end of the month, at the rate of two regular meetings, two dinners a week, plus a provision for two emergency meetings without dinner. Is Number 5 agreeable to a vote on my proposition?"

"Certainly," said Abéraud. "Let's vote. By the end of the month our business will be done."

We voted the supplementary contribution unanimously. Le Rantec took the floor again, unrolled a huge map and fastened it to the wall with thumbtacks.

"My dear colleagues, you have before you a map of the subsoil on which our glass-and-steel office building stands. Everyone knows that the city of Paris is situated on a network of subterra-

157

nean passages and galleries. Here's the tunnel that winds under the Avenue de la République and ends in Père Lachaise cemetery, beneath which it ramifies into at least thirty secondary passages. Here's the subsoil under Rue des Amandiers and this is where we are at this moment, just above this inextricable tangle. And now open your eyes and prick up your ears. Look at this thick black mark—it represents an orifice in the wall that faces our basement conference room. The other, thinner lines indicate various openings smaller than this orifice but which would permit the passage of a man of medium height and weight. To confirm that, all you have to do is consult the scale and measure with a decimeter rule.

"Now, you must bear in mind that below our office building, and more especially below the crack, a passage opens whose entrance was condemned by the contractors but which still exists and—follow my thumb—descends abruptly, then seems to enlarge and even to form right here a sort of hall or crypt, the dimensions of which I can't very well make out but which certainly is large enough to contain men and materials. Then this passage contracts again, resumes its original diameter and winds for some distance like a serpent, only to enlarge once more, this time in three places, so constituting three halls of the same dimensions as the crypt. Here we perceive a kind of appendix, a dead end. After this the passage stretches out and leads in a straight line to a truly gigantic hall, nearly ten times the size of the preceding ones. And here is a curious phenomenon: the passage widens, distends, becomes in itself a hall, but in the center of that hall appears a second passage, with an opening like a well, which descends vertically, then turns, descends once more, rises almost vertically and ends at the top of a hump in the terrain, a sugarloaf, a small subterranean mountain. And from the foot of this pointed hummock there begins a twisting passage, very narrow, which makes an abrupt right-angle turn and rises vertically toward the surface of the ground. That is to say, it traverses in a straight line the whole path that we've followed from halls to passages and from passages to crypts and hummocks. And do you know where it comes out? At a point in Père Lachaise

158

cemetery where a sumptuous vault of green-and-black marble has been built.

"Gentlemen, our trip is over. But I cannot finish without revealing who it was that put us on the right track. Just as in the most complicated riddles, the solution to our firm's mystery was simple: it was necessary to think, or rather, observe. Observe what, gentlemen? That the colors of the ribbons tied around the scrolls were those of this vault. And who, my dear colleagues, observed that? Our Number 5 one day when he was strolling in the cemetery. Instead of contenting himself with attacking us, our adversary wanted to taunt us! That was his mistake. He didn't foresee that one of us might slap himself on the forehead one fine day and cry: I've got it! The colors of the vault! Why the colors of the vault? Would our dear Number 5 continue?"

"Willingly." Thierry Abéraud picked up his cue. "The idea that this vault, this cemetery and the subbasements of the company could be linked to the crack, to the distribution of the scrolls, began to haunt me. I confided my suspicions to Roustev, who didn't take them seriously. The only decision that resulted was an expedition one evening to the Impasse Ronce to visit our unused storeroom. We discovered nothing there, but one must believe that we should have kept it under surveillance, because later it housed the stock of the second wave of scrolls. This incident reinforced my conviction that the area bounded by our office, the Impasse Ronce and Père Lachaise represented the battlefield. But it confirmed the uselessness of warning the general management, frozen in immobility after handing over the affair to two private detectives.

"So then a project took shape in my head—to assemble the senior executives and rally them to my views. A single man would have failed if only because of the extended surveillance needed. We'll discuss that presently. I'd like to stress this vault. It's not impossible to think that the agitator kept the colors of the vault to symbolize the death of our company, its destruction. Perhaps this vault has an even greater importance—I have my ideas about that—but we must be prudent and obey the law. This vault excites my curiosity, and if I were to follow my impulse, I'd go take a look at it. It would be awkward, however, to alert our adversary to our intentions and risk expulsion from the cemetery. You're not unaware that the latter is frequented by a large contingent of regulars, who'd notice very quickly that we were prowling around the vault a little too much. No, what we have to do is organize two or three descents into the passages and equip ourselves accordingly.

"I propose that we let ourselves be locked up in the subbasements tomorrow night and inspect the area. I'll try a reconnaissance during the day. If one of the entrances to the passages has been opened recently, that should be noticeable. Whatever happens, it's easy for us to communicate with one another within the company, and tomorrow at eight o'clock you'll know all the details of the operation. The discussion is now open."

The feelings I had at this stage of the meeting were mixed and contradictory. On the one hand, I felt I was dreaming, so closely did Abéraud's hypothesis approach my own. My intuition had not deceived me. I too had perceived the role of the realm of the dead in this sinister adventure. On the other hand, I experienced a certain frustration: Saint-Ramé had never made me feel that he'd even listen to my proposals. The evening when I'd told him about the comings and goings of Roustev and his band, he'd advised me to get some rest. Think of the glory of it: a director of human relations solving this mystery for the benefit of the directors of the most powerful multinational corporation of its epoch! I was the one at that table who, aside from Abéraud, had come closest to the truth, and I had gained no advantage, no precedence.

Finally, an aberrant sensation contributed to my discomfort: it was becoming clear that this group of executives was trying to replace a faltering general management in defending the interests of our firm. Far from pleasing me, however, this prospect caused me embarrassment. I surprised myself by preferring the elegant and feline nonchalance of Henri Saint-Ramé to my colleagues' wholly Anglo-Saxon aggressiveness and lack of romanticism, to their furious desire to win through where, according to them, the French directors had failed. And this train of thought led me toward an image of the Americans becoming aware of their French executives' activity and of that action's style and results, and then praising Abéraud and his lieutenants for their initiative, reproaching Saint-Ramé for his inability to make use of their intelligence and energy. This affair, I told myself, will produce great changes in the hierarchy of the company, and isn't that Abéraud's real objective? The possibility of a sort of coup d'état fomented by the principal cadres against Saint-Ramé's management diminished my enthusiasm and led me to questions: Why had they coopted me so eagerly? Weren't they afraid I might betray them? Since my information about the suspicions they entertained was very incomplete, I took the floor and inquired:

"May I have your view of the facts and the identity of the provocateur or provocateurs?"

"What we think is simple," Abéraud replied. "Someone having extraordinary means of action has taken it into his head, for reasons that we don't clearly understand, to ruin Rosserys and Mitchell–France and probably in doing so to strike a blow at the concept of multinational companies. This is how he might have proceeded: Experts consulted at my suggestion have stated that it was possible, either by calculating the power of an explosive or by concrete blowtorch or water injection, to damage the pillars that support the building, to cut through them or to make them sink, thus cracking the walls. That's not easy, but it's within the ability of a saboteur with a thorough knowledge of such matters. The civil engineering corps breaks down walls at a predetermined spot with astonishing precision. In the case of our office building, for example, an explosion that cut through the post of reinforced concrete situated at the top of the bend in the passageway between the crypt and the next room could produce the crack that we know about and yet not be heard outside. At the same time the man sends the tracts to the employees, being careful to invest them with mystery and ambiguity. He tries to strike men's imagi-

161

nation by a novel method that will take the directors by surprise. The man is thoroughly at home in the subcellars; he moves about in them like a fish in the water. Finally, he imitates Henri Saint-Ramé's voice so perfectly and so boldly that he brings consternation to a head by circulating false rumors. Our chiefs are disconcerted and don't know how to react. Either they suppress or minimize the facts, and thus magnify them, or they respond with humor and relaxation and thus aggravate them."

I remembered then that Saint-Ramé had invited me to play the game without any restrictions and that my mission was to report faithfully the senior executives' actions and intentions. I told them in detail about that eventful night, softening my terms to describe Musterffies' state. When I had finished, my colleagues remained silent for long minutes, then Abéraud added an epilogue in a cavernous voice.

"So it was just as we thought: the masquerade was organized by that man, and everyone jumped." He added, between his teeth, "Everyone, directors in the lead! What depravity! Thank you, Number 7, for enlightening us and confirming my suspicions. We now possess an enormous advantage over our adversary: surprise has changed camps. He is unaware that we've discovered the area he haunts. Tomorrow night we go hunting. Let him distribute his final imprecations—he's run his race. By the way, who christened these texts *imprecations?*"

"It was Saint-Ramé," I said, "the night of the wake."

"Aha, there's something interesting," murmured Abéraud, after which he concluded, "If no one has any further questions, supper awaits us. Tomorrow morning don't be surprised if I'm not in the office. I'll stay home to make preparations for our nocturnal expedition. In the afternoon I'll have instructions sent to you."

Then I had a smart idea: I questioned the principal cadres about the advisability of my collaboration with Rumin and the general management.

"That will be very useful to us," Abéraud observed, just as I'd hoped. "Don't change your attitude; keep us abreast of manage-

162

ment's plans, take the pulse of the employees. The next few days will be decisive in many ways."

We rose and followed Abéraud, who, rather ostentatiously, quitted the room at a slow pace. We traversed a corridor lighted by scattered violet illumination, and I had the impression of descending even farther into the bowels of the earth. It was hot, but I didn't dare take off my cape. I realized the control Abéraud exercised over his colleagues. We walked in single file in our numbered order. Chavégnac turned and gave me a forced smile distorted by the violet penumbra. His face streamed with sweat. I must have returned a strange rictus, for he turned away hurriedly. Finally we arrived in a circular dining room, feebly lighted. A round table was set in the center and armchairs identical to those in the meeting room awaited us. Beside each chair stood a tall man with a mustache, a white napkin over his left arm. Abéraud stopped and said to us:

"Gentlemen, the temperature here is bearable. Let's keep our capes on and sit down."

The temperature in fact was appreciably cool, so much so that shivers ran up my spine and my hands were suddenly cold. We seated ourselves. A roast pig was brought in and the emaciated lackeys filled heavy pewter cups with wine. Songs without words rose from I know not where, and Abéraud lifted his cup.

"We drink the health of all headquarters executives in the Western world and Japan!"

We drank. Meanwhile the pale lackeys skillfully carved the pig. Pork fat and fillets soon adorned our plates and floods of wine were downed by the principal cadres of Rosserys and Mitchell–France. Abéraud proposed a toast to the Western democracies. The pale lackeys changed our plates and replaced them with gigantic ones on which lay thick slices of beef. Spirits grew warm, heads feverish; we headed toward a binge that would have deserved admonitions from our directors had they surprised us there. Each rose and selected the subject for a toast. Presently it was my turn. Despite adroit manipulations I had not been able totally to avoid quenching my thirst, and this caused me a slight vertigo, a sort of haziness, not disagreeable but conducive to exaltation. And so I got up, holding my goblet high, and I began a prayer.

"O Lord, you who have deigned to favor the birth, expansion and multiplication of giant corporations, multinational and American, grant us the strength necessary to preserve them! Thanks to them, the goods and merchandise manufactured in this lowly world increase and soon will provide food, clothing, comfort and leisure for all human creatures that you have created in your image! Thanks to them, Lord, international finances are healthy, men and women of the entire world, beyond frontiers, beyond national egotisms and religious fanaticisms, hold one another by the hand with feelings of solidarity and fraternal love.

"But right here, Lord, the global propagation of happiness may be compromised by the contrivances of Satan's envoys. Lord, you drove the money changers from the temple; expel the demon beyond our walls! May your divine bounty and your infinite power favor the expansion and the growth of giant companies, American and multinational, which bring bread to those who hunger, water to those who thirst, shade to those who are hot, warmth to those who are cold, and may there rise, where now lie arid and scorched lands, numerous office buildings of glass and steel, and may you protect their treasuries from the obscurantist persecution of the destroyers!

"Lord, I drink to your omnipotence and beseech you to forgive the trespasses of the twelve headquarters executives, your humble servants, who by meeting here tonight are attempting, with their modest means, to repel the invader and defeat his hideous, pagan offensive. Let us drink!"

We drank. And I read in their radiant faces that my prayer had proved effective. So God too would be one of us that night. Brignon, the last to raise his glass, cried:

"We drink to Japan, we rejoice at the unlimited construction of glass-and-steel buildings which honor and embellish that archipelago blessed of the gods!"

164

We drank to the industrial and commercial empire of the Rising Sun. Some of us were half-seas over when, on a sign from Abéraud, the pale lackeys opened a double door set in one of the walls in order to admit an orchestra. The musicians had only wind instruments such as trombones and hunting horns. The music I had noticed at the beginning of the supper and which had aroused my curiosity sounded again, but this time fortissimo. Abéraud rose, clapped his hands and cried:

"Come! Everyone into the Great Hall."

Preceded by the musicians and followed by some of the emaciated lackeys, we paraded back up the corridor illuminated by violet light and so made a thunderous entrance into the room with the puzzling contours. Women in long dresses and high chignons, with severe faces and opulent, tightly corseted bosoms, came to meet us. The musicians played again, more enthusiastically, that strange air in a rhythm that might be a polka or mazurka. However, it lacked words worthy of it, and a sudden inspiration swept me into the limelight. I interrupted Abéraud, who was prancing about in the embrace of one of our haughty, muscular hostesses.

"Hey, Number 5, what a shame not to have lyrics for such a melancholy, fatalistic tune! I've just thought of some, simple and pleasant. Would you like to hear them?"

"Fine idea, Number 7!" Abéraud approved enthusiastically. "Gentlemen," he shouted, whirling around. "Number 7 is going to improvise lyrics! Long live Number 7!"

The musicians gathered round me, and I intoned words which had sprung to my mind one evening as the result of indescribable exasperation. They matched the rhythm, marrying the music as though predestined for it. To those who look after me and surround me with kind attention, and more generally to those who will finally read me, I cannot too strongly recommend that they sing this song in moments of depression and vacuity of soul.

> Ah, ah,
> let's import, export, package and sell

165

and long live beets
and long live soybeans
praised be cereals
corn and wheat
long live pork and prime ribs of beef
let's import the choicest cuts,
the round steak and rump steak,
top sirloin and fillet,
rib steak and strip,
and the eye round—
oh, Lord—
and the eye round.
Let's export the tail and gristle,
brisket and dewlaps,
soup meat and neck
and the rolled shank—
oh, Lord—
and the rolled shank.
Ah, ah,
and long live Père Lachaise
and long live Rosserys and Mitchell the fair—
fair throat and fat rump,
fair throat and fat rump.

My lyrics were a considerable success; repeated in chorus by the
whey-faced lackeys, the haughty, corseted ladies and the company's headquarters executives, they reechoed cheerfully beneath
the vault of the Goulim. And when we brought that eventful night
to a close by snake-dancing in front of the doors of Rosserys and
Mitchell beneath the scandalized eyes of the chief watchman, we
sang steadily, stretching our arms toward the summit of the glass-
and-steel building: "Oh, good morning, fair one! Fair throat and
fat rump, fair throat and fat rump!" Dawn was breaking when taxis
delivered us to our homes. The day it announced was destined to
be trying and troubled.

19

I was awakened at ten o'clock by the ringing of my telephone. My head aching from a violent migraine, I dragged myself to the instrument. It was Saint-Ramé, who expressed surprise at my absence, deplored it in sharp terms and demanded my presence at his side with the least possible delay, for, he explained, new elements had arisen in the early morning. I protested weakly, citing a serious physical ailment, but he dismissed this dryly and gave me an appointment for eleven o'clock in his office. He hung up, neglecting the usual formalities.

I had an hour's time, which was sufficient to prepare myself and make the trip, but not to dispel the nocturnal vapors that clouded my mind. I swallowed some headache tablets, took a shower that was almost cold, absorbed some coffee and called a taxi.

By the time I emerged from the vehicle in front of the company's main entrance, I had decided to respect the official, legal hierarchy and to serve it. My migraine had disappeared and the

167

strong coffee was showing beneficent effects. I plunged into the elevator and went straight up to the general management's floor. Saint-Ramé received me at once, but he wasn't alone. Musterffies, Ronson, Roustev, Rumin and the two detectives were also there, prey to a definite excitement. The managing director's desk was piled with journals and notes and out of this litter emerged a scroll beribboned in green and black. Then I understood Saint-Ramé's impatience, his dryness and the laconic tone of his telephone call. The third imprecation had come.

WHAT DO THOSE WHO RUN
ROSSERYS AND MITCHELL
REALLY KNOW?

They know, most importantly, about self-funding and internal organization. The ignorant masses and executives in the field find it easy to have fun in troubled times since none of them has control of our companies, the continuance of employment and the payment of salaries, without which men and women, their children and their aged, would be doomed to want, to cold and to great calamities that occur regularly. Our epoch is marked by ingratitude toward those who, at the heart of our corporations, administrations and government, master the arduous theories and techniques that have brought about the unprecedented progress of our civilization. Furthermore, this ingratitude is nourished by the profound ignorance which, through an astonishing paradox, characterizes the vast majority today. That is why it is well from time to time to survey—if not to explain—certain essential notions that determine contemporary industrialized peoples' quality of life.

Thus it is with the concepts of *cash flow, staff and line* and *integrated management*. Millions of workers, employees, executive trainees, ordinary and even senior executives, pass through the doorways of our superb companies each morning as a matter of course, as if, in the name of a sort of natural right, the walls, the offices, the machines, were set up and installed there through the will of the Holy Ghost to afford them employment, remuneration and paid holidays, plus an impressive share of material and intellectual enjoyment! It never occurs to any of these people to ask themselves what would become of these walls, these offices, these machines and these enjoyments without a steady cash flow, and a vigorous system of integrated management.

As for the men and women workers who hear reference all day long to *cash flow*—what do they think it is? They imagine simply that *cash flow* means the flow of money that permits payment in cash. According to this definition the cash flow of a family budget, for example, would be the liquid money in currency or in the bank that remains for the family after the total expenses have been deducted. Picture that! Look where sacrosanct popularization leads! If this were the definiton of *cash flow*, would it be necessary to spend a long time studying esoteric books and enrolling in courses taught by great American professors and their eminent German, Japanese or Dutch disciples? No. The fact is that cash flow is a more elevated, more inscrutable concept. Only those with consummate practice in the act of directing and a natural aptitude for modern methods of management are in a position to apprehend it. And Henri Saint-Ramé, our managing director, who will perhaps be the first European to rise to the presidency of a giant American multinational corporation, knows what a company's cash flow is. May it please Heaven that the present text, despite its inevitable limitations, serve to reconcile the mass of those who are directed and the handful of those who direct, at least insofar as cash flow is concerned.

What then do they really know about cash flow, the directors of Rosserys and Mitchell? Well, they know how to reply, clearly and frankly, to the following questions: Whence come the receipts of the company? From the sale of the machines it manufactures. For what are these receipts used? First of all, to pay the suppliers' bills; then the salaries of the workmen, the employees, the technicians and the executives employed by the firm. Then these receipts serve as well to pay for the energy used, the electricity, the fuel, etc. And finally, they pay the general expenses. Any remaining small change is used for amortization and to provide certain supplies. Last of all, if there's anything left, is the profit.

Does Saint-Ramé's knowledge stop there? Not at all. He must display supplementary intellectual fireworks. Such as? He will consider this profit and divide it into three parts: one for taxes (hence the formula, so often misunderstood by subordinate workers, profits before or after taxes); a second part will be allocated to stockholders, bondholders and administrators in the form of percentages and dividends. What does a percentage mean? Saint-Ramé knows this. He knows that it means a certain part of a fixed total. And dividend? Well, that is the opposite of divisor. It is the portion of the interest or profit that goes to each stockholder. To determine it, all one has to do is divide; still, one must know how. A third part of the profit will be retained by the company in the form of reserves, these being divided into legal and statutory reserves. And now we approach *cash flow,* that little heart that beats within the great heart of companies. We have just seen that the company has sold its machines and collected the return from these sales, set aside amounts of money corresponding to amortization, supplies and nondistributed profits placed in reserve. This hard and critical cash which the company does not owe to anyone but itself, which it locks away in its vaults, serves it for self-funding. That is, it can, without depending on the help of a third party, of lenders whether banks or individuals, buy new ground, build new structures, acquire new machinery, finance research; in short, invest. The cash flow is officially this. It is this amount of money expendable at the company's discretion which it has tucked away in its vaults.

One might think that Saint-Ramé's knowledge of *cash flow* would end there, which would not be bad at all. But our managing director and his peers know even more; especially they are unequaled in the judicious utilization of this cash flow. What the devil more have they learned? It is this: They have reflected long and have asked themselves: How will our cash flow render humanity the maximum of service? And one day, striking their bulging foreheads, they reply: By growing. It is important here not to be taken in by the apparent simplicity of this reply,

170

for in truth it was not absolutely obligatory to reply in that fashion. One could have said: By diminishing. As this famous cash flow is made up of amortization and undistributed profits, the less one amortizes, the more profits one distributes, the less money remains in the vault for self-funding.

We have seen, however, that amortization is to include cost of the wear and tear on machinery, buildings, etc., in the price received; consequently the more rapidly one amortizes, the more the price of the machines rises, and the more reserves one takes from the undistributed profits, the less money the stockholders of the company receive. The cash flow becomes the principal source of investments. And thanks to the dexterity of Henri Saint-Ramé and his peers, the world is witnessing a spectacle of gripping originality: the more corporations grow, the more their cash flow increases, the more the price of their products rises and the more the profits distributed to the stockholders remain constant. Saint-Ramé and his peers have found the solution to the problem of abundance and well-being in the Western world: instead of money being a means of production and construction, production and construction have become a means of amassing money. So it seems infantile and supererogatory to study the size of a company's profits in order to determine its health. The official profits distributed being small, it is no longer the curve of profits that is symptomatic but that of the *cash flow*—in short, the independently financed investments.

Has this been understood? Has the point been made clear that the cash flow is not simply a stream of money used to make cash payments? Saint-Ramé keeps watch day and night at the bedside of the fat, suave cash flow of Rosserys and Mitchell–France. Those who direct the innumerable companies of Rosserys and Mitchell in Japan, in Greece, in Holland, in Germany and everywhere else, whose office buildings of glass and steel rise in all the countries of the earth, also watch over their respective cash flows. And all these cash flows are then accounted for, adjusted to one another, over in Des Moines, in Iowa, that splendid state of North America, and they make up a single unique cash flow, voluminous, majestic, winding across the planet, from the plateaus of French Provence and caressing the rugged massifs of the Italian Alps,

171

suddenly swollen by tributaries of the ruble and flooding Japan, then irrigating Amazonia and the Andes, and finally returning to Washington to sink and suddenly disappear from the view of millions of fascinated men. This is the cash flow in whose warm waters the peoples of the West, habituated to rising salaries and prices, bathe and refresh themselves without worrying about the huge alligators that roam beneath strange water lilies. Yes, Saint-Ramé knows what the cash flow is. Perhaps you who have just read these lines will feel a little compassion and affection for these men who, after the model of your managing director, sacrifice their leisure and their family life to growth, to expansion, to the stability of employment, to the maintenance of a level of life, by keeping watch ceaselessly over the amount of *cash flow*.

Does this mean that Saint-Ramé only busies himself with cash flow? Obviously not, since he also has to organize the hierarchy and the work within his empire. Formerly the relations between superiors and inferiors in the bosom of a firm were simply copied from the mechanisms of the economy, which were themselves elementary. But with the coming of the postindustrial age, when monetary and commercial relations became established on a global scale, transcending frontiers and nations, minds of good intelligence were no longer enough to control the circulation of merchandise. The laws of banking and economics were beyond the grasp of any but a handful of minds of genius, and this sudden rise in the intellectual value of managers had its repercussions in the internal organization of companies. So today Rosserys and Mitchell, which showed the way for cash flow, now shows the way for *staff and line*, a method permitting employees to be happy at their work and to obey fair regulations.

And if no one had invented staff and line, how would these merry, carefree men and women who people our giant American multinational enterprises live? Happily, Saint-Ramé and his peers have inspired the human warmth indispensable to the climate of these corporations. There once more they sought and they found. What did they discover? Well, it was this: the system of command and the division of responsibility that the military authorities of all countries have worked out over centuries were actually more subtle and effective than had been commonly thought and, adapted to great corporations, would certainly work wonders. And so a distinction was made between administrative directors and executives on the one hand and the operating executives on the other. The administrative executives are the experts, and advisers. They exist by their functions and not by their operations (which they never conduct). It is the operating executives who carry out the operations. A general on Foch's staff was an administrator; Pétain at Verdun an operator. The first belonged to the staff, the second was on line.

With us at Rosserys and Mitchell–France, Saint-Ramé is surrounded by twelve eminent executives who give expert opinions and advice from morning till night and so make a capital contribution to the development and success of the firm. They are, then, what the masses commonly designate as *staff*. The subordinate employees say of the headquarters executives: they belong to the staff. The others, the directors of departments, of factories, of commercial areas, those who manufacture, crate and sell the machines, are the operators. They are on *line* —in short, at the front. And they depend directly upon the managing director. Henri Saint-Ramé has learned how to set up and control such a system, and that mastery explains the harmony and joy that reign at the heart of his company. When did he learn this? From Douglas McGregor, who formerly taught at the Massachusetts Institute of Technology, he learned those revolutionary and inspired principles which reconcile the growth of a firm and the profitability of its capital with a passion for work and human fellowship.

This has been a cursory view of what our managing director knows. Certainly it is arbitrary to interrupt the enumeration and explanation of his skills at this point, for Henri Saint-Ramé has assimilated many others, especially since the advent of giant computers which have given birth to systems of integrated management and remote control. Thanks to those who know, the administrative tasks will be more and more centralized and the operational decisions more and more decentralized. The man and the woman thus freed from routine tasks will devote themselves to works of the mind and imagination. I hope that now the enthusiasm of the employees of Rosserys and Mitchell–France will rise to new heights. Meanwhile let us pray God that our company will win the economic war for the greatest happiness of all men, and let us beseech Him to preserve the health of the leaders who watch over our growth and expansion. By revealing a little of what they know, and of their burden, I shall have contributed to the respect due them.

The war cabinet of Rosserys and Mitchell and the two detectives had sat silent during my reading, which could be interpreted as either deference or ill humor. It was in fact customary that when an important officer arrived late for a meeting he should be allowed time to acquaint himself with the principal points under discussion; but though recently promoted and frequently congratulated on this during recent days, I dismissed that possibility. On the other hand, a director of human relations, comfortably in bed at the moment when the third imprecation appeared, deserved to have the gravity of his dereliction pointed out. So it was in great embarrassment that I laid the scroll on Saint-Ramé's desk. They waited for me to speak, which increased my embarrassment. Two or three minutes passed before I inquired timidly, like a schoolboy at fault:

"How was it distributed this time?"

Saint-Ramé answered: "Notices were posted last night on the bulletin boards, one on each floor, announcing that a stock of scrolls was available to the employees in the large basement conference room. The watchmen had thought of everything except counting the printed notices and other announcements permanently posted on these bulletin boards; the provocateur took calculated risks. To be sure, he might have been taken by surprise, but he only had eleven notices to put up. As to when and how he accumulated his stock of scrolls in the basement, that's the real mystery."

At those words I remembered the headquarters executives' wild night—their suspicions and investigations had focused on the cemetery and the tunnels. I told myself that the imprecator had succeeded in making a secret entrance and exit in the obscurity of the subbasements, and then I realized the difficulty of being a double

174

agent when one is not used to it. Adams J. Musterffies' haughty voice brought me back to reality.

"Well, what do you think of this text? And the situation it creates?"

I was now completely awake, my brain reactivated by this new event, and I indulged in an analysis, certainly rather shrewd, for it aroused the interest of all my interlocutors. Here is the substance of what I said to them that morning:

"Gentlemen, I notice that this text is much longer than the preceding ones and that it has an almost desperate air, an exacerbated attempt to make the definitive round of certain fundamental questions such as cash flow, staff and line, informational management integrated by telemetry. These texts follow a sharp ascending curve: in the first, a truly sketchy summary, economic subjects are treated with humor and irony—one has the impression that the author is entertaining himself and taking his time. He's in no hurry. He's plotting his aggression. In the second text the rhythm accelerates, and if the irony remains, the style sometimes skids, departing from the framework chosen at the start. The first text, which is ambiguous, gives way to a more significant second one. Remember such an expression as 'a round and salty tear,' which seems to have slipped out inadvertently and is inappropriate to the rigid and gratingly ironic style of the first text.

"In the third, the provocateur seems to be rushed; he doesn't encumber himself with grace notes. The text I've just read, gentlemen, is urgent and goes straight to the point. It makes unhesitating fun of our managing director and through him of all managers of multinational firms, and of the global community of technocrats. The end of this text is cut short and even bungled. One feels that the author would have liked to describe at much greater length the phenomena peculiar to the staff and line systems of organization and informational management, but he gives the impression of being forced to hurry, to finish up as quickly as possible. Here, gentlemen, is something interesting. Why? Note that this evolution of the texts is rigorously linked to the methods of distribution:

for example, the first text was distributed everywhere, almost nonchalantly, in complete quiet, in every office, on every desk, by someone exceptionally well informed about the company's inner workings. The second text proceeded in a manner astute but nevertheless tortuous. Finally, the third text reached the employees by an indirect route, a kind of ricochet, and with the least risk, since it was enough for the adversary to deliver the stock of scrolls downstairs at a moment chosen by him and to post eleven notices. In doing this the man knew very well that the employees would go looking for the scrolls if only through curiosity and that management couldn't forbid them to do so without exposing itself to various difficulties and even to ridicule.

"To sum up, these texts, by their content and their successive styles, and by the nature of their distribution, testify that the provocateur is running out of wind. This, gentlemen, may signify: *(a)* that our efforts and those of our detectives are paying off, the adversary having more and more difficulty in perpetrating his misdeeds within the company; and *(b)* that his end is nearer than was thought. By hurrying, the provocateur shows us that he himself is convinced of that. Who knows? This scroll may be the last."

During my exposition, Saint-Ramé constantly tapped the leather frame of his blotter with his eyeglasses while staring thoughtfully at I know not what distant horizon. He reacted to my words before Musterffies and said in a soft and most surprising tone:

"My boy, I have no wish to fly to the aid of a victory, a victory largely yours, but I can assure you that since I have been managing director, rarely have I heard a colleague express such penetrating views so briefly. Not only am I in agreement with your analysis, but I envy you for having made it. This proves to me, if that were necessary, that you really understand this case, the case that our American friends, Monsieur Roustev and I entrusted to you several days ago, the dark and startling case of the imprecator of Rosserys and Mitchell–France. I thank you."

Saint-Ramé, although incarnating in the highest degree the vir-

tues and defects of that race produced by postindustrial civilization, had never incurred the charge of hypocrisy. In this respect
he enjoyed the reputation of a well-balanced man, courteous,
knowing when to reward or rebuke, but little inclined to excess
in either direction. This reputation explains the profound surprise
caused by his reaction. The Americans, Roustev and Rumin could
not believe their ears. Being accustomed to consider the affair
from its *unthinkable, supernatural* angle and to see in it only a
gigantic anomaly, a formidable boil, the psychic and calamitous
by-product of the affluent societies' unbridled rush toward the
gulf, I was not unduly moved. I'd already perceived that the congratulations of my managing director needed to be deciphered. I
was, I'm obliged to say, in the grip of the furious forces that I'd
seen unleashed the night before. If headquarters executives could
slip into burlesque and dramaturgical psychology, why shouldn't
their boss succumb in his turn? And the idea that Saint-Ramé
cherished a secret but genuine admiration for the man who was
disturbing his company naturally occurred to me and added a new
dimension to the battle we were fighting.

In the course of this meeting we agreed to reinforce our staff of
watchmen, then we listened to the two detectives' report.

I understood the Americans' indignation at my arrival. It wasn't
because I was late, but because of my participation in the recent
revelries. I readily furnished various explanations: Yes, we'd ban-
queted joyously. Yes, we'd offered toasts to fair and open-handed
America, to our company, to the directors of the Western world.
Yes, we'd paid the check with our own money and not the company's, but the wine had been good, the meat savory. Yes, just like
the detectives, we'd suspected one another, no, that hadn't spoiled
our feast, yes, that was the reason my eyes were swollen, yes, the
mental state of my colleagues was sane, no, even when a little
drunk they had not denigrated the values of our Western society.
Yes, they were in favor of selling and buying from the countries
of the East, of making a financial arrangement with them, of maintaining the status quo politically and forgetting ideologies and

liberties, of not thinking of anything except the increase of trade. Then the Americans, relieved, cheered up, and it was in almost happy tones that Adams J. Musterffies, delighted at the state of mind of the French firm's senior executives, questioned Roustev about the enlargement of the crack. The son-in-law of Gabriel Antémès, the man who had sold to our American friends his experience of the French and African market in machines for public works, spoke in a muffled voice:

"This morning, called to the spot by the employee I had specially ordered to keep an eye on the crack, I discovered that it had grown larger. Our master architect, summoned instantly, couldn't explain this enlargement, and that's what worries me. If the experts don't succeed in discovering the causes of this devilish crack, I'm afraid it will continue to grow, to wind hideously and thus to compromise the soundness of the building in short order."

Roustev stopped speaking. Upon hearing the last phrase I felt a delicious shiver run through me. This was where he, Roustev, was losing his marbles too! Saint-Ramé, a strange smile on his lips, stared curiously at his assistant. Musterffies, irritated by the freedom of André Roustev's language, demanded rudely:

"When you say that the crack may 'wind hideously,' do you simply mean us to understand that the building is in danger of collapsing?"

The unhappy Roustev then became pathetic and unrecognizable. He replied, groping for words:

"I beg your pardon, Mr. President, but go and take a look—it's terrifying. That crack looks like a hideous serpent . . . that crack is of a repellent ugliness."

"Now look here," exclaimed Ronson, who only intervened on crucial occasions. "What's got into you, Roustev? You're usually more cool. Have the French directors of the richest and most powerful enterprise in the world, whose cash flow for last year alone exceeds the budget of Argentina and Paraguay combined, gone crazy? This is a strange disease that seems to attack our best minds and corrupt our language! To begin with, Roustev, have you

178

ever seen a pretty crack? What distinction do you make between a pretty crack and a hideous crack? You can't be serious! Why were the American experts allowed to leave after the first repairs? They must be brought back this very night. You'll end by persuading me that these events are more serious than they appear to be. Finally, let's reflect: here it is barely a week since our French firm was flourishing and prosperous; it aroused the admiration of our board in Des Moines; the directors were proud of our company. Thanks to the competence and brilliance of Henri and his general staff, our principles were penetrating little by little into a country as impermeable to modern concepts of profit and self-funding as France, and suddenly because some harebrain gets the idea of circulating trivial tracts, and because this coincides with the death of a senior executive and the appearance of a crack, these results are compromised!

"Come, gentlemen, let's rub our eyes, stop flirting with phantoms, come to our senses. The crack is enlarging; all right. Well, a crack doesn't enlarge by chance; that certainly comes from an undiscovered defect in the subsoil, the earth subsiding slightly. With the technical means at our disposal we'll get to the bottom of this crack. But I beg you, let's forget about its appearance, its beauty or its ugliness, and watch our vocabulary. I don't like to make any trouble for people I have confidence in, but the board in Des Moines—to whom I am responsible—has given me carte blanche and complete freedom to use it. I've done so. Let us together resist the intoxication that seems to be spreading among us."

Instinctively we turned our eyes toward Adams J. Musterffies. He had the floor. Officially Ronson, in his capacity as Des Moines' representative to Paris, did not occupy a position in the hierarchy. Musterffies was one of the great multinational leaders, Saint-Ramé the uncontested and powerful head of the French firm. But I'd always scented a gray eminence in Ronson, a sort of police chief for the company, comparable (allowing for exaggeration) to a sort of company Gestapo. In my eyes, he had unmasked himself. Or rather, he had involuntarily lowered his mask. I concluded that so important a decision would not have been taken without absolute necessity. The firm's home office therefore considered the situation in France extremely serious. Musterffies himself had been short-circuited by this commissar, most of the time silent as a carp, but in whom I had noted an implacable inquisitor, always on the alert. The American vice-president remained placid, knowing (as he surely must) Ronson's exact role. Very skillfully he even picked up his American friend's words:

"In saying that to you, Bernie's done his duty and saved me the task. Coming from me, the words might seem a reprimand; coming from him, they accomplish their purpose, which is to give you useful advice. We no longer live in the Middle Ages and our enemies don't prowl around at night dragging chains and wearing transparent robes. Our enemies have names and faces, they are called workers, artists, intellectuals; depraved, long-haired young men; authoritarian and nationalistic governments; countries jealous of us which, if they're hungry and have no money, owe that to their own lack of will, to their incapacity to work, and not—as they pretend at the U.N.—to periods of drought and nature's ingratitude.

"And what did we Americans find when we landed over there? No Statue of Liberty, but inhospitable forests teeming with ferocious beasts, venomous serpents and cruel, barbarous Indians. Floods and droughts were the daily lot of our pioneer ancestors. Our oil didn't spout by itself from the depths of the earth; our cotton and our wheat didn't grow by magic from hostile soil, often half sterile; and we didn't voyage up the Missouri in ferryboats but in primitive canoes. Our enemies are indeed alive and unless some drug has been poured into our teacups each night, I see no valid reason to babble and chatter as if onstage. If, when I promoted our director of human relations, I seemed to be using purple prose, I beg pardon of my colleagues for misleading them. But there were mitigating circumstances: I was promoting an executive on the field of battle for the first time. Now the incident is closed. . . ."

180

"I didn't think this business of the scrolls would go so far," murmured Saint-Ramé.

"I'm in favor of referring the matter to Des Moines," Ronson said. "Otherwise we'll never hear the end of it. We're too far implicated in the business and we'll have trouble handling it. Vice-President Musterffies himself, who's involved by accident, will agree with me, I'm sure. The entire board of directors must come and join us—secretly of course, so as not to arouse the curiosity of the press and the employees. I admit that I no longer know how to tackle this situation, which is getting worse every day. I pray this provocateur may be caught as soon as possible. Frankly, I've never seen anything like this in my whole career!"

Thus the solid and cynical Ronson in his turn fell into the trap. I noticed that only Saint-Ramé, a fixed smile on his lips, was looking with curiosity at Adams J. Musterffies. What went on at that precise moment between the two men? Today I know.

The vice-president approved Bernie Ronson's proposal, then, tired out, he broke up the meeting without consulting the managing director. They left the office with heavy steps, backs bent, foreheads creased. As I was going through the door, Saint-Ramé called to me:

"Have you another moment? I'd like to discuss all this with you tête-à-tête and to find out especially what happened last night in that tavern—what's it called?"

"The Goulim, sir."

"Oh, the Goulim. That's odd."

"What is, sir?"

"That name, the Goulim. Doesn't it mean anything to you?"

"No, sir."

"It's like the Golem."

"The Golem?"

"You don't know what the Golem is?" Saint-Ramé exclaimed, maliciously astonished, then regaining his gravity. "The Golem, my boy, is a lovely legend. In 1589 a rabbi of Prague, Löw ben Bézabel, is said to have constructed a human figure from clay and endowed it with a soul in the name of the Eternal. This figure, this terrifying automaton, escaped and aroused panic in the streets of the city. . . . That's disturbing, isn't it?"

"Yes," I said, not much impressed.

Saint-Ramé walked to his window, appeared to meditate; then coming back toward me, he met my eye and murmured; "And if the Golem had got into our enterprise? What do you think? Tell me about your night in that tavern. Did you by any chance meet someone with a grotesque face?"

In my presence that morning Henri Saint-Ramé discussed a number of subjects which he treated calmly, sometimes with detachment, and at moments I had trouble recognizing in him the man the Americans had chosen to direct their French firm. I'm practically certain that my attitude in the course of these events had earned me his active sympathy and that in this tête-à-tête he was trying to clarify my ideas, to hold out a helping hand to me. But how could I grasp it? The shadows in which I had become shrouded were too thick for one pale and simple light to dispel.

"So then, this evening," said Saint-Ramé, "you're going to make an expedition to the subbasements? That's fascinating! Do you suppose I am the only managing director in the world whose senior executives are preparing to explore the company's subcellars in disguise?"

"I believe so," I replied sincerely, then remembering my ambiguous position, I added:

"I've reported my colleagues' actions to you, as was my duty, but if they hear about it I'll be in trouble. Besides, I'd like to ask how you plan to use this information."

"Oh!" exclaimed Saint-Ramé. "Don't be alarmed. I'll use it with circumspection. For the moment the best thing is to let this interesting initiative develop, since it happily complements our detectives' investigation. Let it be said in passing, they knew about your libations but not your intentions. As soon as we have unmasked the imprecator, I shall invite all of you to a soirée at the Goulim. . . . Tell me, what do you yourself think of that crack?"

"I think it's due to sinking subsoil."

"You don't believe it could have been contrived?"

"Good Lord," I said. "I don't see how."

"Didn't you tell me that Abéraud considered the possibility of sabotage?"

"Yes, but I'm no expert and, *a priori,* that seems to me incredible."

Saint-Ramé reflected for long minutes, after which, staring me straight in the eye, he asked; "Who do you think I suspect is the imprecator?"

I hesitated several minutes before replying, "I have the impression that you suspect Abéraud and Le Rantec."

"Would you believe it—and I confide this to you under the seal of absolute secrecy—that's what the detectives and Vice-President Musterffies think."

"And Ronson?" I asked. "Whom does he suspect?"

"Oh, with Ronson it's different. He has an idea in the back of his mind, but it must be a horrible one, because he obstinately refuses to mention it without irrefutable proof. . . . Perhaps," the managing director added jokingly, "he thinks you're the culprit."

I only half enjoyed that joke, because I'd been running on my nerves for several days and I longed for rest. After all, I didn't belong to any clique; I'd withdrawn from commercial functions to find some peace and quiet. I was passionately interested in human relations and determined to develop them, come what might. I thought it timely to remind Saint-Ramé of that and I declared in conclusion: "What's happened to us is due to the meager interest shown by our company directors in the lives of individuals and their dignity as workers."

"That's exactly it," said the managing director. "I'm aware that you were hurt by my putting you on the list of suspects, but truly I was joking. Besides, don't worry. I, Henri Saint-Ramé, know who the culprit is."

"What's that!" I cried. "You know him? Are you sure?"

"Absolutely. . . . I've known the imprecator from the beginning, and I'm waiting for the opportune moment, as well as certain supplementary proofs, to reveal his identity and to confound him. Did you seriously believe that I've done nothing all this time? I have confidence in you and I count on you not to noise abroad what I have told you. I haven't said this to anyone else. You must know in any case that Abéraud is on the right path. I wouldn't be surprised if tonight is crucial. It's by no means certain that I myself won't make a tour of the subbasements. The net's tightening; the solution is almost certainly buried somewhere beneath our foundations. Our American friends and the detectives are at the point of believing this. Now it's only a step to meeting everybody down there tonight! And if the imprecator is one of the twelve cadres, he'll necessarily be among us. That promises to make for a fine suspense drama, in the style of *The Mystery of the Yellow Room!*"

And Saint-Ramé ended his tirade with a burst of laughter. I took my leave and went thoughtfully to my office. My secretary handed me a note, which Abéraud had delivered in person. It contained instructions. *For the attention of Number 7—at the end of the afternoon, shut yourself up in the closet opening off the audiovisual hall in the cellar. Wait silently until eleven o'clock or midnight. Number 3 will come to get you. Provide yourself with a bag containing your cape, your neckcloth, your badge, a flashlight, a rope at least thirty meters long, a bottle of water, two sandwiches, a pair of waterproof boots. Message ends.*

Although warned in advance, I remained nonplused at this material evidence of the decisions taken the night before. So it really was true, then—I hadn't been living in a dream. I, director of human relations for Rosserys and Mitchell–France, was going to plunge into the entrails of my company that very night in the line of duty, and with me eleven headquarters executives. I shuddered at the thought. The directors of the company, impelled by the same sort of intuition as ours, might meet us there. What would be their reaction to the sight of twelve phantoms armed with flashlights and ropes, haunting the foundations of the firm in search of the specter of subversion?

20

That afternoon at twelve-thirty, as I was preparing to go out for lunch and then shop for a rope and rubber-soled boots, Bernie Ronson entered my office unannounced and seated himself before me without a word. This behavior on the part of the delegate from Des Moines, which would have stunned me two days before, left me almost unmoved. Nevertheless I had no doubt that a serious reason had led him to present himself to me this way, gliding into my office like a cat. His face was anxious. But after all, might he not once more be playing a game? I waited for him to speak. Finally, in a low voice he said:

"The Arabs don't want to sell us oil anymore. Did you know?"

"No," I replied.

"The news just broke. It's been confirmed by Des Moines."

"By Des Moines?" I said, with an involuntary touch of irony.

Ronson lifted his eyes toward me in astonishment. "That doesn't seem to impress you much," he observed.

185

"It doesn't surprise me," I said. "This decision by the Arab countries will probably add to the firm's difficulties."

"Add to them?" Ronson was amazed. "Add to them? It's going to create them. The trivial incidents that have upset us recently are nothing in comparison with the enormous problems that we multinational companies are going to face from now on if the Arabs, the yellows, the blacks and the half-breeds refuse to sell their minerals, their wood, their wool or their oil."

"I don't know how to prove it to you," I said thoughtfully, "but I'm convinced that these events are connected in one way or another."

"Ah," said Ronson, "you constantly surprise me, Mr. Director of Human Relations. But now let's drop oil; I did not come to talk to you about these questions. I have an ultrasecret order to communicate to you. Listen carefully."

The American leaned toward me and whispered, "At precisely three o'clock you must be in the rear dining room of the Café de la République; a man with black tortoise-shell glasses will be waiting for you. He'll also be wearing a white turtleneck sweater. He'll be holding a big round gold watch with the initials R.M. engraved on it. This man has instructed me to tell you that he wishes to talk to you."

"May I know his name?" I asked, making an effort to remain calm.

"This man would prefer to give you his name himself; nevertheless he has authorized me, in case you insist, to reveal it to you. Do you insist, Mr. Director of Human Relations?"

"Yes," I said in a steady voice. "I insist."

"Well, then, this man is no other than Ralph McGanter in person."

"What does he want with me?" I exclaimed.

"Hush," said Ronson. "Don't talk so loud, and above all be discreet; now my mission is accomplished. Do not question me about McGanter's reasons; I don't know them. But once more, you and I must remain silent as a tomb. No one is *au courant,* neither

186

Musterfflies nor any member of the board of directors in Des Moines. So now go and have your lunch in peace and prepare yourself for this interview. Understand that this is an immense privilege for you, to have a chance to talk to this man in the flesh and in such circumstances." Ronson got up and before leaving he repeated: "Above all, not a word—be silent as the tomb. . . ." And he went out.

"As the tomb," I muttered to myself. And I understood that my adventure was entering its decisive phase. Ralph McGanter, the mysterious and powerful president of Rosserys and Mitchell International, would be waiting for me at three o'clock in a turtleneck sweater in the rear dining room of a Paris bistro. Why? What did he want? From whom had he heard about me?

I decided to walk a little, to take the air rather than shut myself up in a restaurant; my instinct, or simply habit, led me to Père Lachaise. When I arrived at the main gate my attention was attracted by the groups of executives and executive trainees who, in greater numbers than usual, were strolling along the cemetery paths. I entered the cemetery and here and there nodded to those who saluted me. The employees of Rosserys and Mitchell–France seemed very excited by the problems of oil and gas. They moved about between the tombs gesturing violently, and sometimes one or another of them, forgetting the solemnity of the place, punctuated his opinion with a loud exclamation. Suddenly I noticed one group more numerous, more agitated and noisier than the others. I recognized most of my staff colleagues crowded around the imposing tomb of green-and-black marble. I would have liked to avoid them, but Fournier saw me and called:

"Eh, Director of Human Relations—over this way. We're almost all together."

I had to resign myself to joining them. Abéraud, who was holding forth in the center of the group, welcomed me with a big smile. "Well?" he asked me. "What do you think of the news?"

I shook my head. "Upon my word, I don't know any details; Ronson simply told me. I don't know precisely what's involved."

"Ronson told you?" Abéraud asked in astonishment. "Hold on now, when was this? You've seen Ronson this morning?"

I had committed an error. I tried to retrieve it. "I met him in the elevator as I was leaving my office."

"Ah, good," said Abéraud. "You were lucky. I've been trying to get hold of him all morning."

Le Rantec's arrival produced a welcome diversion. He was in a state of extreme agitation. "Have you stopped to think that we're headed straight for recession and unemployment?" he cried. "We are about to enter a period of economic scarcity! Now here's a pretty problem! Should we or should we not base our policy on revenues?"

The cadre Le Rantec then went on expressing commonplaces drawn from the press. To make himself more easily heard, he had perched on the highest step of the green-and-black marble tomb.

"The whole problem hinges on a proper understanding of the Seven Majors! It's extremely difficult to explain that expression: Seven Majors. Let's say, to give you some idea, that you might call them the 'seven great ones' or—why not?—the 'seven graces'! As a matter of fact, they're the seven largest global corporations dealing in oil! Five are American, one English, one Dutch. And it's altogether proper that these companies should be gigantic. They have to take a hand at many stages in the operation of the petroleum industry and for this they have to have huge amounts of capital at their command. What are those stages? Well, first of all, there's the search for underground oil; and then the procuring of the oil—that is, the erection of derricks and drills that pierce the surface of the earth. And afterward the oil must be transported and refined and then sold. Finally, there's the colossal petrochemical industry. Everyone talks about petrochemistry without knowing precisely what it means. Well, it means the whole chemistry based on petroleum! The Seven Majors control the whole range of those activitties. What will become of them now that the Arabs want to take over their wells? And without oil, what's to become of us? The subject is as vast as it is fascinating; we could discourse

188

for hours about it. It's better to proceed through questions: who out there wants to ask a question?"

"Is coal going to come back?" asked a junior executive seated astride an ancient headstone.

At my side another cadre burst into laughter and shouted, "Is coal going to be reborn from its ashes?" which showed that despite being overworked, the executives of this period had not lost their sense of humor.

"It's not impossible," Le Rantec replied. "It's all a question of profitability and investment, and also a question of the cost of recovery. At the moment investments are below the cost of replacement and our cost of recovery is at 67 percent. But if the Arabs blow up their wells someday, we may see these figures change. Meanwhile, of course, there's competitive and profitable nuclear energy."

All of a sudden sounds of wailing and lamentation arose very close to us. It was a funeral procession, which we had neither heard nor seen approaching, fascinated as we were by Le Rantec's remarks. The priest, the family and the friends of the deceased were passing close by us and observing us with curiosity. Brought back to reality, no doubt, by this funeral, the cadres and employees of Rosserys and Mitchell–France dispersed themselves and then withdrew in haste. They had abruptly become aware that it was bad form to hold a meeting on energy and the oil shortage among the tombs. Death decidedly was following our company everywhere, both indoors and out, and had been doing so for almost a week. But that day it was making itself obtrusive.

I disappeared as discreetly as possible and well before three o'clock I was at the Café de la République, where I ordered sauerkraut while I waited for Ralph McGanter, the man in the white turtleneck carrying a gold watch. I profited from my lunch by reading the newspaper. I lingered over the comments occasioned by growing shortages of oil and the threat that hung over zinc, copper, bauxite and even the phosphates. So the West, led on by North America, had in sum been living beyond its means. And if the inhabitants of the industrialized countries had known a spectacular improvement in their scale of living, this was, after all, due not simply to their intelligence, to their work, to their skill, but also in large measure to the low prices they had paid for their raw materials. Here was the explanation of the almost universal famine in an immense part of the world and the prosperity and pollution in the other part. I promised myself to discuss these questions with the president of Rosserys and Mitchell International. I was amazed not to feel worried at the prospect of such a meeting. At other times I would have been overcome. But the events upsetting my company, combined with the crisis unsettling the values of postindustrial society, encouraged me to defy the hierarchy and to relax in its presence. After all, wasn't it Ralph McGanter's downfall that was in prospect? Was the man so eager to meet me still so powerful? This too I would ask him, I told myself; unless he had great need of me he would not make the effort to see me. At precisely three o'clock I observed a small man wearing black tortoise-shell glasses and a white turtleneck sweater, conspicuously playing with a large gold watch. He was strolling among the tables in the rear dining room. I approached him.

"What time is it?" I asked in English.

"See for yourself," he replied.

In the middle of the dial I saw the interlaced letters *R* and *M*. I bent over and said, "Are you Ralph McGanter?"

"In person," the man whispered, "and I'm very happy to meet you, Director of Human Relations. Here, let's find a seat over there in the corner. We'll be able to chat undisturbed."

We took our places, face to face, at a little square table set apart. A waiter approached, and we ordered—I an anisette, he a Coca-Cola. It was not up to me to speak first, but that's just what happened, and my interlocutor seemed surprised.

"You know," I said, "my nerves are in such bad shape that I'm no longer impressed by anything or anyone. I don't even know if you're really Ralph McGanter and I admit I don't give a damn.

Maybe Ronson's setting a trap for me; he's carrying on his personal investigation into the mysteries that have recently beset our company. And maybe you're just one more detective? You should know in any case that I have nothing to reproach myself for unless maybe exhausting myself by taking my job as director of human relations too seriously. At present I'm playing the role of buffer between my fellow headquarters executives and the general management. In these circumstances whether you are or aren't Ralph McGanter is really of little importance."

The man inspected me with glaucous, myopic eyes. They were very different from the descriptions that the publications of Rosserys and Mitchell or even the special journalists of the great Western weeklies had given of the famous "piercing glance" of Ralph McGanter. "The glance of an eagle," they had written, or a bird of prey, a falcon, a vulture, a rattlesnake, a cobra. One writer had especially distinguished himself by saying: "History furnishes few examples of men endowed with so strange a glance, at once so intimate and so distant, the right eye fixed on the infinite horizon of the future of the world, the left fixed on you, your own future, pitiless, cutting like a steel blade." I had before me and behind the black tortoise-shell glasses two glaucous, myopic, globular eyes. As he still said nothing, I felt a kind of dim irritation, which I expressed by speaking to him.

"I don't know," I said, "whether you're the president, but your expression would rather indicate the contrary."

This observation seemed to interest him. He finally consented to speak.

"My expression? What's so special about it?" he asked in a tone I could recognize as that of a man accustomed to command.

"Well," I said, hesitating a little this time, "it's just that there's nothing very special."

"Why should there be?" he asked, slightly impatient.

"I don't know," I replied, "but I've read several descriptions of your glance by journalists and they all describe it flatteringly."

191

"Well, they have to. I pay them!"

"All of them? Even those from the great international week-lies?"

"Yes, of course," he said, almost dreamily. "In one way or another, I always pay them."

"But some have compared your glance to a vulture's or a rattle-snake's."

"And why not? That's what's needed. People love it. I've had a lot of research done on the kind of glance I ought to have or people believe I have. Don't think a multinational president would be criticized by the people or his colleagues because his glance is a vulture's! That's no longer at all pejorative. But you, now, how would you describe my glance? What do you see behind my glasses?"

"Sir, begging your pardon, I see two glaucous and globular eyes."

"Bravo! I knew you were my man!" exclaimed the American potentate. "It's true that my eyes are glaucous and globular, but it's been a long time since I've heard that! This matter of my glance is an excellent introduction to our conversation. At first it got on my nerves, but actually it constitutes an interesting test. Yes, truly you are the man! My colleagues aren't bad, but as soon as a problem departs somewhat from the ordinary, they're all at sea! I've had enough of it, this ridiculous business of our French affiliate; and above all at just this time of economic crisis I had no wish to see this silly panic continue to develop here in France. So I took the file in hand myself day before yesterday. I examined it minutely, as I do every affair I take up. I studied the *curriculum vitae* of Rosserys and Mitchell–France's senior executives, and way back in the States I found the answer: you're the man! And your comments on the subject of my glance confirm this abundantly.

"In the dossier I'd noticed the strange and powerful personality of this director of human relations we had in Paris. Then I got on the move myself—no one knows this except Ronson. I came here

192

to meet you and talk with you. I need colleagues of your caliber, my friend! I didn't come to punish you but to reward you, to promote you, to bring you over to my side. Have you thought about it? Have you taken in the fact that Ralph McGanter is sitting here before you in a turtleneck? That's something, you know, but all the people sitting at those tables over there, they don't know it! To whom did the waiter serve the Coca-Cola just now? To Ralph McGanter! Yes, I came to you without hesitation, without shame, without pride; that's the way it always is when I handle my affairs. Last month I left home to go personally and see a subordinate, an obscure member of the Bolivian cabinet. My colleagues had no idea of it! I, McGanter, went to Bolivia, and it wasn't the president that I went to see but an obscure person. Why, then? Aha, that's the question! Why indeed? Well, I'll tell you: the obscure person is going to be, beginning next Monday, minister of agriculture. Do you understand, my boy? Not of transportation, not of the interior, but of agriculture. Are you beginning to see the picture? Our sales of machines will expand formidably in exchange for a few trivial favors! For example, I'll see that these Bolivians get a loan from the International Bank in San Francisco. That way they'll be able to pay for our machines and at the same time equip their army. Aha! Do you understand? When McGanter hits the road it's because something is going on! And you, I know now, are the man that those idiots Musterffies and Saint-Ramé have been looking for for days! Come on, admit it, don't be afraid. Far from being angry at you, I admire your intelligence, your audacity, your sang-froid!"

Completely disconcerted by this slightly mad tirade, I asked, "But exactly who do you want me to be? What man are you talking about?"

"All right," said McGanter, shooting me the sly glance of an accomplice. "I understand, you want to hear me say it: Mr. Director of Human Relations, you are the man your French associates have named the imprecator."

"What?" I exclaimed, completely dumfounded.

"Yes, Mr. Imprecator, allow me to congratulate you. You fooled

193

everyone—except me, of course, except Ralph McGanter, who at this moment is unquestionably one of the three or four most powerful personages in the world! From now on you'll work at my side, in Des Moines and in New York, you'll be my personal colleague. You'll begin next week. And now tell me all the details. Your story fascinates me."

And the president of Rosserys and Mitchell International brought his head close to mine, a voracious and sardonic smile at the corners of his lips.

So I was the imprecator! There it was. Mr. McGanter had succeeded where his private police, his vice-president, his French directors had failed! The case of Rosserys and Mitchell–France had actually amused him. It was an odd case well suited to relax a man occupied elsewhere in destroying governments or regimes that interfered with his interests, and now and then debasing some country's currency.

This man saw in me the imprecator. All right. What attitude should I adopt? Well, I didn't undeceive him immediately. And to properly convey why, I should make clear the mentality of the leading cadres of that period. First of all, it was rarely granted to an executive of my rank to encounter in flesh and blood one of the corsairs ravaging the world in those days. These men considered themselves more important than political leaders and, unhappily, they were often right. They stirred up wars and arranged peace at will, in their own interests, fixing the volume of merchandise to be produced and prices and conditions of trade. Consequently a director of human relations worthy of the name couldn't pass up an opportunity to make a prodigious leap forward in the hierarchy of his company, or on the other hand, to pour out on the spot whatever was on his mind. When you meet a man as powerful as that, you either heap insults on him or try to gain advancement from him. But that day I perceived that my case was special. The imprecator did not especially seem to love his company and its bosses. And what McGanter appeared to admire in this provocateur was just that. And so by playing the role of the imprecator I could kill two birds with one stone: express my resentment while at the same time emphasizing my value. The more hostile I was to Rosserys and Mitchell, the more I adopted the imprecator's line, the better my chance of passing for him and therefore being congratulated by McGanter. From then on, I conducted myself with a skill which even today, long after these events, it pleases me to emphasize. First of all, I set about a half-hearted denial.

"Mr. President," I explained, "although I believe I understand that you love this imprecator, I owe it to the truth to say that I am not he. I am embarrassed to assert you are wrong—but once doesn't count."

"I love the way you talk to me, and I see it as an additional proof that my hunch was right. Having said that, I do not love the imprecator. *Love* is a word I long since banished from my vocabulary. It's not that I am incapable of tenderness; babies, little birds, move me, and thanks to me, the annual contribution of Rosserys and Mitchell to the British Society for the Protection of Animals is exceptionally high. But one has to choose: power, the ability to influence the events of time—or an uneventful life among the little birds. No, I do not love the imprecator, I do not love you, my friend, neither you nor anyone else, but I've learned to be efficient, and the qualities or, if you prefer, the faults that have made it possible for you to upset the company can be used for other purposes by me and to serve a more important objective commensurate with your ambition. And so, when at this moment everyone is looking for you, it is I who have found you. And so, when everyone wants to punish you, it is I who wish to reward you. And so, when everyone wants to banish you, it is I who intend to promote you. Once more, my directors the world over won't understand my decision at all, but that's why I'm president, why I'm Ralph McGanter. Without that, today I'd be a commonplace marketing director, or better still, a sort of Musterffies, characterless and grossly overpaid."

"Why did you overthrow the president of Chile?" I asked suddenly.

"Oh, I love that! Really and truly, I love that! Yes, you're my man! Next time it'll be you who overthrow a government!" McGanter said jauntily. "Why? I'm probably going to surprise you. It wasn't for a political reason. You should know I've changed a great deal and today I don't give a damn for political reasons! At this very moment I'm preparing a vast and very profitable marketing deal with the countries of the East and with China! Yes indeed, China! I even have a special envoy in Albania. I realize that Comrade Enver Hoxha is hard to convince, but he too will come along! In any case, at the moment, I've already won a victory over there: my special envoy hasn't been expelled! Well, then, in Chile it wasn't for economic or financial reasons either. I'm close to losing money in that country and I'm beginning to make it in the Soviet Union. Why do you suppose I'd overthrow a government to gain so little? Eh?"

"I admit," I said, sincere and attentive, "that you surprise me. Why did you?"

McGanter took my hands in his. His were round, white and plump.

"You know," he replied, "it's true I've spent most of my life making profits, exploring new markets, manufacturing more and more. But for several years now I've kept watch over our cash flow, principally so my stockholders will leave me in peace, so they'll be reassured, proud, and so they won't demand excessively high dividends. What interests me now is power."

"The power of money," I said.

"No, not the power of money," McGanter replied forcefully. "If you only knew the extreme satisfaction I feel when the world accuses me of having overthrown the democratic regime in Chile! That's power, that's true might. To create economic and monetary crises, to promote the armament of this or that nation, to launch them one against the other—that's a power money alone cannot supply! It requires a gigantic organization, the shaping of minds, the mentality of a commando, a real commando, a crusader, a conqueror! Today all these conditions are combined in Rosserys

196

and Mitchell International. We're not far from dominating the world. There's nothing in common between me and the richest oil magnate or banker in the world, even if our interests are closely meshed. They're powerful because they are rich. I'm powerful because profit no longer interests me, because either I or my successors will force governments to authorize Rosserys and Mitchell to raise armies."

"Raise armies!" I exclaimed incredulously.

"Yes indeed. That surprises you? But wait and see. Our properties will be threatened everywhere, because we'll arouse hatred and jealousy everywhere. No state, not even America, will have either the means or the will to defend its properties from attack. See where the war in Vietnam brought us! Picture our properties being attacked, our influence contested everywhere. How do you think the Western powers, even united, even in a coalition, could defend our interests on sixty or two hundred battlefields like Vietnam or Angola? Nations' resources are too feeble, governments wouldn't be sufficiently motivated; their citizens would end by demanding peace and the withdrawal of troops. No, the Western democracies are incapable of defending us. Whereas if I organize the colossal power of three or four multinationals on a global scale, if I arm mercenaries on the spot, if I pit well-paid multinational Bolivians against hunted, skinny national Bolivians, if I draw up Indonesian regiments against the students and the maquis of the Jakarta countryside, then I'll rule the world. Then the Western governments, freed from the concerns of war, can pacify their citizens, can concern themselves with social matters, city government, transportation. Thieu is a bad example. Since he was supported by the American government and we supported the government, it was thought that we supported him. But that's false. I guarantee you that if a coalition of multinationals had backed Thieu, he would have won. The mistake in Vietnam was to support Thieu because he was not a communist. Those quarrels are antiquated; the criterion of support is the agreement of interests in the service of a new type of hegemony. Sometimes we have to suppress anticommunist regimes and support communist ones. Take Castro. I really have nothing against Castro today. Do you think I love the Chilean junta? They're not criminals; they're idiots. A coalition of multinationals would certainly not have supported them."

"Whom would they have supported?" I asked in a low voice.

"I don't know. Probably they would have made a clean sweep. The idea is to get possession of ground, mineral rights, forests, oceans, to establish a hierarchy that knows no god."

"But," I asked, "why tell all this to me, an insignificant person, a humble staff executive of one of your innumerable companies?"

"First of all, by chance: I tell you all this by chance. There is no danger it will hurt me. Chance having brought me in disguise to this rear room of a Paris bistro, I find it convenient and pleasant to pour out all this to you. And if one day you should take it into your head to say that Ralph McGanter, the great McGanter, told you his life story while wearing a turtleneck sweater and sitting in a Paris bistro—don't worry, no one will believe you. But I've been patient with you. Tell me the details of your method. That interests me more than you can imagine. For example, how did you go about cracking the wall and day after day arranging the enlargement of that crack which so terrifies poor Musterffies?"

It was then that I changed my approach and staked everything. Weighing the advantages that the role of imprecator would win me with that singular man, I declared:

"Mr. President, having formed a clear idea of your exceptional personality while listening to you and having been greatly impressed by your flair, your astonishing ability to read the unreadable, I can admit to you that your view is correct. I am indeed the imprecator. I shall be honored to serve you as you have proposed, but I ask a favor, or rather, I take the liberty of making one condition, the first and last I shall ever make: Let me pursue my diabolical plan to the end. Don't force me to reveal the details now. Moreover, only a man of your stature could fully appreciate it. In exchange I promise you to stop the progress of the crack, to respect the walls. I'd planned the total destruction of the building, but I shall spare it. In return for the beautiful climax, for the surprise and refined pleasure it will give you, allow me to execute the remainder of my plan."

McGanter beamed with joy and pride. His features even softened slightly. He pressed my hands between his and looked at me almost with affection, and he said:

"My friend, why talk to me about that devilish building? Haven't I told you that I am neither a banker nor an industrialist? What would remain of your magnificent plan if those walls did not crumble? Not only do I authorize you not to reveal to me—at present—the details of your superb machination, but I further hope—what am I saying?—I *order* that the crack grow bigger and that other cracks appear, and that suddenly our office building of glass and steel be swallowed up in the depths of the disemboweled earth! I'll leave for New York tonight by regular airline, but I'll be back tomorrow morning accompanied by my general staff of imbeciles. That's what was planned. Musterffies, at his wits' end, apprised the board of the troubles of the French firm. We decided day before yesterday to move to Paris and examine the question at first hand. Nobody but you and Ronson knows that I've come to Paris. In Des Moines they think I'm in Paraguay. No one but you and me knows the imprecator, a fact that promises me a great deal of fun tomorrow. As president I'll be annoyed by so minor a question, forced on me by the carelessness of my colleagues and the French directors. No one must guess that we've already met; but before we separate, may I also ask a favor?"

"A favor, Mr. President?"

"Yessir! A favor for the great McGanter! Can you at least tell me when and how your plan will be completely executed?"

"Yes, sir. I'll tell you," I replied, this time absolutely sure that I foresaw correctly. "In the next few days, the senior executives of the company, their bosses and no doubt the members of your general staff from Des Moines will perish horribly, having previously undergone agonizing ordeals. Only you and I will be spared.

The earth will open up and swallow the glass-and-steel building."

"Impossible," McGanter murmured between his teeth. He emitted a soft, admiring whistle, then he repeated slowly, "They will undergo agonizing ordeals, after which they'll be swallowed up in the bowels of the earth. . . . What a program! My instinct didn't deceive me: I knew you were the imprecator. But the personality of the imprecator surpasses my fondest hopes. You're worthy to be my successor someday. I'll teach you international management and the manipulation of capital, but you already have as much hatred of humanity as I, the taste for tyrannical power, and for you as for me, men are no more than wooden posts; fields no more than plots of earth that produce grass; mountains simply rocks and minerals; the sea has never been anything but a reservoir of salt, of energy, of fish. Today you've provided me with the only emotion of my career and very likely the last.

"Yes, carry out your plan in detail. Bring death down on our French company—that will allow me to force public opinion to sympathize with the misfortunes that lie in wait for the great productive combines, if they are not more respected. It will highlight the problems of growth and employment, it will allow many governments to shoot and imprison thousands of revolutionaries! I'll make it an argument on a global scale. The fact that our French company is the one to pay the price of this policy doesn't displease me. France has often served as guinea pig for other nations. Truly, once more, I congratulate you. And now, Mr. Imprecator, I'm close to admiring you." McGanter rose, pressed my two hands with feeling and said, "I'll leave without you. I don't want anyone to see us together. No one would recognize me, but with you it's different."

McGanter left. For a moment my eyes followed this little man as he pushed his way between the waiters of the brasserie and the customers standing up to pay or waiting for their coats. Soon I lost sight of him. I waited some ten minutes, then I left.

As I was entering Rue de Jean-Pierre-Timbaud in search of a sporting goods store to buy equipment for that night's expedition,

I gave a sudden start and plastered myself against the wall. What I saw brought an unexpected piquancy to the already complicated situation in my company: a man and a woman, pressed against each other, were talking softly, apparently debating a crucial question: Were they going into the nearby hotel or not? Both consulted their watches. Did they have time? Yes, they had time. They disappeared into the hotel. Stunned, I stood for several minutes with my back against the wall. I'd truly had the wind knocked out of me. The liaison I'd just discovered had something sinister and salty about it, like blood. Then I left, uneasy and sad. What a nasty, mad affair! How long had Abéraud and Mme. Saint-Ramé been sleeping together?

21

Night had descended on my office building. The personnel had departed. Only the senior executives, each concealed in the hiding place Abéraud had assigned to him, and the watchmen, who were ignorant of this expedition, remained within its walls. In the darkness of my closet, I waited, as instructed, for Number 3—Samueru—to come and fetch me. I passed the events of the day in review. The game I'd been playing with the world president of the company was not without danger to me, whether or not he, and later the others, became convinced that I was in fact the imprecator. The liaison of Abéraud and Saint-Ramé's wife upset me greatly. Abéraud had shown on various occasions that he was not fussy about the means of gaining his objectives. There was in him a cynical determination that was no less reprehensible for being effective. By seducing Saint-Ramé's wife had he brought into play another piece on his chessboard? And then—what did this liaison really conceal?

Today, in my little white room, I meditate on this aspect of the Rosserys and Mitchell–France affair. It carried a lesson: the heart and the mind decay together. It does not seem true to me that a man uniquely preoccupied with making money can truly love his wife and family. And it seems clear to me that a society affected in its mind cannot preserve a great heart. And so, creating employment and assuring economic prosperity mean nothing unless accompanied by altruism and charity. It is said that only the end matters; that if cold and arrogant men, who love only themselves and their machines, increase family allowances and reduce taxes, well, they are honest and good. But I know now that this is not true. And that if they have no heart, on the day their machines break down they become wicked and mad.

I am approaching—with reluctance, anguish at my throat—the verge of the horrible climax. Those who surround and look after me feel this and are disturbed. They understand that I must proceed to relate facts that are far from pleasant. The chief doctor did not like that liaison between Abéraud and Saint-Ramé's wife either. However, he is still unaware of what I know, and so when I said to him, "Some souls decay as much and as rapidly as the body," he replied, "Yes, that's true." What then becomes of the just man?

Impavidum ferient ruinae. The ruins will strike him and leave him unmoved. The ruins.

And so, at the time when the countries that possessed oil and rich mineral resources in their soil decided to keep them or to make the countries that enjoyed abundance pay more dearly for them, a strange expedition got under way in Paris, France, in an office building of glass and steel that rose at the corner of the Avenue de la République and Rue Oberkampf, not far from Père Lachaise cemetery. At midnight, the twelve senior executives, led by Abéraud, assistant director of forecasts, after removing a small slab, crawled flat on their bellies into a narrow, dripping passage and wriggled silently as far as a gallery about two meters wide and two meters high. They were not on their way to visit the innumerable skeletons embedded in the celebrated catacombs down there. They were advancing, irritable and angry, in search of someone who for a number of days had been sowing trouble in their company, calling into question its very foundations, someone who, through his dirty tricks and taste for mystery, had set nerves on edge, and in particular those of the dozen cadres here, who through this aggression saw their abilities, their moral and political values, questioned. Their conviction that the aggressor was unquestionably one of them created an atmosphere of suspicion hard to endure, and one might read on their faces, though ill lit by their flashlights, a mixture of fear and ferocity.

Anyone who had met them one by one or as a group a week earlier would have had trouble recognizing in these animals, dressed in capes, wearing boots, carrying packs, panting, floundering in the mud of the subsoil of their office building, the same ambitious, dynamic young men, sure of themselves, juggling figures and graphs, dreaming of an extraordinary mission to the Near East or to Washington, a finger hooked in their vests, showing off around Saint-Ramé's antechamber. We advanced slowly in silence, very close together, sometimes tripping over invisible rough spots, reaching out to touch the slippery wall with our free hands. Thus our fingers were quickly covered with a nasty substance, a kind of malodorous and viscous paste.

Suddenly we heard Abéraud say, "Hush!" and we stopped. Number 5 was lighting the left side of the gallery with his flashlight. Since we could not crowd together to see what he was looking at, he passed the news back: strange figures had been cut into the side of the passageway, as well as various numbers. Abéraud let it be known that the hieroglyphs left him perplexed. Then he moved on, permitting each in turn to file past the inscriptions and designs. With the exception of Abéraud, who, though Number 5, was leading, we were in the order of our numbers. After Abéraud came Fournier, Number 1; then Portal, Number 2; Samueru, Number 3, etc. When I—Number 7—arrived at the hieroglyphs I

204

tarried a minute or two. I thought I saw the outline of two faces and beneath them figures. Just above what must have been meant to represent untidy hair, I made out two red death's heads. I went along, leaving my place to Number 8, who was Brignon, and ignoring what happened behind me, I followed the column. Suddenly a strangled exclamation reached our ears. Abéraud halted and the others with him. I heard whisperings and Vasson, who was now in front of me, inquired softly, "Who cried out and why? Pass the question." I handed it on to Chavégnac. The reply came by the same route and I passed it on to Abéraud. It was a message from Sélis: "I've identified the portraits and seven or eight numbers. It's horrible."

Abéraud spoke: "In a few minutes we'll come to a wide bend before the first sharp descent and we can regroup; let's go forward. Number 10 will explain to us there." We obeyed. And in fact three or four minutes later we found ourselves crowded together on a sort of platform such as one finds in certain turns of mountain passes. Sélis approached Number 5 and we surrounded them, eager to hear. "Put out your flashlights. Mine and Number 10's will be enough," Abéraud commanded. Suddenly we were plunged into obscurity, for Abéraud and Sélis lighted only themselves and those who were very close to them. And this is what Sélis announced:

"The two portraits are of our two founders, Bill Dolfuss Rosserys and Richard Kenneth Mitchell. There is no possible mistake. Each of us has seen those portraits often in Saint-Ramé's office. I'm absolutely sure it's they, and above them each has a death's head. Underneath is the date of birth but not of death; instead of that, there's a question mark. And among all the numbers I recognized several. There's the total of cash flow for last year, the profits declared to the French government and next to it a figure that few people know, the amount of undeclared profits. And another figure is the sum of exports for the last six months. Aside from Saint-Ramé, Roustev, the financial director and myself, I'm certain that's unknown to everyone, including you." Sélis, visibly shocked

205

by this discovery, had blurted this out very quickly and in a panting voice. We were no less shocked than he. After a moment of silence Abéraud said, "We absolutely have to go back one by one and verify Number 10's conclusions. I'll go first." So Number 5 went back and returned ten minutes later, wearing a thoughtful air and completely covered with mud.

"What happened to you?" Le Rantec asked.

"I fell down in the passage. It's nothing. I was only able to recognize a single number, the date of Bill Dolfuss Rosserys' birth, but I positively identified the portraits, the two question marks and, of course, the red death's heads. Sélis is right. This proves that the evil begins here in these subterranean passages and catacombs, and that the man is more crazed and dangerous than we would have thought. If you want, go back and make sure yourselves."

These words fell on an audience that I felt was unresponsive. The atmosphere was hostile. To plunge into the passageway alone, four minutes to go, two minutes to examine the hieroglyphs, four minutes to return, added up to ten minutes' absence in a dripping black tunnel and beneath signs connected with death and lethal magic. By all evidence the senior executives of Rosserys and Mitchell–France would have been much more at their ease at a business lunch. Abéraud felt this and like an officer who must launch his troops to the attack, he delivered a short inspirational speech.

"Gentlemen," he said, raising his voice slightly, "I know what some of you must be thinking: you're asking yourselves what you're doing in these dripping passages when there are important reports to study, especially at the present moment. Who knows if at this very moment Arabian sheiks and the governments of South America aren't thinking of increasing the price of a barrel of oil, or the price of copper or of bauxite? Who knows whether at this moment the Dutch aren't suddenly deciding to float the florin! Who knows, in fact, whether at this very minute, as I speak to you, the President of the United States and his brilliant adviser aren't deciding to send troops into Libya or into Venezuela, or better yet, to provoke the collapse of the franc? I know that, I feel all that, my dear colleagues, but for just this reason, one day soon we shall be praised for having borne our part of the burden, our part in the defense of basic human and social values. We assume these burdens in somewhat unspectacular fashion for the moment, but before long it will be enthusiastically acknowledged by the successors of Bill Dolfuss Rosserys and Richard Kenneth Mitchell. What we are doing here tonight is pursuing someone who furiously desires the death of our company and all it stands for.

"Let's not be upset to find ourselves here, surrounded by signs of death and magic. Besides, if someone has taken the trouble to carve portraits of our founders on the wall of this passage, and to inscribe the sum of last year's cash flow, it's certainly because our efforts have not been in vain. The author of these infamous graffiti hates us, despises us, is spying on us and threatening us. We'll find him wherever he is—even, gentlemen, if he's one of us."

The conclusion of this exhortation increased our uneasiness, but the discourse itself had the merit of reviving the cadres' fury, their irritation, the jealousy they habitually and constantly felt for one another. They'd probably lost sight of the fact that the man might be one of them. Abéraud maliciously and skillfully reminded them of that. Then Fournier, Number 1, committed himself by saying: "I'll go. I admire what you say, Number 5. I'll go and confirm Number 10's ideas about these damned hieroglyphs."

And he made his way into the dripping passage. When he returned he confirmed the opinions of Sélis and Abéraud, and he was completely overwhelmed.

"What do these question marks in place of the founders' dates of death mean?" he managed to ask.

"Perhaps," Terrène hazarded timidly, "that means they were born but haven't died and perhaps their phantoms . . ."

"No, no." Abéraud cut him short a bit nervously. "This is poisonous. The enemy wants to lead us astray, to frighten us. He is trying to touch man's most primitive instincts in us: superstition, the tendency to daydream. I've come to a double conclusion: these signs, these drawings, these numbers are not mysteries—we know what they represent. Their purpose is to numb our minds and dissuade us from going on. I'm quite persuaded that each of you would bravely go back to that place alone, so much so that no one need supply proof of his courage. I know you're all determined. I propose that we not waste any more time reviewing these hieroglyphs. We have better things to do and the night's passing fast. Let's tarry no longer."

These words were greeted with obvious relief. Each one hurriedly agreed and we started on, in single file, in improved spirits. Suspicion, however, persisted. And I caught myself hoping that the expedition would proceed in darkness, so greatly did I fear the prospect of my eyes meeting those of the others. If I was not the imprecator, who among us could be? We made our way forward, following a passage as narrow and wet as the first one, but descending abruptly toward the depths.

Although a vast amount of time has passed since these events, and although tragedy attended them, I cannot evoke that descent down the steep, slimy tunnel without a smile: it was the only moment of relaxation that night. The difficulty was that the slope became more and more slippery. After five minutes of careful advance, we had to hunker down practically on our behinds. Each one supported himself on the shoulders of the man ahead of him. Only Abéraud had no one in front. And now he shot down the slope. We tumbled after him through the mud and ended on level ground that was even muckier. We had considerable difficulty in getting up, so entangled were we with one another. Many of us had lost our flashlights. Abéraud judged, rightly enough, that it was necessary to recover them. Le Rantec was charged with this task. And we were witnesses to the gripping spectacle of a staff executive, familiar with graphs, long-term funding and objective management, climbing on all fours up a steep passage some thirty meters below the computer hall of our company. When he had swarmed up a good third of the slope, Abéraud asked him to unroll his rope and attach it somewhere above in preparation for the return trip.

Le Rantec acquitted himself of his task perfectly: he descended again by holding on to the rope and sliding. We then examined the place we had come to. It was a large circular hall with smooth, gleaming walls. The passage through which we had entered this hall was continued through an opening in the wall opposite. Our dozen recovered flashlights gave adequate illumination for a crypt of this size and we had time to look at one another. Our clothes muddy, our faces highlighted by the flashlights, our hair disheveled, our eyes staring, we made a wild and forlorn group. Perhaps there was really something comic about us, but no one dreamed of laughing. Abéraud consulted his watch and announced:

"It is one-ten. We can go on for another hour. After that, we must retrace our steps if we're to be back at our point of departure around five A.M."

I got the impression that these gentlemen were not very enthusiastic. Moreover, Portal asked timidly, "Exactly what are we looking for here? Is the point of our expedition simply to reconnoiter the subsoil of the building?"

He had spoken aloud what the majority of his colleagues were thinking to themselves. Abéraud was not taken aback and he was magnificently justified by circumstances a few minutes later. First he replied:

"We're searching for the man who's toying with us at the very heart of this company, who's trying to diminish us in the minds of the personnel, who maintains that we serve no purpose and have usurped our power—the man who is stirring up the employees against us. I'm sure he's taken up his quarters in the underground passages, and it's there that we'll fall upon him. Once more, it'll take patience. We have to explore these premises and he knows them well."

With these words, Abéraud had shown himself cunning. This time he had not talked about a crusade in the service of Rosserys and Mitchell, symbol of a society that we must defend, but of the specific and personal interests of the principal cadres. And it was true that in the long run the activities of this mysterious aggressor would at least have the effect of diminishing the *staff* executives, who were often detested by the *line* executives. We were preparing to go on—that is, to plunge into the passageway opposite the one through which we had arrived—when we heard the noise of footsteps, coming straight from the tunnel we were about to explore. Silence fell, and our interest in the expedition, grown doubtful for an instant, was reestablished. Abéraud whispered, "Turn off your flashlights," which we promptly did. For a long time we stood listening. No sound. Then once more footsteps approached. There we were, with pounding hearts, awaiting the man who unwittingly was approaching us. When the steps were quite close, I had the feeling that the man was not alone.

Abéraud whispered, "This may well be the man we are looking for. Be ready to capture him. Stay where you are and when you see his light let him proceed toward the center of the room and then surround him. Above all, keep him from escaping through the passage we came through, or by the one he is coming from."

A man emerged from the tunnel, flashlight in hand. He advanced toward us. Abéraud raised a cry.

"Forward! Block both exits! Corner him!"

We made a rush. Then the man began to scream, "Help! Help!"

Others appeared and a free-for-all followed. Several of us were knocked to the ground. Flashlights went out.

"I've got him! I've got him!" cried Brignon.

"Let go of me, you idiot! It's me, Vasson!"

"No, you're not Vasson. Bring a light, someone!"

I turned my flashlight in the direction of these cries and immediately recognized Vasson, whom Brignon was beginning to strangle.

"It's Vasson," I cried. "Let him go!"

Brignon, confused and overexcited, apologized and picked up his flashlight. Nevertheless the melee went on in various parts of the crypt. Suddenly we heard the voice of Musterffies.

"Gentlemen, this is a misunderstanding! Stop, I beg of you. There is no imprecator here!"

The tumult ceased instantly. Flashlights that had gone out were turned on again and soon we were able to take stock of the situation. Together in this chamber were Musterffies, Ronson, Saint-Ramé, Roustev, King Voster, the French detective and the twelve senior executives of Rosserys and Mitchell–France. Then explanations began. Knowing Saint-Ramé was aware of the expedition planned by the cadres, I was not at all surprised to hear him say that he had decided to make a tour of the underground passages on his own. Roustev and the French detective had decided to go together. The reason for the presence of all these people in the underground passages of the company was thus explained. What was less clear was the lack of coordination. If I'd understood properly, Saint-Ramé had come down alone. Then the Americans and King Voster had descended from their side. Finally Roustev and the French detective had thought up their own expedition. Then each had to tell how he had arrived in this crypt. This is what transpired: Roustev and the French detective had removed a different slab from ours, then they had followed a small passage that brought them underneath the round crypt. The Americans had made an opening under our audiovisual hall, and this led them straight to the steep passage down which we'd slid. Then they'd explored the tunnel prolonging that passage, and hearing our voices, they'd retraced their steps.

Saint-Ramé said, "I came in through the cemetery."

"Through the cemetery?" Abéraud repeated.

"Yes, I had an idea that I could reach the subterranean passages of the company by making an entrance through a brand-new green-and-black marble vault."

"When did you get that idea, sir?" Le Rantec asked in a tone of surprise and respect.

The hierarchy is resuming its rights, I said to myself, and it's natural and proper that it should do so through the mediation of that superb technocratic pseudo economist Le Rantec.

"Well, now," Saint-Ramé replied, as simply as if he were seated at his desk during the weekly conference, "I must say that one detail struck me about these scrolls. That was the green-and-black ribbon. And while I was strolling down one of the paths of Père Lachaise the other day I was brought up short before that vault. Something clicked in my mind and I associated the colors of the marble with those of the ribbons. Once this caught my attention, I observed that the tomb was close, as the crow flies, to our office building. The theory that an individual of evil intent toward Rosserys and Mitchell–France might use this tomb to penetrate the subcellars occurred to me.

"So far it was only a hunch. But I proceeded to verify certain points. On the one hand, the City of Paris assured me that no one was lying stiff and cold inside the vault. Furthermore, through one of my friends at the Ministry I acquired a map of the underground above which our office building of glass and steel rises. From this I concluded that it would be child's play to reach our building by way of the tomb if I broke a hole in the cement floor. Not to hide anything from you, I got hold of certain information according to which the defenders of our company who plan to unmask its malign enemy were going to explore the passageways and all the tunnels tonight, by different routes. This made me decide to experiment with access through the tomb. I was sure of meeting most of you here. Have you actually found anything of interest?"

"Think of that: we had the same idea as you," exclaimed Yritieri. "We too, or rather Thierry, was struck by the similarity of the tomb's colors and the ribbons."

"That doesn't surprise me in Monsieur Abéraud," Saint-Ramé observed gravely.

"We haven't found anything very significant," Abéraud replied to the managing director's question, "but I hope it won't be long now."

I meditated on the ambiguous tone with which Abéraud had said: "I hope it won't be long now." Not far from me, I made out

Musterffies and King Voster, who were listening intently to what Roustev had to say. No doubt he was translating the words of Saint-Ramé and Abéraud. I began to feel cold, and though warmly dressed, experienced the chilling effects of the underground humidity. So it was with understandable relief that I heard Abéraud propose in English, "Mr. Vice-President, if you see no objection, I think it's time now to climb back to the surface. We've fastened a rope to facilitate the ascent of the slippery passageway. If you'll allow me, I'll take my place behind you in case you should need any assistance."

"And I in front of you, if you will permit me!" cried Le Rantec. "I know the way well—it was I who anchored the rope."

The expedition was at an end. The executives' reflexes had revived. The customs of the company were once more in force.

"Very well, gentlemen. Thank you; I accept your proposal," said Musterffies. "Despite my age and the hectic life I have led—that's true, isn't it, Bernie?—I hope I can manage by myself. Ah, Bernie, just tell them whether I needed anyone to push me or pull me five years ago in the Indian quarter of Asunción! Aha, you remember, don't you, Bernie?"

Ronson did not reply. In general, though not talkative, he always answered Musterffies' appeals. "Hey, Bernie, where are you? Everyone was here a minute ago. What the devil! He hasn't disappeared! This is no time for me to lose you, Bernie!"

Then we heard a voice, more cavernous than ever and slightly husky, coming from the end of the round room with smooth, gleaming walls.

"Yes, Adams, I'm here. I remember Asunción. But just look what I've found. It's something very odd."

All the flashlights were turned simultaneously toward Des Moines' representative in Paris. Legs apart, he had his feet firmly planted in the muddy earth in the attitude of a marine sergeant, an unreal figure bathed in the pallid light of the wavering flashlights which the senior executives, their bosses and the detectives were beaming at him.

"What have you found, Bernie?" demanded Musterffies in a slightly cracked voice.

"This," Ronson replied dryly, showing to his ghostly and petrified audience a long sheet lightly spotted with mud. This scene and the one that followed are among the most intense memories that I retain from this adventure. We had no time to make a gesture or take a step when a cadre cried out hoarsely:

"A stencil!"

It was Abéraud. Abéraud, who despite that distance and that uncertain light, had nevertheless succeeded in identifying the paper. I myself think that he had guessed rather than seen, so strong was his conviction that the solution to the problem lay there, thirty meters below the glass-and-steel building. Abéraud knew what he was looking for, so he was naturally expecting to find it. It was indeed a stencil. Musterffies advanced toward Ronson, and we formed a group around them. "It's in French," said the vice-president. "Who wants to translate it?"

I was immediately behind him. I took the stencil from his hands and with the aid of my flashlight read what was to have been the fourth imprecation. This is what I saw and spoke aloud in English that night in the vast circular chamber with its smooth and gleaming walls.

WHAT DO THOSE WHO RUN
ROSSERYS AND MITCHELL
REALLY KNOW?

They know that making money is the only activity that counts, and that all the rest, as they say, is just literature. They know that temporal power is more important than nontemporal power. They love dead writers and musicians, but not those who are alive and working at the same time they are. They do not fear God except when they are small or close to death. They know that relations between individuals and between peoples are founded solely on power and wealth. They know that in this base world a good banker is more useful than a good confessor or a loving wife. They know that man and the earth were created to dominate the universe and that nothing under the sun equals a good deposit of copper, a vast pool of petroleum or an immense herd of cattle and sheep. They know that men are not born equal, that this is a fairy tale and that if nations write it into their constitutions, it is simply because that is more satisfying to the mind, more convenient for social contracts. They know that it is the same for those who say they believe in God. They know everything is bought and sold. Thus they buy large numbers of politicians and churchmen, whom they then resell at a good profit. They know that everyone has just one life and that that alone counts. All the excesses of a man are finally either forgotten in the night of time or pardoned by history.

Who could be angry today at a rich Missouri planter for having, all his life, raped Negro women and buried their slave husbands alive? Is that planter in hell? And where is hell? The fact is that he lived comfortably to an old age, rich and respected, that he had numerous children and grandchildren, and that these were not stricken by any divine malady, but increased the ancestral acres and had children in their turn. Who today still despises Judge Sewall, who cruelly and stupidly condemned the "witches of Salem"? Those who run Rosserys and Mitchell know all this; they have learned their lesson well. They know too that they are citizens of the most powerful country the world has ever known. They know that their military leaders command enough arms and armies to knock sense into any country in the world, including the dictatorship in the East. They know that what is called patriotism or the dignity of a people is utterly meaningless. They know that all nations are flabby, think only about business, profoundly admire the wealth and the generosity of the United States, the wisdom, probity and foresight of its leaders, and in particular the geniuses who, starting from scratch, have built empires—those who began by selling overshoes and ended at the head of powerful industries producing goatskins, sealskins or chocolate biscuits. Those are mankind's exemplars, and it is for them that God created rubber trees. They know, those who run Rosserys and Mitchell, how to transform one box of pickles into several boxes of pickles, then into several boxes of biscuits, then into several bottles of turpentine, then into real estate, cast-iron pipes, refrigerators. And beyond that, they know how to build ships that carry thousands of cases of all kinds, and tons of fuel, and moreover, they know how to off-load these cases and this fuel on the docks of distant countries, whence they return laden with carpets, coconuts, cinnamon and coffee, and then they buy, sell and rebuy, borrow and lend.

In this they demonstrate the true meaning of life: they deserve to lead the world. They know that poems are written by madmen for madmen, sonnets and concertos by the superficial; and that prayers are said for the feeble by the feeble. They know that ideologies play no part in international relations or human groupings, and that in the final analysis everyone is reconciled with everyone else at the sight of a large bag of gold. They know that a dollar or a ruble must always produce two dollars or two rubles and that the way to accomplish that result is ruse, cynicism and mercantile imagination. Today they know how to best use science's discoveries to increase the production of money, even before that of merchandise.

They can as easily sell a car rental agency in the U.S.A. as a cannery in the Low Countries, or tomato juice factories in France. They know that the important thing is to buy everything, to have everything, to manipulate everything rather than to adjust financial, industrial and commercial forces to the needs of the people. They know that manufacturing chairs or automobiles is not necessary or primary; the only thing that counts is the annual profit. In our day the directors of Rosserys and Mitchell know how to overthrow governments, undermine international agreements, debase currencies, ignite wars and end them when it's in their interest to.

As you see, they know many things. And as one might suppose, they must command immense intellectual and moral capacities to assume such heavy tasks. Fortunately they do. That is why we should pray God that our company wins the economic war for the greatest happiness of all men, and why we should beseech Him to preserve the health of the leaders who watch over our growth and expansion. By revealing a little of what they know, and of their burdens, I shall have contributed to the respect due them.

I'd barely finished reading when the two detectives detached themselves from the group and silently went to post themselves, one at the entrance of passage number one, the other at passage number two. So the two exits were guarded and none of us could flee. It was now certain that the stencil had fallen from the pocket of someone in that hall that night. No one breathed a word. In our hearts, although we'd repeated a hundred times that the provocateur was surely a man highly placed in our company, with access to the firm's files, we hadn't truly believed that he was one of us. But now we were forced to surrender to the evidence and face the ugly truth. Someone here had planned in advance to sow confusion, then fear and even dread and terror within Rosserys and Mitchell–France. Who? And why? The pitiable spectacle provided by these costumed, muddy, shivering gentlemen assembled in this kind of crypt—distrustful, hate-filled, incapable of reacting—testified to the failure of the human relations they'd pretended to establish among themselves.

Even as I struggled against the chills that ran up and down my spine, I composed a sort of epitaph that would summarize for future generations the adventure I was living: "Here stood the steel-and-glass building of Rosserys and Mitchell–France. Within its walls, trained and competent men successfully instituted pragmatic management. Here the theories of staff and line and integrated management were skillfully applied. From here once streamed one of the world's most splendid cash flows. In short, satisfied directors worked here, assiduous, powerful, contented and, above all, human. Nevertheless they disappeared into the depths and no one has seen them since. Peace be to their brains."

Don't worry. That night we succeeded in climbing back to the surface.

217

But those unfortunates in the spot where we left them in the subterranean crypt were overwhelmed, except Abéraud, by the startling evidence that one of them had lost the stencil of the fourth imprecation, which he was preparing to print and distribute. This text sounded like a conclusion. It no longer took up specific questions but developed a single theme. Money. Profit. In short, piracy and paganism. It no longer indulged in humor. All this sounded like a man at bay, hard pressed to reach an end, expressing all his grievances at once. A short inquiry was held on the spot. At the end of my reading no one had dared speak. It was Adams J. Musterffies' duty to say something. I realized that McGanter was right: the vice-president was not a man for difficult situations. He was afraid to face the sad truth that there was a traitor on the staff.

He said in a thin voice, "We can't leave it this way. If someone here had this paper in his pocket, the best thing is for him to confess, and remove the frightful suspicion hanging over all of us. How can we take our comfortable seats this morning and make judicious decisions to augment our self-funding powers if we aren't free of this? Let the man who wrote, rolled, tied, distributed, imitated, raise his flashlight, then put it under his chin to light up his face. If he turns himself in, much will be pardoned. Specifically, Bernie and I will use all our influence with our dear and brilliant President McGanter to see that the culprit's identity is not divulged, that it remains the staff's secret and is never known to the on-line executives and employees. I'm sure Ralph will listen to us. After all, we're his best and oldest buddies. Right, Bernie?"

"Yes," Ronson agreed. "We're dear Ralph's best and oldest buddies."

Listening to Musterffies, I remembered the speech I'd dreamed up at the big meeting in the basement conference hall. I'd imagined, in fact, a speech something like this: Let him who wrote, rolled, tied, distributed, imitated, rise. Yes, let him rise and be praised by us and even recompensed! It was surprising that Musterffies had been led to speak a little in the same way.

No flashlight was raised in response to the international vice-president's plea. No face was lighted up. Then Ronson, somewhat annoyed, announced, "The vice-president is right on one point: before we go back up we'll profit by this *flagrante delicto* to search everybody's pockets. Raise your flashlights in the air and hold them with both hands!"

We obeyed. The scene turned fantastic. Eighteen flashlights were raised at the same time, for Ronson raised his too.

"And now," he went on, "Voster, you begin the search and take charge of any paper or object that seems incriminating. Your French colleague can help you. Begin with the vice-president, then take me, then Henri, then Roustev, after that anyone you like."

Thus the hierarchy was respected. The two detectives searched our pockets and our bags minutely, felt our clothes, and discovered nothing. We were obliged to leave without having in the slightest dissipated the tension or attenuated the suspicion. Abéraud and Le Rantec exerted themselves to hoist Musterffies to the top of the slippery passageway. The troop passed without a word in front of the portraits and figures carved in stone. Toward five o'clock in the morning we found ourselves, muddy, dripping, haggard, close to the audiovisual hall. We had only one idea: to get home, take a bath, sleep for a few hours. But that wasn't how Ronson saw it. His voice cracked out: "I apologize for delaying your return home, but I consider it indispensable that we hold a meeting and discuss the night's events while they're still hot, if I may so express myself. Let's go into the audiovisual hall. It's well heated, and that's something anyway."

"Fine idea; exactly what I was going to suggest," said Musterffies, more and more insignificant and outranked.

We entered the audiovisual hall. Musterffies presided, with Saint-Ramé at his right and Ronson at his left. The meeting was about to begin when suddenly there was a knocking at the door.

219

We all gave a start, including Ronson, which says a good deal about the state of his nerves.

"Come in," he said.

The door opened and one of the night watchmen appeared.

"Excuse me," he stammered, astonished to see us there, rigged out as we were. "I heard a noise and I came to find out what . . . How did you get in?" he asked abruptly.

"Don't ask questions just now, my dear sir," Ronson replied amiably. "You've done well to come and investigate. It proves you're on the job. It will be held to your credit. . . . Now listen," he added severely. "Just one thing: don't tell anyone, under any circumstances, what you've seen tonight. Any individual who questions you on this subject must be reported to me or to one of the company directors. You can go home now. Thanks and good night."

"You . . . you don't want a little coffee?" the honest fellow asked hesitantly, obviously not yet recovered from the spectacle.

"Ah, some coffee . . ." Ronson did not answer immediately. A little coffee would have done everyone good, but the delegate had decided to profit by our fatigue to provoke blunders. Anyway, that's how I interpreted his reply: "Thanks, my friend. We'll have coffee later on."

No one protested and the watchman departed, not without a last glance around the room, as if the devil had gathered his commandos in the audiovisual hall of Rosserys and Mitchell–France. And then a phantasmagoric meeting began. The heat of the room rapidly made our wet and muddy clothes steam. Whitish vapor mounted slowly toward the ceiling. I tried to keep alert, for I had the feeling that I was now living through minutes that few cadres in the world would have a chance to experience, and even fewer directors of human relations. Through the little white clouds that floated here and there I perceived that three men had preserved their calm and a command of their intellectual faculties: Ronson, Saint-Ramé and Thierry Abéraud. These men's glances were lively and often crossed like sword blades. Ronson stared at me with extreme insistence. I supposed that was because he alone in that room knew I'd met the international president the day before, the absolute master of the firm. Had McGanter confided to him his opinion that I was the imprecator?

Bernie Ronson announced: "With the agreement of Vice-President Adams J. Musterffies and Henri, this is what I have to say to you. In the first place, I let myself be dragged into this silly adventure against my better judgment. In all my career of thirty years with Rosserys and Mitchell International, this is the first time I've held a meeting like this. Look at yourselves, gentlemen; let's *all* look at ourselves! Are these the executives and French directors of the most powerful company the world has ever known? Who, in these steaming, stinking, mud-covered phantoms, would recognize distinguished personalities whom our society and our universities have educated and for whose sake our company has spent large sums, hundreds of thousands of dollars, to teach them our laws, our regulations, the conditions of a good cash flow, the techniques of accelerated amortization, the transfer of capital, the modern rules of the Treasury Department and of international fiscal policy?

"And what's the reason for this grotesque metamorphosis? An earthquake? A bombardment? A war? A revolution? Not at all. There's no reason. I see nothing but automatic reaction, a series of automatic reactions triggered by ineptitude, a monstrous error of judgment engendered by panic. Really, what difference does it make to us that some idiot, innocent or fanatic, has printed and distributed tracts lampooning the directors of our company, and mystified the executives and employees by imitating the managing director's voice? We'll discover him soon enough. Why do we need to take this seriously? Are you aware that the dollar's rising and will shortly regain its strength, thanks to the State Department's shrewd maneuvers? Do you even know the prominent role that a company like ours has played in that operation? Are you indifferent, you muddy cadres, to the spectacular recovery of the North American economy, before which there is now opening a new era of domination over the peoples of the earth, and protection against the enemies of man's liberty—that is, against themselves? Don't you realize that consequently the effulgence of giant American multinational companies will intensify, and that those who have the wickedness and impertinence to oppose, attack and scorn those companies will have to pay the price?

"In this connection, you doubtless noticed the portraits of our founders, Bill Dolfuss Rosserys and Richard Kenneth Mitchell, down there in that narrow, slimy passage, carved by the provocateur, and you wondered why their dates of death had been replaced by question marks. Well, that imprecator, as you call him, was right: they're not dead, they still live, they'll live forever!" And as he shouted that, Ronson smacked the table savagely. "Yes, they'll live through you, and their work will go on! And this imprecator's given me an idea that I'll submit to President McGanter this very evening when he lands in France: to hang the portraits of our founders on the walls of all our companies, with their dates of birth beneath them but question marks instead of their dates of death!

"And now, gentlemen, some final observations: This minor affair ceases to be minor when it threatens our image and the unity of the French affiliate's management team. Not only is it vital to unmask the traitor, but we must punish him severely. After his capture he'll appear before a disciplinary committee, a company high court composed of those here present, plus the financial director. The culprit, need I remind you, is here among us, listening and plotting. But believe me, gentlemen, he won't have much to say for himself. The company's justice will be terrible, pitiless, exemplary! Moreover, if these proposals shock any of you, let him say so at once!" Ronson shouted this, suddenly beside himself, pounding the table before an audience now dumbstruck, but fully awake. Musterffies, Saint-Ramé and Roustev themselves seemed not to believe their ears and looked at one another in amazement.

A quick glance at certain of my colleagues confirmed that they shared the enormous apprehension now chilling me. Ronson frightened us. We were no longer in a company at the peak of Western and global economy, whatever its faults, the egoism and baseness of its policy, the cynicism of its theories and regulations. We were somewhere else. The man before us, foaming with rage, his eyes bloodshot, now hammering out almost every sentence, aroused sinister memories. Scenes from that meeting still wring my withers. Everything contributed to the horror of it: our attire, our white, unshaven, crumpled faces. And that vapor gently rising from our garments.

"Yes!" Ronson shouted. "I'm talking to you for the first time about company justice. Undoubtedly others have stupidly taught you that there are only two valid and sovereign justices, God's and man's. Soon, gentlemen, you'll see the third justice, the global corporation's. Remember this: on the day when the world is a single and unique corporation, then there will reign on this earth only a single and unique justice: ours! Our multinational sisters' combined with our own! Rosserys and Mitchell's!

"What would our man be sentenced to by an ordinary tribunal? To nothing at all. His only risk is being fired, and even then we'd have to give him severance pay! Is that what you call justice? No, you'll render justice yourselves, gentlemen, and we'll preside over your honorable court. I for one don't ask the culprit to turn himself in, because I pity him already! We'll judge him at the scene of his crime, down there in that crypt where God made him lose the stencil of his foul imprecation!" Ronson pointed menacingly at his audience. "Hide yourself, vermin, hide yourself well. We'll find you just the same, and sooner than you think! Today would be ideal, to mark our great Ralph's visit! If only I could offer him that grand gift! I haven't given up yet! Gentlemen, that's all I have to say to you. I'm not going to open a debate. The time draws nigh when the company will open its doors. It's in our interest that nobody see us in this state—you with your silly capes, old women's scarves and clowns' numbers. Get moving, gentlemen. Au revoir."

We did not wait to be asked twice. Overwhelmed by these terrible words, we dispersed in silence on Rue Oberkampf under the fearfully astounded gazes of people hurrying for the first subway. As I was going through the door I heard Ronson say to Musterffies:

"You're an asshole!"

I hailed a taxi and gave the driver my address.

"Are you ill, sir?"

"No, just a little tired."

"You been in an auto accident?"

"No," I said. "Just an accident."

I closed my eyes, no doubt a little feverish.

22

The nurse assigned to me, the one constantly at my bedside, was bending over me and looking at me intently.

"Am I sick?"

"No," she replied gently, "you're not sick, simply a little tired, but the periods when you're yourself again are more frequent and last longer."

"Was I in an automobile accident?"

"No," she said hesitantly. "You just had an accident."

I closed my eyes, no doubt a little feverish.

That morning, unlike the mornings after my other sleepless nights, I thought I ought to go to work pretty nearly on time, instead of sleeping till noon to recover. It was just as well; as I came out on Boulevard Voltaire I ran into a police line diverting traffic. And the section of Rue Oberkampf between Boulevard Voltaire and our glass-and-steel building was black with people. I realized quickly that the people standing there in the street were my company's employees.

"What's going on here?" I asked a policeman.

"I'm not quite sure," he replied. "I think that they're afraid the glass-and-steel building down there at the corner of the Avenue de la République and Rue Oberkampf is going to collapse."

In other circumstances I would surely have pondered his vocabulary and style, most unusual in a member of the police department. But the news he'd just given me was so important that it completely absorbed my mind.

Showing my identification, I said, "I'm director of human relations, especially responsible for security problems. I must get through."

"Right," said the policeman. "Go on and good luck."

In a few minutes I was among my fellow workers, who this time were expressing neither gaiety nor joy but rather great uneasiness. When I arrived in front of the office building, I found a second police cordon, keeping the crowd some ten meters away from the great front door. Firemen were entering and leaving constantly. The staff of Rosserys and Mitchell was there. Their faces showed signs of the mad expedition, of fatigue, of lack of sleep. I went up to Saint-Ramé and asked:

"What's happened since we left this building?"

The general manager made a face, an expression of irony and fatalism, not at all like him when confronted with a grave situation.

"What happened is that at about nine-fifteen Roustev panicked, discovering not only that the initial crack had grown considerably larger but that others had appeared in almost all the pillars of the subbasement."

"But don't Roustev's experts have any ideas about it?"

"You know," Saint-Ramé explained, "it's not always easy to find out what causes cracks in buildings. Some are completely normal; that's why they don't bother anyone. The architects are used to seeing cracks and often it takes a good while to specify the causes.

226

But this situation is complicated," Saint-Ramé added, "because the watchman who saw us last night couldn't hold his tongue, and as a result most of the employees now know about our nocturnal expedition. . . . I really don't know how this is going to turn out," the managing director concluded soberly.

"What are the firemen doing?" I asked.

"They're helping our architects, and experts from the City of Paris, make sure that the building's safe despite all the cracks."

The employees were agitated. There was no talk of anything but the expedition to the subbasements by the cadres and directors the night before. It was then that I understood the genius of the imprecator's methods. His activity was truly on the verge of destroying the company. By recapitulating, I analyzed his Machiavellian scheme. The man had avoided beaten paths. He'd eliminated all the orthodox methods: meetings, the usual tracts, sabotage, denunciation, etc. He'd left strikes to the unions. Then he'd pursued a concept, very confused at the start, but now becoming clear to me: an attack on the company's spirit. If a company possessed a body, in its machines, its administration, its management, its workers, it also had a soul, a mind. Like an individual, then, a company would be vulnerable to fear, magic, superstition.

I had arrived at this point in my reflections when a voice rang out, overriding the chatter. I gave a start and lifted my eyes toward the glass-and-steel building. From the window of my office, Saint-Ramé was talking to the crowd through Rumin's bullhorn. He was alone. Was he going to repeat his earlier performance? In any case, everyone was surprised. I found proof of that in the dazed faces of Musterfflies, Ronson and Roustev, not far from me. What did the managing director, whose conduct was decidedly becoming more and more unpredictable, have in mind? How was he going to get himself out of this mess?

"Ladies and gentlemen, listen closely. I have news for you and then I have to explain certain facts which touch you closely and which each of you has in mind even as I speak. First, the news: the experts have just informed me that our glass-and-steel building is in perfectly sound condition and that there is no reason to be alarmed. The cracks result from a slight subsiding in one area of the subsoil, something perfectly normal on this terrain. It may even be that a slight additional subsiding will follow, about which no one should feel undue concern. After that there will be no further sinking for at least one hundred years! There you have the news. But you can understand that without this diagnosis we had to take exceptional security measures and that is why this morning we thought it advisable to evacuate the building.

"And now, ladies and gentlemen, I should like to explain something I have just heard is worrying you. If presented in a distorted way, it might make you think your directors had gone mad. As a matter of fact, last night Vice-President Musterffies and I, accompanied by our principal colleagues, went down into the building's substructure, precisely because some of us were worried about an enlargement of the crack in one of the bearing walls of the eastern subbasement. So in order to keep a clear conscience, we decided upon an expedition. All night long we inspected the pillars that support our glass-and-steel building. Numerous passages were dank, muddy and slippery. And we fell often. When we came back up in the early morning, satisfied by our inspection, we decided to hold a meeting on the spot and pin down the conclusions from our examination of the subsoil. Then an alert watchman, attracted by the noise, opened the door of the room where we were meeting. I admit that in his place I'd have been as surprised and perhaps frightened as he was! That, ladies and gentlemen, was because we didn't look our best and were covered with mud. I may add that the room was so warm our clothes steamed, and we were wrapped in whitish vapors, which might have made our staunch watchman believe he was dealing with an assembly of phantoms!"

At these words hearty and spontaneous laughter shook the employees. Saint-Ramé had won the game. And he concluded:

"Ladies and gentlemen, you should know that this watchman will receive a special retroactive raise in pay at the beginning of the year!" The crowd applauded. "I invite you now to return to your work. You surely know that raw materials are going up and a petroleum war has broken out on our planet. And in that war, ladies and gentlemen, you yourselves, the personnel of Rosserys and Mitchell International, are our infantry, our forward echelon! And I can assure you that throughout this ordeal, your directors will be worthy of you, that the corporation will be ably managed. Ladies and gentlemen, I thank you for having listened so attentively and I invite you to reenter the building in orderly fashion."

The crowd applauded frantically and marched toward the building in close order. Just then, glancing at Ronson, Roustev and Musterffies, I saw that a fourth person had come to join them during the managing director's talk. He no longer wore a turtleneck sweater, but I recognized his black tortoise-shell glasses, his nervous silhouette, his snakelike head. Ralph McGanter was there, virtually incognito, for only the directors had so far met him in person.

His French firm had, to say the least, prepared an original welcome for him.

23

That morning an extraordinary meeting was held, the first of its kind, on the eleventh floor of the glass-and-steel building—a meeting presided over by Ralph McGanter, one of the ten most powerful personalities in the world, who, surrounded by his vice-president Musterffies, his creature Bernie Ronson, his French general managers and the ranking staff executives, asked for a detailed account of this unprecedented situation. The presence of the staff executives accentuated the exceptional character of that meeting. It was, in fact, not the custom in giant American multinational companies of that period to invite staff executives to discuss an important subject with the global president. Ordinarily the latter first deliberated in secret with his general managers; after that they decided to summon or not to summon some particular executives on a specific question.

I myself felt, and indeed was, in a unique position. Besides, McGanter and I played to perfection the game whose rules we'd laid down in the brasserie. Aside from Ronson, no one knew that we'd met. Moreover, McGanter was the only one convinced—and what's more delighted—that I was the imprecator. And this certainty of being alone with the solution to the enigma, and having discovered it so fast, had obviously put him in a good mood. In short, McGanter was rubbing his hands with morbid satisfaction, the sort a president feels when he is aware of having solved a problem insoluble to his general staff. And so the meeting took on a slightly burlesque air, the reason for which I alone understood.

"But what about this imprecator?" the president inquired. "Where is he, where in the world is he hiding himself? Are you sure he's one of the personnel? What have you planned to prevent his wicked deeds today and tomorrow, and to unmask him?"

"We're tracking him down, Ralph, we're tracking him down," groaned Musterffies. "This time we have proof that he's among us, since he dropped the stencil of the fourth imprecation, the one I just read to you."

"But," McGanter observed, "if he's among us he knows he's being tracked. From now on, aware of what's being planned, he'll take his own measures and will escape you. . . . What's more," he added, and I had the impression that he winked playfully in my direction, "this imprecator, as you call him, doesn't seem at all stupid and is even, I'd say, rather intelligent. Of course, I wouldn't say more intelligent than you, gentlemen, but at least—how shall I put it?—aha, at least equally clever."

A heavy silence fell. Everyone knew how to translate this kind of presidential language, which meant: Gentlemen, you are all egregious asses and this imprecator is much brighter than you, and so more interesting to me, therefore more interesting to the company. Turning to Saint-Ramé, McGanter declared:

"Having said that, I must congratulate you, my dear Henri, for your shrewdness this morning. You cleared up a delicate situation in the wink of an eye."

Then an astounding event occurred: a staff executive took the liberty of making a speech. This was certainly seizing an opportunity, but also running an enormous risk. The more important and worrisome the subject of debate is to a president, the less judicious or profitable it is to volunteer an opinion. The audacious executive was no other than our assistant director of forecasts. Like us, his features were drawn, his face marked by weariness. No doubt he'd realized that if he remained silent before McGanter, his prestige as a leader would be undermined with his colleagues and later on it would be hard for him to keep them in line. His voice was husky, his English excellent.

"Mr. President, I take the liberty of giving you my blunt opinions, and first of all informing you of certain facts you may not know about. For example, several investigations have been going on simultaneously within the company since the beginning of these events, which I'd call hostilities. For the affair, despite certain folkloristic aspects, carefully planned to distort reality, is serious: someone is trying to ruin our company and through it all companies like it. Aware of this and angered by it, a dozen staff executives, not allowed full participation in general management's investigations, decided to intervene as a group, commando style. So it was because of our initiative that we were found underground in those tunnels last night. Why? Because we'd discovered, by our own means, that the key to the machination was hidden thirty meters below our computers, and that between Père Lachaise cemetery and our glass-and-steel building strange plots were being hatched.

"It was not taste for theatricals that led us to put on capes, wear green neckcloths, pin on green-and-black badges. These colors are those of a vault not far from the building and are also the colors of the ribbons tied around the scrolls. Finally, Mr. President, you've said that this imprecator is clever, intelligent, perhaps more so than your collaborators. I can assure you that you're right, with a shade of difference. I take the liberty of mentioning it for the good of our company, which—thanks, it must be said, to your genius—dominates almost the entire world. Now, the shade of difference is this: first, don't regret the imprecator's intelligence,

232

for, Mr. President, he is undoubtedly one of your colleagues, seated at this table. If he is indeed assuredly one of the most intelligent among us, it follows that to unmask him, we can limit our researches and choose among those who, right here, are the cleverest and most intelligent. I conclude by saying this: the imprecator's identity is a problem that, to me, has become easy to solve. On the other hand, it's very difficult to prove his guilt. There's really only one way: to catch him red-handed.

"And on that subject I have some ideas: Tonight, however tired we are, we must return to the subcellars. If proofs exist, they're there. Tomorrow they'll no longer be there. The culprit cannot in fact go down during the day. He'll wait for night to destroy the evidence. So it's certain that if we continue our exploration: *(a)* the imprecator will descend with us since he's one of us; and *(b)* he'll choose a propitious moment to escape from our company in the darkness and destroy the proofs; or, on the other hand, he will get hold of the compromising documents at the same time we do but will destroy them without our knowledge. Let's not forget that he knows the passageways much better than we do and the electric flashlights give only a minimum of illumination. It's child's play for someone familiar with these locations to hide himself for five minutes while the group passes by his hiding place, then to rejoin us. If we surprise him, he can even deny the fact, maintaining that he lost his way, that he took the wrong turn. That's all I have to say, Mr. President. I beg your indulgence for having taken so long."

Abéraud had got himself out of his difficulties brilliantly, and besides, he was gambling without risk. He had extricated himself because he had succeeded in telling McGanter, with elegance, that the latter was a genius. At that time this was the flattery preferred by magnates. Practically all bank owners and captains of commerce and industry believed in their genius and greatly appreciated being told about it, provided this was not done too blatantly, in which case everyone else jeered and they became furious. Abéraud was gambling without risk, as I say, for he was speaking to a man delighted by the imbroglio, believing that he had discovered the imprecator in my person. I asked myself how this would really end, what it would mean to me, to the others and to the company, and I had a foreboding of the end. I felt it coming, close and not pretty.

"What's your name, sir?" McGanter inquired.

"Thierry Abéraud," my colleague replied, getting to his feet.

"Are you on staff or on line, Mr. Abéraud?"

"I'm on staff, Mr. President."

"Have you already been on line?"

"Yes, Mr. President."

"Very good, Mr. Abéraud. I appreciate your views. We Americans love to hear plain blunt language when it comes from a staff executive. . . . Listen. I think we'd do best to wait until evening. I tell you now that I plan to go down with you. I don't want to miss this. . . . Adams, you'll see to my equipment." This was said to Musterflies.

"Dear Ralph," the latter murmured, "some of those passages that wind below our computers drip horribly and others are slippery as ice."

"What about it, Adams? You went down yourself, didn't you?"

"I went down, Ralph."

"Then are you insinuating that I can't go where you yourself have gone?"

"Oh, not at all, Ralph. I'll see to your equipment."

The meeting broke up on these words. As we were leaving, Saint-Ramé called us back:

"Ralph has asked me to introduce you to him individually. Can you stay for a moment?"

He presented us in the order of our seniority, indicating for each his name and position. But since seniority had also been the basis for the choice of the numbers Abéraud had given us, we were filled with amazement to hear Saint-Ramé calling out: Number 1, Fournier; Number 2, Portal; Number 3, Samueru; Number 4, Vasson; Number 5, Abéraud, etc.

We gathered again in the hall on the eleventh floor, still short of breath. It was a little as though our names had been called out in front of a monument to the dead. The voice of the imprecator might have punctuated the roll call lugubriously, saying: Dead on the field of honor for his company . . . Dead on the field of honor for his company . . .

24

That day was the vigil of arms. The directors were not to be seen. Ralph McGanter, contrary to his custom, did not visit the offices or shake hands with his deserving co-workers. The staff executives avoided one another. It was not until almost eleven-thirty that I received my second coded message from Abéraud: *Number 5 to Number 7—Meeting at the Goulim at twelve-thirty. No badges; business clothes. Counting on you.*

The atmosphere of the company was dismal. It seemed that the personnel, like animals, instinctively scented unhappiness and tragedy. Rumin asked to see me and I received him at once. The man was neither vindictive nor distrustful, but concerned. In a weary voice he asked:

"What can anybody think about all this, Director?"

"About what exactly, Rumin—the cracks?"

"The cracks and the rest. I don't understand anything anymore."

236

"I don't understand much myself," I said. "How's the employees' morale?"

"Strange. People are uneasy. They have no new complaints against management, but first the scroll . . . It's very odd. You might say they're afraid for management."

"Afraid for whom?" I asked, intrigued.

"Saint-Ramé and Roustev haven't been normal recently; neither have the directors. And by and large they've never been so kind and so distant with their colleagues at the same time. You'd say they were afraid too."

"Afraid of what, Rumin? That the building's going to collapse? Every precaution's been taken."

"No; afraid of something else. . . . I was sure this business of the scrolls would turn out badly. In the beginning it was fun, and then . . ."

"You know," I said without conviction, "everything's going to be all right."

Rumin got up and shook my hand almost cordially. When he'd left I had an odd feeling. It touched me that simple, honest people were worried about their bosses, who were neither simple nor honest. I leaned back in my chair, warned my secretary to wake me at noon and fell fast asleep.

Later, at the Goulim, I learned that Abéraud had not called this meeting. Chavégnac, a nonpolitical Christian cadre, Samueru, a Jewish anarchist, and Portal, the son of a wealthy Gascon family, had demanded the meeting and had prepared the agenda themselves, to analyze the proposals made the night before by the American Ronson. Abéraud could only bow to their demands. The reaction of these three cadres and the subject of discussion delighted me and took a load off my conscience. I too had been shocked by Ronson's ideas, but I hadn't dared speak to anyone, so heavy was the air of suspicion. At the beginning of the meeting, Chavégnac explained the reasons for his initiative.

"Last night," he declared, "I heard words that still echo unpleasantly in my ears, and, gentlemen, I'm going to put the question to you at once: What does the idea of Company Justice conceal? I confess that I was shaken listening to those words. Let me tell you that if companies arrogate to themselves the right to sit in judgment on people, we're headed straight for a pagan and fascist society. I am very much concerned about the fate that may befall this imprecator if we finally succeed in finding him. Who's going to judge him? Are we? By what right? Under what law? Since last night, I've been tormented by worry, and my colleagues Portal and Samueru and I decided to tell you about it. To be perfectly frank, gentlemen, we would like to reach an agreement on the following proposal: In case we finally capture the imprecator, we demand that he be discharged according to the usual rules, that he not be made the victim of any violence and, *a fortiori,* that he not appear before any company tribunal. Such courts are arrogant, they destroy liberty, spread intolerance and corruption. We can't agree to any such ridiculous and arbitrary parody."

Chavégnac ceased speaking and the moment of truth finally sounded for the senior executives of Rosserys and Mitchell–France. They had got to the heart of the matter. This time it was no longer a question of margins, markets, cash flow, invoices, crude oil, zinc, exportation. It was a question of what sort of men they were beneath the presumptuous disguise of energetic, knowledgeable technocrats drawing the chariot of the postindustrial world. In that epoch a young cadre leaving his family and homeland to enter and succeed in one of the branches of Rosserys and Mitchell International truly left his family and his homeland. He entered a universe living on the border of families and of nations, with its own laws and regulations written and unwritten. Even before Abéraud, visibly bored, had given his opinion, I declared myself in agreement with Chavégnac's position. I said very forcibly that I shared his fears and that I strongly urged my colleagues, when the moment came, to oppose the creation of such a tribunal. After me Le Rantec, the high-flown technocrat, pseudo economist and member of the Revolutionary Socialist Party, took the floor

238

and made some astounding statements which revealed much about the tragedy of then current ideologies. Here is Le Rantec's opinion of company tribunals:

"Our excellent colleague Chavégnac's reactions, and those of his friends, are something to delight a citizen like me, a democrat devoted to justice. But in this case I think they exaggerate the weight that Bernie Ronson meant to give to his proposals. When our American friend talked about a company court, I think he was alluding to a disciplinary committee or, if unhappily the imprecator occupies a sufficiently high position, a court of honor. So I advise you, my dear colleagues, not to be unduly alarmed. If Bernie Ronson gets the impression that some of us are misinterpreting him, that is, are turning against him, that will complicate our situation. It's complicated enough as it is. I add that if we take our friend Chavégnac literally, he's brought a grave accusation against the methods and customs of the company and the ends it pursues. We know our colleague well enough to be sure that his words exceeded his thought. He himself is an ardent fighter for our company, a steadfast defender of its values.

"So I propose that a note be made that aside from divine justice and the justice that men have legally and freely established for themselves, there exists no other justice as such. But I'd be willing to sit on a court of honor or a disciplinary committee that would, within the framework of the company, demand an accounting from whoever's made so much trouble. There can be no harm in that, no impropriety, no diminution of our dignity as staff executives. I might add that a disciplinary committee not only has the duty to punish but also can pardon or establish attentuating circumstances. And I'm glad to know that some of our colleagues like Chavégnac, Samueru, Portal and our dear director of human relations would be sitting on such a committee, striving for moderation. So the judgment will be as equitable as possible."

Chavégnac and his friends fell into line with Le Rantec's opinion. I did not agree at all, but I foresaw that shortly I'd need all my forces to defend myself and I didn't want to throw them into

239

the battle too soon. It remains true that the debate held that day in the Goulim displayed to perfection the mentality of staff executives at that time. The best of them were aware of the danger to freedom in a world oriented toward production, sales and currency. But they never found the necessary strength to push their analysis to a conclusion. They hoped to the last moment that a minimum of morality would be retained. It is this characterless psychology that led right-thinking but essentially ego-ridden political movements to pave the way to power for the cohorts of fascism. And when the latter seized the levers of government, they turned upon their supporters as well. How many democrats, Christian or otherwise, then regretted having compromised with the booted villains!

Once this subject was exhausted, a discussion opened about the second nocturnal expedition in preparation. Abéraud took the floor:

"Gentlemen, this is how I think we should behave tonight. In the first place, unless President McGanter decides otherwise, I'm in favor of not changing our procedure: we'll wear our capes again, our scarves and our numbers. The only difference from last night is that this time we won't need to hide. This expedition is in a way official. Discretion and secrecy are no longer needed. I am convinced that tonight we'll lay hands on very compromising documents and material which the provocateur had no time last night to destroy or remove. And he couldn't get down to the company's basements today because all the entrances are under surveillance. Ronson's even posted a man in front of the green-and-black marble vault. So the watchword will be: Let each spy on his neighbor without exception.

"I admit that this is not a pleasant task and that neither our education nor our professional training has prepared us for such work, but circumstances demand it. After this, no one will jeer at staff executives, the technocratic managers who—despite a few inevitable black marks—bring many benefits and inspiring models to the world and its youth, if only by keeping the wheels turning,

240

thanks to what they know, in mechanisms as complex as Rosserys and Mitchell International. One cannot repeat these simple truths too often, and if tonight I ask an ultimate effort from you, if I request you to retain your uniforms, it is to affirm, especially in President McGanter's eyes, the eminent and original role that you've played in this affair."

It was clear that Abéraud had no intention of foolishly sacrificing the rewards of his cogitations and activities. Now that the denouement was approaching, he was trying to demonstrate that without him things would have turned out differently. The discovery of the imprecator was not to be put down to the general management's credit or anyone else's but the cadre Abéraud, who had directed the investigations, taken the bull by the horns and, before anyone else, mobilized, galvanized, organized the senior staff executives. Le Rantec was exultant. Brignon, Yritieri, Vasson and Sélis rubbed their hands at the enticing prospect of this manhunt. Terrène smiled fiercely, showing his gleaming long white teeth. They dispersed in the street and I, succumbing suddenly to the effects of my sleepless and exhausting night, decided to go home and get some rest.

I set the alarm for six o'clock, lay down and fell asleep.

A bell woke me. It was not the alarm clock. Someone was at my door. I sat up in bed and looked at my watch. Who could be coming to see me? I got up, put on my dressing gown and opened the door. Saint-Ramé, on the landing, looked at me with a smile.

"Excuse me, sir," I stammered. "I fell asleep for a bit. . . ."

"Don't apologize. You have good reason to rest. Tonight will be rough. I hesitated a good while before coming to disturb you, but I needed to see you. I needed to talk with you about developments in the affair. You know that I'm very fond of the conversations that we two have, especially, let me say, during recent days."

"Everything's in a mess. Won't you sit down there?" I pointed out an old-fashioned easy chair beside my bed.

"If you don't mind, I'd like to stretch out a bit myself," said the managing director, and to my surprise, he undid his tie, took off his shoes and lay down on my bed. I seated myself in the easy chair. I couldn't get over seeing him there on my bed—the man the Americans described as the ablest manager in Europe and the one with the most brilliant future. Saint-Ramé fascinated me more and more. He behaved more like a friend with me than the general manager of an affiliate dominating world markets. Had he discovered that his wife was deceiving him with Abéraud, something that still seemed incomprehensible to me? If not, should I tell him? He was silent for a long moment, and I respected his silence. With half-closed eyes and hands at the nape of his neck, he seemed lost in a dream. "Director," he said finally in a soft voice, "what are my senior executives up to now?"

Without hesitation I told him in detail about the midday meeting at the Goulim.

"Ah, so some of them questioned dear Bernie's proposal after all. That means they're not completely drugged by their salaries and expense accounts. . . . They remembered that self-funding and company graphs do no good and make no sense unless they're at the service of man. A man is harder to order around than a regiment of computers, isn't that true? What do you think?"

"I think as you do, sir."

"And a woman," he said suddenly, shutting his eyes completely. "Isn't a woman harder to love than a man is to order around? Do you believe, Director, that someday people will choose their wives by computer? I think it's already being done by matrimonial agencies."

Obviously this sally caught my attention. I was well enough acquainted with Henri Saint-Ramé's subtlety, with his taste for what was called at that time the second or third level, not to imagine that this reflection was made by chance. Was he aware of everything? In that case why was he talking to me about it? What did he want me to say?

"Why are you talking to me about a woman?" I asked, rather awkwardly.

242

"Because tonight a woman will be the turning point," he answered gravely. "But I can't tell you more than that."

Brusquely he got up and sat on the edge of the bed.

"Director, I'm going to reveal something to you. That's why I came here. Listen carefully. Tonight they're going to try to assassinate me. . . . I want you to know that. You're my only interesting colleague, and the only one worthy of confidence. I'd have liked to help you more all through this affair, but I couldn't. One or more persons will try to assassinate me. I don't know whether any of us will escape from this adventure, but in case you do, I entrust this conviction to you. Later, if you have occasion to reestablish the truth, or simply to establish it, don't forget what I am telling you now."

"But," I said, trying desperately to keep hold of reality, "what's going to happen tonight that's so terrifying? Why these ideas of death? Is Roustev planning to stab you under cover of darkness so he can take your place? Who'd want you dead?"

"Not you, in any case; that's the one thing I'm sure of. . . . For the rest, we'll soon see. Now I must leave. Don't be upset about my wife. I know she's sleeping with the assistant director of forecasts and I also know why. Despite appearances, you see, I'm still the best-informed man in the company. That's as it should be, isn't it? As befits my reputation? Am I not the managing director?"

With these words Henri Saint-Ramé rose and took his leave. I took a shower immediatley, but for once this exercise failed to clarify my thoughts. So I went to my office with a fairly fuzzy mind. My secretary, all excitement, came to my desk and told me:

"Sir, I didn't know where you were. Hurry. President McGanter asked to see you almost an hour ago."

Everybody is setting out his pawns, I told myself. At that precise moment I wondered whether Saint-Ramé hadn't manipulated me and whether McGanter wasn't getting ready to do the same thing on his own account. I had temporarily lost sight of the fact that neither the president nor the managing director was exactly a choirboy. Both had successfully crushed many people on various occasions, people almost as intelligent and vicious as they were. What vast operation was unfolding in my company? Wasn't this whole affair more serious and brutal than I'd imagined? After all, did a president and a managing director have time to waste with a modest director of human relations? Were the staff executives and I only these gentlemen's playthings? Pawns in a game whose meaning and rules escaped us?

Ralph McGanter received me in Ronson's office. He was alone. I had retired within myself and felt full of distrust and aggressiveness. McGanter rose and said to me, "Well, Mr. Imprecator, how goes it?"

I resolved not to engage any further in this dangerous and ambiguous game. I replied forcefully, "Mr. President, I'm truly as sorry as can be to disillusion you, but I assert that I am not the imprecator and moreover I do not know who he is."

McGanter, noting the firmness of my reply, raised his eyebrows for a moment, then resumed his playful expression and repeated his act. "I'm not asking for a second confession. You already answered me in the brasserie; don't forget that."

At this instant his face became cruel. I bitterly regretted my attitude in the brasserie. A crude trap had been set for me and I had walked into it with my eyes shut. The directors had searched for a victim and had found him in the person of this naïve and unhappy director of human relations. A victim who satisfied everyone, for by the proclamation of my guilt the reputations of the staff executives, those technocrats and pseudo economists, would be saved. So I was a convenient victim. Now I perceived the trap in all its vileness and, horrified, I saw the scenario unfolding: Tonight they'd descend into the entrails of the company. There in the dark they'd seize me, demand a confession and then judge me. An easy and innocent prey.

How was I to get out of this? To be sure, I had the chance of resigning, clearing out, fleeing from this disgusting company and thus sparing myself tonight's expedition. But it was not that simple. Aside from the fact that I'd deprive myself unjustly of my job,

244

by fleeing I'd admit my guilt. And in that case, I knew, I'd have trouble rehabilitating myself, in finding other employment. Who'd hire the imprecator? Finally, there was my dignity, reinforced by an irritation that was quickly becoming fury. Meanwhile McGanter was going on:

"Tonight we'll have a good laugh, you and I. They'll all be keeping an eye on one another, and we'll be there enjoying the spectacle. We'll let them slither around for a few hours and then we'll call them together and I myself will bring this affair to a brilliant climax by presenting you: 'Gentlemen, now that you've made a thorough search, the moment has come to tell you the truth: here is your imprecator.' In the light of their flashlights," the president concluded, "you can't deny it—it'll be splendid!"

"Listen," I said. "Once more, even if, in a light-hearted moment, you got me to say that I was your man, I warn you, Mr. President, if you introduce me that way I'll deny it firmly."

"That'll be even better, my boy. More normal. Come on, cheer up. See you this evening."

We parted, I preoccupied and worried, he, it seemed to me, somewhat thwarted. Well, all the bets aren't down, I said to myself. I'll try to be brave, and besides, you can always count on the unexpected.

As a matter of fact, the second nocturnal expedition was bursting with the unexpected.

How had the directors and senior executives of a company like Rosserys and Mitchell reached the extremities I'm about to describe? The question can't be asked often enough. The reply can't be pondered sufficiently. My own answer is clear and commits no one but myself: they had lost sight of the fact that they were simply men. And in the pursuit of their careers, they had shown not the best of themselves but the worst. We've always known that man does not live by bread alone. Even more, he cannot live by machines alone, by self-funded investments, interest rates and holding companies. The habit of love, once it is lost, cannot easily be regained. And man, who has required millions of years to raise

245

himself above the animal level, sometimes reverts to it in an instant, to his woe. Simplistic and melodramatic, these reflections nevertheless assumed a singular importance in the light of the vicissitudes shortly to be described. The actors were powerful managers and their staffs. Men who mocked priests and poets. Who said to Heaven: Help yourself and we will help you. They would have carried their arrogance to the point of lending their souls to God at a yearly rate of 14.5 percent.

Make way! The managers are thirsty. Make way! The marshals and their lackeys are about to descend into the entrails of the earth and quench their thirst in the dark! Let them drink deep!

25

So just when all the newspapers, all the radios, all the television sets in the world pulsated with anguished information about a rise in the price of beef, restrictions on crude oil, the dizzying cost of wool, bauxite and phosphates, somewhere in France, at the corner of the Avenue de la République and Rue Oberkampf, not far from Père Lachaise cemetery, a dozen senior executives, two managing directors, two international presidents, a member of the CIA and two private detectives plunged beneath the computer hall of Rosserys and Mitchell–France. They followed numerous narrow, dripping passageways and arrived, not without frequently losing their footing in the mud, at a sort of crypt, a round chamber with smooth and gleaming walls. And there they held the first meeting of the night. The voice of one cadre, assistant director of forecasts, rose and echoed beneath the vault.

"Let him who has betrayed and soiled our splendid firm turn himself in. This will allow us to stop here, to save our time and energy, and above all, the time and energy of Mr. McGanter, here present, the most powerful and most feared president in the world!"

"Yes!" Several voices took up the plea. "Let him confess. It will be held to his credit. He's already cost the company a great deal of money; he's attacked its cash flow!"

"We refuse to have our cash flow attacked!" the executives shouted in chorus.

"Gentlemen, thank you for those appropriately aggressive words," McGanter called out. "I agree with you: the cash flow is sacred. You've grasped that point admirably. I say solemnly to the one who has attacked our cash flow that if he denounces himself now, we'll go back and he'll suffer no harm. He'll be free to hand in his resignation, and what's more, we'll offer him a handsome compensation. If he denounces himself, I promise that he will not be judged by us. I'm going to count to sixty—if he hasn't denounced himself in one minute, I'll consider his felony compounded."

McGanter began to count. The light of the flashlights threw fragments of faces oddly into relief. Each was spying on his neighbor's gestures, his slightest shiver. The minute passed and no one confessed. We took up our march, making our way deeper into the entrails. A single passageway was open to us. We advanced, bent over, one behind the other. We must have been about thirty meters below the glass-and-steel building. Suddenly the American detective, who was leading the column, exclaimed; "Hey, look at this!"

The column stopped. "What have you found?" McGanter asked.

"I've found an empty oxygen cylinder and a length of tubing."

"What does that mean?"

"I don't know yet," said King Voster.

"I think I know!" cried Abéraud. "I suspected it. That oxygen cylinder proves that someone's used a blowtorch near here, a special blowtorch designed to cut through concrete. . . . I have a diagram in my pocket and when we reach the galleries I'm sure we'll find the cause of the cracks. The man must have cut through several pillars and we'll be lucky if the building doesn't collapse on top of us tonight."

"Who's talking that way?" McGanter inquired.

"The cadre Abéraud, sir, assistant director of forecasts."

"Ah, it was you who organized a group of staff executives to take action? You're the one who spoke at the meeting this morning?"

"Yes, Mr. President."

"You seem to have handled the matter very well, my boy. McGanter congratulates you. Come over here by me. . . . Let him pass, you others. I promise you that if we find the sheared pillars you predict, I'll promote you to full director."

"Thank you, Mr. President. I'm coming."

We flattened ourselves as best we could against the wall and Abéraud succeeded in squeezing past and reaching McGanter.

"Forward!" ordered the latter, and we set out again. The map Le Rantec had secured and Abéraud carried proved to be accurate. We came out in a series of three spacious square rooms which together formed a long gallery. There we paused to catch our breath. As in the course of the first expedition, our faces, hands and clothes were covered with mud. We explored the gallery. Several of the great concrete pillars that supported the building stood bare in that place. Three of them had been cut through. In a corner of the third hall we discovered two more oxygen cylinders and a pressure gauge. But no trace of the blowtorch. McGanter, who by all appearances had not expected this, examined these objects minutely. There could be no further doubt: someone had tried to provoke the collapse by attacking the pillars. Just a few centimeters of settling had sufficed to open the cracks. The man had carefully calculated his effort.

One question remained: would he or would he not have continued his criminal activity? Was his object to sow panic by causing the cracks, or to go on and cut through all the pillars, thus causing the collapse of the building? In that case had he thought of the murderous consequences of his action, especially during the day when eleven hundred persons might perish in the ruins, not counting passers-by and neighbors? I confess that the sight of this infamous sabotage was painful; and whatever one might have against Rosserys and Mitchell, such means were highly reprehensible. Why risk the lives of hundreds of innocent persons this way? I was a little chilled, and anger rose in me against this imprecator, who, on certain occasions, had seemed to me rather sympathetic and shrewd. Now things had grown serious. I had no doubt that the director's and my colleagues' sentiments agreed with my own, and I foresaw how thoroughly Ronson's threats would be carried out if we unmasked the wretch.

The silence that had reigned for some minutes was eloquent. I was frightened. What would happen to me if McGanter decided to put his project into execution? If what Ronson had called company justice was nothing but a kind of manhunt, could I hope to emerge alive from these catacombs? Would Chavégnac and his friends still support me? I considered the possibility of flight, of letting myself drift to the end of the column and then of retracing our course with all speed. But I was not sure of getting away and my flight would testify against me. So much the worse: I was there, I must stay and face up to the situation as best I could if obliged to do so.

We resumed our progress. Shortly afterward we saw an immense hall, a sort of subterranean esplanade, completely enclosed, with a round hole at its center, the opening of a passageway identical to the one we had encountered at the start and almost as steep. We formed a circle around this narrow black hole and took counsel. One of us, equipped with a long rope, would have to go down first. McGanter asked for a volunteer. *"Moi,"* said the French detective. So it was done. He wrapped a rope around his body and King Voster, Terrène and Vasson held it to allow the detective a gentle descent. A good twenty meters were unrolled. The detective's voice reached us from a distance, muffled.

"What does he say?" asked McGanter.

"He says we can go on," said Ronson.

We went down one after the other and found ourselves at the bottom of this pit in a tunnel as narrow and slippery as the preceding ones, but with an almost level floor. We set off again in single file. The tunnel grew narrower. Soon we could proceed only by crawling. We all felt oppressed and haunted by claustrophobia. We were in the dark, in the mud, flat on our stomachs, one behind the other, and our flashlights of little use.

"Abéraud," said McGanter, "check your map and tell us where this damnable tunnel comes out. If it doesn't lead anywhere we're going to die of suffocation, and it doesn't really pay to tempt fate."

"I know the map by heart, Mr. President. One more push and we'll come out at the foot of a kind of hillock, a little underground mountain with an opening at the top like a volcano. We'll go down through that sharply. Then there's no serious obstacle between us and the green-and-black marble tomb in Père Lachaise. At the foot of the hillock I expect to find the tools that were missing in the gallery and perhaps documents. We should redouble our mutual surveillance: the provocateur may fear the discovery of the documents even more than that of the tools."

"Very well," said McGanter, "but we've got to keep him from getting away. . . . Ronson, you crawl last. Voster, you go first: Forward!"

Having placed the two Americans, the only persons in whom he seemed to have complete confidence, McGanter chuckled. "What an adventure! I've had lots of them in the dog's life I've led, haven't I, Ronson, but not one as incredible as this! If the President of the United States could only see me crawling in the mud of this tunnel under my French company! Ah, what an adventure!"

Decidedly, Ronson seemed to know everything and McGanter called him to witness just as Musterffies had. I noticed too that Saint-Ramé, Roustev and Musterffies were quiet as mice. We crawled on, our noses in the slimy mud. Suddenly the column halted.

"What's going on?" Roustev asked.

"I have the feeling," King Voster replied, "that the tunnel is

251

getting narrower and may cave in. . . . I hesitate to go on. . . . What should I do, President?"

There was silence. I was terrified. Were the directors and the senior executives of Rosserys and Mitchell going to die absurdly of suffocation in the collapse of this tunnel? Finally, McGanter spoke:

"King, I leave the decision to you. Only you are in a position to make a proper choice. . . . Abéraud, are we very far from the hillock?"

"No, sir; perhaps thirty meters away."

At this moment a wail reached us, a sort of sob punctuated by bizarre yelps:

"I don't want to go on, I don't want to die, I'm smothering, don't go on, please, don't go on."

It was the cadre Fournier, head of the New Machines Department, husband of a splendid, flirtatious female whom the coxcomb Vasson, head of Eastern Bloc exports, was impudently courting.

"Who's crying like that?" snapped Ronson. "No matter, we're committed to going ahead. It would be even harder to crawl backward."

"No, no; kill me right here. I won't go any farther!" Fournier cried.

I guess Fournier was a few meters behind me, in the grip of full-blown hysteria. Because of him we were suddenly in an impossible situation. The tunnel was so narrow that no one could get past anyone else. How were we to get Fournier out and ourselves along with him? I selfishly rejoiced at being in front of him. In case of panic, I could press forward because he blocked the passage only for those behind him. King Voster reported.

"I've just moved forward some twenty centimeters and I'm almost certain, President, that we'll have to turn back."

"Yes, but how?" stormed McGanter. "How can we go back with that ass having a nervous breakdown there behind us! And if you can't go forward, Voster, we're trapped like rats. Who is that imbecile going crazy?"

Fournier was now in fact in a terrible state and his howls were

252

a serious threat to morale. His attack reached a paroxysm and he began to curse the company and accuse himself of being the imprecator.

"Yes," he yelled. "I've always known I'd drop dead in your stinking American sweatshop—but I'll take you with me! We're all going to die—all of us, you understand?—in this shitty tunnel! You too, McGanter, you pig, you assassin, you fascist—you're going to die buried alive, and it'll serve you right for all the blacks, all the poor bastards you've massacred all over the world! And the rest of you dumb sons of bitches flat on your bellies in a muddy tunnel, don't you look great now! You can have your pimps' pay, your graduate work, your Harvard, your business school, my ass! They're just right for you, you pigs! You'll never fuck my wife, Vasson, because you're going to die, and all the better for her; you'd have clapped her up! And Abéraud, you dirty bastard, no more fucking old lady Saint-Ramé, that whore who puts in for family allotments! Ah, help, help, we're all going to die!"

"Who the hell unloaded that one on me?" McGanter cried. "Roustev, Saint-Ramé, who *is* that poor fool?"

"It's Fournier, Mr. President. He's a graduate of the Engineering College, has a diploma from the Advanced School of Marketing in Cincinnati and took a course at Harvard summer school."

"Then why is he so sensitive? And this business about Abéraud and your wife—is that true, Henri? Oh, damnation, that Abéraud; if we get out of here alive, he'll be cited in the presence of the whole Grand Council!"

"I'll be cited for what, Mr. President?" asked Abéraud, who disliked uncertainty.

"You will be cited. Hell and damnation—isn't that enough? We'll see for what later on. Just now we've got to get out of here . . . but shut him up, for God's sake! Who's just in front of Fournier?"

"I am, sir, cadre Le Rantec."

"Le Rantec, what's your position in the company?"

"I'm attached to general management, Mr. President, a staff

executive in charge of U.S.-European relations."

"Aha! Then I'm sure you've never been on line."

"Never, Mr. President."

"All right, you're on the line now, my boy, and for the first time. Fetch that madman a good kick in the head and knock him out! I can't stand his raving!"

Fournier called on his mother, whispered that his true vocation was to farm, to raise sheep peacefully in the country. In his delirium he threw in all the stereotypes then fashionable among executives. All of them had stated at least once at some dinner party that they no longer wanted to live like imbeciles on a high salary and in congested traffic, and that one day they would raise pigeons or pheasants or trout or, of course, the sacrosanct sheep. When I heard Le Rantec ordered to brain Fournier with a kick on the head, I trembled. Flat on my stomach in the mud of the tunnel, I instinctively put my hands over my head in case Yritieri, lying in front of me, went crazy and tried to knock me out too.

"Well, Le Rantec, what about that kick? Are you going to shut him up or aren't you? Hurry up if you too want to be promoted. As a matter of fact, Le Rantec, *do* you want to be promoted?"

"Yes, sir; of course."

"But do you really want it? Every executive in Japan and the West wants to be promoted, I know that, but some of them really want it, hot and hard! Are you one of those, Le Rantec?"

"Oh, Mr. President, I promise you that since I left school I've never dreamed of anything else."

"And what sort of position would you like, Le Rantec?"

"Oh, sir, what I'd really love to do is direct a holding company —a little one to begin with, of course."

"Well, my boy, if you silence that idiot demoralizing our troop immediately and completely, I'll give you a company that includes a car rental agency, one of the hotels we're planning to build, and a chocolate-caramel biscuit factory, recently enlarged. Will that suit you?"

"Oh, sir, that's all I need, a pretty little holding company. In one

254

year I promise you a pretty little cash flow."

"Well, then knock him out, my boy."

We heard the sound of a blow followed by a cry of pain. Le Rantec had kicked Fournier in the head.

"Have mercy, Le Rantec, I'm bleeding!"

"Shut him up, for God's sake!" shouted McGanter.

"I'm stomping, sir, I'm stomping," Le Rantec apologized. "But it isn't easy. I can't see anything and the pig is protecting his head with both hands."

"Then stomp with both feet at once!" Ronson suggested.

We heard Le Rantec strike several times more. Fournier's cries redoubled.

"My eye, my eye! Have pity, please, I'm doing better. I'm not afraid now . . . I can crawl. . . . Forgive what I said. I don't think that . . . Aiee! Oh, my eye. Le Rantec, stop . . . stop!"

"It's a mistake to knock out Fournier," cried Brignon.

"Who said that?" asked McGanter.

"Brignon," Roustev informed him. "He's the man responsible for the success of our mower-thresher with vertical intake."

"Ah," McGanter said in a softer tone. "That was an excellent operation, young man. I congratulate you. . . . But why shouldn't we brain this madman?"

"Because, Mr. President, once he's unconscious the tunnel will be blocked; we'll have a real job getting him out of here. But if he keeps the use of his arms and legs he'll be able to get out by himself."

"That's a reasonable point of view," McGanter granted. "What do you think, Bernie?"

"All things considered, I think Brignon is right."

"All right, stop kicking, Le Rantec!" McGanter ordered.

"Yes, sir . . . but I'm afraid it may be too late. I can't feel Fournier moving anymore."

"The devil . . . Who's behind Fournier?"

"It's me, cadre Sélis, specialist in prices."

"Sélis, do you think Fournier is unconscious?"

"His feet and legs have stopped moving, sir."

"This is tiresome. . . . How're you doing, Voster?"

"I think we can make it, President. I'm almost through this dangerous place and I think maybe I overestimated the risks. It seems to me you'll all get through all right."

"Have you any idea, Voster, what to do with this Fournier, who's unconscious and blocking the tunnel?"

"Yes, President. The man in front of Fournier should tie a rope around him and we'll drag him with us until we get out of the tunnel."

"Le Rantec, can you tie Fournier?"

"That's impossible for me, Mr. President. Like you, I'm stretched out flat on my stomach and there's no way I can turn around."

"In that case," said King Voster, "it will be easier for the man who's behind. All he has to do is crawl between Fournier's legs, pass the rope around his body and if possible under his shoulders, then give it to Le Rantec, who will pass it on to us. I think the rope will be long enough. I see the tunnel widening ten meters ahead of me."

Sélis and Le Rantec executed this operation, not without difficulty. Le Rantec crawled forward, dragging with him the rope that Sélis had passed around Fournier's body. The first part of the group found themselves in the tunnel at a point high enough for them to stand, and they began to drag Fournier. Behind him Sélis was at work, disengaging a foot caught in the mud, a jammed arm. No one spoke. The progress of the body was halting and took a good half hour. When Fournier appeared, Voster took hold of him under the armpits, hauled him out and turned him over, for the unhappy man had been dragged with his face on the ground. He was unrecognizable. The second part of the group rejoined the first. King Voster had bent over the inert body of the director of the Department of New Machines of Rosserys and Mitchell–France. He wiped his face with his handkerchief and cleaned the

256

mud from his eyes and mouth. Then he straightened up and said, "He's dead."

"Are you sure?" Ronson asked. "You're not a doctor."

"Examine him yourself," the American detective replied.

But Saint-Ramé, who in turn bent over the body, confirmed the diagnosis.

"You don't have to be a doctor to see that Fournier is dead," he said.

Instinctively a dozen of us turned toward Le Rantec. The latter felt these glances directed toward him in the dark. A terrible silence hung over us. The American detective, who had once more bent over the corpse, then said, "I don't think he was killed by a kick in the head. His mouth and nostrils are full of mud. You must have knocked him out. Then he died of suffocation."

"Le Rantec is not the only one responsible for this death," said the brave but feeble Chavégnac. "We all are."

"Yes, we all are," McGanter agreed. "But it was just an unfortunate accident. Was Fournier married? Did he have children?"

"Fournier," Saint-Ramé announced in a funereal voice, "was married and had two children whose births were widely spaced. One was fourteen years old, a son. The other six, a daughter. He was the oldest of the senior staff executives. He was honest and conscientious. He got his secondary education at Montpellier Lycée, then his first year of political and economic science at Toulouse. After that he came up to Paris. Upon graduation he went to work in the United States, exceptional for a French cadre. He was not a discoverer of markets, but despite that he directed our Department of New Machines, for he had no equal in preparing a promotional budget. Beyond doubt there was no one among my colleagues who personally contributed more to the healthy state of the French cash flow."

"Yes, it's true the cash flow of our French firm has always been the envy of Europe, Japan and even us back in the U.S.A. Voster, can you carry poor Fournier on your shoulders? Where are we now? What's become of Abéraud?"

"Here I am, sir, just behind you."

"Good. Are we far from the vault in Père Lachaise?"

"Not far, Mr. President, but we're going to have to climb the hill, then go down the shaft. After that, the tunnel becomes a large passageway which leads almost in a straight line to the vault."

"Where is this hill?"

"According to the map, sir, it must be about a hundred meters from here, straight ahead."

"Well, then, forward march," McGanter ordered.

And the troop moved on, still in single file, Voster at the head, carrying Fournier's body, Ronson at the end, keeping an eye on everyone. I found myself near the middle of the column. In the distance I made out King Voster's massive figure with my colleague's body on his shoulders. The erratic illumination of the flashlights made the scene unreal. Perhaps it was actually a dream —a nightmare.

We walked in silence, half shamed, half ferocious, with empty minds and yet with fear in our bellies. It was thus that we emerged at the foot of the heralded hillock. This was simply an extrusion of the ground and in fact one could guess that there was some sort of opening at its summit. We had all had enough of these tunnels and passageways, and so we felt relief at reaching this place. King Voster put down Fournier's body and we were able to gather around it and pay a kind of bizarre homage by directing our flashlights in turn at his poor, mud-streaked face. Who could have foretold, when Fournier was making his brilliant scholastic record at Montpellier, then at Toulouse, that he would end this way, fifty meters below the computer hall of the French affiliate of the most powerful multinational corporation in the world? Portal, a practicing Catholic, recited the Pater Noster. He had just come to the end when Ronson shouted, "Look, over there. He's climbing toward the top of the hill. It's him! Quick, come with me!"

We caught sight of a shadow clambering rapidly. We turned our flashlights toward him. Abéraud, Ronson and the two detectives rushed after him and we followed.

The fugitive gained ground and for a moment we lost sight of him.

"Don't climb, don't climb!" Voster shouted to us. "Stay down here and surround the base of the hill. We'll have him cornered!"

"We'll have to keep him from going down the shaft," Abéraud pointed out. "It's the only way you can get from here to the tomb."

We stopped our climb and began a circling operation.

"There he is!" Voster shouted. "He didn't have time to rope up so as to get down the shaft. He'll have to come down. Look, he's headed toward us!"

"I've got him!" Terrène cried. "I've got hold of him!"

"No, you haven't, you idiot!" cried Musterffies.

"Well, was it you who were running?"

"What do you mean, was it me? I was running, of course, but running after the man!"

"Terrène, you're crazy!" Brignon shouted. "There he is—quick, this way!"

We bumped into one another trying to capture the fugitive, who, quite close to us, took advantage of projecting ledges to disappear from sight. Our flashlights were not of much use. We listened, panting, for the slightest sound. I told myself that if the man was clever and bold enough to leap out among us, he'd never be identified, so heavy was the suspicion and so minimal the visibility.

From the top of the hill Ronson called, "Have you spotted him?"

"Yes," McGanter replied. "He's a few meters away, in the shadow."

"We don't have to catch him to find out who he is," Ronson said. "Stay where you are. Ralph, call the roll. Here am I with Voster, Abéraud and the French detective. Tell those around you to give their names. The one missing in the roll call will be our man."

"Great idea, Bernie. I'll start. Terrène!"

"Here!"

"Yritieri!"

"Here!"

"Sélis!"

"Here!"

"Brignon!"

"Here!"

"Portal!"

"Here!"

"Chavégnac!"

"Here!"

"Vasson!"

"Here!"

"Samueru!"

"Here!"

"Fournier!"

"He's dead!" Ronson shouted from the top of the hill. "The director of human relations!"

"Here!" I said.

"Ah, you're there after all," muttered McGanter. "You fooled me, all right, you did. We'll talk about that later, when we've got out of this damned bog. . . . Roustev!"

"Here!"

"Saint-Ramé!"

There was a silence.

"Saint-Ramé!" McGanter shouted again. "Henri, where are you?"

"Here," replied a voice I hardly recognized. "I'm here, McGanter."

And the managing director stepped out from behind a shelf of rock where he had been hiding.

"What is this, Henri!" McGanter exclaimed, stupefied. "What were you doing back there?"

"Well, Mr. President, let's just say I was thinking," Saint-Ramé replied ironically. "I said to myself, What shall I do? Shoot down at them or put an end to this revolting comedy? I opted for the second choice."

And Saint-Ramé tossed a pistol to the ground. Then Ronson, Abéraud and the two detectives climbed down from the hill and joined us. We lined up, actually petrified, like children, practically in ranks in front of Henri Saint-Ramé, managing director of Rosserys and Mitchell–France, born in Poligny in the Indre, graduate of the Institute of Political Science in Paris and of the Harvard Business School, Master of Science from the Massachusetts Institute of Technology, Chevalier of the National Order of Merit.

The first to react was McGanter.

"Henri," he said, "this is a weird sort of joke. This nocturnal expedition, this long, terrible crawl and the accidental death of one of your executives have addled your mind. You're not the man we're looking for. If you are, Henri, I expect you to come clean with me, and what's more, to explain. We're not going to leave this place until you've given me a full explanation of your behavior, and one that I can understand."

"My dear McGanter," replied Saint-Ramé, who in my eyes had just brightened these putrid shadows, "I'm afraid we mustn't stay here long. It would be dangerous. The office building of Rosserys and Mitchell–France is going to sink very soon. It won't collapse, but there will be various landslips and we run the risk of ending our somber days in these tunnels like rats in a trap. It's not that I'm unwilling to explain anything at all to you, but you and the others will never understand, with the possible exception of one man whom I am very sorry to see here: I did everything I could do to prevent him from coming down tonight. In particular, McGanter, it was I who slanted the reports to make him look guilty. I told myself that if he knew he was suspected, he wouldn't join us. He decided otherwise. Alas, I couldn't bring more pressure on him, or I'd have aroused his suspicion. Ronson and Abéraud were already on my trail, and I was pressed for time to accomplish my purpose. Later on I'll tell you what that was, if you wish. This man, who alone perhaps will understand my reasons and explanations, is the director of human relations. He has character, he is honest and sensitive and therefore out of place among you."

"Who are you making fun of, Saint-Ramé?" roared McGanter. "Voster, grab him!"

Saint-Ramé let himself be taken without resistance.

"I've suspected you for some time, Saint-Ramé," said Ronson, his voice trembling with rage, "and someone here knew it! It's not the director of human relations, the most valuable and intelligent of your cadres, but the assistant director of forecasts, Abéraud."

"I did too," helped Le Rantec, who no doubt was afraid that his little holding company would go glimmering. "I suspected him too. Only he could imitate his own voice so well."

"So you'll be stupid, superficial and cowardly to the end, my poor Le Rantec," said Saint-Ramé. "For the sake of your Revolutionary Socialist Party I hope you're the only one of your kind."

"You don't have the floor!" roared McGanter, now beside himself. "Ronson, you were right! We'll try him! Let's make a court! Ronson, where can we hold it?"

"I think the platform beside the hill, where Voster and I were posted, should serve our purpose. It overlooks the tunnels we've come through. Let's make up the court. Ralph, I think it's proper for you to preside, and then you can choose the others."

"Very good; it won't take long," McGanter declared. "You, Ronson, and you, Adams, will be associate justices, and Abéraud district attorney, and Brignon, the fellow with the reaper-thresher from Kansas, assistant district attorney. Voster and his colleague will be sergeants at arms. The director of human relations will be Saint-Ramé's defense attorney. We Americans love justice. With us the accused has his rights. One cannot condemn a man on common sense alone. Let's overcome our legitimate fury in order to render justice. Let's give a lawyer to this villain, who may even be out of his mind! Let us not dishonor America. All the other cadres will be the jury. Let's hurry; it's almost three o'clock."

After that we moved to the platform attached to the side of the hill. At our feet we had only an immense black abyss. The flash-lights merely served to light up the platform itself. A rock was brought up and placed for McGanter to sit on. Musterffies and Ronson sat on the ground, one to the president's right, the other to his left. The other cadres seated themselves tailor fashion, form-ing a semicircle on either side of the presidential rock. King Voster and his colleague brought in Saint-Ramé and forced him to kneel. I noticed then that his hands were tied and his ankles bound. I took my place at the right of the accused. Everyone was ordered by Ronson to turn his flashlight toward Saint-Ramé, who was forced to hold his own in both hands so as to illuminate his face.

"We must see this blackguard's face throughout the trial," Ron-son had decreed. It was a weird vision, the countenance il-luminated from below by a flashlight. Sometimes it was as if the yellow, creased face of a phantom were hovering in the dark. And the "trial" of Henri Saint-Ramé began. During the preparations the company executives had not whispered a word.

Only Ronson and Abéraud recovered rapidly from their semi-surprise to exhibit a hatred, a contempt, a desire for vengeance that they no longer tried to disguise. McGanter, who in general thought very fast and who had absolute confidence in Ronson, was not far from sharing their appetite for punishment. But mainly, they all wanted to know everything, understand everything and thereby bring to naught Saint-Ramé's eventual rationale. That night I observed at close hand the shameful mechanisms made famous by the Inquisition and by Stalin's trials. At first it was more important to demonstrate by any means that the accused was guilty than it was to destroy him physically.

"Confess!" they shouted in the ears of their victims. "Confess and save your life! Acknowledge your errors, confess your crimes. Go to prison and not the stake!"

And to Saint-Ramé: "Admit that overwork has driven you mad, or that being threatened by Roustev, who was about to replace you, you decided to reestablish your position by confusing the personnel. Admit one or the other of these motives and then come

263

back up to the open air with us, on condition, of course, that you submit your resignation to the Grand Council—for reasons of health. Come on, Saint-Ramé, speak up, damn it! Were you afraid of Roustev or not? Or have you recently had more and more lapses of memory, attacks of vertigo, inexplicable moods? When you talked to the employees through Rumin's bullhorn didn't you use bizarre terms and phrases? Isn't that so, Abéraud? Tell us about it, Abéraud. Take the oath, Associate Director of Forecasts, to tell the whole truth and nothing but the truth. Raise your flashlight and say: 'I swear.' And then isn't it true that Saint-Ramé's statements on that day were completely incoherent? And at the cemetery, at the tomb of our lamented Arangrude, what happened? Cadre Le Rantec, you remember that? Come, sir, attaché to the general management. You too raise your flashlight and tell us about those references to Tolstoy at the tomb of a marketing director. Madness! Would a man who practically invented the marketing of cellophane-wrapped pork in France reread a great classic novel every year during his vacation? Madness! What have the sighs of Anna Karenina to do with Korvébon hams? Madness! Isn't it right, Le Rantec? Besides, none of that was true, and there's someone here who can so testify, isn't that right, Vasson? Take the oath, Vasson, swear to tell the truth in the name of the United States of America, refuge of liberty. Raise your flashlight and say, 'I swear!' Well, then, Vasson? Take the oath, Vasson. You're well acquainted with the Arangrudes? How often have you slept with his wife? Six times! Thanks, Vasson!"

"That's a lie," I protested.

"The defense will shortly have its turn and all the time it requires," roared McGanter, tracing arabesques in the air with his flashlight. "At present the witnesses for the prosecution have the floor. Well, Vasson, did Arangrude read Tolstoy? Thanks, Vasson. Why would he read Tolstoy? And you, Roustev? You, my dear André, henceforth general manager of Rosserys and Mitchell–France, take the oath too, swear, swear, Roustev, raise your flashlight. Tell us what Saint-Ramé was preparing to do to our cash

264

flow. How many times was he mistaken in his forecasts? How did he conceal his errors or plan to conceal them? Come, dear Adams, lift your flashlight, describe the procedure for falsifying accounts! How has Monsieur Saint-Ramé been operating for two years? Listen to that, you executives of Rosserys and Mitchell–France, listen to that. Did you hear? And now let the cadre Abéraud return to the bar. And let him tell us, yes, he who has touched the round white thigh of Mama Saint-Ramé, let him tell us what she told him on the pillow!"

"Aha, on the pillow!" seven or eight cadres repeated in unison.

Abéraud came to face the fallen managing director and said, "For almost a year now he has alternated between impotence and the most sordid peculiarities."

"That concerns Henri Saint-Ramé's private life," I protested, "and is irrelevant."

"What do you mean, irrelevant?" exclaimed McGanter. "A man who's going mad goes as mad in his bed as in his office! Go on, Mr. Associate Director of Forecasts!"

Abéraud described with relish and in detail what it was in Saint-Ramé's conjugal relations that proved he was going mad. All this was truly disheartening.

"And I understand that this swine behaved in the same way with a number of secretaries, isn't that so, Brignon?"

"Absolutely true, sir."

"Swear, Brignon, raise your flashlight!"

Brignon raised his flashlight.

Yes, his own secretary had almost been raped by the managing director and he, Brignon, had not dared tell about it.

When the testimony satisfied McGanter, the floor was given to Saint-Ramé.

This is what the managing director of Rosserys and Mitchell–France had to say:

"You'd like me to be mad. Well, as it happens, I am not. You, on the other hand, are completely so. I shall tell you what has happened in our company during the last few days. You'll see that it's simple, and not worth blowing up to such proportions, still less worth bringing us where we are now, here on this platform in the subcellar of our building, me bound and kneeling, and you, to be frank, monstrous. But these developments are no accident. Now I know that you were even weaker and more incompetent than I'd imagined. Listen, and you'll be ashamed. But I foresee that having been dragged past the point of no return by your attitudes and insane actions, you won't be strong enough to rise above your abjection; and that whether you believe me or not, you'll become even more vile, more insane.

"I didn't write the first imprecation. As some thought at the beginning, it's the work of a more or less anarchistic student who, to earn a little money, got himself hired by the maintenance crew that cleans our building at night. I know the young man; he admitted it to me, laughing. But the effects of that imprecation caught my attention, effects our student was far from foreseeing.

"During these last few years I have become convinced that the essential function of the managing director of a company like ours is to make people work together, to watch over working conditions, to devote himself almost entirely to questions of education, rotational employment, psychology, reforming internal relations, new methods of communication. I brought it up with my director of human relations: 'You watch, human relations are going to develop spectacularly. Our great corporations' nerves are strained past the breaking point.' A company is like a human body in many ways and that's even more true of firms of global scope. They have their heads, their hearts, their entrails, their muscles. But if in the last twenty years our companies have acquired solid powerful muscles, if their capacity to produce has hugely increased, their brains, alas, have remained small.

"I apologize for saying it, but the learned theories of our American friends and their European and Japanese disciples on methods of management are not up to their theories on production, exploitation of markets, diversification and purely financial problems. First of all, after the war we had to produce. Then to sell. Now the

266

time has come to talk, to talk to one another, to live—let's risk the word—relatively happy and relaxed at our place of work. Now the psychology of the company, the art of communicating information, the ability to respect one individual among hundreds and thousands of others, have become productive factors in themselves; that is, if the management can't achieve those objectives, productivity falls off. Whereas up to the present these factors were exclusively matters for our psycho-sociologists, or later personnel directors, then directors of human relations, they'll soon be an essential function of general management. This means quite simply that at the heart of our great companies power will change hands, and this change will give rise to ruthless battles between finance and management on the one hand and psychology and politics on the other, battles that will go so far as to compromise the prosperity of the firms.

"The era of technocracy is coming to its end. The living word is going to reassert itself powerfully and put the theoreticians of management back in a subordinate place. And it is well that we, who believe in liberty and initiative in matters of political economy, should be the first to apply these necessary reforms, for lack of which other men will undertake to accomplish them abruptly by destroying our companies. How could you think for a second that you have before you a provocateur, an irresponsible urchin? Let's come to our senses: the harm is reparable. We've given ourselves an electroshock. Let's react sensibly. I'm still the same Henri Saint-Ramé that you know and all my activity has just one goal: to diagnose our sicknesses before the revolutionary factions send their doctors to replace us.

"Well, gentlemen, one fine day fate incarnate in that student's thesis gave me the chance to experiment with the ideas I've just sketched. I decided to use the situation to test what I've called the nerves of the company. So I transformed the joke into an experiment. I made up my mind to continue it and I wrote three more texts. I made use of the late lamented Arangrude's death to depress the company's psychology and atmosphere. From a practical point of view, my position made everything easier. No one could easily suspect me and I myself issued false rumors and fantastic instructions. At the end of a certain time my intention was to call a meeting of my close associates and explain to them what I'm explaining now, to analyze before them and with them the mistakes that have been made, to imbue them with my point of view.

"Just think, Rosserys and Mitchell–France could again have impressed the whole world with a method of management far in advance of its time, and I, Saint-Ramé, could have become the prototype of the progressive boss! But why have things turned out badly? Why couldn't I control what I'd started? For two reasons: first, Abéraud's initiative poisoned the situation. When a group of colleagues on such a high level got away from me, I could no longer control events as I had planned. Abéraud's actions turned my experiment into a tragedy. Secondly—and no doubt this will displease you, but you should reflect on it—Abéraud and his colleagues wouldn't have aggravated the situation at all if my view hadn't been right. The result exceeded my expectations. I had counted on my colleagues' nerves giving way. I knew their characters were weak. But I never dreamed the company's highest officers would fall into the trap. I thought McGanter, Musterffies and Ronson were safe from this sort of test. Alas! And tonight, because that funeral and my language seemed strange to you, and because three times the employees received a scroll with an intentionally polemical text, look what you have come to!

"When Le Rantec is reduced to breaking a colleague's head to become manager of a holding company, I say that our system is sick, very sick, gentlemen! The best thing now would be for you to untie me and for us to get back to the surface—and before dispersing, to give a little thought to poor Fournier!"

"Hold on!" said McGanter. "I have some questions for you, and this one first: Where did the cracks come from? Did your experiment include destroying the building?"

"Those cracks are none of my doing," Saint-Ramé replied with spirit. "They were due to sabotage. I told you a moment ago that

268

this affair stimulated the battle of the cliques inside the company. Someone cut the concrete pillars with a blowtorch. Knowing what you were capable of tonight, I don't doubt that someone, for his own purposes, one of you, ambitious and unscrupulous, would have been capable of causing the building's collapse to blame it on the imprecator later. I was the first to be surprised by the enlargement of that crack, and I think that Roustev, who, as everyone knows, has practical experience in the building field, could explain it to us."

"What are you insinuating by that?" Roustev shouted.

"Nothing at all—just calm down, Roustev. Weren't you officially in charge of cracks and splits?"

"What of it? We all know how to patch them. You make me sick, Saint-Ramé."

"Poor Roustev. I make you sick and I feel sorry for you."

"I'll have none of your pity!" roared Roustev, who, mad with rage, left his place and rushed toward Saint-Ramé. I intercepted him. "What are you going to do to a man tied and on his knees?" I cried, ready to fight. We turned our flashlights on each other, and the assistant managing director's rictus frightened me.

"Come back, Roustev. Let's keep calm!" cried McGanter. "I have another question for you, Saint-Ramé. In your system, where the managing director's supposed to devote himself to the happiness of individuals, to working conditions and information, etc., etc., who'll look after the cash flow?"

"A good assistant manager and a competent, honest financial director could handle it easily."

"The way you go at things, Saint-Ramé!" exclaimed McGanter. "Never mind. . . . Let's get back to the rest of your explanations. They don't convince me at all, and your conclusion's actually silly. So we untie you and go back up. Then we separate. And tomorrow you give an interview and announce that thanks to your genius, a great step was taken here tonight toward new command methods at the heart of giant American multinational companies! Saint-Ramé, you're out of your mind! What do you think, gentlemen?"

269

"He's out of his mind," repeated the others.

"Saint-Ramé, I demand a confession that for some time you've been suffering violent migraines, that you have lapses of memory, that sometimes you lose your self-control. If you admit that, we'll go up and have you sign a declaration to that effect. I forbid you to make a spectacle of yourself before the whole Western world. You've been managing director of Rosserys and Mitchell–France and your reputation is international. If you publicly denounce what you once idolized, you'll be striking a terrible blow at our company, you'll be sowing doubt in the minds of hundreds of millions of students and children, minds already undermined by revolutionaries, and they'll start to wonder about the meaning of our society. If you, Saint-Ramé, so representative of our hierarchy, if you yourself create doubt, the values we incarnate will be truly and violently shaken. And those values are good, Saint-Ramé. We must defend them. And the best way to do that is for you to draw the right conclusions from an affair that got out of control. Stand aside, Saint-Ramé, resign for reasons of health. The company will make your apartment over to you, or its equivalent, and will pay you an unprecedented compensation. What the devil, Saint-Ramé —make up your mind, for God's sake!"

"You will make me say what I do not think," the ex-managing director replied in a firm voice.

Then the voice of Bernie Ronson rose, echoing and sinister: "There are a thousand ways of making people talk, Saint-Ramé. I know some of them."

This time there was no answering echo. I was dumfounded by these words and thought for a moment that this savagery might turn the situation in Saint-Ramé's favor. But the silence was short. McGanter resumed:

"I'd be very sorry to have recourse to such extreme measures, but the overriding interest of my company is now at stake. I absolutely oppose exposing it to ridicule or having it doubted openly by the managing director of the French firm. Saint-Ramé, I beg you to accept my deal!"

"I thought I knew all of you over in Des Moines so well," Saint-Ramé said in a subdued voice. "The newspapers even called me the European manager who'd best assimilated your methods and your techniques, but that was false. You've surrounded yourselves with assassins; money, profit, financial power have turned your heads. You have denatured and degraded the intellectual and moral patrimony of young America. You're shameful!"

"You're talking like a communist, Saint-Ramé. Shut up!"

"I'm talking like a man who's just understood that he's in more trouble than he thought. You're crazy, McGanter. The books about you by left-wing authors were true after all. You're crazy, and Ronson's your slave. And look at the men seated around you in the shadows. Despite the darkness they have lowered their flashlights, they are so afraid I may look them in the eye! They're cowards! They represent a sterile generation. They've had twenty years while the ruins of their country were rebuilt by their elders, survivors of prison camps and of the war. They're servile, without ideals; they've grown fat too fast and their children will never forgive them! They're flabby and touchy! Egotists and playboys! Their idea of adventure and creativity is a change in the menu at their favorite restaurant! Don't be afraid, gentlemen! I can only distinguish your silhouettes, but I know you through and through. You're afraid! Afraid of McGanter, afraid of Ronson, and also afraid of me! Kneeling here, bound, I terrify you! You'd like me to call myself mad, then you'd be relieved!"

"Abéraud," Ronson said, "have you a nail file?"

"Yes, sir."

"Good. Just drive it under his fingernails."

Abéraud jumped up. I saw his flashlight coming toward me.

"Don't come any closer, Abéraud," I said, revolted. "Stay where you are. I've got a knife and I'll slash your belly open." (That wasn't true, but I'd have said anything to stop him.)

"King, just put that director of human relations out of harm's way."

The American colossus approached and made short work of me.

271

He drove his thumbs into the hollows under my shoulder blades and forced me to walk to the edge of the shaft at the top of the hill.

"If you budge," he said, "I'll pitch you to the bottom."

I'd had enough. I promised not to move. And he went back to Saint-Ramé. That shaft at the edge of which I now sat reminded me that from its foot a passage ran in an almost straight line to the green-and-black vault in Père Lachaise. I unrolled the rope I was carrying and lashed it firmly to a block of stone. It was dark and no one noticed what I was up to. Why these precautions? Because I was afraid. Things were going badly. After Saint-Ramé my turn might come. By praising me, the ex-managing director had singled me out for persecution. He had made me an accomplice, a witness who later on might not hesitate to recount what I had seen and heard. Moreover, what was I witnessing at that moment? Voster was holding Saint-Ramé. Abéraud slid a file under one of the ex-managing director's nails. He howled with pain. Le Rantec spoke up again. "Sir," he said, jealous of Abéraud and afraid of being supplanted by him, "may I go to work on his other hand?"

"Bravo! Le Rantec, go to it, but slowly, slowly!"

"Stop, stop!" cried Chavégnac, who could no longer stand the sight.

"No nervous breakdowns here! One was enough, and you know the consequences!" Ronson warned. "All you have to do is stop your ears."

From that moment on, no staff executive of Rosserys and Mitchell–France had a word to say. Le Rantec and Abéraud, whom Saint-Ramé's suffering seemed to excite, accompanied their tortures with degrading insults.

"You impotent dog! You've shat on me for the last time! No more of that, huh?" cried Le Rantec.

"Dirty little bourgeois fag! If you don't confess we'll split you!" growled Abéraud.

Could it be possible! I was seized by nausea. Saint-Ramé's wails gave place little by little to groans. I decided to flee. I was checking

272

my rope, knotted around the rock, when a dreadful apparition paralyzed the torturers, the cowards and myself. In impressive silence, broken only by Saint-Ramé's moans, a phantom appeared. A terrifying figure which moved slowly, waveringly, toward the tribunal of Rosserys and Mitchell–France. Terrène was the first to recognize it.

"Fournier!" he cried.

There was a stampede. I saw flashlights flickering in all directions, I heard cries for help. What a dreadful memory! And then a dull sound overhead. A sound that was soon to become the rolling thunder of an avalanche.

"It's collapsing on top of us!" someone cried.

I let myself slide down the shaft as fast as possible, and slightly scorching my hands, arrived on level ground without meeting any obstacle. Then the rumblings echoed around me and became an uproar. Fragments of earth and rock were falling everywhere. I flung myself flat on my belly with my hands clasped over my head, and closed my eyes. For a long time I held this position. Then silence returned. I patted myself to be sure no bones were broken. Where was my flashlight? Luckily it was beside me and in working order. I was at the bottom of the shaft, and in front of me a tunnel opened. I was alive. I thought of Fournier. So he wasn't dead. We had thought him assassinated by Le Rantec or smothered by the mud or both. No doubt he'd revived by himself.

For a long time I proceeded underground. Often I had to crawl. Sometimes I had to clear away debris from the great collapse. I heard their groans, their curses and their blasphemies, coming from somewhere on the far side of the wall. They too were alive. The platform on which they'd held their mad, shameful court must have fallen, and they'd probably been thrown to the foot of the hill. There they must have tried to clear a passage through the rubble. That was why their groans reached me in my tunnel, and yes, their imprecations. There was even a moment when I could communicate with them.

"Where are you?" McGanter asked.

"In the tunnel that leads to the green-and-black marble vault."

"Then you have a chance of getting out. . . . As soon as you're free, give the alarm so they can get us out of here."

"Of course, I'll do it at once."

"Bastard," cried a voice.

"Don't insult him!" McGanter ordered. "He's our only hope of getting out of here alive."

"How's Saint-Ramé?" I asked.

After some moments of silence, McGanter said, "He's doing all right. We're looking after him."

Then a long scream burst out. I recognized Chavégnac's voice. "It's not true. It's not true. They've strangled him. Ronson strangled him with his bare hands. He'll kill us all. . . . Lord, forgive us. . . ."

Then the voice broke. I had only one idea in my head: to save them. To reach the vault as fast as possible. So I couldn't linger. Before leaving the area where I could hear them, I cried to those buried alive, "Listen, can you hear me? Answer me."

"Yes, we hear you faintly but distinctly," replied McGanter.

"I'm going for help. Don't try to call to me. I'm starting now. Save your strength. Courage!"

"Thanks!" cried several voices.

And I moved on. The tunnel grew larger and finally I came to an opening. By flashlight I explored the spot. It was indeed the famous vault. Its concrete floor had been cut through with a blowtorch. This was the way Saint-Ramé had been able to get into the tunnels and from there into the office building. A mass of paraphernalia littered the vault: imprecations not yet distributed, a map of the tunnels, a multigraphing machine, a pair of boots, several coils of rope. A thick envelope caught my attention. I opened it. It contained the proof that Roustev had done his part by cutting through the pillars. Saint-Ramé had taken his fingerprints from the oxygen cylinders and the blowtorch. I had listened very attentively to Henri Saint-Ramé's explanations and they had convinced me. The man was intelligent and proud. To play at cat and mouse, to mystify his colleagues, all that was well in accord with his style and temperament. But he had aroused much hatred, much rancor. In transforming his firm to a theater, he had overestimated his powers. Nevertheless his ideas seemed to me essentially correct. It would be necessary henceforth to worry seriously about the nerve of giant American multinational corporations, and more generally about the minds presiding over the economic prosperity of the West.

But how to get out of the vault? I searched in vain for some mechanism. I had no other recourse but to call for help. It was not till midmorning that an astonished voice answered me.

"Who's that talking inside the vault?"

"It's me," I said. "Open up, hurry!"

"Who are you?"

"I'm the director of human relations for Rosserys and Mitchell–France, whose steel-and-glass building stands at the corner of the Avenue de la République and Rue Oberkampf, not far from Père Lachaise cemetery."

"You mean it used to stand," snickered the man, heedless of my predicament.

"Oh," I said, "has it collapsed?"

"And how!" the man exclaimed. "Fortunately the watchmen had been sent away. What's more, it surprised everyone. Maybe you'll be able to explain it all!"

"I'll explain it to you," I said in a tired voice. "It's a long story."

And I stretched myself out in the vault, exhausted, waiting for someone to be kind enough to open it.

"Hang on. I'm going to look for help. If they want to hear your long story, they can't let you die in there."

Now I can remember only one thing more: McGanter and his troop were never found. Oh, my chieftains! Oh, my colleagues on the staff! Where are you now? Do you sleep in peace or do you wander forever blaspheming through the labyrinths?

26

Today the medical team that has been looking after me are all gathered around my bed. Some smile, others are frankly laughing. They are pleased with the results of their efforts. I've emerged from my coma. It seems I've been in a coma for a week.

"But what happened to me?"

"You had a silly accident," the head doctor explains. "For a reason you may recall, you went down into your firm's subbasement, you slipped, you fell backward, and you took an extremely severe blow on the back of your head. . . . You might easily have been killed!"

"But," I say, still incompletely recovered from the dream, which, as I regain consciousness, is fleeing swiftly. "My company —surely that's Rosserys and Mitchell?"

"Bravo! Bravo!" my audience applauds, obviously delighted at the return of my memory. "And what was your position?" asks the head doctor. They await my reply in silence.

"My position? Well, now . . . wasn't I associate director of human relations?"

"Hurrah!" they cry in self-congratulation.

"Well," the doctor exults, "you've come back from a long way off! I'm going to tell your employers and colleagues that you've not only regained consciousness but are rapidly recovering your memory."

He leaves the room, to return a few minutes later and announce, "They're all delighted over in Rue Oberkampf. I've given them permission to visit you for ten minutes, no longer. . . . And now, rest."

At twelve-thirty they come into my room, excited and happy to see me restored.

"Come on, Pilhes, you had us all worried," Le Rantec jokes.

"Sir, we were beginning to be bored without you," says young Brignon.

"Well, my dear Pilhes," Saint-Ramé inquires gently, "how do you feel? We're waiting impatiently for you, and I have some good news: you've been named director in chief of human relations for Rosserys and Mitchell–France."

"Bravo! Congratulations!" exclaim Vasson, Terrène, Yritieri, Fournier, Sélis, Chavégnac, Portal and all the rest.

"Your gauze bandage is very becoming," Roger Arangrude says in affectionate mockery. "It makes you look like a pasha!"

They laugh heartily. They are still just as dynamic, as well behaved, as happy to be alive and at work, to produce, to sell, to conquer new markets. And I'm reassured to see them this way, as I've always known them, enterprising and in good health.

"With a month's rest, you'll be your old self again," Roustev declares.

"This evening," says Henri Saint-Ramé, "our American friends are arriving in Paris. McGanter himself will be happy to see you again. They'll drop in to say hello this time tomorrow."

"I thank you for all these expressions of sympathy," I say. "And how's Monsieur Ronson?"

"Monsieur Ronson's doing very well," says a voice. And Des Moines' representative in Paris, who's kept to the background until now, discreet and courteous as is his custom, approaches my bed, eyes me with his penetrating gaze and says, "I wish you a prompt recovery, Mr. Director."

"Thanks, Mr. Ronson."

"Come, come, the visit is over," the head doctor decrees.

I reflect with surprise on all those kindly faces bent over me. I've been in a coma for a week. Has nothing whatever happened during that time? I search desperately in my reviving memory, but find nothing at all.

This morning I resume my work after more than a month of inactivity. I'm in fine fettle. I whistle as I emerge from the Métro at the Filles du Calvaire station. How good it is to be at work again! My office, my files, my secretary, my bosses, my colleagues, all my co-workers are waiting for me. My company is prosperous, powerful, gigantic, American and multinational. And this gives me a feeling of security, warms my heart. In a similar company my job might have been in danger, especially with my high salary. I proceed slowly along the sidewalk of Rue Oberkampf. Over there majestically rises our glass-and-steel building.

And here I meet Chavégnac, associate director of the Spanish-American Department.

"Well, old Pilhes, how goes it?"

"Couldn't be better," I say, patting him on the shoulder.

"Listen, you probably haven't heard the news," Chavégnac goes on. "I hate to have to tell you on your first morning back after the accident, but Portal telephoned me during the night. . . ."

"What about?"

"Well, it seems Arangrude was killed last night driving home on the belt parkway. . . . Did you know?"

278